James Barnes, A. J. Keller

A Loyal Traitor

A Story of the War of 1812

James Barnes, A. J. Keller

A Loyal Traitor
A Story of the War of 1812

ISBN/EAN: 9783337117603

Printed in Europe, USA, Canada, Australia, Japan

Cover: Foto ©Andreas Hilbeck / pixelio.de

More available books at **www.hansebooks.com**

A LOYAL TRAITOR

A STORY OF THE WAR OF 1812

BY

JAMES BARNES

AUTHOR OF

"NAVAL ENGAGEMENTS OF THE WAR OF 1812"
"FOR KING OR COUNTRY" ETC.

ILLUSTRATED

BY A. J. KELLER

NEW YORK
HARPER & BROTHERS PUBLISHERS
1807

Copyright, 1897, by HARPER & BROTHERS.

TO

CARLTON T. CHAPMAN

WHOSE PAINTINGS OF THE SEA FIGHTS OF THE DAYS
OF 1812 GIVE US BACK THE DEEDS OF MEN AND
SHIPS THAT SHOULD NOT BE FORGOTTEN

THIS BOOK

Is Dedicated

EDITOR'S NOTE

The manuscript from which the following autobiographical story is printed was found in an old desk that had been hidden away in the garret of a shipping-office in the town of Stonington, Connecticut. The story is written in an aged ledger, and parts of it required a great deal of care in the putting together, as the mice had unfortunately commenced their work of destruction. However, it has been deciphered, and, it is to be hoped, contains sufficient that will interest the reader. John Hurdiss is well remembered by one or two of Stonington's oldest inhabitants, although he moved from that town some time in the forties. His grandchildren (for whom he probably wrote the story) are now given a chance to read of the strange adventures of their ancestor under three flags. Thus, without further preamble, the tale is presented as it came from his pen and in his words. The main title is taken from one of Captain Hurdiss's own expressions; the titles to some of the chapters had to be supplied, as the original author left them blank.

CONTENTS

CHAPTER   PAGE

I. AB INITIO 1

II. A DEFERRED SOLUTION 12

III. THE BURNING 21

IV. WHEREIN I FALL IN LOVE WITH THE SEA . . 26

V. THE LION'S GREED 34

VI. A LAND VOYAGE 44

VII. HARDSHIPS 59

VIII. A REVELATION 68

IX. FREEFOOTED 74

X. A NEW BILLET 78

XI. A PRIVATEERSMAN 85

XII. TEST TRIALS 98

XIII. UP ANCHOR! 107

XIV. THE SWORDFISH AND THE WHALE 113

XV. A PRISONER OF WAR 125

XVI. IN DURANCE 139

XVII. A FRENCH LEAVE-TAKING 147

XVIII. A MASQUERADER 157

XIX. FRIENDS IN NEED 162

XX. A BEGGAR A-HORSEBACK 168

XXI. A GENTLEMAN VALET 177

XXII. A VALET AND A GENTLEMAN 182

XXIII. A DISCOVERY AT A DISCOUNT 190

XXIV. IN THE CHOPS OF THE CHANNEL 196

XXV. IN TRUE COLORS 205

CHAPTER | PAGE

XXVI. THE "YANKEE," PRIVATEER 212

XXVII. I WITNESS SOME REMARKABLE PROCEEDINGS . 220

XXVIII. AN OBSERVER OF HISTORY 225

XXIX. DANGEROUS DELAYS 237

XXX. A CUTTING OUT 242

XXXI. A CRUISE ON MY OWN ACCOUNT 247

XXXII. WRECKED AGAIN 258

XXXIII. A SURPRISE PARTY 270

XXXIV. STRAINED RELATIONS 287

XXXV. THE REDEMPTION OF MY PROMISE 296

ILLUSTRATIONS

"'I AM AN AMERICAN CITIZEN'" . . . . *Frontispiece*

"ONE BEFORE WHICH MY MOTHER USED TO STAND
AND WEEP" . . . . *Facing p.* 6

"'HARK! WHAT NOISE IS THAT?'" . . . . . . " 18

"'OUT THE WINDOW WITH IT'" . . . . " 22

"THE SOUND OF SCURRYING ON DECK CAUSED ME
TO START UP SUDDENLY" . . . . " 30

"A MAN IN FLOWING SATINS AND VELVETS" . . " 56

"'ANCHOR'S ATRIP,' HE CRIED" . . . . . " 72

"HE SAT DOWN BACKWARD IN THE EMPTY FIRE-
PLACE" . . . . " 84

"'GOOD-BYE, MARY,' SAID I" . . . . " 90

"'YOU WILL END THIS CRUISE AN OFFICER'" . " 104

"WE ROLLED OVER FAIRLY" . . . . " 122

"'WE'VE A DYING MAN DOWN HERE'" . . . . " 134

"THE MAN INSTANTLY DREW HIMSELF ERECT" . . " 150

"I STRUCK OUT INTO A LITTLE CHANSONNETTE" . " 170

"'OH, THAT MARY COULD SEE ME NOW!'" . . . " 184

"A GREAT, BLACK-WHISKERED MAN STEPPED OUT
OF IT" . . . . " 200

"I CAUGHT THE COMBING OF THE WINDOW" . . . " 244

"HE LEANED HIS FACE OVER THE HOLE AND
    SHOUTED" . . . . *Facing p.* 254
"DOWN WENT THE *DUCHESS OF SUTHERLAND*
    LIKE A LITTLE *ROYAL GEORGE*" . . . . . " 266
"'SURRENDER!' I CRIED" . . . . " 272
"I PUT OUT MY HAND. SHE TOOK IT" . . . . " 302

A LOYAL TRAITOR

CHAPTER I

AB INITIO

In sitting down to write a tale in which I myself am the central figure and most prominent actor, I cannot help, at first, having a fear that any one who perchance shall read all that is to follow (if I ever succeed in the finishing of it) will judge me a person whose opinion of himself is high in the extreme.

While possessing the proper self-respect, without which no man is ever truthful or successful, I do not claim to have accomplished anything for the reason that I am gifted beyond the ordinary — I am not; but circumstances of my early youth gave to me chances for adventure, and fate led me, under the guiding hand of Providence, through much probably that is outside of the usual walks of life.

Although, as I write, I am only in late middle age and hale and hearty, all that I intend to chronicle here seems long ago indeed ; yet truthfully, and in such ways as memory recalls it, do I intend to put it down.   If I am discursive, it is because I am led away by the vividness with which my eye puts the scenes before me — and that is all there is to it.

In going over many events of the past in the half-waking hours at night—a habit I have long been prone to—I have felt, often, my heart-beats quicken, and more than once I have scarce restrained an inclination to speak or to cry aloud in accordance with my feelings. Perhaps the placing of all this upon paper may reduce the intensity with which I relive a life that is gone—and thus, to begin :

My earliest childhood's recollection is of a warm summer's day. I know it was warm, because the sand in which I was playing sparkled and shone as it ran through my fingers, and the long stretch of beach, the whiteness of which dazzled my eyes, was hot to the touch of my bare feet. A big brown dog was playing up and down the water's edge, and an old colored mammy, crooning softly to herself, was shading my head with the green branch of a tree. By-and-by a rowboat hove in sight around the point, and soon a tall man with gray hair came, and, lifting me on his shoulder, carried me through a wood where the trees seemed to touch the clouds. Then we turned out of the shadows, took a path through a meadow, and came at last to a large house, where a beautiful woman gathered me in her arms, kissed me, and called me pet names that I was glad to hear.

This, I say, is the first day of all my life that I can remember—which is beginning at the beginning, and no mistake.

There were many such days, but gradually it came to me that I began to enjoy life and to love things. I loved my beautiful mother, who spoke to me in a language very different from that of the three old colored people whom I saw every day—namely, Aunt Sheba, Ann Martha, and Ol' Peter ; I loved them also, and I loved the dog.

I seemed to understand the two kinds of speaking very well (my mother's and the rest of the world's, I mean), although I did not know that one was French and the other darky English pure and simple.

The tall man, whom I sometimes called "*père*," and at other times "daddy," was not always with us. Very often it was long months between his visits, and he generally remarked how I had grown and how much heavier I had become since last he had lifted me up on his shoulder.

Then came the time when I began to think—strange thoughts that were never answered, because for the most part I confided them to no one except, maybe, to the brown curly dog, who was called "Maréchal" by my mother, and "Maa'shal" by the colored people. Like myself, he seemed to understand either language perfectly, and replied to each in his own fashion.

I well remember the day I first began to wonder at the vastness of the world. It was upon an occasion when my father and Ol' Peter took me for a sail in a *tremendous* boat, that they afterwards hauled up on the beach out at the mouth of the river, and the very next morning after this excursion I went down with my mother to the end of the little wharf, and lo and behold! a great ship was lying at anchor in the broad stretch of water beyond the reedy point of land. My mother was weeping softly, and my father kissed her, and me, too, over and over again. Then he stepped into a boat rowed by dark men with beards on their faces, and put off to the ship, that spread her sails and like a great bird swept out into the bay.

When she had gone beyond the point, and we could no longer see the tall figure standing on the after-deck waving a hat, my mother's tears fell faster than ever, and we went back to the house. I never saw my father again.

I call him "my father," in thus looking back at the great spring-time, because I always think of him as such, and because I bear his name. Long years afterwards I learned much that this story will tell, if it goes on to the

end, but it is now too early to indulge in explanations—
I must relate things as they come to me.

Well, when I was six or seven years of age—and these
first days I have touched on even then but a memory
—I began to enjoy life in new ways. I had never a
playmate but the dog, who had grown too old for romping;
but my mother would read long and wonderful stories to
me in her beautiful low voice, in French, of course, and
I, listening, pictured the outside world as something
strange and beautiful, and just waiting and yearning for
my coming to see it and enjoy it.

Of course, by this time, I knew that the name of the
river on which our plantation bordered was the Gunpowder, that the blue waters were the waters of Chesapeake
Bay, that I lived on the shores of Maryland, and that the
ships were bound not to fairy islands (except now and
then when I *wanted* them to be), but to Baltimore and
Annapolis and Havre de Grace, and to a dozen other
places whose inhabitants sought their living by trading
and sailing on the sea.

I had also heard from Ol' Peter that there had been a
war between our country and another, named England,
and that a great man named Washington had once
stopped at this very house in which we lived. Ol' Peter
described to me the surrender of Cornwallis (at which
he had been present, according to account); but my
mother's talk and all she read about was of France, that
I gradually came to believe must have been the most
delightful country in the world. Yet my mother always
spoke as if France were dead, which puzzled me not a
little. Of a truth, there were many things that puzzled
me in those days; I had so many times received the
answer, "You will learn all some time—*On vous dira tout
ça un de ces jours, mon petit*," that at last I learned to
hold back my curiosity, or to answer with my own imagination.

Our neighbors, who were not very neighborly, lived at long distances from us.   They had no children, and up to my tenth year I had never exchanged a thought with any one of my own age.   To tell the truth, I am afraid my mother did not encourage the people near us to be very friendly, and I suppose that they talked much, and perhaps said spiteful things about her.   I can remember how I began to notice that she seldom walked farther than the rose-bush at the end of the garden path, and that she was growing thinner and thinner, yet more beautiful every day.

We led a very simple existence, depending mostly on what we raised in the garden and what Ol' Peter brought back from the "cross - roads" — a collection of three houses and a tavern five or six miles distant from our plantation.

But I was growing big and strong for my age—so strong, indeed, that I could handle the heavy oars when Peter and I went out on the river to tend the nets; and never shall I forget the first time I was allowed to fire the old fowling - piece that occasionally brought a fat canvas-back duck, lusciously reeking of wild celery, to grace our table.   The kick the old gun gave me, upon this first occasion, blackened my shoulder and bruised my jaw.   But what cared I for that!   Had I not survived the proudest moment of my life?

But to continue my descriptions:

The furnishings of the big house we lived in I can recall in detail; they were very rich, although there were no carpets in any of the rooms except in the room my mother slept in.   But there were great nail - studded chairs, and two carved oak sideboards, and a wonderful clock, upon which, by-the-way, I took my first lesson in geography; it was shaped like a golden earth, with the hours marked upon its circumference, and a hand that pointed them out as each came around in turn.

The rooms up-stairs were empty, except for some packing-cases and rubbish—all but one small chamber, to which my mother alone had the key, and which contained a great iron-bound chest that I stood much in awe of.

In the wide hallway down-stairs were three portraits; one before which my mother often used to stand and weep (I knew it to be he who had sailed away in the ship and who used to carry me on his shoulder). The second was a handsome pale-faced man whose hair fell in long ringlets over his steel armor, and who looked forth, very proud and haughty, from his piercing gray eyes that would follow one even out of the door on to the piazza. (I have often peered around the corners to see if they would discover me, and they never failed in it.) The third portrait was a beautiful one of a woman whom I thought to be my mother. One day she told me, however, that it was not—that it was her sister, at which I marvelled.

A score or so of books were in a great case in one of the bare front rooms, some of them bound in handsome leather bindings and filled with fine engravings. Ah, what would I not give to possess them now!

One day was so much like another that, were it not for the seasons that flew by quickly, the world would have apparently been standing still; but the oars were becoming less heavy and the distances not so great. Very soon I tended the nets alone or wandered along the shore with the old flintlock fowling-piece over my shoulder; ducks, or perhaps a wild goose or a swan, during the spring and fall, were always hanging ready to be cooked, in the spring-house at the end of the garden.

I began to roam farther and farther in my lonely excursions. Poor old Maréchal would follow me no longer; he stopped within the shadow of the house.

I suppose that many people who travelled by the

"ONE BEFORE WHICH MY MOTHER USED TO STAND AND WEEP"

coach that passed the cross-roads every day wondered who the boy was that used to stand there with a tall gun beside him at a fence corner, silently watching the lumbering vehicle go down the highway in a cloud of dust. I must have presented a quaint sight, no doubt, for my clothes were of home manufacture and I kept growing out of them. But the gold buttons on the rough cloth were very fine, and were inscribed with the same crest that was painted in one corner of the portrait with the flowing brown hair; these buttons played an important part in subsequent adventures, and I would give a finger to own one at the present writing. A person often possesses little things, whose value appears of the slightest, that in the course of time become priceless—lucky is he if he happens to retain them! But I am forging ahead of my story. To get back to it in quick order:

One day my mother and I and Ol' Peter mounted the rickety wagon to which our one lone mule was harnessed, and drove to the cross-roads. It was the first time that I could remember my mother leaving the plantation; I did not know then that it was on my account that she was making this departure, but I can see it plainly enough in looking over the time. A question that I had asked of her some days before had more than probably decided her upon doing so.

"Are we always going to live here?" I had inquired.

I remember that she had looked at me strangely, and the next day the preparations were made for the great changes. It is little things that occasion them usually in life, I notice.

When the coach stopped at the cross-roads tavern the passengers gazed at us most curiously. The guard nudged his companion and whispered something, and a tall man in an officer's uniform politely handed my mother to a seat inside—then the horn blew, the driver touched up the horses, and away we went.

I began to feel frightened; but this feeling wore off mighty soon. We passed houses and plantations with hundreds of colored people working in the fields, and at last, a little past noonday, we entered the town of Baltimore, and drove to an inn.

The crowds of busy people and the sight of boys of my own age playing in the streets, the near-by glimpses of the shipping at the wharfs, thrilled and excited me; and as we descended from the coach I held fast to my mother's skirt and would have hidden. The landlord of the inn hastened forth, and received us with the greatest consideration. After much bowing and scraping, and many orders to the negro servants, he turned from my mother, and, poking out his finger, pistol fashion, in my direction, addressed a question at me, to which I falteringly replied, in a manner that was evidently unintelligible, from the look on his face—I must have spoken French in my embarrassment.

We did not stay long at the inn—two or three days at the most; then we went to live in a little house that my mother had rented at the corner of the street. Aunt Sheba and the two other servants joined us, and soon we were comfortably settled. It was surely my mother's intention to go back to the plantation for the rest of the property she had left behind her; but, alas! she put off the expedition time after time—although she often spoke as if it were a duty neglected.

Now I went to school at a Mr. Thompson's, a heavy-faced, snuffy individual, who wondered at my knowledge of Latin and marvelled at my simplicity. I began my studies auspiciously enough, but for a long time I could not overcome my aversion to the use of slate and pencil —a well-nibbed pen and linen paper were much more to my liking. As to the scholars, it did not take me a week to adapt myself to circumstances; after I had fought two or three battles with the lads of my own age they decided that I was better as a friend than as an enemy, and I grew, more than likely, to think and behave as any one of them.

And so two years went by—two years like those of any boy's life: playing along the wharfs, climbing into orchards, talking with the fishermen, swimming, racing, fighting, and all. But my poor mother could now hardly leave her room; she passed most of the time in a chair by the window—waiting for me, I take it. The people near us were very kind to her, and the doctor who lived at the inn used to come and see her frequently. Major Taliaferro (pronounced "Tolliver") was a devoted attendant; he was captain of the county train-band, and made a fine appearance in his regimentals, I can assure you, with his big cocked hat and plume. He and I grew very friendly, and, by-the-way, he was the officer whom I have mentioned was so polite to us on the stage-coach.

One afternoon when I returned from school I found my mother sitting talking to a gentleman whom I recognized as a Mr. Edgerton, a lawyer of the neighborhood—a handsome, kindly man of some parts and learning; he afterwards went to the Legislature, and became well known. Good cause have I to remember him with gratitude!

Upon my entrance the gentleman regarded me most curiously. He had a smattering of French phrases, although he could not speak or read the language. "Then it is *à demain, madame*," said he, rising, and picking up his hat. As he left he bowed low at the door.

The next week was to be the saddest and perhaps the most misfortunate of all my life.

I was seated on the hard little bench in Mr. Thompson's school-room, longing to be back once more with my old gun and my boat paddling along the marshy shore of the Gunpowder, when a shadow fell across the threshold. I looked up; it was the doctor. I cannot recollect his name, which is a pity, as I would like to set it down; he was a kind man, and I owe him much that I never can repay. Quickly he stepped to Mr. Thompson's side and whispered a few words in his ear. The school-master coughed and looked at me over the great bows of his spectacles; then he called my name.

The doctor caught me by the hand, and I followed him out into the sunny street.

"Be a brave lad; be a brave lad, John," he repeated.

He almost dragged me up the road, so fast he walked, and a nameless fear coming into my heart, I began to sob aloud.

There were two or three people gathered in front of our little house, and back in the garden I saw a strange sight. It was Ol' Peter leaning across the picket-fence; his head was bowed on his arms, and his shoulders were moving up and down. The people spoke in whispers as we went up the little path. Once inside the door the doctor bent and kissed me on the forehead.

"Be a brave lad, my son," he said. "Your mother has left us—" He turned away without finishing something he was going to say.

It did not require the sight of Aunt Sheba's tearful face beside me to tell what had happened—I knew it with a chill all through me. Boy that I was, I fainted dead away.

After a while, when I came to myself, they brought me to the room and left me there. . . .

The second day after was the funeral. It seemed to me that all of the town was present—from curiosity, mayhap, the largest part; yet, since she had come to the town, my mother's gentle manner had made her many friends. The doctor said she had long suffered from trouble of the heart.

But I could scarcely realize what had happened. What it meant to me of course I did not know.

It was the fall of the year; the blackbirds were chattering in the hedges, and off in the fields a bob-white had begun to pipe his cheery whistle. It was all the same, but there was a great blank somewhere. I could not even weep. My heart and senses were deadened by my sorrow, and yet I felt angry, as though I had been robbed.

When we returned to the house after the funeral, Mr. Edgerton, the lawyer, was waiting.

"I have here Madam Hurdiss's warrant to examine her effects, and the key to a certain strong-box which she has directed me to open and take care of," he said. "We will start for the Gunpowder to-morrow morning. You will go with us, doctor?"

My kind friend nodded. "To a certainty, and the young gentleman will accompany us," he replied, with a hand on my head. "He is the party most interested. That there is no denying."

"Of course," returned the lawyer. "And we will start early."

Then he said something about its being "a most interesting case," and the two gentlemen left the room.

This night, for the third time, I sobbed myself to sleep, Aunt Sheba holding my hand and crooning the old Congo song that had lulled me many times on her wide bosom.

CHAPTER II

IT was very early the next morning when we started
southward along the turnpike. The doctor and I were
driving in a tall chaise that swayed on its hinges, up and
down, to and fro, like a small boat in a tide-rip. Mr.
Edgerton followed on horseback.

The sun had not risen when I had been awakened,
the morning chill was in the air; a mist hung low over
the marshes, and the waters of the bay looked dull and
cold. I had begun to shiver, and the kind physician
threw a heavy cape around me, and tucked me in carefully beside him; we had not spoken, except for a morning's greeting, but now he began a fire of questions, and
I could not answer even the simplest.

I had never heard that my mother was a widow before
her marriage to the man whom I called my father; I did
not know her maiden name, nor where she came from;
and if I was not born at the plantation on the Gunpowder, my birthplace was a mystery to me; for, as I have
said, my first recollection was of the warm day on the
beach.

My mother had told me nothing from which I could
formulate a suggestion or give a reply that would throw
any light upon my family history; apparently she had
left no will, and my appearance upon the day of her conversation with Mr. Edgerton had interrupted, most probably, any disclosures that she had intended making.
What was to become of me I did not know.

The lawyer had ridden alongside of the chaise as we slowly ascended a slight hill.

"Know you anything, Master Hurdiss, of a large iron-bound chest in a room on the second story of Marsh-wood House?" he panted, digging his heels into his nag's ribs to keep him abreast of the wheel. (I have forgotten to mention that the estate upon which we lived was known in the neighborhood as the "Marshwood plantation"—whether from the name of a previous own-er or its location, I have never been able to ascertain.) "Know you aught of this chest?" Mr. Edgerton re-peated.

To the question I could only reply that I had often seen the box and had caught glimpses of the interior, that it was full of papers, and I had noticed it must have contained some money, for I once saw my mother take some gold pieces from a heavy leather bag that she had afterwards most carefully replaced.

"Never mind; we will solve it all," grunted the man of law, "so soon as we get there—I have the keys. Come, doctor, press ahead!"

The horses lurched forward into a trot—we had now reached the top of the hill—and, tired and sleepy, I leaned back on my friend's shoulder and fell to dozing.

When I awakened the sun was high, but the chill was yet in the air, and a damp breeze had sprung up from the eastward that presaged rain. Aloft against the heavy clouds a V-shaped line of wild-geese were winging their way to the south; their coarse honking fell down to us; the sound caused me to look upward, and I fol-lowed the steady flight. I have always been well versed in the signs of nature, and there is nothing so sure to judge by as the actions of wild-fowl.

"We are going to have cold weather," I remarked to the doctor.

"Yes, the old gander is setting a pace for them as if

the snow were after him," he replied, leaning forward and putting the whip in its socket.

To my surprise, as I gazed about near to hand, I saw that we were almost at the cross-roads, where it was our intention to stop and procure something to eat, as we had tasted nothing since the gray of the morning.

Two or three houses had been added to the group that lined the road-side, and a new sign-post waved its arms at the corner. A number of negroes hurried out, at the sound of wheels and hoofs, and took the horses.

As we entered the low-ceilinged front room of the tavern I overheard the talk that the doctor and lawyer were having together. "It was certainly most careless to leave such property unguarded," the latter was saying. "Perhaps we are too late." This made me listen.

"But no one would suspect anything in the way of treasure, that I'll warrant, and they are honest people hereabouts," returned the doctor, reassuringly.

For some reason I could scarcely swallow a mouthful of the meal that was served for us, although it smelt most savory. As a special honor the landlord himself insisted upon waiting upon the table, and I shrewdly suspect, putting things together, that he was of a curious nature, and longed for a chance to listen to the conversation ; but if this was his desire it was not gratified, as the doctor and the lawyer were most reserved in his presence.

At last, however, we were on the move again, a fresh horse having been placed in the shafts of the old rattle-trap, upon the possession of which I found that the doctor prided himself most mightily. Well, off we went at a tremendous pace, the new horse charging down the road in a clumsy, heedless fashion, and the chaise rocking behind him fit to capsize us.

The doctor at last succeeded in pulling the nag down

to a steadier gait, and Mr. Edgerton, coughing and choking, came trotting up beside us through the trailing cloud
of dust that, despite the damp, hung in our wake. For
two miles we drove on in silence, and then turned from
the main road into the lane that led to Marshwood. The
old fields on either hand were grown breast-high with
brambles, and the lane wheel-rucks were almost hidden
in the tall grass that swished softly under the box of the
chaise.

Marshwood House was built partly of brick and partly
of wood. The brick had come from England at the time
when the colonies, because of the tax on industries mayhap, brought even their building material from over the
water. It had once been very handsome, but during the
Revolution the outbuildings had been destroyed, and the
right wing of the house had fallen into sad decay. By
the expenditure of some not inconsiderable sum, however, the whole estate could have been restored to the
beauty it must once have possessed (but alas! that never
has or never will happen, I suppose). Now, at the time
of which I speak, ruin was writ on everything.

When the horses had been tied to two rusty staples
driven in the trunk of an oak-tree that stood before the
door, we all stepped up on to the piazza. The boards
were sagged so badly that they had fallen away from the
body of the house, and even the stone-work had crum-
bled along the foundations.

It appeared like the old place, and yet it was not; but
there was the same hornets' nest that I had watched
building (ages and ages ago, it seemed to me); yes, and
there, hanging on a nail, was a fishing-rod with a rusty
iron hook dangling from a bit of rotten fish-line. I had
stood on tiptoe and put it there; now I could touch it
with my elbow.

The lawyer had some difficulty in opening the door.
However, after some manipulation, he succeeded, and

gave a sigh of relief as he saw that there were no traces of any one having preceded him.

"Come in, come in, doctor," he said, cheerily, his voice echoing oddly down the empty hallway.

"Come on, John, my son," repeated the physician to me.

I turned, before I crossed the threshold, and looked out over the sloping meadow and the stretch of yellow marsh to the blue-gray waters of the Chesapeake. The rain that had been threatening all the morning had begun to fall with that depressing, sun-filtered drizzle that promises hours of it.

It was on such a day that I used to lie with my head in my mother's lap while she read to me. I remembered this with a certain calmness, for there had settled upon me a firmly assured belief that I should never be happy again, and I accepted the feeling with a stoicism that now I wonder at.

But my pen runs from the main task of putting facts on paper. To return :

I entered the house, and insensibly caught the doctor's great hand in mine.

There was a musty, locked-up odor greeting us that checked full breathing. The big room on the right smelt like a cellar, dank and unhealthy.

The doctor drew aside a chair, and, opening a window and the shutters, admitted some light. Dust was all about, everywhere ; the heavy oak centre-table was littered with dead, starved flies ; the whole place was so chill and unhomelike that I shuddered. The doctor closed the window.

"By Jove, it grows cold !" he said.

The lawyer, who had deposited a pair of large empty saddle-bags on the floor, stamped his feet.

"Heigho !" he cried, "let's cheer things up a bit. Here's a fire all ready for the lighting ; that's a godsend."

In the wide fireplace were some good-sized logs and a handful of fat-wood. Drawing a flint and steel, he struck a light, and soon a tiny blaze crept up the old chimney, broadening with a burst of flame at last into a cheerful, roaring, warming glow. It cleared the room of its unhealthiness, and all three of us spread our hands out to it as if it had been winter.

"I think the look of things has made us exaggerate the inclemency of the weather," remarked the doctor, with an attempt at a laugh. "Come, squire, let's set to work."

The lawyer drew from his pocket a small bunch of keys. "We will have to try for it—they're not numbered," he replied, thrusting one into the keyhole of the desk in the chimney-corner.

He tried them all before he found one that would fit. Then he turned the bolt with a sharp click, and lowered the lid. I began to feel excited, and I could see that the others were, and did not conceal it.

"Ah, no one has been here, that's evident!" the doctor exclaimed.

Plain to view were some French coins, a shining little tower of gold. The lawyer opened one of the drawers on the left. It was empty. Then another, with the same result. In the bottom one, on the right hand, however, was a paper and a miniature on ivory.

I remembered the last—the side face of a large, heavy man in a white wig. His nose was very prominent, and despite the massive jowl he had an air that suggested the effect of a noble presence. His costume was magnificent. From beneath a broad sash that crossed his breast peeped a great diamond star or cross, and lace and jewels decked him.

"An excellent likeness, I judge," murmured the doctor, looking at the portrait with one eye shut.

"Ecod! I should know it across the room," replied the lawyer.

2

"Who is it?" I asked, for I had seen it in my mother's hands.

"It is the French king who lost his head by the guillotine," the doctor answered—"Louis the Sixteenth."

"Did your mother never speak to you about this portrait?" asked the lawyer, who was untying the ribbon with which the paper had been fastened.

"Once I saw her looking at it," I replied, "and I asked her who it was. But I never did so again, because she began to talk so fast and in such strange words that I could not follow. Then she began to weep, and her hair fell down all about her—Aunt Sheba came running in and held her in her arms. It was a long time before she grew calm again. She never told me."

"Humph! that was strange," quoth the doctor, beneath his breath. "H'm, very strange."

By this the lawyer had spread the document on his knee. He gave a grunt of vexation.

"This is Greek to me," he muttered. "See what you can make out of it."

He extended the paper towards us. The physician took it, wrinkled his brows and shrugged his shoulders.

"I give it up," he said, half smiling.

I peeped beneath his elbow.

"Why, it's French," I cried, "and my mother's writing, sir!"

"Can you read it?" asked the doctor, spreading it out on the desk lid.

In reply I began without hesitation:

"' *To Monsieur Henri Amédée Lavalle de Brienne.*

"' DEAR BROTHER,—Although I have not written you and have received no word from you, I am writing these lines, trusting and intending that they will meet your eye should you survive me. My husband, whose memory I cherish, is dead—lost at sea. Despite

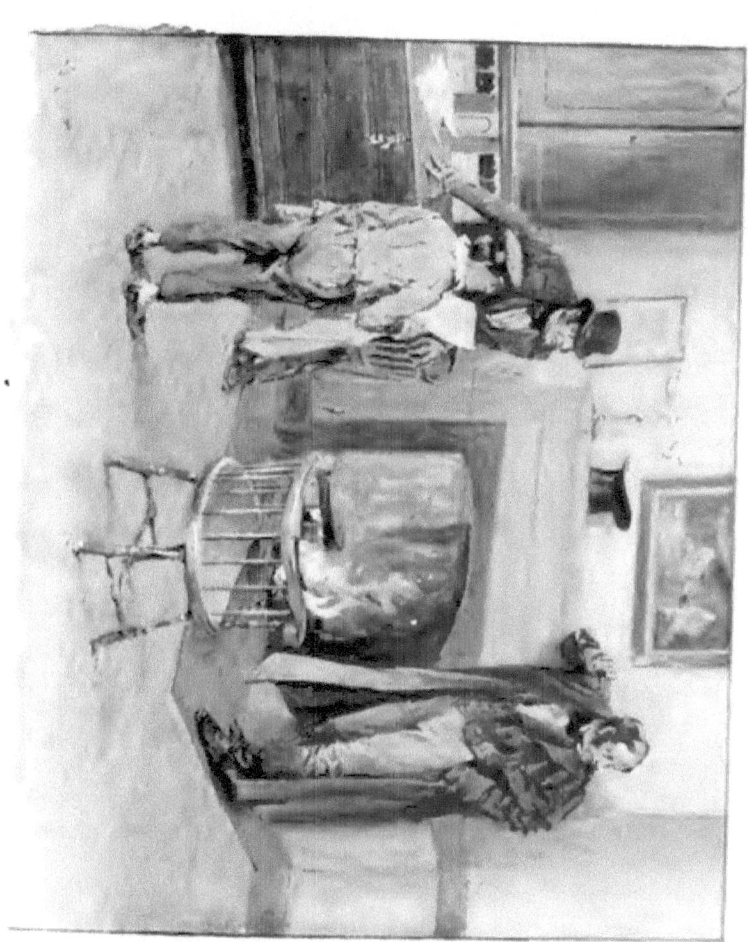

the injustice with which you have treated him, and me also since my second marriage, I recommend to you my son, who bears the name of his step-father.'"

I started and read the last words over twice.

"Go on!" interjected the lawyer, rapping the mantel-piece sharply with his knuckles.

I continued, with my face burning and my lips atremble:

"'For the sake of the name *that he might claim*, and all that it may mean, you may receive him. I have told him little of the past. In my judgment it was not needed, nor could it now produce anything to his favor. If circumstances should alter, you may divulge the secret; but I pray you not to do so unless this happens. This I beseech you for the sake of her whom you have loved. My son will bear with him the chest that contains the papers that I brought from the château at A. They will be unopened and addressed to you. The portraits and other possessions that my husband brought from England I leave to my son, and there is enough money in the two bags to pay for my Jean's education. I have never been able to bring myself to talk about the dreadful happenings. I cannot even think of them, or I should go mad. Somehow it has appeared that silence has been the better part; but to your discretion I leave this, and to you I intrust my son's future. The papers he will bear will be sufficient proof of his identity. May God watch over him and direct you!

"'It is evident to me from your letter, in answer to the one I wrote so long ago, that you were uncertain which one of your sisters was writing to you. I am *H. de B.*, who inscribes here what will be carved upon her tombstone:

"'"*Madam John Hurdiss*, widow of Captain John Hurdiss, merchant and trader, of Cornwall, England."'"

This was all the letter contained. It did not seem to lessen any mystery that existed, and for some minutes neither the doctor nor Mr. Edgerton spoke a word. Suddenly the latter kicked back one of the logs in the fire-place with his foot.

"Confound the fire, it smokes like a smudge!" he

grumbled. "So we are not to open the papers, after all! But there may be something lying loose. Let us up."

All at once the doctor raised his hand. "Hark! What noise is that?" he exclaimed.

A roaring, crackling sound came from overhead. Something fell heavily on the floor of the hallway outside. The two men sprang to the door and pulled it open. The hall and the other rooms were filled with stifling smoke! The old portrait (the one with the long, brown curls) had fallen, and a blazing bit of wainscoting burned through the canvas that had smouldered to the frame.

"The strong-box!" shrieked the lawyer—and he plunged up the stairs.

"It's in the room on the right!" I cried, as the doctor and I followed him, feeling our way with the aid of the banisters.

CHAPTER III

THE BURNING

The fire having ignited the soot must have eaten through the aged chimney, and had probably been burning in the walls along the staircase and in the floors of the rubbish chambers for some minutes before we had inkling of it. It was almost beyond imagining, the way it had spread. But the steps of the staircase itself were firm underfoot, although inside the walls, and even to the roof, the roaring, crackling flames were gutting the left wing of the house.

The doctor did not stop to help Mr. Edgerton find the key; he threw his weight against the door I pointed out again and again—it went open with a crash at last, after I had thought that he would have stove his own side in first.

There was no smoke on this side of the house, but it followed us from the hallway, choking the throat and stinging the eyes. There was the box in the middle of the room.

Now we were all three encouraging one another and shouting for haste. Twice did the lawyer drop the bunch of keys as he tried to fit the lock.

"Take them, lad," he cried, at last, looking over his shoulder; "your fingers are the nimbler. But make haste!"

The tears were pouring down his face; hurriedly he rose from his knees, and, making a leap for the window, kicked out the glass and the shutter that had been nailed fast, and thrust his **head to** the air, coughing, struggling, and gagging as **if his last** day **had come.**

In the meantime the doctor was bending over, with his face close to mine, and whispering admonitions **to be** cool ; but his hand **on** my shoulder shook as if **the ague** had possession of him. Upon my soul, I think I was the coolest **of the three !** Key after key **I** tried without success. Suddenly **the** doctor slipped his fingers into the handle **at** the end.

"Out the window with it !" he spluttered. "What jackasses ! What dunces ! Bear **a** hand here, Edgerton !"

The lawyer turned back into the room. He took the other end of the box, and they heaved with all their strength, I, still on my knees, helping them.

We might as well have tried to pull the big oak before the house up by the roots.

"It's nailed down !" roared the lawyer, **with a** curse, running his fingers along the edge.

There was a crash in the lower hall, and a great tongue of flame licked in at **us** through the doorway. There was such a roaring now **in our ears** that we could not make ourselves heard except by shouting.

"Out of the window for our lives !" cried the doctor. "The stairs have fallen !"

The lawyer bestowed some angry but useless kicks on the lid of the box, and **we** crowded out of the window on to the roof of the back piazza. **The** wind, blowing strongly from the eastward, had kept most of the smoke **and** the flame away from the north side of the building. But it was a fearsome sight to see the way things were going. **The** whole of the west wing, and **the** south also, **to** the roof, was **one** red smooch of flame against the tree-tops. The dark smoke curled over and hung close to the damp earth.

It was some twelve or fifteen feet from the piazza roof

to the ground, but a chinaberry-tree grew close to hand,
spreading to the eaves. There was no time to hesitate!

The lawyer made one leap of it into the tree and
crashed through it; then just as the roof on which we
were standing shook and sloughed away, the flames
bursting up from below, the doctor and I caught at a
branch and swung off together—but the limb broke beneath our weight! Down we came by the run, I landing
full and fair upon the doctor's chest, which almost did
for him for good and all.

Scrambling to our feet, Mr. Edgerton and I hauled
him away some distance from the house, and the cool
rain helped to revive him, but for some minutes he drew
breath with difficulty.

Then the three of us sat there on the wet grass and
watched the house burn.

I shall never forget it, or the mixture of feelings which
filled my mind and bosom. A sense of unreality, an in-
ability to grasp the idea that it was really *happening* probably was uppermost.

The lawyer, whom I had always thought a cold-tem-
pered person, was squatted cross-legged, Turk fashion,
grasping the toes of his boots in either hand, rocking
himself to and fro, all the time muttering and scolding
like a child, and, whether from the smoke or his anger
and disappointment, the tears following one another down
his cheeks.

The doctor, who had raised himself on his elbow, was
the first to speak coherently.

"The burning of a mystery," he said, with a gesture
of despair. "Now what's to be done?"

A shrill, frightful scream, the like of which I had never
heard before nor since, roused us to our feet.

"In the name of all the powers, what's that?" cried
Mr. Edgerton.

"The horses, man! Damme, we've forgotten them!"

answered the doctor, starting on a run to the front of the house around the east wing.

The oak to which the two beasts had been made fast was close to the wooden building. One of them had broken loose, and had made off into the garden, towing the chaise behind him. The other (the saddle-horse) had wound the halter around the trunk of the tree, and, half strangled, was snubbed close to it, backing away with all his might. The heat had shrivelled the upper branches of the oak, and even the bark on the side towards the house was singed and smoking. As we saw this, again he emitted the horrid cry of fright and agony. I had never known that such tones were in the voice of any animal.

The lawyer drew out a knife, and, hastening up, shielding his face, cut the poor beast adrift. He galloped away towards the swamp, and did not stop until he was belly deep in the water.

The wooden wing was completely eaten by this time, and the flames were pouring from every window of the brick portion of the older part of the dwelling. Soon the walls alone would be left standing. I turned away from the sight and looked out to the river.

A long white row of wild swan swayed in the current. Their halloings and cries, like those of a crowd of school-children at recess, came down to us on the damp wind. The smoke had evidently been seen from one of the plantations up the Gunpowder, for a boat under a small spritsail was making out from the farther shore.

The doctor was back in the garden examining the chaise, which had been overturned in a patch of brush-wood. He tried each wheel mechanically, and I could see he felt relieved that no damage had been done.

"Well, what are we going to do now?" I nervously asked of Mr. Edgerton, speaking for the first time, and repeating the doctor's words of a few minutes before.

The lawyer fumbled in his pockets, and drew forth the miniature and the paper he had taken from the desk. I remembered having noticed also that the doctor had slipped the coins in his pocket.

"This is all we have to go by," he replied. "Lord only knows what you've lost, Master Hurdiss. Oh, confound the thought that made me light the fire!" he added, kicking and pawing at the soaked ground like an angry bull.

Well, to make a short story of a long one, we watched the house burn down to a mass of smouldering, heated ashes, and then we started to drive back without speaking. On the return we met a number of men on foot and horseback, who had sighted the conflagration from the cross-roads and were coming down the lane, but it was too late to do anything, and in a few words we explained what had happened.

That sorrowful night we spent at the tavern, and the next day we drove over to Marshwood again, followed by many curious persons.

We dug in the still warm ruins, and there, to show the heat of the fire, we discovered nothing of the strong-box but the hinges, melted out of shape, and two or three small bits of metal as large as bullets that had once been gold pieces. These were turned over to me as being my lawful possessions, and they made, with what the doctor had saved, and the miniature and the paper, my sole inheritance—the annuity upon which my mother had been living had ceased with her death.

When we returned to Baltimore I accepted the lawyer's invitation to go to his house, pending any action on the part of my relatives, should they be discovered. Matters seemed to be all in a fog generally, and my grief at my bereavement made me rather careless of consequences.

CHAPTER IV

How Mr. Edgerton smoothed over the affair of the conflagration I know not—some explaining must have been necessary, for the plantation did not belong to us, having been only rented to my mother for a term of years. But the lawyer must have appeased the proper owner in some way; no trouble followed that I heard of.

And now comes the time when I must act for myself.

On the twelfth day of November, 1809, my new life began. But before I go on I should explain that on the outside of the paper which I had deciphered on the day of the burning of Marshwood House (and which has stayed in my mind, as I transcribed it also), an address had been found. In some way it had been overlooked upon the first reading. It was important, however, as it gave the address of my uncle, Monsieur Henri Amédée Lovalle de Brienne, as Miller's Falls, near Stonington, Connecticut.

The lawyer had written to this place an epistle at some length, but we had waited in vain for a reply; letters often went astray in those days, and, as I afterwards discovered, this one was most likely lost *en route*. In the meantime I had become a member of Mr. Edgerton's family, and had lived with them a year. I was treated with kindness, but of course it was not expected of him to take charge of my maintenance, and the proposition for a change came from my own lips.

In walking along the water-front one day I discovered

that a little brig, the *Minetta*, was about to sail for Stonington, and I proposed to Mr. Edgerton to take passage in her and search out my relative, if he were living.

The lawyer, who I could see felt himself responsible in some way for the beginning of my misfortune, exacted a promise that should I fail in finding M. de Brienne, I would return to him, and I should have done so had affairs terminated otherwise than as they did.

The consultation in which this decision was arrived at took place on the evening of the 10th of the month; and it was two days later, as I have written, that my new life began, for bright and early that morning I was standing at the taffrail of the little brig that was being warped out into mid-stream.

Mr. Edgerton and his family, consisting of a maiden sister and a grown daughter (he had been a widower for some ten years), together with Mr. Thompson, the schoolmaster, the major, the kind doctor, and some of my boy companions, were on the dock. And I must not forget that Aunt Sheba, Ann Martha, and Ol' Peter were there also—all three of them in tears.

The lawyer had promised to take care of Peter, and the doctor had taken Aunt Sheba and Ann Martha into his household. I am glad to say that I had not sold the old people, although I had a perfect right to do so, as they were my property, but had given them their freedom, and knew they were left in kind hands and keeping.

Soon the faces on shore became indistinct. The brig took in her kedge anchors, the trilling of her capstan falls ceased, her jibs rattled up the stays, the yards creaked aslant, and we caught the light westerly breeze. The tide was setting out, and we made good travelling of it.

I was not the only passenger. There was a Virginian, by the name of Chaffee, a tobacco-planter, who was going on the voyage as a sort of supercargo, and his wife (a slight, black-eyed woman of much spirit) accompanied him.

The captain and first mate were both New Bedford men, and tip-top sailors, as circumstances proved afterwards. The crew of nine men were Americans also, so far as I could judge, three of them being negroes—great, deep-chested black fellows, worth large sums of money in the market; but they were free men, and held themselves differently from slaves, although one, Pompey, waited on the cabin table.

Whether the *Minetta's* crew was a picked one or not I do not know, but no man would have felt ashamed of being over them — I can say that much. As for the brig, she was something over one hundred and eighty tons' burden, and loaded with tobacco, sole-leather, and turpentine; she was light in ballast, and in good trim for fast sailing.

The crew, for the most part, slept in a tall deck-house built abaft the foremast; the cabin was given up to Mr. Chaffee and his wife; the two officers and myself bunked in a little cubby-hole forward of the after-skylight.

The *Minetta* was old-fashioned, and her high poop and top sides gave her a clumsy look; her spars and masts were very heavy for her tonnage, and I think had been built for a larger vessel; but she spread a great show of canvas, and the way she boiled the water up in front of her proved she was no laggard I watched, with a sinking heart, familiar landmarks fade into the distance.

Here I was, scarce fourteen years of age, starting into the wide world alone, verily with my bridges burned behind me! Mr. Chaffee had entered into conversation with me, and he and his wife displaying great interest, I told him as much of my story as I thought proper. So far as the captain and first mate went, I might not have existed.

That night as I lay on my narrow little shelf, I was so full of thinking that at first I could not sleep. I longed for comfort, and would have given worlds to have rested my head on Aunt Sheba's shoulder (such a comfortable resting-place it was). I half sobbed aloud from loneliness, but at last I dozed off, and was awakened some hours afterwards by feeling the vessel pitching heavily.

Strange noises sounded all about me. Every plank overhead and on each side seemed to have a voice of its own. It was the first time I heard these sounds. Some loud bawling and the sound of scurrying on deck caused me to start up suddenly, and I almost cracked my skull against a beam. After that I could not sleep, and, lowering myself from the bunk, I dressed and climbed out to the air.

I had imagined, from the patter and stamping of many feet, that I should find the whole crew trying to save the ship from some distress, and I was not prepared for the calm sight that met my eyes. It was moonlight, and all sail was set. The brig rose and fell steadily, occasionally taking a sea *chug* under her broad bows with a jar which made her quiver, and the water would fly up in a gleaming sprinkle and scatter along the wet rail. Only four men were in sight—one at the wheel, two gathered in the lee of the forward deck-house, and the first mate leaning back against the sky-light, smoking a long clay pipe. (Oh, I have forgotten to mention that I had noticed the captain snoring in his bunk as I left the cabin, which had been reassuring.)

The cool breeze and the damp on my cheeks were grateful to me, and then and there I felt a love grow within me for the sea (and I have truly never lost it). I stayed on deck breathing a strange freedom until the morning watch.

About noon of this day, some time after we had

doubled the capes, the breeze freshened, and we were carrying only our lower sails. The planter and his wife both kept the cabin, suffering much from the unusual motion; but as for myself, I can here record I have never felt a touch of that sickness which is expected to accompany a first voyage or to follow a long stay ashore. I revelled in the swinging of the vessel, and wished it would blow harder—which it did.

At four o'clock in the afternoon a sail was made out to the northward, and holding the course that we already were on we would have passed close by her, as she was bearing down on us before the wind. I noticed, however, that as the stranger became clearer, and her lower courses could be seen, the first mate went aloft with a glass, and, hurrying down, held consultation with Captain Morrison. In pursuance to orders, the brig's course was altered a few points, and we stood to the eastward to give the approaching vessel a wider berth.

But no sooner had we done so than the latter bore away a trifle, as if it were her intention to intercept us, and twenty minutes' more sailing brought her into plain view.

She was a vessel the like of which I had never seen up to that day. Her hull appeared as large as one of the many-windowed warehouses on the wharves of Baltimore, her towering tiers of canvas gleamed in the sunlight, and a smother of foam rolled under her forefoot.

A few more turns of the wheel now, and we were holding a course due east, sailing with the wind almost abeam.

"She means to head us off," said Captain Morrison, looking about with an oath. Then he thundered an order to set the steering-sails.

Why he should have had any cause for alarm I did not know; but soon I could see that the crew were much disturbed. Gathered in a whispering cluster at the break

of the forecastle they were watching the vessel with anxious eyes. I timidly approached Mr. Norcross, the mate.

"Is she a pirate?" I inquired, half fearing.

"Yes, about that," was the gruff return. "She's a British line-of-battle ship, and keeps the seas, with all her kind, by robbery."

"Will she harm us?" I inquired again.

"Not you, my son," he answered, quietly. "But she would like to get her clutches on some of our brave lads yonder." He jerked his thumb towards the group of seamen, and spoke so softly I could scarcely hear his words; but an instant later, at a nod from the captain, he was all voice and eagerness, bellowing orders at top lung.

We took in some of the lighter sails, and, with a turn of the wheel and a heave, there we were, close hauled on the port tack! The big one followed suit majestically without a flutter of her canvas.

Slowly but surely we were nearing the huge vessel, now holding the same course as our own.

It was a grand sight! The shadows on her white sails were as blue as the sky overhead, her ports were opened, and the muzzles of the black guns could be made out plainly. The red coats of a party of marines on her forecastle made a bright patch of color, and some men sprawling out on her great yard-arms were no bigger to the eye than midges.

The captain was giving nervous glances at our shaking foresail. Then he took a look across the water, as if measuring the distance and the rate of the other's travelling. Suddenly a smile wrinkled his cheeks.

"We're outpointing the old whale, and going faster, Mr. Norcross," he said, grinning.

"Aye, sir; given the wind hold as it is and she will pass astern of us."

The crew by this time had noticed the fact, and a

movement began among them. One, a tall fellow with light hair and a well-set-up figure, took a few steps of a hornpipe.

"Not this time, Johnny Bull; not this time," he laughed, slapping one of his companions on the shoulder. "I know her—'tis the *Plantagenet;* and I'd go overboard with a shot in my pocket before I put a foot on her deck. She reeks of the cat!"

I was soon to learn why this man, whose name was Dash, knew so much. As soon as he had finished his dancing, the tall sailor and another man ran aft.

"Shall we show our colors, sir?" the former asked of Captain Morrison.

"Ay; toss them out," replied the captain, whose good-humor had now returned.

In two minutes the Stars and Stripes were crackling at our peak. The line-of-battle ship was almost even with us by this time. Faces showed above her bulwarks; we could see the officers clustered on the quarter-deck.

Suddenly a puff of smoke burst out from one of her forward ports, and a ball skipped and plashed across our bows—so close that we heard the slap of it against the water; then the report came to us. The captain mounted the bulwarks, and, taking off his hat, made an elaborate bow.

"Sorry I cannot stop, you great big hog," he said; and then, standing there bareheaded, he burst into such a torrent of cursing that Mrs. Chaffee, who had come out of the cabin, and was anxious to see the sight, sought its refuge again. But we had outpointed the battle-ship, and crossed athwart her bows.

Not three hundred yards astern of us she roared past.

"She dassent fire a broadside at us, or she'd do it in a minute," muttered Mr. Norcross, looking over his shoulder.

He had taken the wheel himself during the last few minutes, and had handled it amazingly, I can tell you.

As if afraid to acknowledge her discomfiture, the three-decker went on in silence, like she had not seen us, and our men, who were now all in the rigging of the brig, burst out into a cheer.

But they were cheering too early in the game, and, alas! this was soon to be proven.

Somehow, despite Captain Morrison's excited profanity, I had begun to admire him hugely.

CHAPTER V

THE LION'S GREED

So we ran on with the wind holding fair until late in the evening, steering northeast by east. I had overcome a great deal of my timidity already, and had asked so many questions and paid such close attention to the way the brig was being handled, that by nightfall I thought I knew not a little about the working of a ship.

Captain Morrison, seeing my interest was so real, and put in a good-humor, as I have said, by the escape from the 74, explained to me something about steering by compass, and the wherefore of several orders. One of the sailors, a Hercules in a blue knit shirt, amused himself by teaching me a few simple knots, and before the day was out I had dropped the mister from his name and was calling him "Silas," like any one of the crew.

The planter's wife had so far recovered from her indisposition as to take a seat at the swinging table in the cabin, and we made a very jolly party at supper. The skipper, warmed by a bottle of port which Mr. Chaffee had set upon the table, began to tell tales of the sea.

I have heard many stories in my life, but I do not think that I have ever been thrilled or excited by any in the way that I was that evening.

Mrs. Chaffee must have noticed it, for she closed her fingers over mine, that were tightly gripping the edge of the table, and stroked them in a gentle, motherly way. I resented this (although I'm glad I did not show it), for was not I at that very moment employed with the captain in repelling an attack of a Barbary corsair? and Mrs. Chaffee's kindly act recalled me to myself; reminding me that I was but a boy, after all, who a few hours before had been almost in tears for the lack of what she had shown me—a little sympathy and the comfort of a friendly glance and touch.

The captain had not finished his yarn-spinning—in fact, he was in the middle of it—when the first mate thrust his head down the companionway.

"Will you come on deck, sir, and take a look at the glass on the way up?" he said.

To my surprise, the skipper cast his tale adrift without an apology and hurried out, pausing for an instant only to give a hasty look at the barometer, which hung against the bulkhead at the foot of the ladder.

"'Tis evidently fallen calm," observed Mr. Chaffee, looking to see how much port there was left in the bottle, and giving a little whistle.

"And very glad am I that it has," answered his wife. "I think any more of that pitch and toss and I should have died."

For the last three-quarters of an hour, indeed, the *Minetta* had been stationary, heaving a little now and then, but in such a small way and keeping on such an even keel as scarcely to move the wine in our glasses. The captain had been gone but a few minutes when we all decided to go on deck.

The seas were round and oily, and the brown sails hung in lazy folds against the masts. The man at the wheel now and again gave the spokes a whirl this way and that, and he was forever casting his eye aloft as if by some motion of his he might catch a breath of wind.

It was past sundown, and there was a strange suffused glow everywhere, more like early dawn than the twilight of evening. But off to the northwest towered a black tumble of clouds that were edged with a fringe of lighter color. They were stretching upward and peering grandly above the horizon-line like a range of growing mountains.

A brilliant quiver of light flashed all around, and then a streak of forked lightning ripped horizontally, like a tear in a heavy curtain, against the pit of the cloud. A low, distant grumbling followed.

The captain went below at this, and bent over to look at the barometer again.

"It's falling, Mr. Norcross," he said, raising his head. "Shorten sail, sir, and be lively!"

The men tumbled out from the deck-house. The topsails which we had carried all the afternoon were taken in, and a reef put in the foresail and mainsail.

I watched all this bustling about with much delight, and then my attention was drawn to the sky. The clouds had now spread so that they were almost over us. It had begun to rain; a few big drops spattered the deck in spots as large as dollars; they could be heard falling in the stillness against the dry sails overhead. Then there came another flash of lightning and a deafening thunder-roll.

A slight puff of wind trailed the heavy blocks on the spanker-boom rattling across the deck.

The captain, who had been watching the clouds, suddenly pointed to the westward; then he jumped to the wheel, and immediately began shouting orders to haul up the mainsail, get in the jib, and make all snug aloft. Every eye had followed the skipper's gesture—a line of white below a wall of gray was coming towards us on the rush! The rain fell softly, mottling the surface of the water; but all at once there came a glare of pink and violet lights, and the thunder began to crash and roar on every hand.

Warned by the captain, Mr. Chaffee and his wife, pale with fright, went below to the cabin. I, however, kept the deck, and in some way (I cannot account for it) was overlooked. And here nearly comes an ending to my story.

So suddenly and so fair abeam did the wind strike us that it was almost a knock-down then and there, and the first thing I knew I slid across the deck over against the lee bulwarks. The scuppers were running so full that I went under from head to foot; I thought surely I was going to be drowned—in fact, I think I took a few strokes and imagined myself overboard. The masts were extending over the water so far that the yard-arms almost dipped, the crew were hanging on by anything they could lay hand to, and the wind raised such a screeching in the rigging that the captain, who was bawling at the top of his lungs, might as well have held silence; his voice apparently blew away from his lips. Nevertheless, some of the crew must have understood him, for they clambered into the shrouds. This I noticed as I tried to crawl up the slope of the deck. Then there came a loud report; the foresail blew out into tatters, and the brig righted. A turn of the wheel, and she was put before it, crashing down into the sea (that came tumbling under her quarter), and now and then lifting her stern, yawing and twisting as if she would roll over like a ball—any which way.

I managed with difficulty to make the after-ladder, and stumbled down it head first, some one slamming the sliding hatch with a bang almost on my heels as they went over the combing.

Looking about me, I found Mr. Chaffee and his wife engaged in prayer. They were much bruised from having been flung about the cabin, and were in great fear that we were about to founder.

But the *Minetta* was going so much steadier now that we all three sought our bunks, and managed to stay in them, and I had so much confidence in the captain and

crew, and was so unfamiliar with terror, that probably I
did not recognize the nearness we had come to disaster,
so after an hour or so I went to sleep.

When I awakened the sunlight was pouring in at the
transoms, and we were slowly heaving up and down.
There was nothing to give me an idea of the time of day,
but I could smell the brewing of coffee, and dressed
hastily.   No one was in the cabin, and the breakfast was
untasted on the table; so, hearing the sounds of conversation, I went on deck.

We were hove to, and, within an eighth of a mile of us,
another vessel was coming up into the wind.   She was
very trim to look at, well sparred and lofty, and I saw
that a boat was being lowered over her side.   She had
the weather-gage of us.

The captain was walking up and down with his arms
folded, and our crew were gathered in the waist, muttering in surly and half-frightened voices.

"We are in for it this time, Master Hurdiss," said
Mr. Chaffee, casting a bitter look over the taffrail at
the stranger, from whose peak was flying the British
Jack.   "We are under the lion's paw, and no mistaking it."

Norcross, the mate, leaned over the rail and spoke to
one of the men on the deck below him.

"Dash, do you know that vessel, my man?"

"Indeed I do, sir," was the reply from the light-haired
seaman who had appeared so elated at the escape of the
previous day.   "It's his Majesty's sloop-of-war *Little
Bell*, if I'm not mistaken, and she is a little floating hell,
sir; that's what she is!"

Nevertheless, as I have said, she was a trim-looking
craft, and I could not but admire the way the men tumbled into the boat and the long, well-timed sweep of the
oars as they pulled towards us.   When alongside, with-

in a few yards, a young man in a huge cocked hat stood
up in the stern-sheets.

"What brig is that?" he asked, brusquely.

Captain Morrison answered, giving our name and destination.

"I will board you," was the short reply of the cocked-
hatted one, and he gave orders to the bowman, who was
ready with his boat-hook, to make fast to the forechains.

The English seamen, a sturdy-looking set, were all
armed with cutlasses, and four or five of them followed
their officer over the bulwarks.

The young Britisher's insolence must have been hard
to stand.

"Muster your crew and let me see your papers," he
ordered, with a toss of his head ; " I would have a look
at both of them."

Our captain's politeness in replying, however, was
quite as insulting.

"You have only to mention your wish, my courteous
gentleman," he sneered. "Here are my papers and
there are my crew. Will you help yourself to the cargo
also? And pardon my not firing a salute, but we have
a lady with us who objects to noise—and loud talking,
maybe."

At this the English lieutenant lifted his great hat ;
but he glared at the captain as if he would have liked to
have laid hands on him ; then he ordered, in a lower
tone of voice, two of the crew to rout out the forecastle,
and the rest of them to give a look into the cabin and
deck-house. He waited until they had returned, and
then taking the papers that had been extended to him,
he called off the names of the American seamen. Each
one stepped forward in turn, but without saluting, and
replied to the lieutenant's questioning; apparently they
all hailed from New England. Three of them, however,
he told to stand over to the larboard side.

The men obeyed, and I have never seen such hate on any faces as they had on theirs.

But the scene, that was tragic enough in all conscience, despite the grinning of the armed men-o'-war's men who stood behind their leader, was to be broken by a climax as unexpected as a bolt from the azure heavens.

"John Dash," read the officer. There was no answer, and he called it louder again, without result. "Where is this man?" he asked, impatiently.

Our captain made a low bow. "Thanks to your honor for your kind inquiry," he replied. "But the man failed to report on the morning of sailing—so careless of him!"

It might have gone well had it not been for the interference of a low-visaged petty officer, who, with his fingers to his cap, here spoke.

"I saw some one go over the bow as we came up, sir," he said.

Two of the men hurried forward and leaned over the side. I, being near the rail, looked over also.

There was John Dash, holding on to the bobstay, his frightened face just above the surface of the water. In an instant he was hauled on board.

"Ah, there's where you've been all the time, Mr. Dash!" observed Captain Morrison, sarcastically. "And how strange I not knowing it! Are you clean and sober? This gentleman has been asking for you very kindly."

The poor man, dripping wet, was standing erect before the boarding-officer. The titter that had run through the English sailors ceased as they saw the look on his face. He was drawing quick breaths, half-snarling like a dog, but he was trembling from head to foot.

"Oho!" said the servant of the King, lifting his eyebrows, "and here we are, eh? I think you know me, as I remember you, Charles Rice! You left us at the Port of Spain one fine day a year ago, and forgot to return, you may remember. You owe his Majesty an accounting."

"I am an American citizen," returned the sailor, hoarsely, "born at Barnstable, Massachusetts! I was impressed from the ship *Martha* on the high seas, and owe accounting to no one but to my God!"

"None of your insolence!" cried the Englishman, drawing back his closed hand. "We'll see about that, sirrah! You'll come with me, and these other fine fellows also."

Dash, or Rice (I understood afterwards the latter was his real name), gave a leap backward and ran into the deck-house. The officer turned slowly.

" Bring that man out," he said to two of his bullies.

Before they had crossed the deck something happened, and no one who witnessed it can ever shake it from his memory. The tall sailor appeared at the doorway. His hands were behind his back, and his blue eyes were absolutely rolling in his head.

" No, by the powers of Heaven, you shall not be served!" he cried. "*There* is something you cannot command, at least, to do your bidding!"

With a swift motion he drew his left arm from behind him and flung something on the deck. *It was his right hand, severed at the wrist!*

Such a horror possessed us all that not a word was said. The planter's wife sank in a heap to the deck, and as for myself, I went sick to the pit of my stomach with the misery of it, and reeled to the side.

The lieutenant fell back as if struck a blow over the heart, and, without a word, followed by his men, he clambered weakly down to his boat and shoved off. Dash lifted the bloody stump above his head; a curse broke from him, and he fell senseless into the arms of one of the black seamen. They carried him into the deck-house, and all hands followed, even the wheel being left deserted. As for myself, I crawled below into my bunk and wound the blankets about my head—Mrs. Chaffee was screaming in hysterics.

Then and there was born in my heart such a hatred for the sight of the cross of St. George that I have never confounded my prejudice with patriotism, and this may account for some of my actions subsequently.

No one referred to the happening in our talk after this —it might not have occurred.

However, in such ways as we could we made the poor fellow comfortable; but John Dash, seaman, existed no longer; a poor, maimed, half-crazed hulk of a man was left of a gallant, noble fellow. But he had lived to teach a lesson.

Two days later we sighted Sandy Hook, and, beating up the bay, anchored in the harbor of New York, where the planter and his wife and the heroic seaman were put on shore.

As the wind and tide were ripe to take us up the East River and through the narrows of Hell Gate into the Sound, we tarried but long enough to drop anchor and get it in again, and I caught only a panorama of houses and spires and the crowded wharfs of the city.

The voyage up the Sound was uneventful, and my landing in Connecticut and what followed I shall make another chapter.

But we passed many coasting-vessels and towns (whose number seemed past counting on both shores), and at last we entered the narrow sound of Fisher's Island, and crept up close to the wharves of Stonington. I made up my mind not to go ashore until the following morning, as it was after sunset before we had found a berth that suited the skipper.

Oh, I have forgotten to add that when I returned to my bunk, after we were boarded by the party from the *Little Belt*, I had missed the miniature which I had left hanging by a nail driven into one of the stanchions. That one of the British sailors, in the hurried search of the cabin, had helped himself to it was beyond doubting.

CHAPTER VI

A LAND VOYAGE

As soon as breakfast had been finished I bade farewell to Captain Morrison, to the mate, and to all of the crew, with whom I had somehow gained popularity, and then I was set on shore, my friend Silas rowing me off in the dinghy, and parting from me evidently with some feeling.

When I felt the solid ground beneath me and smelt the familiar odors of a seaport town, my fears almost gained the upper hand, and I was tempted to stay by the brig and return to Maryland in her. But finding that Miller's Falls was distant only some thirty miles up in the country, and getting the right direction from the first person I asked (a blacksmith standing at the entrance to his forge), I set out bravely on foot with my belongings on a stick over my back, the way I had seen sailors start on a land voyage from Baltimore.

Hill country was new to me, and the stone walls and fences and neat white houses gave me much to wonder at as I plodded along the road that was deep in dry dust, and such hard travelling that after I had made twelve miles, or such a matter of distance, I grew very tired, and determined to rest.

Although it was November the day was quite warm, and I sat down by the edge of a little brook and bathed my feet, that had blistered badly. The cold water felt very comforting, and I took my ease.

Many thoughts came to me. What would my dear

mother have said to have seen me at that moment? Why had she not told me something of myself? Who was I? Why all this mystery? I gave it up.

While drawing on my shoes I heard a strange sound, and saw coming down the road a two-wheeled cart drawn by a team of swaying oxen. Climbing up to the roadway and hailing the man who was walking at their heads (calling out "Gee!" "Haw!" every other minute), I asked my whereabouts and the hour.

The farmer, even before he replied to my questions, began to subject me to many of his own: "Where was I bound?" "Where did I come from?" and, "Who did I know in the parts?" To these I replied as best I could, and with a directness that seemed rather to disconcert him.

But he was a kindly man, and noticing that I limped, and that I was in no condition to travel, he proposed my stopping the night with him, and he would carry me part way on my journey on the morrow. To this I agreed, as I found I had wandered somewhat out of my way.

At supper that evening I tasted for the first time the delicious cakes made out of buckwheat, and had to relate again, for the benefit of my host and his wife (a tall, sharp-featured woman, who spoke with a whining drawl), the story of my adventures and the eventful voyage of the *Minetta*.

When I told of the affair of the severed hand, and the action of the English, the woman quoted a passage from the Bible that was quite as much as a curse on the heads of the offenders, it breathed so of vengeance. But we had not burned half a candle before we all were yawning. Well, to be short, I slept in a great feather-bed that night, and the next morning, after breakfasting on more cakes than was good for the stomach, I started northward, mounted astride, behind Farmer Lyman on a jolting gray nag.

When my friend put me down he bade me a farewell, and told me I had but five miles before me to the town of Miller's Falls.

It was up and down hill, slow going, and noon, I should judge by the shadows, before I saw the village, nestling at the bend of a small valley. On the wind came to me the shrieking and clanking of machinery and the jarring of a waterfall.

I sat down on the top rail of a fence, and surveyed the village for some time before I descended the hill. Once more afoot, as I walked along I saw in a steep gorge, a sheer descent of some fifty feet to one side of the roadway, a rushing brook, and I could perceive, almost in the centre of the town itself, a pond that spread back into the hills.

The mill that was raising such a clatter stood at one side of a dam built of stone and timber that had backed the water of the pond; and I walked up close to the building, looking with wonder at everything. A huge overshot wheel was turning and splashing busily, and the water was roaring over the dam and breaking on the brown, slippery rocks below. It fascinated me, and I stood for some time leaning over the rail watching it. I grew so interested, in fact, that I almost forgot my mission or where I was, and was recalled to myself by a voice hailing me from only a few feet above my head.

"Well, sonny," said a drawling voice, "be ye wondering where all that water is goin' to?"

A thin, cadaverous face, with a very pointed nose and chin, was thrust out of a little window, and two long hands on either side gave the man the effect of holding himself in his position by the exercise of sheer strength.

"I suppose it goes into the sea," I replied, perceiving that he wished to chaff me.

"Correct," he answered. "Go to the head."

"May I come into the mill?" I asked, for I had never
seen one, and the varied noises excited my curiosity.

"Why, certainly," the man said. "Pull the latch-
string in the door yonder and come in."

The Fall's mill not only sawed the long pine trunks
into planks and squared timbers, of which there was a
profusion about, but also ground most of the grain for
the neighborhood. As I entered, the stones were grumbling and the air was full of dust that clung to everything.

"What is it you're making?" I shouted into the tall
man's ear. He had greeted me at the doorway.

"Buckwheat cakes," he replied, thrusting his hand
into the top of an open sack. " Ye're a stranger here,
ain't ye?"

I knew what to expect by this time, and that probably
my appearance had determined the miller to find out all
he could about me merely for his own satisfaction. So,
half shouting in his ear, I related (by the answering of
questions) part of my story—at least, I told him where I
had come from and the why and wherefore of my trip.
When it came to asking for my uncle's place of residence I ran against trouble, and my heart sank.

"What is the name?" asked the thin man when I had
first mentioned it.

"Monsieur Henri Amédée Lavalle de Brienne."

"Eh?"

I had to repeat it.

"No such person in these parts," the man answered,
shaking his head positively. "And I ought to know,"
he added. (I dare say he did, and most people's private business besides.)

But here was an uncomfortable position! What was I
to do? Somehow the hum and groaning and rumbling
of the mill appeared to prevent my thinking, and I
stepped to the door.

The village of Miller's Falls stretched down one wide road that curved about the edge of the mill-pond. It was not a cheerful-looking place, taking it altogether, but it had a certain air of prosperity; there was some movement, and a number of horses and carts were on the streets.

All at once the chatter of voices and the familiarly shrill cries of boys at some rough merriment arose from the road at the right. I looked about the corner of the building and saw that a half-dozen youngsters of about my own age were coming down the hill, and before them rode an odd figure on a small brown horse.

It was a little man, who sat very erect, and who had a semi-military hat set aslant his gray hair, which was gathered in a long queue behind. His coat was of a very old fashion, made of velvet, and heavy riding-gaiters encased his thin legs.

The horse he was riding was by no means a bad one, and it was clearly all the old gentleman could do to keep him from breaking into a run; and to accomplish this last was the evident intention of the crowd of small boys, for they were tickling the horse's heels, or giving him a cut now and then with some long switches; they varied this by pelting small pebbles at the rider. The latter, however, kept his seat and controlled the horse exceedingly well, although it was easy to see that he was both angry and frightened, for he would stop and scold at the boys and often turn his horse's head threateningly in their direction. This would excite a scattering and shouts of derision and laughter.

Some one spoke over my head at this moment, and I saw that the lank miller and one of his crew, attracted by the noise, had perceived the approach of the old man and his tormentors.

"Why, it's old Debrin, from Mountain Brook," said the miller. "Come down to get his corn ground, I reckon."

Slung across his saddle were two bags, and the rider was now headed towards the mill and restraining the horse with difficulty. When he drew up at the little platform it was all he could do to throw off the bags, and when he had lifted his legs from the stirrups and slid to ground I thought he would have fallen, and for the first time I perceived how old a man he was. Moved by some impulse, I jumped down from the door-sill and helped him tie the rope halter of the little horse fast to a post; his hands were trembling so that I doubt if he could have accomplished it unaided.

My action had so surprised the boys that they had gathered in a circle about us in silence and astonishment. When I had finished, the old gentleman looked at me with his black, beadlike eyes and raised his hat.

"Thank you—thank you very much." he said, in broken English, in which I recognized at once the manner in which my mother had spoken. The trace of the French tongue was there beyond all doubt. So I lifted my own cap, and answered in what I may well call my native tongue, and told him in French that I was very glad to have been able to help him.

His astonishment at hearing me address him thus was so great that for a minute it deprived him of the power of answering, but then he burst forth into such rapid speech and into so many violent gesticulations that it was all I could do to follow. The little crowd pressed us so close that I became embarrassed, and the old man, who had been complaining of the conduct of the boys and the temper of his horse, and at the same time stating how welcome it was to hear his own tongue again, suddenly saw that he was creating a deal of amusement for the gaping, snickering circle about us. He drew himself up proudly, and his lip curled with infinite contempt.

I now, for the first time, had an opportunity to ask a question that had been forming itself in my mind.

"Are you Monsieur de Brienne?" I ventured.

"I am; and you?" he replied.

"Am Jean Hurdiss, your nephew, who has come all the way from Baltimore to see you."

Instantly his manner changed. I thought he was going to fling his arms about me. But if such was his intention he controlled himself.

"We will not talk before this canaille," he said, quietly, "but I cannot here express my delight at seeing you."

This must have appeared very strange to the on-lookers, who, of course, understood no word of what we were saying, and what happened afterwards must have been stranger still; and I can now readily see why I was regarded as a mystery by the inhabitants of Miller's Falls during the whole course of my stopping in the neighborhood.

The old man, with a great deal of dignity, laid hold of the sack of corn, and seeing that nobody volunteered to help him; I took up the other end, and we carried it into the mill. There we flung it on the floor, and M. de Brienne pointed at it with his finger.

"Grind me this," he said, in a commanding tone, despite the broken and twisted accents. "I will pay for it when I return."

Then he spoke to me: "Come, my child; we stay here no longer than necessity demands of us."

The surprise occasioned by our actions at the meeting had struck the crowd of ill-bred youngsters dumb, but they were soon started again in their shouts and deviltry by the difficulty that my uncle and I immediately had with the little brown horse. How so feeble a man as he appeared to be could ever manage the restive beast at all was more than I could see. Full half a dozen times he failed to make the saddle, even with my assistance, and this even drew laughter from the windows in which some of the mill-crew had gathered.

At last, however, I succeeded in getting the old gentleman into the saddle, and, obeying him, I crawled up behind him and placed my arms about his waist. But between my lack of knowledge, the horse's scampering, and the old man's weakness, we almost came to grief more than once.

Three of the little rapscallions, who of course could not follow us, for we had started on a run down the road, cut across the meadow by a path, as if intending, for some reason, to head us off.

They reached the main roadway first, and were waiting in an orchard at the end of a stone wall for us to go by. I noticed that they had gathered some apples, which they held in the hollows of their arms, much as boys carry snowballs in an attack. I had been angry before, but now my one desire was to get at them. I often fear that I must be a vindictive person indeed.

As we approached they let fly, of course, and one of the apples caught my uncle squarely in the forehead. He would have fallen, I believe, had I not held him for an instant. Reaching forward, I caught the reins and brought the little horse to a sudden halt. Then I slipped from my seat to the ground, and with no weapons but my closed fists I charged the enemy.

It is not bragging to say that from some ancestor I have inherited immense strength, and even at the age of thirteen I believe I should have been a match and more for some lads four or five years older. (Since I have been seventeen years old even I have never met a grown man who could force down my arms or twist a finger with me.) But to return : I caught the first boy a jolt with my knuckles on the side of the head, and, seizing the second, who came to his rescue, I fairly believe I threw him over the fence without so much as touching it. He landed on some loose stones on the other side, and set up a tremendous bawling. The third lad did not stop to get a chance, but legged it as **fast as** he could across the meadow.   I **was so** angry now that I believe murder was in my heart, and I **picked up** the broken branch of a tree and stood **over the first** boy whom I had struck.   **He looked at** me and began to beg for **mercy.**

"**Bravo!**" called **my** uncle from **the horse, that for a** wonder was standing still.   "Bravo, *mon enfant.*"

He was wiping the juice of **the** apple **from** his eyes, **but** catching my glance **he** threw **me a kiss** from his finger-tips, and laughed **a** laugh of congratulation and sympathetic triumph.

I covered my fallen antagonist with added chagrin by scooping up with **a** sideway stroke of the foot some dust out of the road on top of him, and, walking to the horse, I clambered **up** behind again.   Then, digging my heels into the nag's side, we started on a gallop up the hill **and** entered the woods that lined the crest.

I had been so **angry that I** dare say **I** had shed tears **even at the** moment **of my** victory (what **varieties of** weeping there are, to be **sure**), and I had such **a lump** in my throat that I waited for my uncle to begin any conversation he might wish, but he did not speak **until** after we had progressed some distance in among the trees. Then he pulled the horse **up** with a jerk (that caused me almost **to** break my **nose** on the back **of his** head), and he ordered me to dismount.

I did **so.**   Monsieur de Brienne leaned from the saddle and **turned** me **around** by the shoulder, much **as I** have seen a planter look at a negro before **purchasing.**

"Very like, indeed ; very **like,**" he muttered.   "A true De Brienne."

Then he leaned farther over and **told** me to embrace him.   I complied, and **he** kissed me on each cheek and between the eyes.

This quite embarrassed me.   I dropped my glance to

the ground and shuffled uneasily; but the old man had
begun to talk, and I dare say it was an hour that we
stood there, for I had to tell him, of course, of my mother's death and of the burning of Marshwood. When I
came to relate of the loss of the strong-box and its contents, the old gentleman grew pale; then he drew a long
breath, and ripped **out** into a frightful burst of temper.
For some reason I could not help but feel that it was directed against me, and I waited until he had calmed before I went on. Suddenly I remembered the letter which
had given me the only clew that had led to this meeting,
and I thrust my hand into **my coat** pocket. It was not
there! Fruitlessly I searched with a growing fear upon
me, and I saw that my uncle's little black eyes were following **my every** movement; I could see that there was
a **certain suspicion** in his look, but the **letter** was not
forthcoming, and was not to be found in my bundle, **al-**
though I undid **it from** the strap of the saddle-bag where
I had tied it, and spread its few contents on the road-
side.

"Where is the miniature that you spoke of finding?"
inquired Monsieur de Brienne, in a cold, harsh voice.

I told him what I imagined had become of it.

"Ah, bah!" he cried at this, and raised his hand as
if he would have struck me. Had he done so I believe
I should have pulled him from **the** saddle. He was
scarcely **larger** than myself, and I was growing angry at
his unnecessary and unjust words.

"What have you done?" he cried, restraining him-
self. "**You have** lost all the proofs — all the papers,
you fool! Now we can prove nothing. A curse on such
stupidity! What use are you without them? Why did
you come?"

I had gathered up my possessions, and was tying to-
gether the corners of the handkerchief, making up my
mind to burden him no longer with my presence, and to

return whence I had started (I still had a number of the gold pieces sewed in the lining of my cap, where Mr. Edgerton's maiden sister had placed them), but suddenly M. de Brienne spoke in rather an eager tone, and asked me to come closer to him. I did so, wondering. He leaned forward and caught one of the buttons of my coat between his thumb and forefinger, and looked at it closely. Then he heaved a sigh.

"All there is left," he said. "Ah, my child, my child, you do not know what you have lost! Pardon my rough speech of a moment since, but what you told, and what has happened, appeared to turn into ashes what little hope I had left in life."

I was softened by the sadness of his tone and the real grief that showed itself in his small, pinched features. So I looked up at him and tried to smile.

"What is your name?" he questioned of me, eagerly, in a whisper, as if to extract a secret that I might not care to disclose aloud.

"John Hurdiss," I replied. "That's all I know; but I can tell you what the letter that I lost contained." I repeated it word for word.

The old man drew a long sigh. "Was your mother's name Hortense or Hélène?" he questioned again, suddenly and hoarsely.

"I don't know," I said. "I have no idea. My mother told me nothing."

"So be it," he replied, as if accepting a decision against which there was no use railing. "Come, son; up with you, and we will ride on to my château."

We followed the well-worn road, and then turned off through the woods, and came to some pasture bars at the edge of a clearing: I slid to the ground and opened them at a command from my uncle, and replaced them after he had gone through. The field that we entered had been sheep-grazed, and was poor pasturage. Here and there crumbling, hoof-worn patches of rock showed through the sparse, close-nibbled turf ; clusters of rank fern and hardhack bushes were dotted about, and we threaded them, following a narrow path until we were stopped by a second gate, which I opened in the way I had the first. A half-mile of travelling through an expanse of soft, swampy ground, grown with alders and dogwood, and I heard the sound of running water. Soon we came to a clear brook that gurgled beneath overhanging banks, and purled about gleaming, time-smoothed stones ; crossing it, and clambering up the steep bank, we arrived at a second clearing, hardly five acres in extent. A half-score of large apple-trees and a diminutive garden were to the left, and at the edge of the wood was a small, unpainted house ; close behind it a little barn, whose foundations extended into the hillside.

"Gaston! Gaston!" called Monsieur de Brienne, at top voice, "where are you hiding?"

In answer a head was thrust from the doorway, and the oddest-looking figure that I had ever seen came into view. It was an old man, whose frame when covered with flesh or muscles must have been enormous, but now so scantily cushioned were the bones that the quaint clothes hung on him much in the way that a coat hangs on a fence-post. But the man moved with incredible swiftness. He gave a strange look at me, and took Monsieur de Brienne's stirrup-leather in his hand and assisted him to dismount. I pushed myself backward over the horse's hind-quarters.

"A guest, Gaston, to Belair! My nephew, Monsieur Jean Hurdiss. . . . This is Gaston, my valet, chef, major-domo, and standing army."

My uncle smiled as he said this, but the other's face was most serious. As I eyed him closely his countenance looked more like a ball of tightly wound twine with ears and features than anything else I could imagine. I had never seen such a mesh of wrinkles, or imagined that age could stamp itself so wonderfully. That the old servant was not decrepit, however, was evident from the deft way in which he unsaddled the little horse and threw the trappings over his shoulder.

Now my uncle turned to me again. "Welcome, my son," he said. "Consider all here as yours entirely."

He ushered me through the doorway. I could scarce control an expression of astonishment as I looked about. Immediately facing the light I saw something that caused me to give a start. It was the figure of a man in flowing satins and velvets; great curls fell over his shoulders, and torrents of lace poured at his wristbands and knees. He had on high red-heeled shoes, fronted by wide bows, and his slender, bejewelled hand rested on the top of a tall walking-stick.

It took me a second glance to perceive that it was but a portrait that extended from the floor to the ceiling, being merely nailed, without framing, against the wall. A rough table made of pine boards but covered with a handsome cloth was in the centre of the room. It was heaped high with books in embossed leather covers. Tacked about everywhere were many portraits of times long since. One especially, before which I drew a long breath—dumfounded (it was so like my mother)! But Monsieur de Brienne had gathered me by the elbow, as it were, and marched me around.

The portrait whose resemblance had struck me so vividly he told me was my grandmother, and then went on, stopping before each, "Your great-grandfather, your great-uncle, your aunt," and so forth, and so forth.

One might have thought that I was being introduced in person to all my ancestors and past family — in fact, I caught myself bowing as if it were expected of me.

But after a few minutes I found a chance to look about. There were but four rooms on the ground-floor of the

little house and three above, and if the furniture of Marshwood had been an odd assortment, that of Belair was odder still. I had noticed, as I have said, that the portraits were not in frames; they had evidently been brought from their former resting-place rolled in some shape or other for convenience. Many of them showed traces of rough handling, and were much cracked and soiled.

My uncle slept on the first floor in a great four-poster bed hung about with heavy curtains of embroidered silk, but the rest of the *ameublement* was made up of clumsy wooden benches and stools, not the workmanship of a joiner, but clearly made by unskilled hands.

The room up-stairs to which I was shown contained nothing but a mattress stuffed with corn-husks, and, hanging on the wall, a beautifully painted landscape. A bench, on which stood an ebony cross, and a large brass blunderbuss made fast to a nail over the door, were all the other things in the room. The one small window looked out upon the bleak hillside.

Wonderment at my surroundings gave a zest to the situation. I awaited new developments most anxiously while I sat there on the floor, leaning against the window watching the sunset. But hunger soon told me it must be near meal-time, so I arose, put on a clean shirt-frill, and shifted my jacket. Hearing my name called a minute later, I descended the stairs.

At dinner we were waited upon by the great wizzened-faced servant. My uncle, who was taken with a sleepy, tongue-tied mood, had attired himself in such a brilliant-ly faded costume that he resembled nothing less than one of the pictures that looked down at us. I could not but smile.

Before the meal was half finished, however (it was exceedingly well cooked and toothsome), I received a shock.

Monsieur de Brienne suddenly and without a warning gave a little cry and fell back in his arm-chair (a home-made affair, cut from a barrel of some sort), and I, frightened, ran to his side.

But the old servant appeared quite used to this, and together we got my uncle into his bed, where we rubbed and chafed his limbs until I grew so tired I could hardly move. The next day I thought he was like to die. He would not let me leave him, and talked so incoherently that I could make no sense out of his maunderings at all.

Now begins such a strange existence that if it were told to me by any one who claimed to have led it I should be most doubtful. It would make a volume in itself, maybe, but I intend to hasten over this period, and to get quickly into that from which has developed the present.

To this end I shall do my best to resist any temptation to dwell at too great length on the life I led at the lonely farm-house on Mountain Brook.

CHAPTER VII

HARDSHIPS

Behold the third attempt that I have made to condense this part of my narrative.

In desperation, for I wish to push on, I have adopted the measure of giving but an outline of my personal history covering two years nearly.

So I jump to a day in June, after I had been living in the little house on Mountain Brook one year and seven months.

During this time I had been to Miller's Falls but once or twice with my uncle; so insolently was I stared at, however, that I did not care to withstand again the ordeal of pointed fingers and the whispered conversations of the curious. But now, on this June day, here I was standing at the edge of the pasture waiting for some one most impatiently.

From the door-step of Belair nothing could be seen except ranges of hill-tops. But just a mile below the pasture lived a farmer named Tanner, who managed by hard labor to gain his living from the ground.

But I was not waiting for him, nor for my uncle, nor for Gaston, who, by-the-way, had been constituted, or had appointed himself, my guardian to such an extent that I might at times consider myself a prisoner. No, I was not waiting for any of them, but for some one who soon hove in sight across the slope of the opposite hill.

It was a little girl of fourteen years, and the only living being at that time who knew anything of my thoughts or life ; and they were both strange enough for a boy to possess or to endure.

Perhaps if I should tell of our conversation on this day it might recount something that would show how things were with me. Our first encounter was by accident—she gathering flowers and I hunting bird's-nests ; in our meetings afterwards there was nothing but the friendship of two lads, to put the case exactly ; so this morning, when she had climbed up on the top rail of the fence beside me, and hooked the hollows of her feet behind the bar to keep her balance, the way I was doing, we began, as children do, to speak without preliminaries of any kind in the way of greetings.

" Why weren't you here earlier ?" she said, as if accusing me. " I was here long ago."

" He had one of his fits on and kept me at work," I replied. " First I had to practise with the small sword for two hours. If I don't look out he will run me through some day. I almost wish he would !"

" I heard you shooting," said the girl.

" Yes, he wouldn't let me off until I had placed three pistol-balls inside a horseshoe nailed to the side of the barn ; but I'd rather do that than go through the fencing."

" Down at the village and at our house every one says you're all crack-brained." The girl laughed, making a grasp in the air at a yellow butterfly that flitted over her head. " What else did you do ?"

I was ashamed to say that I had been at my dancing-lesson, so I grumbled : " I had to translate four odes of Horace and learn all about a lot of stupid people named De Redun. I'm glad they had their heads cut off."

" Why did that happen to them ?" asked the girl. " What did they cut their heads off for ?"

" Because they were nobles and offended the French

Republicans by being polite and well dressed and clean,
my uncle says."

"Tell me all about it."

I had had the history of the great French revolution—
at least, one side of it—drilled into me ever since my ad-
vent at Mountain Brook. I had learned that my uncle
had escaped to America from France, where he had
fought for the King, and that my mother and her sister
had also managed to get away from the frightful prison
of La Conciergerie with their lives, but that my grandfather, two uncles, and an aunt by marriage had all lost
their heads by the guillotine, for the sole reason that
they were rich, very well dressed, and very polite indeed,
so far as I could make out.

I had learned by heart the family histories of any
number of the great noble families of France, and all
of this I considered most dull work indeed, and wasted
time.

However, the story that I related to Mary Tanner, as
we sat on the top rail of the fence, seemed to interest
her greatly.

"You see," I was saying, after I had finished spinning
the long yarn, "my name is not John Hurdiss at all; it
is something else."

"What is it?" asked the girl.

"I have no idea," I replied; "but my uncle always
calls me Jean, which means John, and, to be honest, I
don't think he knows himself."

"I don't see why *he* shouldn't be able to tell," replied
Mary, "if he knows so much about other people."

"No more do I," I answered. "But who cares? . . .
John Hurdiss is good enough for me."

Now, the fact of the matter was this, and it may as
well be stated here as afterwards: I had guessed about
the truth. My uncle did not really know my name, and
for this reason:

You see, as I have told, my grandfather was the Marquis de Brienne (I have forgotten to set down that Gaston always called my uncle "Monsieur le Marquis," or something that might be resolved into that). Well, the old gentleman (my maternal ancestor) had five children —the present proprietor of the Château de Belair on Mountain Brook, two younger sons (guillotined), two daughters, Hortense and Hélène, who afterwards married two of the well-dressed and well-hated ones at a time when they had more titles than gold.

Now it happened these two latter gentlemen—my real father and uncle-in-law, of course—had each the same initials (it is no consequence what the names were, but each ended in "de B."). Early in the great troubles they had sought refuge in England, having better luck than their future wives, who were taken by the revolutionists. But the two ladies escaped through the aid of an adventurous sea-captain, and they joined the colony of refugees in England, where they each found a husband waiting. But affairs did not prosper with them. In the year 1796 the Duke de B—— became entangled in a plot of some kind for the restoration, was caught in France, and lost his head like the rest of his family; and in the same year the Comte de B—— had an unfortunate duel with an English major of infantry, and was killed. This left the two noble ladies widows, each with an infant boy of a few months old to take care of. For some reason they packed up their belongings and set out for America on a sailing-vessel, commanded, it appears, by no less a person than the sea-captain who had assisted in their first escape from France.

Sad to relate, the ship in which they sailed was wrecked, and one of the ladies was lost with her infant in the disaster. Whether it was the Duchess de B—— or the Comtesse de B—— was not placed on record, but the commander of the ship, Captain John Hurdiss, married the survivor at some place in the West Indies, I believe, whence they moved to Baltimore.

Now there was no way of finding out which one of the ladies the gallant Captain Hurdiss had married; I had never heard my mother's first name mentioned that I could recall. My uncle did not know it, of a certainty.

The loss of the letter and the burning of the strongbox were two misfortunes that had prevented me from knowing really who I was.

This was the situation in a nutshell, and I trust that I have made it plain, for I have endeavored to do so in the very shortest manner, to the best of my ability.

It may all seem complicated, but I have tried hard to make it lucid. Let me return to the day in June, and to the boy and girl talking together, balanced on the top rail of the pasture bars. . . .

"Did you bring the book with you that you were speaking about?" I asked of my companion.

"No," she replied; "but I will leave it under the flat rock this evening."

"I'll get it, then," I answered. "Halloa! Look at that."

"It's a woodchuck!" cried the girl, jumping from her perch, and we both charged at a small brown animal that scurried into a hole beneath some loose stones. We were busily engaged routing him out and he was whistling back defiance (we had almost got at him) when I heard my name called. I looked up and saw my uncle and old Twineface approaching along the path.

"Jean, Jean! Come here at once!" called Monsieur de Brienne, in French.

"I'm going to run," gasped Mary, and without another word she turned and fled, jumping over the tall ferns like a deer.

My uncle had now approached within a few feet's distance.

"Who was that with you?" he inquired, angrily.

"Mary Tanner, the daughter of the farmer below," I replied. "I have known her for some months. She is very nice—and—and pretty," I faltered.

"Bah! You shall have nothing to do with her! Never speak to her, d'ye mind me? And here's where you have been spending your time instead of being at your studies! Come back with me; I will fence with you."

"But, uncle," I began, curbing my rising anger and making a bad job of it—"but, uncle, listen to me."

"I shall not listen to one word!" M. de Brienne returned. "You forget who you are!"

"Perhaps if you told me I might endeavor to remember," I retorted.

This pleasantry did not amuse; the old gentlemen turned livid, and, thinking I had said enough, I started for Belair, my uncle and Gaston falling in behind me.

It was one of my uncle's *young* days; and here, to put down something that I myself could not account for, and that no person of real learning to whom I have related the facts could explain: At varying periods my uncle, who was past sixty, seemed to be gifted with an agility, a nervous force and strength, that I have never seen equalled in a man of his slightness. This rejuvenation, during which he often sang rondeaux and tinkled an accompaniment on an old theorbo, would last for some ten hours, perhaps, and would be followed by two or three days, or sometimes a week, of collapse, during which he appeared on the verge of dissolution, and either Gaston or myself had to be with him every minute, administering from time to time a few drops from an acrid-smelling vial.

But, as I have said, this was one of his youthful days. I had been awakened in the early morning by a strange sound, and had found him jumping the colt backward and forward over a hurdle on the grass-plot before the house, Gaston standing by, a grim spectator, with no interest in his dull, lack-lustre eyes. For an hour the old man had put me through an exercise with the small sword (he was the best fencer I have ever seen), until I almost cried out from weariness, and we changed the proceedings for pistol practice. Now we returned to Belair, and, despite my complaining, I was forced to take up the foils again, and actually to defend myself, for my uncle kept me up to my work by now and then giving : a clip over the thigh or forearm. At last I grew angry, and pressed him so close that a smile of pleasure drew his lips, and he muttered " bravo " two or three times beneath his breath.

Suddenly I noticed a gray shadow cross his face, his eyelids drooped, he raised his hand, and, without a word, fell forward at my feet !

It was one of the worst attacks that he had experienced, and for five days Gaston and I nursed him ; thus I found no chance to get away to the pasture bars, or to the flat rock where Mary had placed the book we had spoken of.

On the sixth day my uncle was up and as spry as ever, but now I found that I was practically under surveillance ; wherever I went the frightful Gaston would go also. He was a most unpleasant person to have around, for although his senses were most acute and he possessed the cunning of a wolf, it was impossible to carry on a conversation with him. He had an impediment in his speech, a combination of a stutter and the result of having no roof to his mouth, that made his utterances sound like those of a savage or wild beast. To say " yes " or " no " was an effort for him, and he usually expressed his meaning by making signs.

One day, I remember, I had determined to test my authority over him ; for in most things he obeyed me implicitly, so far as the fetching and carrying went—but upon this occasion, as I say, I determined to give him a test.   I had walked as far as the edge of our clearing, then paused on the bank of the brook.

"Gaston," I said, "go back to the house—I'm going on alone."   The only reply was a shake of the head. "Do you hear me? I'm going on alone."   It was my intention to make my way to the Tanner farm-house, where, by-the-way, I had never been, and ask for Mary.

Now, seeing that Gaston did not intend to obey me, I jumped down the bank and dashed across the stream, but I had not taken a dozen strides before the old servant had me by the arm.   His long fingers closed on my flesh like a steel clamp.   The result was that I went back to the house.   But that evening I managed to get away, and went to the flat rock, under which the book had been hidden.   I had to wait until daylight before I could examine it, although Mary, a week or so before, had told me of its contents.

It was an old volume relating the adventures of an Englishman named Robinson Crusoe (I can recall the musty smell of its pages at this very instant).   Oh, the delight that I had for the next few days, reading the greatest story, to my mind, that was ever penned!   Oh, the desire for freedom and the longing to see the world which was builded up within me as I turned each page! Ah! Robinson, Robinson! despite the moral you intend to teach, you have turned many lads' minds to the sea ; you have given them a burning, dry thirst for adventure not to be quenched at home!   I had read few stories in English up to this time, but I fairly shook over this one with the intensity of my sensations.

I am afraid that living this life gave me a tendency for dissimulation, although in my jailer, Gaston, I had a hard one to deceive.   Nevertheless I succeeded in escaping one afternoon, and made off through the woods to Farmer Tanner's. Suffice it to say that I was chased out of the door-yard by the hired woman, with a broom in her hand; she informed me that Mary had gone away —where, she did not state. I was threatened, incidentally, with the ox-goad, if I should return; so my errand was not altogether successful.

Week after week, broken hearted, I cruised about the woods, hoping to get a sight of a welcome figure or to hear an answer to my whippoorwill call—our signal. It was to no purpose.

CHAPTER VIII

A REVELATION

HERE to give a big jump over time! Two years went by—and the misery of it all! The long, snowed-in days of the winters when, although my uncle had money, I think, I had scarcely sufficient clothing to keep me warm, and barely enough to eat. The lonely days of spring, summer, and fall, studying, working, or roaming the hills companionless and moody — I do not see how I survived, truly! M. de Brienne's conduct and manner by now had become so strange and his mind was so volatile that what little affection I held for him dwindled and dwindled. I had begun to hate Gaston generously.

But when spring came, to amuse myself, I delved in the garden, and was rewarded by seeing all my green things prosper wondrously. An illness that had lasted over a month almost brought me to my grave in April, and left me thin and weak ; but, notwithstanding, there had entered my mind but one idea—to escape, and that right soon. Why had I not thought seriously of it before must excite wonder, but the determination to prepare for an actual separation from my surroundings came to me in this fashion.

Owing to the strangeness of the costumes I was forced to wear I had much hesitancy in going abroad ; people would have taken me, I fear, for a mountebank. My coat, much too small, was of velvet ; my breeches of stained and heavy brocaded silk, much patched ; and my hose tattered and threadbare. Nevertheless, I was well shod, as my uncle possessed a box of shoes and boots of curious fashion and superior workmanship that fitted me, even if those I wore were not always mates. I determined, however, that I must have other clothing.

I knew nothing of the goings on of the outside world. Now to come to the day on which I was enlightened.

June again—June of the year 1813. I had escaped from Gaston's eye (the old man had begun to show some signs of age), and had gone down to the highway that led to Miller's Falls. Half hid in the bushes, I was seated, hoping to catch a glimpse of some human being, when I saw walking down the hill a figure whose appearance made my heart give a leap. It was a tall, broad-shouldered man, dressed in a sailor jacket and wide trousers. A great bundle, that he carried as if it was a bag of feathers, was on his back, and he was whistling merrily as he swung along the road.

I knew him in an instant, and his name came to me. It was Silas Plummer, who had been one of the crew of the *Minetta*. I sang out to him by name. He came to a halt, but showed half fright upon my appearing through the bushes.

"What in the name of Moll Roe have we here?" he cried. "Who are ye?"

"It is I, Master Plummer," I answered, and I told him who I was. In my eagerness I must have appeared half crazed, I judge, for he looked at me askance as I grasped him by the arm.

"What are you doing, lad?" he inquired. "Lord! I know ye now—and how you've grown!"

In a few words, and in an incoherent fashion, I fear, I told him of my life and my virtual imprisonment. Evidently the explanation set his mind at rest in regard to my sanity.

"Why don't you clear out—take leg-bail?" he said.

"There's a chance for a fine lad like yourself to the southward. The sea is not far away" (how my heart leaped at the word "sea"!), "and there are great goings on there. Harkee; we've taken their frigates, and given the lion's tail a twist until it is kinked like a fouled hawser."

"What do you mean?" I inquired, hesitatingly.

"Hear the lad!" Plummer responded, setting down his bundle and going into the pocket of his jacket and drawing out a newspaper. "There's a war between America and England! I'm just in off the *Comet* privateer. Listen to this," he said. He slapped his trousers-pocket, and it chinked to the sound of gold. "And listen here," he repeated, tapping the other side; it jingled musically. "Ho, but we are getting even with them for all their man-stealing!"

"A war with England!" cried I, taking the paper that had "Victory!" spread across it in large type. "Do you remember Dash, and his hand there on the deck?"

"Aye, like a glove thrown at the feet of the King," said the sailor; "and the news of it is about the world."

"Plummer," I said, "sell me some clothes; I'll pay you for them. If you'll wait"—I had hidden three or four of the gold pieces under the flat rock—"I will run and fetch you the money," I continued, eagerly.

"Not a penny, not a farthing," answered my old friend, giving my shoulder a push. "Come into the woods. I have some duds that might fit you here in my kit."

My hands and, indeed, my knees also, were trembling so that I had to have assistance (a strange tiring-maid) in getting into the clothes. But in ten minutes I was rigged out all-a-taun-to in the outfit of a swaggering privateersman, even to the shirt opened at the throat and the half-fathom of neckerchief—I recollect that I was mad to see how I looked in it.

"And here's a cap, too," laughed Silas. "It has a Portugee rake to it, but never mind—ah! man alive! now you're ship-shape."

He stood off and looked at me, with his head side-wise, as if I was wholly some workmanship of his own hands.

"Anchor's atrip," he cried, imitating the shrilling of a boatswain's whistle; "set sail and away!"

"How—*how* can I thank you?" I said, half faltering, and blushing, for I felt hot all over.

"By meeting me ten days from now in New London, my lad! There's a crack brig, the *Young Eagle*, about to sail from there; and though they'll take few green-horns, togged out that way you can pass muster. Ship with me, messmate. I'll help you out!" He grasped my hand. "Ah, you've got a good grip for a rope! And look at the chest and the arms of you! Big as my own, I'll warrant."

I had never realized what a size I had become; but I had been finding out that it was only my uncle's skill that kept me from disarming him in our fencing-bouts of late, and Gaston had not laid hands on me since some time before my illness. Now I was fully recovered and in fine fettle.

"I'll go with you," I replied, grasping Plummer's hand again; "I will be there, trust me for that, Silas, my friend."

"The *Young Eagle*, then, at New London, eh?" He slapped his pockets and started off. "I'm bound up-country to see my sweetheart!" he shouted back from over his shoulder, and I heard him chanting the "Sailor's Return" as he disappeared about a bend in the road.

I gathered my rags and made for the brook, where I looked at myself until I became fairly ashamed, and threw a stone at my reflection in the water. Then tak-ing off my clothes, I donned the old ones, and hiding my bundle beneath the big flat rock where I kept the *Robinson Cruso:*, an old horse‑pistol, and many treasures—including a half‑score of the De Brienne buttons —I went up to the house. I could see that my uncle was in a strange excitement; he was pacing up and down the front room muttering and frowning. He did not notice my presence, but Gaston cast a suspicious look at me, in return for which I, elated by the doings of the day, made a threatening gesture. I think the man had grown afraid of me, for he cringed.

At twelve o'clock that night I was awakened by some one stirring in my room. I looked up. It was my uncle. He was in his night‑dress, barefooted, and his gray hair straggled over his ears. Held close to his side, as if it rested in a scabbard, was a narrow court sword, whose naked blade flashed in the ray of the moonlight that came in at the curtainless window.

"No, by St. Michel, they shall not enter!" he cried, and he stopped suddenly, rigid, as if he were listening for some one coming up the stairs. Then he turned to the bed on which I lay.

"The Swiss guard is beaten back! Arise, your Majesty!" he said. "They're upon us. Come, gentlemen, stand fast!"

Again he listened. "No, they're gone," he whispered, softly. "Is the Princess calling for me?" He made as if to sheathe the sword, and I saw, in doing so, the sharp blade cut into the palm of his left hand; but he paid no attention to it, and, making a profound bow in my direction, he hurried down the stairs.

To say that I had shuddered would not express it. And suddenly, as if a burst of light had come upon me, the idea that I need no longer stay flooded my brain.

"Why, he might murder me!" I thought, the conviction coming then for the first time that he had turned

"'ANCHOR'S ATRIP,' HE CRIED"

madman. Quickly I arose, and putting on only half my clothing and my shoes. I lowered myself out of the window.

It was cloudless, and the moon was at the full. My shadow chased before me as I ran down the path. Freedom! freedom! seemed to beckon me. I breathed the same sensation that I had on that clear moonlight night when the salt breeze was in my hair; when the wide sea rose and fell, and the little brig dashed through it as though she had caught my exultation or I hers.

I leaped the brook, and scattered the sleeping birds out of the bushes up the banks. "Ho for the sea! Hurrah!" I cried; and I never turned to give even a farewell look at the Château de Belair.

CHAPTER IX

FREEFOOTED

When I arrived at the flat rock I shifted into the suit of sailor toggery, damp from the wet of the dew; and making a pile, and a very small one, of my treasures—all but the *Crusoe*—I ripped out the back of my embroidered waistcoat and tied them up in it.

Striking out for the highway, I soon gained it and started on a dog-trot, headed south. My lungs and legs must have been in good condition, for I kept it up steadily for an hour or so. (It may seem imagination, but I believe people can run faster and longer at night; maybe the distance seems shorter because we observe less clearly.)

Soon I began to recognize the well-known signs of approaching dawn. I had heard a fox bark up in the hills some time since, and now, as if in challenge, the crowing of cocks sounded and drowsy songsters fluttered twittering in the branches of the trees along the road. Before the sun had risen, round and red, the robins were piping and the thrushes tinkling their throat-bells on every hand.

I was in a new country, a much richer one than that of a few miles farther north; the farms were nearer together, and prosperity was plain on the face of the earth. The damp morning mists that hung over the brown new-ploughed ground smelt of growing things, and the buds on the trees, as they opened to the warmth of morning, scattered their scents lavishly.

I had signalled out at the bottom of a hill a house at which I intended stopping and getting a meal if I could; but as I went by a pasture I saw a man driving some cows through an opening in the fence. He saw me also, and hurrying about his work, he came walking towards me.

I now perceived that my costume was a password to people's hearts.

"Good - mornin', lad," hailed the farmer, who was a man past middle age. "Goin' off to sea again, be ye?"

"Yes," I replied, stepping to the fence. "Am I on the right road for New London?"

"Air ye in the navy?" he asked, without replying to my question.

"No; but I'm to ship aboard the *Young Eagle* below."

"Oh, privateersman, eh? More money in it, I reckon. But there's no lack of glory in the sarvice. I have a son aboard the *Constitution*. He was in her when she fit the *Guerrière*. When I think of it I allus feel like cheerin'."

And then and there the farmer took off his hat and gave three lusty cheers—in which, despite myself, and not knowing anything about the subject, I joined.

"My name is Prouty," the old farmer went on. "And my son's name is Melvin Prouty. Ye'll heard tell on him afore long. He's got promoted already. He's a quartermaster."

"Good!" I exclaimed, for, notwithstanding my sailor's rig, I was supposing a quartermaster must be next to a commodore at least.

"Well, I won't keep ye. Ye're on the right road. Good-luck and good-bye," he said, extending his rough hand across the fence.

I shook it warmly, and, picking up my small kit, trotted down the hill. I covered some two miles more before I stopped at a farm-house for breakfast. Here I was received with as much honor as if my short stopping was to cast a blessing. I found that I had to adopt some subterfuge; and when asked what vessel I had served in, I replied, and with truth, "the *Minetta*, from Baltimore," and that I was bound to join the *Young Eagle*. Her fame evidently had spread broadcast, and I cannot forget the envious looks that were cast at me by a couple of youngsters, who requested to know if I had any pictures on my arms. As I had none, and had seen them on my voyage, and often before that, pricked into the skins of the sailors on the wharves, I determined to remedy this defect as soon as possible—surely 'tis a relic of a savage ancestry.

The goodwife of the house where I got my first meal almost insisted upon my carrying away enough to stock me for a voyage of two or three days; but it was mostly pie, for which I care little, so I declined.

The main road was so well travelled that there was no mistaking it now. My legs, as well as my heart, seemed gifted with a desire to get ahead, and every one I met had for me a kindly wave of the hand, and would have questioned me breathless had I not made haste and hurried on.

By four o'clock in the afternoon I had mounted to the top of the hill. From there I caught a glimpse of the ocean; close to, the wide opening of the river Thames, and, stretching to the westward, the blue Sound. How the picture comes to me! The sparkling sea; here and there a white sail dotted on it; the breeze, that was from the south, bringing the smell of it to my nostrils, setting my heart beating and thumping in my throat! Overhead a great hawk spun about in widening circles. I knew how he felt, for was not I free, and the world before me at my feet?

Out of pure joy and the loftiness of my spirits, I threw

the Portuguese cap into the air and caught it as it fell. And nothing would do but I must start at a headlong pace down the hill, jumping the water-bars and kicking my heels behind me as if I were a colt escaped from a pasture. By the time that I had entered among the houses that clustered about the outskirts of the village of Groton it grew dusky, and I began to feel a trifle tired, for I had covered the distance of some thirty miles that day.

As the dwellings became thicker and I could see across the river the clustering lights of a large town, I felt a little trepidation. People had not paid so much attention to me as they had farther up the country, and I had run across one or two sailor-men, dressed much as I was (save the cap), who had hailed me good-naturedly. But I longed for a bed and a warm cup of coffee, and seeing a citizen leaning over a fence, smoking meditatively, I inquired my way to the best inn in New London.

"I should 'a' reckoned that you'd 'a' known them all by this time, lad," he said; "but the best hotel is the United States, down near the wharves. Keep straight ahead for the ferry."

At the end of a lane on the water front I found a man with a small boat, who rowed me across the river and disdained to ask pay for it. He left me standing gaping about on the pier like the veriest country loon. Groups of sailor-men were everywhere; to all appearances they had gained possession of the freedom of the town, and, moreover, they seemed to have captured the prettiest girls, or bargained to drink the place dry, for from a grog-shop a number of them reeled out, arm in arm, singing a song to a tune that I learned to know and sing well afterwards myself—"Hull's Victory." The sound of fiddles and merriment were to all sides.

CHAPTER X

AT last, pulling my wits together, I asked my way, and found it was only a few steps to the United States Hotel. So I turned from the street and entered.

A number of loungers were on the broad veranda. A group of men—one in a cocked hat and blue coat with brass buttons—were sitting about a table on which there was much to drink, and they were not slighting it. But here no one gave me more than a glance, and I entered the coffee-room, where I found a corner.

A hubbub of conversation and much strong tobacco filled the place, and the waiters were so busy that I did not know enough to insist upon gaining their attention; thus no one sought me out. I had sat there but a few minutes when I became engrossed, listening with dropped jaw to a group of seamen talking within a short distance of me. One of them was telling of the action between the *Hornet* and the *Peacock*, and he interspersed his talk by constantly calling to those about him to drink the health of " Lawrence, the bravest officer that ever trod a quarter-deck !"

I here learned that a man may be a hero by mere reflected glory, for each one who drank with him nodded to the speaker as if Lawrence were his name. Suddenly I perceived that a man in a long apron was standing at my elbow.

" What is the order, messmate ?" he asked, familiarly.

I replied by asking for some coffee, and stating that I would like to get a room for the night. This evidently caused him some surprise.

"Rooms come high," he smiled, looking at me, "but I can get you the coffee, right enough."

I had seen one of the sailors, in paying his reckoning, wave back the change due him into the waiter's palm, so when the man returned I offered him one of the gold pieces I had in my pocket. He looked at it curiously, bit it, and crossed over to a table and showed it to some of the sailors. The man to whom he handed it rang it on the bottom of an upturned plate.

"Good gold," he said, "and French. I've seen 'em often."

Whether he told the value of it or not I do not know, but soon the waiter advanced with a half-handful of silver coin. I waved it back at him, and the man's eyes grew large. He returned to the sailors and spoke to them.

"Just home from a cruise, I dare say," said one, looking over his shoulder, but not addressing me.

"He doesn't look it," replied another, who had "Success to the Fox" painted on the ribbon of his cap. "But one can't tell nowadays. There was a girlish-looking lad—" Here the man began a yarn in a low voice, and I buried my face in my coffee-cup, and almost scalded my throat.

"I've got a room for you, messmate," said the servant, leaning close to me, "and the best one in the house. If you've got your kit ashore, I'll take it up myself."

"No, thanks," I replied. "I have nothing with me." I noticed that the man was looking very carefully at my hands. Although they were not soft exactly, as they had been hardened by the chopping of wood and the handling of hoe and spade, the life of the sailor-man stamps the hands so distinctly to the eye of a close observer that there is no chance for going wrong in judgment.

"Will you follow me? I'll show you up," said the waiter-man.

I picked up my bundle, squeezed it under my arm, and followed him out of the room, creating no little comment, I dare say, for not a few craned their necks to get a look at me. In the hallway my guide stopped and spoke to a large florid person in a stained satin waistcoat.

"Here is the lad who wishes a lodging, Mr. Purdy," he said.

The big man looked at me from head to foot.

"It will cost two dollars, and we will give you your breakfast. Is it a lark of yours, youngster? Eh? Gad! I know of a sailor with money giving a dollar bill to a cow to chew on for a cud. But 'tis your game to play the gentlemen, eh?"

"I trust I am as much a gentleman as any one under your roof," I returned, hotly.

"Heighty-tighty! what have we here?" exclaimed the landlord. "I forget. The price is three dollars, and it's the last room in the house. I had partly engaged it to a *gentleman* in a cocked hat, but he has failed to appear. Pay in advance, please, or you don't ship for the night."

I gave him one of the gold pieces. He slipped it into his pocket without comment, and told the servant to show me up-stairs.

The room was quite large and comfortable, the soft bed with the white sheets looked inviting, and I was so stiff and tired from my walking that I tumbled out of my clothes and drew the covers over me.

I thought that I should go to sleep at once, but as is often the case, thoughts prevent the proper closing of the eyelids, as if they were the doors of the mind. What was I to do on the morrow? It was full eight days ahead of the time that I had promised to meet Plummer, and I had but four gold pieces. A thrill of fright took hold of me when I thought that perhaps my uncle might follow me and fetch me back with him. The noise of shouting and loud talking below in the tap-room, and the singing and chattering on the streets, continued for a long time, and I tossed uneasily.

To the best of my recollection I had not lost myself in sleep at all when I heard some stumbling and laughing out in the hallway; then the door to my room was pushed open, and a hand shielding a candle, the light of which dazzled my eyes so that at first I could not see clearly, extended through the doorway. A man entered, talking loudly to some one who was following him.

"Come in, come in, Bullard; and don't drop that bottle for the life of you."

A thick, growling voice answered.

"I've had all the bottle I want, Captain Temple," were the words I caught in answer, and the second man came in. He also carried a candle.

"What is it you wish to discuss with me, sir, that we couldn't say before McCulough?" he went on.

"'Tis just this," replied the one addressed as Captain Temple (I recognized him as the officer who had sat on the piazza): "McCulough thinks to tie us down in some way, because he happens to own a few planks of the ship. Now I— Damme!"

The speaker had placed the light on the mantel-piece, and the other man did the same with his candle, snuffing it with his fingers as he did so ; but what had broken off Captain Temple's speech was the sight he had caught of me sitting bolt-upright in the bed, and blinking, I dare say, like a startled owl.

"In the name of Davy Jones, what is this?" he exclaimed. "What are you doing in my room?"

"A drunken sailor-man," interrupted the larger one, holding one of the candles over his head. "Kick him out where he belongs. They're getting too high and mighty, anyhow."

6

The captain, seeing my bundle lying on the floor, sent it flying through the open doorway down the hall, and the other man, with a stroke of his foot, swept up the rest of my belongings.

"Get out of this, you swab," cried the captain, "or I'll keelhaul you well! No chin music, now! Come, get out!"

I was mighty angry by this time.

"I'm no swab or no drunken sailor, I'll have you understand," I replied, "and this is my room, and I paid for it."

The captain muttered a curse.

"I'll spit you like a goose!" he roared. "How dare you talk to me like that?"

With this he drew his sword and made one or two passes at me. Of course I do not suppose it was his real intention to inflict an injury, but the point came dangerously close to my throat—I had drawn the covers to my chin.

"Don't kill him, captain; don't kill him," snickered the big man.

At this, moved by some impulse, I jumped to the floor. There was a narrow poker leaning against the empty fireplace. Shaking with fear, I picked it up and fell into the position of defence. The big one's laughter changed to an impatient tone.

"Rout him out, the impudent rascal," he cried, "and I'll boot him down the stairway!"

The captain could not reach me across the bed, so he came about the foot-board. He made a swift pass at me as if he would give me a good slap with the back of his sword. I parried it, and, aiming a quick stroke at his head, sent his cocked hat flying across the room. His return to this showed that he intended me some harm, for he thrust straight at my breast. Again I parried, and a second time the captain lunged. He had swept the point of his sword a little too far down this

time, and I got over it a bit with the poker. I remembered the disarming-stroke that my uncle had shown me
so often. With a quick turn of the wrist I caught his
blade aright and absolutely hurled it from his hand. It
clattered across the floor, and, darting forward, I caught
him just below the shoulder with the point of the poker.
Had it been a cutlass or a small sword it would have
surely run him through! As it was it staggered him,
and he sat down backward in the empty fireplace.

The big man was roaring down the hallway for help,
and I could hear a charge being made up the stairs.
The captain looked up at me, however, curiously.

"Where on the green earth did you learn that?" he
grunted.

I was so full of emotion and fear of the consequence of
my action that I could not speak, and stood there panting. A dozen faces appeared at the doorway. The
captain extended his hand.

"Give us a lift, lad," he said. "I'm badly grounded."

I pulled him out of the fireplace, and picked up his
sword for him—a strange picture we must have presented,
I in my shirt, and he slapping me good-naturedly between
the shoulders so hard that it set me coughing.

"No harm done, friends," he said, addressing the crowd
that had now half filled the room. "Some pleasantry between me and this young gentleman. Bullard, you old
squillgee, gather the lad's trousseau from the hall, and
fetch it in here."

Affirming that it was just a joke, he and the captain
cleared the room and gathered up my things. The
shorter man was looking at me curiously.

"Gadzooks!" he said, "but that was a master-stroke!
Who are you and where do you come from?"

I was drawing on part of my clothing, and a fit of embarrassment had hold of me. Now why I spoke as I did
I cannot account for.

"My name is Debrin," I replied, taking the name that my uncle was known by at Miller's Falls. "I've come to ship on board the *Young Eagle.* Si Plummer spoke to me about her."

The captain threw back his head and laughed.

"You'll ship all right, lad—I'm Temple. of the *Young Eagle.* What's your first name?"

"John," I answered.

"Go below, Bullard, and make out articles for this lad to sign—John Debrin, instructor in small arms. Never knew of one in a privateer before, but I'll create the billet, begad!"

Then and there he made me show him what I knew about handling a weapon. In fact he treated me as if I were altogether his equal, and I soon lost any feeling of discomfiture.

As this is the only time that I ever saw Captain Temple in such a mood, I have dwelt on it. But to shorten this part of my log: I signed the articles that Bullard brought up with him, and insisted upon giving up my room, which the captain apparently took with reluctance, and I slept on the floor in a corner of the hallway.

From my clothes Temple must have judged me a seaman, for he asked no questions on that head, and apparently was satisfied with the explanation that I came from Chesapeake Bay, had sailed in the brig *Minetta,* and had been taught swordsmanship by an old Frenchman.

I awakened in the morning with the puzzled consternation of one unused to find himself in new surroundings, and with the feeling that last night's goings-on had been a dream. A glance at the paper in my pocket, however, proved that it was not.

A strange day was before me. I seemed destined in life to be a mystery to the people whom I met, and circumstances kept up this position for some time to come.

"HE SAT DOWN BACKWARD IN

CHAPTER XI

No one was stirring about the inn except a sleepy, draggled-headed pot-boy, lazily sweeping out the tap-room.

Although I was very hungry, I determined on a ramble along the water-front before breakfast, and I headed down the street.

I was surprised at the number of vessels at the wharves. A maze of masts and rigging arose above the tree-tops, but the scene lacked the life and movement of loading and unloading.

The vessels appeared slovenly and unkempt, their yards at all angles, and their shrouds sagging. Close to me, with a long bowsprit extending almost into the front yard of one of the white houses that clustered at the southern bend of the harbor, was a great three-masted ship. Her cut was different from most of those that I had seen, but what held my eye was this: her foremast had been spliced neatly with wrappings of great rope, and three or four jagged breaks showed in her topsides and bulwarks. She was lying close to a great warehouse that prevented a view of the open bay, and I walked down the pier. The great vessel had quarter-galleries, like a man-of-war, and above her rudder-post I read the words, "*Northumberland* of Liverpool"; then I remembered hearing the night before that this vessel had come in under the lee of the *Young Eagle*, and had been one of the richest fruits of her first cruise.

When I reached the pier-head I walked out on the string-piece, and, climbing on the top of a pile of lumber, I looked out across the smooth water. A quarter of a mile from shore lay the tidiest-looking craft. She was not very small, but sat low in the water, a backward rake to her masts gave her a jaunty appearance, and the tall spars that lifted high above her deck looked as slender as whipstocks. Her jib-boom was of tremendous length, but at that time I did not know enough either to criticise or to appreciate her altogether at a glance.

It was setting out to be a scorching day. The smell of sperm-oil and pine timber came from beneath and about me, and so still was it that the sound of a man rowing a dory over against the farther shore sounded plainly — I could hear every thump in the thole-pins. The clicking of a block and tackle broke out, and a musical high-toned bell hurriedly struck the hour from the little brig. That she was the *Young Eagle* I had no doubt, and it flashed across me that maybe I had gotten myself in somewhat of a predicament, and that perhaps it would be better for me to find Captain Temple and inform him that, while I did know something of small arms, I was in truth nothing of a sailor.

I took the paper out of my pocket, and saw that there was no reference made to performing the duties of seamanship, but that I had been enlisted to instruct the crew in a branch with which I felt myself perfectly familiar.

My old friend Plummer had promised to help me learn the ropes, and so I determined to go ahead without any explaining.

Thinking that it would be best to report to my commander at the inn and await his orders, however, I turned my footsteps back into the town, and as I walked the path along the tree-lined street, why I should fall to thinking of Mary Tanner I do not know. I took a squint down at myself in my sailor finery, and rather admired the way the wide bell-shaped trousers flapped about my ankles. The wish grew upon me that Mary could see me as I was. Thus, with my head down, I hastened on, and did not perceive that an open gate swung across the way until I had run afoul of it, bows on.

As I leaned over to rub my shin I heard a laugh, and, looking up, there, not ten feet from me, was the very person who had been in my mind—Mary Tanner herself, but grown so tall and slender! The power is given to women to control the expressions of their feelings in a manner that fails men altogether—at least, I might say, we are more clumsy at it. I was so astounded that I could not speak a word, and stood there on one leg like a startled sand-piper. She spoke first.

"Well, where did you come from?" she laughed, gathering up her apron in one hand. It was filled with roses she had been clipping from a bush.

As time had been long since I had seen her, I confess I felt tempted to reply " From China " or some distant port, as her laughter galled me sharply. But as it was, I answered, falteringly :

"From up there," pointing with my finger towards the north.

"How did you get away from Gaston?" she asked.

At the mention of the old man's name I could not help but give a glance over my shoulder, at which Mary laughed and asked another question.

"Where did you get those outlandish clothes?"

"I'm a sailor," I replied, giving a hitch to my breeches.

"Oh no, you're not," said Mary, throwing back her head. "You're a boy."

"I wish you good-morning, Mistress Tanner," I replied, making an effort to pull off the tight-fitting Portuguese cap, and only succeeding in giving my hair a tweaking. "Good-morning, Mistress Tanner; time has not improved your manners."

I walked away, really angry. It is no evidence of superior wisdom on my part to here make an observation; but a few months of town life will change a woman and teach her more than five years spent on a hill-side farm, and this is no falsehood. I had gone but a few rods when I heard my name called, and, looking back, I saw Mary leaning over the fence and beckoning to me with a rose in her fingers. Affecting a great deal of leisure, I retraced my steps.

"Are you really going to sea?" she asked.

Now although I could see how great the change had been that had come over her, this was spoken after the old manner; and despite the feeling that things were not exactly as they had been, I felt more at my ease.

"I'm one of the crew of the *Young Eagle*," I replied, and, I must confess it, proudly.

"My!" was all Mary vouchsafed to this, but I noticed that her eyes brightened and that she flushed. The rose she had been holding fell from her hand, and I bent over and picked it up. As I offered to return it she looked at me slyly.

"Why don't you keep it?" she asked.

"Because you have not given it to me."

"Then I will give you another."

As I took the flower she extended, an entirely new sensation thrilled me—a strange bounding, fluttering of the heart—and though this portion of our short interview may be interesting or not, I'm glad to set it down fully.

"Oh, I've got some news to tell," went on Mary, looking at me archly, and then lowering her eyes.

"What is it?" I inquired. "Good news?"

"Yes; I may be rich some day, John."

"Rich!" exclaimed I. "How is that, pray tell me?"

"You see, my grandfather who lives in Canada was a Tory," Mary answered. "His name is Middleton—one of the Irish Middletons—and when he left New London my mother would not go with him, for my father was an American soldier. Now my grandfather wishes me to come to him."

"Oh, are you going?" I asked, with my heart beating loudly.

"Well, I won't go now," Mary replied. "You see, my father is very ill here at my uncle's." A shade of sadness came into her voice. "He wants me to go," she continued, "but I won't leave him for any grandfather, no matter how rich he is."

"If you went, perhaps I would never see you again," I said, faintly.

"Why," she answered, opening her eyes wide, "you could come and see me."

"When?"

"When you got command of your own ship." She smiled as she spoke.

"I'll have one some day," I spoke up, bravely. "And that is what I'll do."

But an interruption came to this little dialogue.

"Look up the street," cried Mary, suddenly pointing.

I did so. Here came the frightful old Gaston, shambling along with his arms dangling in front of him; his clothes and head-gear were fit to make a ghost grin. But as if he had been a school-master and I a truant school-boy, I dodged through the gate and hid behind the rose-bush. For years I could not think of this action without shame, but now I laugh at it.

"You had better not let him catch you," Mary observed, joining me, and we peered about the corner of the rose-bush until after Gaston had passed. That he was in quest of me there was no doubt, and I cannot help thinking that my evident fear amused Mary Tanner, for she stood there smiling at me, and pulling at a green branch over her head (oh, I can see how she looked!); but the scene was interrupted by the approach of a slight, quick-stepping man, who rattled a walking-stick along the fence-pickets as he came nearer.

"Here's Captain Temple," I said, straightening up. "Now you'll see if I'm a sailor or not."

When the captain was opposite the gate I stepped from behind the rose-bush and saluted.

"Heigh, oh!" he exclaimed, looking longer at Mary than he did at me. (She was a tall girl, and appeared older than her years.) "Heigh, oh, I'm just in time to rescue you, my lad. 'Tis plain you're a prize to beauty! Aye, and would fly her colors too," he added, pointing to the rose that I had thrust in my bosom. As he spoke he bowed gallantly, and Mary dropped him a courtesy.

"Sorry, lad," Captain Temple went on, "but I may have use for you. Can you read and write?"

"Aye, aye, sir; French and English, and Latin too," I answered.

"Ecod! a scholar, eh?" was the return. "Scholars make bad sailors. But Bullard has gone to Lyme Haven, and I would have somebody come to McCulough's office and help me with the papers. So bid good-bye to your sweetheart, and come along—come along. We'll get under way to-morrow mayhap, or the day after."

"Good-bye, Mary," said I, extending my hand. "Don't forget me."

"Good-bye," she said simply, and thus we parted.

I was filled with the idea, as we went down the street, that I would run across Gaston, and I determined that if this happened, I should not show the fear of him that I had a few moments since. But we met no one except some villagers driving their cows to pasture, and, approaching the wharves once more, we entered one of the warehouses, and found awaiting there a crowd of sea-

"'GOOD-BYE, MARY,' SAID I"

men.   They all touched their hats as Captain Temple and I came to the doorway.   A red-faced man with a great bulbous nose and snuff-powdered coat greeted us.

"You're late, captain," he grumbled; "and look at the gentry that have been awaiting you.   There may be a few topmen among them, but I'll wager we've got hog-butchers and tailors here, at any rate."

He might properly have added pirates in his category, for some were as rough-looking cutthroats as any one might wish to see.

"Here, act as shipping-clerk, lad," ordered Captain Temple, shoving a great ledger towards me.   "And set things down right and ship-shape, too, in plain English. Never mind the spelling—just so one can read it."

Luckily it happened that the page before was but half filled, and I saw at a rapid glance the mode of proced-ure.   I recognized also Bullard's handwriting.   And now began the examination that to me was most interesting.

Temple looked at every man, as he presented him-self, slowly from top to toe, and I noticed that many of them gave a shake to their shoulders when he lowered his eyes, as if a chill had passed over them.   The ques-tions were very simple, consisting in asking the man's name, age, previous occupation, and the vessel that he had last sailed in, and, if satisfactory, he was told to get his dunnage and present himself at the pier some time before noon.

"We have no idlers on board this ship," said the cap-tain, addressing the crowd.   "If you're not doing one thing, you're doing something else.   I want both-handed men about me."

In about two hours the work was finished, and Cap-tain Temple, looking over the ledger, paid me a compli-ment upon my writing, and expressed the opinion that evidently I was an old hand; in which I did not con-tradict him.   Before midday arrived, however, I was al-

most famished, but I found no time to search for anything to eat.

It had got noised about the lower part of the town
that the remaining part of the crew of the *Young Eagle*
were to debark in the early afternoon, and quite a
crowd had gathered along the shore to see them off. I
managed to run up to the inn and to secure my small
bundle, and hastened back again.

Already a boat-load had gone out to the ship, and as I
clambered down the rough ladder the crowd and those
in the second boat were indulging in much rough play-
fulness; it was a very mixed assembly, and there appeared to be no deep feelings shown in any of the fare-
wells. Just as we shoved off I heard my name called—
that is, my first name. "John! John!" cried a voice,
and, looking up, I saw Mary Tanner standing at the
edge of the pier. She waved her hand to me, and then,
with a quick glance about her, kissed it twice.

My return to this, which I kept repeating for fully a
minute, was not conspicuous, because half of the men
gathered in the stern-sheets were doing the same thing
or indulging in mock lamentations. Three or four silent
ones, perhaps, felt more deeply than the others.

As we came alongside the brig I noticed that her
deck was not more than six feet above the water-line
amidships, but that her bulwarks were fully the height
of a man's shoulder. Her sides shone as if they had
been varnished, and the brass-work along the rails
gleamed like gold. But when I set my foot on deck, it
was then that I was astonished. I have seen many privateers and vessels of the regular navy since that day,
but never have I seen such a clean sweep of deck and
such fine planking in my life. All the loose running-
gear was flemished down neatly, many of the belaying-
pins were of brass, and her broadside of six guns was
very heavy for her tonnage.

Amidships, carefully lashed and chocked, was a long twelve-pounder. The others were eighteen-pound carronades. Two large brass swivels she carried besides these—one on her forecastle, and one forward of the wheel on the quarter-deck. Sne was built upon a plan different from most of the vessels of that date, but now become more adopted in America. Instead of having her greatest breadth well forward, it was farther aft, and she was cut away like a knife-blade. I have never seen her equal, I really think, in going close-hauled, or in any point of sailing.

Now, as I stood there with my bundle in my hand, I longed for some one to ask questions of, and then I remembered that if we sailed on the morrow, Plummer would be left behind! Most of the men coming off shore carried their hammocks with them; where I was to get mine I did not know. But as Captain Temple had been so kind to me, I thought nothing of going to him, considering that it would be the best way out of the difficulty, so I stepped up to where he was standing near the binnacle. He looked at me as if he had never seen me before.

"Well!" he said, sternly. "Coming aft in this fashion! If you wish to speak to me, wait at the mast."

"I have no hammock, sir—" I began.

"Sleep on the deck, then," returned he. "Go forward!"

He spoke to me much as one might address a dog, but there was nothing to do but to obey like one, and, biting my lips, I went down the hatchway to the berth-deck.

How so many men were going to sleep in that crowded space I could not see; they were so close that as they moved about they touched one another, and so low were the deck-beams that the tallest could not stand erect. and even I brought up against one with a temendous whack that set starry skies before me. To my relief, I perceived that I was not the only greenhorn, and that there were a few others who knew even less than I did of what was expected of them.

An awkward country lad, who had been standing there gorming about open-mouthed, approached me.

"Tell me, please, sir," he said, "where are our beds."

I explained that the long bundles some of the men carried, and that they were taking up to stow in the nettings, were hammocks, and that he would probably have one served to him. He thanked me kindly, and probably looked upon me as being a very knowing, able seaman.

The men were joking and swearing roughly, and before we had been on board ten minutes a fight started between two half-drunken sailors, which occasioned only merriment among the lookers-on, until a great, thick-set figure, that I afterwards learned was Edmundson, the third lieutenant, ran down the companion - ladder, and sent both of the fighters to the deck with two blows of his great fist.

"If you're after sore heads, you can get them!" cried he. "But avast this quarrelling."

No one said a word ; even the fighters stopped cursing, and the silence lasted long after he had disappeared.

I was mad for something to eat, for, as I have told, I had had nothing since the night before ; but soon the word was passed through the forecastle that there would be no grub until the evening, at which there were many mutterings and more strange oaths. During the afternoon the crew was divided into watches, and the men were given their numbers and stations, but so far as I could see no provision was made for their comfort in any manner ; no regular messes had been organized, and at six o'clock, when we were fed, we sat about in groups on the deck, and ate with our knives and fingers from the rough tubs; but the feed was wholesome, and there was plenty of it. I did full justice to a very healthy appetite.

Before dark Mr. Bullard came on board. As he walked forward I managed to catch his eye, and saluted.

"Ah, here's our sailor fencing-master," he half laughed.

"Might I have a word with you, sir?" I inquired.

"What is it?" he returned, frowning.

"There are two country lads on board that have no hammocks; they know little of shipboard, but are willing. Can you not help them out, sir?"

I did not tell him that one of the country lads was myself. He muttered an oath, and here I found out that asking favors of ship's officers generally makes them cross. But he turned and spoke to an old seaman standing near by.

"Willmot, get two hammocks and give them to this lad," he ordered.

I followed the old sailor to the forward hold, and a few minutes afterwards presented a new hammock to the lank countryman, and kept the other myself; following the example of the other seamen, we marked our names on them in plain, black lettering.

The countryman, whose name was Amos Craig, and I found a hook forward and agreed to swing together. It was near the hatchway, but we took it because the air would be better—the forecastle was already foul from much breathing. I did not turn in early, being in the first watch, which we kept as if we were at sea; but that night, as I looked out towards the lights of the town and realized how great a change the life before me was from that I had been leading, I was half tempted to slip overboard and make a swim for it; I felt that this did not mean liberty. I had yet to learn that there is freedom in faithful and loyal service.

I had been much surprised by the difference in the manners of Captain Temple ashore from those he showed on shipboard. This change, however, is the natural sequence of absolute authority, and the relief occasioned by being able to throw off responsibility. In after-years I felt it much the same with me; but in the writing of this tale, as I cannot claim that I have the power of adding adornment, I also intend to be as free from moralizing as I can. So, to return to what happened. As I leaned over the rail I made up my mind to accept anything that came, make the best of it, and do my duty according to the best of my powers.

Half of the watch on deck were lying sprawled out and snoring against the bulwarks, keeping carefully out of the moonlight, for the reason that sleeping in the glare of the moon addles men's brains; but this may be mere superstition.

Up and down the quarter-deck a restless figure paced in quick, nervous strides. A sailor, with his heavy hair done in a long queue down his back, and two small gold rings in his ears, approached me and nudged me with his knee.

"Old Never-sleep is on the rampage," he said, directing his thumb over his shoulder. "We'll catch it to-morrow, you can wager on that, messmate. I've cruised with him, and I know his tricks!"

"Is he a good officer?"

"Aye, good for those who please him; he never works the watch below, but he'll hound a shirker till you can see his bones. Some men on this 'ere craft will wish themselves overboard before the cruise is over. Jump when he speaks, that's my advice!"

Then the man went on to ask me questions. I dodged them as best I could by asking others, and as he liked to talk, I picked up not a little worth remembering. I found that Captain Temple had various nicknames that described his qualifications and characteristics to a nicety. Every skipper, no matter what his age, is called "old" on shipboard. Temple, I should judge, had not turned four-and-thirty, although he was slightly grizzled and his face was weather-seamed. "Auger-eyes" they called him on account of his keenness of vision. "Old Gimlet-ears," because it was rumored that he could hear in the cabin what went on in the forecastle. "Kill Devil," for the reason that he feared not to fight the powers of hell if they were arrayed against him. But chief of all, "Old Never-sleep," for a very evident reason. He apparently stood all watches when there was aught to be gained by vigilance.

The quartermaster on deck stepped aft as the sailor and I were talking, and spoke to Captain Temple:

"Eight bells, sir."

"Make it so," were the words I caught from the captain's lips.

Immediately the musical high-toned bell struck the hour. On the voyage of the *Minetta* I had learned to tell time after the manner at sea, and I knew that the other watch was coming on. In ten minutes I was below in my hammock.

So great a number of people composed the *Young Eagle's* company that the men were swinging double in the close-crowded space—that is, one hammock was underneath the other, the upper lashed high against the beams, and the lower sagging so that its occupant could touch the deck with his hand.

I had never heard such a chorus of snoring and muttering in my life, and it took me a few minutes to become accustomed to the reeking air. But at last I dozed off into a fitful rest of ever-changing dreams, only to be awakened by the rolling of a drum and a confused sound of stirring, cursing, and piping. Thus began a day in which I had to face some trials, I assure you, and call upon many resources that I did not know that I possessed.

7

CHAPTER XII

TEST TRIALS

WE did not proceed to sea, as it had been expected that we should, but we stretched several new sails, and the captain marked them for alteration by the ship's sail-maker, much as a cunning tailor changes the cut of a coat to secure a proper fitting. The men were made to take their positions at the guns, and I found that I had been given a number at the long 12-pounder, and was expected to work a handspike in getting her into position. For three long hours we were kept at this, slewing the guns hither and thither, aiming and gauging distance, and bringing powder and shot from the magazines. Of course we indulged in no firing, but served the pieces in pantomime.

The men appeared eager, and I could see that Captain Temple was pleased at their performance—the majority were old hands and needed little schooling, and there is no use denying it, they *jumped* to the best of their ability. But my real trial was soon to come.

Most of the greenhorns had been enrolled into a company of marines; they were standing in an awkward row arranged in the waist, and keeping out of the way of the more experienced gunners who were indulging in the mimic battle.

"Debrin!" roared a voice. "Pass the word for Debrin."

A squint-eyed, bowlegged boatswain's mate was bawling about the deck.

For an instant I was so confused that I almost forgot the name I had assumed.

"Here!" I called at last, with my heart giving a wild leap into my throat. I gave over the handspike to my friend of the night before, and the boatswain's mate looked at me out of his crooked eyes.

"The old man wishes to speak to you," he growled in a low voice.

I stepped aft and pulled off my cap, as I had seen the other sailors do.

"Take hold of those gawk-legs and lick them into shape," said Captain Temple, apparently counting up my ribs as he looked me through and through. "You say you know the drill. There's a rack of muskets forward on the berth-deck, and a chest of cutlasses at the after-ladder. If any one gives you a sneer or a back word make him sweat his blood."

I hope that the quiver that went over me was not apparent, but a cold sensation crept from my chest to the end of my spine. Now, as it happened, I had watched closely, as a boy, the drilling of the trainband at Baltimore, where I learned much from my friend the major, and once I had formed a company of my school-mates at Mr. Thompson's, electing myself their leader. I tried to recall the orders of command and the positions as I marched the men below and armed them at the rack. But when we came back to the deck I was again seized with a dire fit of trembling that made me keep in movement to conceal it, for I perceived that those under me were watching with some curiosity to see what I should do. Besides this, it appeared to my imagination that all the crew were standing about with popping eyes, ready to laugh if I should open my mouth. So I took a long swallow, threw back my head and shoulders (ah! there is nothing like it to keep up one's courage!), and adopting a terse mode of speech, I began to sift the men into military shape, according to their heights.

My uncle had impressed one thing upon my mind as the surest way to obtain authority; it was not to make men *hear*, but to make them *listen*; so I did not shout, but endeavored to speak in low, firm tones, explaining clearly, as I gathered them into line, how they should stand and hold themselves. Some were inclined to smile at first, and indeed who can blame them; for despite my size, my youth was evident, no matter my air of authority.

To those that appeared amused I kept repeating my instructions until the grin had faded from their faces, and at last there came that feeling which expands the spirit of the holder of it—the sense of authority over others! So stepping out before them, I picked up a musket and began to drill them according to my recollection of the manual of arms.

If there had been an expert present, he might have found some fault with my method, but we got through without a hitch, and I might claim, without boasting, that I held attention. Over and over again we went through the motions; I was wondering whether there was to be no time limit to the drill, when suddenly some one spoke to me from behind.

It was Mr. Bullard. "Very good, drill-master," he said. "Dismiss the landsmen, and take up the boarders with some cutlass-work."

The muskets returned to the racks, I once more came on deck, and found that I had to face a very different ordeal. There, awaiting me, were thirty or forty sailormen—I could see that at a glance.

They regarded the idea of my instructing them as something of a huge joke, for there they stood nudging one another, half sneering, and all whispering; the cutlasses had been served out, and as soon as I took the position of "on guard" I noticed that some of them fell into it at once involuntarily, but others displayed an awkwardness that I knew must be premeditated. Now was the time for me to stand or fall.

Stepping up to a tall man who topped me by half a head, and bidding him stand two paces to the front, I gently pushed him into the right position, moulding him, as it were, and paying no attention to the anger that flashed in his eyes and drew the corners of his mouth. The rest were becoming interested, but—odds life !—they were not grinning at me now, but at their messmate. Satisfied that the man could do what I wished, I again gave the order for them to act together. The tall sailor twisted his cutlass in his hand and held it upside down. Once more, as if believing this came from sheer stupidity, I went through the same performance, trying to speak kindly and firmly, but really on the verge of breaking down. Three times was it repeated, and then the man succumbed.

But I had not finished. On the left of the line was a short, thick-set foretopman, with brawny, tattooed arms. Apparently he considered himself beyond all this and an adept with the weapon, for he indulged in side remarks that set those near him snickering, and he exaggerated all my motions. I saw that he was a leader in his way, and that for comfort's sake I should have him with me, so I called the others to a rest, and bade the man step forward. He did so in a careless, jaunty fashion, though his face had reddened. Placing him before me, I told all hands to observe closely; that I would show them the bad effect of too open a guard and too lowered a point.

It was a dangerous game to play, perhaps, but I called upon the seaman to make the various cuts and thrusts at my head and body. He did so with a vengeance, and it took all my strength to keep him from reaching me.

Captain Temple and the other officers had gathered in a little knot to one side and were watching. My blood was up, and I would rather have died than fail in what I was attempting; so I called upon the man to guard himself, assuring him that no harm would follow. Keeping my wrist well up, I told him to have a care of his left cheek. He grinned in reply. By a quick motion, the secret of which Monsieur de Brienne had taught me—for he was an adept with the broadsword as well as with the rapier—I got inside the man's guard and laid my blade along his throat. I well believe I could have severed his head from his body with a backward draw-stroke! The fellow paled and clinched his teeth; I resumed my position instantly, with my eyes fixed on his, for I feared mischief. Then using the same movement that I had in my encounter with Captain Temple, I twisted his blade from his grasp and sent it flying, and verily I believe it would have gone overboard had it not caught a stay overhead. Picking it up myself before any one could reach it, I returned it to him, and he stepped back into the ranks. There was no more trouble after that.

Now, strange as it may seem, when I got away I went forward and leaned out of an open port, and there, for some reason, the strain under which I had been laboring almost overcame me, and it was all I could do to control the shaking of my limbs or to keep from sobbing. While crouched there I felt a hand laid on my shoulder, and, looking up, I saw it was Edmundson, the third lieutenant.

"The captain wishes to speak to you in the cabin, lad," he said, kindly. "Bundle aft."

When I entered the plainly furnished little space, for the quarters of the officers were almost as confined as those of the crew, I saw that Captain Temple was sitting at a table, which was covered with open charts; several officers were with him. He looked up, and, seeing who it was, half smiled.

"Debrin," he said, "you have done well. If you are as good a sailor as you are a swordsman you will end this cruise an officer. This is more than I have ever said in the way of praise or promise to any living man. Forget it, and do your duty."

I could not have replied at this moment, my brain-works clogged; so I merely touched my forehead in salute, and went forward again. I believe that I was blushing like a school-girl. I could see that the men were whispering, and it was all I could do to hide my embarrassment.

Luckily there had been no call upon me to display any knowledge of seamanship so far, and I trusted that if it should come to the worst, what I had already done would stand in mitigation for my ignorance; besides, I hoped that Plummer might put in an appearance, and to him I knew I could go for aid. The idea of being an officer raised my spirits mightily also, but unforeseen circumstances were to prevent the fulfilment of my castle-building, and I had begun to build as high as only youth and imagination can erect the promise of future.

The next day was a repetition of this one, albeit the work was quite easy for me, and I grew keen with the very interest. The fourth officer, a Mr. Spencer, arrived in the afternoon; and a sergeant, who had served in the army, was enlisted as a lieutenant of marines; apparently the latter found no fault with whatever they had been taught under my instruction. Sutton, the man with whom I had had the passage of arms, came to me to learn the disarming stroke. As I met him more than half-way in this overture, we became friendly, and I found I had judged him rightly—he was looked up to in the forecastle.

In the evening I endeavored to get ashore (how much

I wished to talk to Mary!), and I was delighted at being one of the crew that pulled Captain Temple to the wharf at six o'clock.

I was no mean oarsman, owing to my training on the Gunpowder and at Baltimore, and I felt cocksure that in this branch of sailor-work I need lay down to no one. But so far as going aloft or navigation went, I knew no more than a plantation field-hand.

Captain Temple's stay on shore, however, was short, consisting merely of a visit to Mr. McCulough's office (the latter was part owner of the *Young Eagle*). But I got a chance to run up into the town, as I had intended, and dropped in at the hotel; the landlord and the serving-men treated me with such deference that had I been more of a sailor-man and less of an innocent, my head might have been turned, and I dare say I should have swaggered dreadfully—to be honest, I may have done so as it was. My wish, if it were possible, to get another glimpse of Mary Tanner, was frustrated, however. That fortune was not to be mine. Oh, one thing that I almost came to forgetting: On the pier, standing in the crowd, was Gaston, his outrageous black hat tied about with a streamer and his long cloak flapping about his shanks. I doubt not the people were making fun of him; but (good-luck) he did not recognize me, and I breathed more freely. I wondered how he had tracked me, and what my uncle would do if he returned empty handed; perhaps he might consider it a good riddance. My curiosity on this point was never satisfied.

As we rowed back to the ship I heard the captain say to a cadaverous-looking man who had joined him at the dock with a big bundle and an oak chest:

"Well, Mr. Flemming, we sail on the early tide to-morrow. 'Tis earlier than we expected, but we're all tuned for starting—ship-shape and Bristol fashion."

The new-comer was the brig's surgeon, and one of the bowmen observed to me, as we hoisted the gig up at the davits :

" Hark'ee, messmate, how would you like old sawbones there to take a hack at you—eh, Johnnie ?"

I might state, if I have not done too much bragging already, that I had received a nickname in the forecastle, and was known as " Johnny Cutlass," which, instead of resenting, I felt quite proud of.

The last boat to leave the shore had brought off to the ship what appeared to me to be a load of old iron—apparently small crowbars fastened on rings, and cannon-balls welded together by solid bars of iron or attached to each other with short lengths of chain. Fearing to ask what they were, although I knew not, I waited for some landsman less ashamed of his ignorance than I to ask their meaning. My lanky friend who swung with me was the means of my finding out what I wished.

" What are they," he inquired—" those things in the boat ?"

" Them's Yankee tricks," answered the squint-eyed quartermaster, "and four of them will do more damage in walking through a vessel's rigging than a frigate's broadside. They're British puzzlers."

They were the dreaded star-shot and chain-shot that the English had declared barbarous and inhuman in warfare, for what reason they or no one else could tell you ; but they were fearsome things in battle, and this I had afterwards a chance to witness and can subscribe to.

The stays and running-gear were tested and made taut before nightfall, and all sorts of stories went from lip to lip concerning our destination. Some said northward to the Gulf of St. Lawrence ; others declared that the Spanish main would be our cruising-ground ; while a few asserted that nothing but the English Channel would please old " Kill Devil."

Now whither we were bound, of a truth I never found out, and of this I will speak at some length. My faith, but I was tired when at last I got into my hammock !

CHAPTER XIII

UP ANCHOR!

ALTHOUGH it was six o'clock in the morning when the tide was at the flood, a large crowd had gathered at the shore to watch us set sail. It was a damp, low-clouded day.

A fifer had been discovered among the landsmen, and hardly had I reached the deck, sleepily rubbing my eyes, when he began to pipe a merry jig step; the men fitted the heavy bars to the capstan, and while some scrambled aloft, as many as could lay hold and find foot room began trotting merrily about to the music. In came the cable, a couple of men alongside slushing it with water to keep the black mud off the deck, and slowly the *Young Eagle* walked up to her anchor. A slight breeze was blowing towards the mouth of the harbor, the foresail and topsail fluttered and caught it; a faint cheer sounded from the wharves, and the crew answered. Then the brass swivel on the forecastle cracked out a salute, and the privateer was off for adventures.

Poor Silas! how bitterly I regretted that he was not with us; I could well imagine his disappointment on finding he had been left behind. Would I ever see him again? Why had I not left a message for him? I wondered if he would ever hear of the fruit his idea-planting had borne. But doings of the present soon drove away all these regrets and thoughts.

A wild exhilaration thrilled me, and I could see that I was not the only one affected in this manner. A double allowance of grog had been served as soon as we were under way; I tasted it, of course, and it burned my throat so like fire, that I handed my allowance to Sutton, thereby cementing the friendship that had sprung up between us; it was not bad policy.

We presented a fine sight, no doubt, as we swung into the dancing tide-rip of the Sound. A fish-hawk rose from her nest on the top of an old mud-beacon, and sailed along with us. I noticed that Bullard pointed her out to the captain, and that the latter smiled. Some fishermen hauling lobster-pots into a dory waved their caps and huzzaed loudly as we tore by them. Every stitch of sail we had was now up and drawing.

Before long Fishers Island and the mainland faded out in the blotch of gray fog that, despite the wind, hung all around us. And now, as if to test the seamanship of the crew, sails were taken in, then spread again; and as the wind increased the brig heeled over until the sea was roaring and tumbling along her rail, and the lower sails were wet with the scatter of the spray as it flew across the deck. But there was no stopping the headway of the privateer; as she met the heavy ground-swell of the ocean there was none of the thumping that I remembered hearing on board the old *Minetta*.

The *Young Eagle* cut through the sea clean as a knife, and, looking over the side, I could see the bubbles race by at a rate faster than I ever thought a vessel could leave them behind her. The crew were on the broad grin of delight at her behavior.

One great, hairy-chested fellow, a fine specimen of a sailor, swung his arms about his head and gazed up at the swelling sails.

"Oh, oh! isn't she a beauty?" he exclaimed. "A darling ship! Aye, she's a sweetheart!"

There was an accent of love and of admiration in this that was not to be mistaken; his speech rang with a worshipfulness that was contagious. I caught it, and could have shouted !

About noon the wind slowly died away, the fog thickened, and we drifted, heaving and rearing in the smooth round seas. I had more of a chance to observe the people with whom I supposed I was to live for the next few months. The great majority of them were fine Yankee seamen, men who had served on merchant-vessels or in the Marblehead fishing-fleet, typical Down-Easters, with a leavening of sailors who had seen service on board vessels of the navy. There were a few foreigners—Portuguese or Spaniards, I should judge—quick, active men with black hair and wiry frames. Some rough-looking characters there were, too, whose faces showed instincts not all the best, and, as I have said before, greenhorns and countrymen, making their first voyage, filled out the complement.

The threshing and moving of the vessel seemed to discommode these latter, and many were ill, and wished themselves ashore, I take it, from their looks—one or two desired to die, I am sure.

In the little steerage six or eight prize-masters bunked together. They were mostly men past middle age, and had the appearance of broken-down seafarers, and the majority of them were prone to the bottle habit, unless they belied their appearance. In all there were crowded on board the *Young Eagle* in the neighborhood of one hundred and thirty souls, perhaps more.

I have never seen any one so careful of detail as Captain Temple. He would permit no slouching in appearance, as he would permit none in duty. There was something of an attempt at uniform, and the forecastle, in fact the whole vessel, was inspected by him as regularly as if she were a man-of-war.

Odd to relate, the skipper himself was a teetotaler when at sea, no matter what his behavior was when dry ground was beneath him. To show his carefulness and regard for neatness, I heard him, only the second day out, rate a man severely for not being clean shaven. His own costume, in which he looked most picturesque, would have attracted attention anywhere. He wore his huge cocked hat set lightly athwartships on his head, his neat blue coat fitted his trim figure to a nicety, and his legs were encased in Hessian boots with gold tassels, ·like those of a dandy. In fine, he was a handsome man to look at, and there were stories agog about his being a great favorite with the ladies.

Junior officers get their key from their commander, and although our lieutenants did not present so neat an appearance or wear their clothes so well, they were a good-looking set, and all young men with the exception of Edmundson, who may have turned forty odd.

All night long the fog hung about us. We had been drilled during the day, and never have I seen a crew pick up so much knowledge in such a short space of time.

After breakfast on the second day the fog-bank lifted, and land was made out to the northeast. I heard one of the officers say that it was the island of Martha's Vineyard; a slight wind was stirring, and we sailed on, steering east by south, and by noon we had sunk the headland. At one o'clock a cry came from aloft that a sail was in sight to windward, so we altered our course, and tacked in the direction of the stranger. An air of eagerness showed in the faces of the crew, and I honestly believe that some of them began to count upon their share of prize-money. As the other vessel was coming fast, it was not long before we could see her from the deck.

She was bringing the wind with her, and had all sail set, stun-sails and royals. Mr. Spencer went aloft, and took a squint from the cross-trees through the glass. All hands were watching him, and the way he hastened down to the deck showed that he had something to communicate, for immediately the *Young Eagle* was hove to, and then put before the wind.

"Old Kill Devil's changed his mind, I reckon," said Sutton, the foretopman, coming up grinning. "And he wouldn't without good reason, you can bet a cotton hat. Now, to my way of thinking, that vessel's an English frigate, unless it be one of our own; the Johnnie Bulls generally sail in company nowadays.'

It soon became evident that it was Temple's intention to give the on-comer as wide a berth as possible, for we spread every rag we had, and steered a westerly course. It was thick weather up aloft, and the sunlight barely filtered through it. But it was one of those days when distance is hard to judge, the sea one dead gray-green, with no flash or change in color, and nothing to tell whether the horizon was five miles off or twenty; nothing but the white sails of the approaching vessel, and occasionally a sight of the dark hull lifting underneath the canvas.

We were holding our own quite well, perhaps, slightly gaining on the pursuer, for such she had become, when the fog began to lower, or better, we ran into it. It thickened, and soon we could see nothing but the heaving water fading away into a gray wall at a distance of a few hundred feet.

We took in our kites (the wind had worked round a trifle), and changed our course to the northward. The interest was less intense now, owing to the other vessel being shut out from sight; Captain Temple's intention was to give her the slip and let her pass well to the south. For two hours we sailed on. It had grown lighter overhead, as if all the clouds had settled down upon us; but occasionally we caught a glimpse of sunlight and blue sky.

I lay on my back against the bowsprit with my hands making a pillow. I was thinking of the strange life that I had led, and wondering what my uncle thought of my sudden disappearance. Why had old Gaston pursued me to New London, and what a lugubrious figure he had presented standing there on the dock in that strange head-gear? Of course this brought me to thinking of Mary also, and I put my hand inside the bosom of my shirt. There was the rose that she had given me, and that I had carefully pinned in a wrapping of strong paper. But my thoughts were interrupted by a sudden commotion. A man who had been aloft for some reason or other—disentangling some running-gear, which had fouled in the blocks, if I remember right—suddenly gave a shout.

"Sail, ho, to windward!" he cried, and never have I seen any one get to deck so quickly. He jumped the last twelve feet off the ratlines at the risk of his bones, and ran aft. Temple and Mr. Edmundson came forward to meet him. What he said was heard so clearly that it brought all hands crowding up much excited.

"I can make out the topsails of a vessel rising the fog, sir, not much above a mile to windward; she's bearing down upon us!"

The way that Captain Temple tripped aloft showed that he was a topman, and one of the best; Edmundson, although a larger man, was not far behind him. And all hands watched them make their way to cross-trees and swarm up higher. Then we could see they were pointing. Quickly they descended to the deck. Mr. Spencer and Bullard and the prize-masters had all come up from the cabin; the crew also were gathered amidships ready to *jump* at the word.

"'Tis the English frigate," said Temple, in a whisper. (As I was standing close by I caught the words distinctly.) "She must have us in sight from aloft. Our top-gallant-masts are plain to view. Ecod, we'll fool them, though," he cried, "if this fog holds! Mr. Bullard, will you follow me to the cabin?"

CHAPTER XIV

THE SWORDFISH AND THE WHALE

THE breeze was light and better for a small vessel than for a heavy, deep-laden man-of-war, and we might have run away in safety if we chose. That something was up, however, that meant adventure no one could help seeing. Again we had altered our course and were going once more directly before the wind.

Orders were given, without any bawling or shouting, to house the top-gallant-masts. Full of alacrity the crew worked like bees. (I loved them for the way they went about it.) The yards were lowered to the deck as quickly as if they were clothes-poles in a drying-yard. I had never seen anything done so neatly and with such despatch. Our headway decreased, of course, as we lost the use of our upper sails.

Mr. Spencer, who was aloft, reported to the deck: "We're hidden now, Captain Temple," said he. "She might pass within a quarter of a mile of us and never see us."

Purposely I had stepped close to him as he spoke to the captain, and the latter's reply was as astonishing to me as it was apparently to the startled officer. Temple was eagerness in every line of his face. He struck his right fist into the palm of his left.

"The closer the better," he exclaimed. Then he turned. "What are the soundings?" he inquired of the bowlegged man who had hastened up. We had been heaving the lead for the past half-hour.

S

"Six fathoms, sir, and shoaling; here it is, sir."

"Prepare to lower away the long-boat, Mr. Bullard," the skipper ordered, after a glance at the lead. "Mount the forward swivel in her, pick a crew, take a boat's compass, and make off due west. Mr. Spencer, you will take command of her—a word with you."

Every one looked at the captain in astonishment, but no one asked a question or put in a comment of any kind. As I was one of the crew of the long-boat, I helped to get her ready and swing her overboard. The swivel was lashed on the forward grating, half a dozen muskets were handed down to her, and we shoved off. Mr. Spencer was pale and nervous. As we left the brig's side we saw that her helm had been put hard down, and that she was headed south. There was just enough wind to move her slowly through the water. In three minutes she was lost to sight.

We had been resting on our oars, and now Mr. Spencer spoke for the first time.

"Make no noise," he said. "Pull slowly, straight ahead."

We gave way, trying our best to silence the thumping in the rowlocks. So light was the breeze that we could have kept apace of a vessel's sailing. For ten minutes we rowed on, and then we stopped again and Spencer spoke.

"Load that swivel and get ready with those muskets," he ordered.

I heard him mutter something in which I caught the words "tomfoolery" and "nonsense," and I looked back over my shoulder. A half-dozen perplexed-looking marines were grouped in the bow, and three sailors were ramming home a charge in the swivel.

"Lads," said Mr. Spencer, "Captain Temple's orders are to fire into that frigate and get away, *if we can*. It all depends upon yourselves and the way this boat is handled whether we are blown out of the water, cut to pieces, or escape with whole skins. I want no talking in the boat."

The man beside me on the thwart pulled his shirt over his head, and several others did likewise. They sat there bare from the waist up, and their torsos looked like those of the men in some of the old engravings in the handsome books I had read at Marshwood.

We were pulling slowly ahead now, rising and falling on the great swell, and for fully a quarter of an hour we rowed without a break. Then Mr. Spencer called for oars, and we drifted a long time.

" Ss-h ! listen !" cautioned one of the men in the bow, suddenly. He was bending over, with his hand making a hollow back of his ear. Half of the crew did likewise. For a minute I could hear nothing. Then I detected a groaning sound and a ripple of the water. It was the noise of a vessel's sailing !

" I can make her out, sir," said the bowman in a thrilling whisper. " She's not five cable-lengths away."

" I can smell her," put in one of the men forward.

The lieutenant rose to his feet, and I could see that his hand was trembling as he fumbled in the breast of his jacket. He pulled a boatswain's whistle out and put it to his lip. But before he blew he spoke calmly:

" Bring that gun to bear," he ordered, drawing a breath.

" Blow her out of water," spoke up the man beside me, with a chuckle.

What utter foolishness it seemed to me even then (and of a truth it was that anyhow) to attack a frigate in a long-boat, armed with six muskets and a broadside that you could carry in the crown of your hat ! But no one seemed to flinch.

" Give way softly," whispered Mr. Spencer, taking the tiller himself from the cockswain. Then, without warn-

ing, the silver pipe shrilled, and he bawled at the top of
his voice, as if he were commanding a ship's crew instead of a handful of mystified seamen in a cockle-shell :
" All hands on deck there, and lively ! There's a vessel
here astern of us ! Port your helm !"

He answered this order himself, with an " Aye, aye,
sir," and, leaning forward, shouted, " Fire !"

Close to the water a great shape could be seen. The
little gun slap-banged, and almost jumped overboard
with the recoil. The six muskets rang, and, animated
more by the gesture of Mr. Spencer's hand than the
word, we laid back on the oars. We took perhaps some
forty strokes or more, when the lieutenant called for us
to cease, with a sound of a hiss betwixt his teeth. The
huge shape was now astern of us on the port hand close
too. We had rowed across her bows ! Now so alive was
every nerve, and at such a tension was my mind, that I
remembered everything I heard and saw, so that I can
repeat it to a dot.

The crash and volley had been followed by a cry and
a great to-do from the direction of the frigate, we could
hear a confused jumble of accents, and above it the shriek
of a man in agony, "Oh, God, I'm killed !" he wailed, distinctly. Then a voice commanded silence, and we could
make out every word that passed.

"Can you see anything ahead there, you men forward ?" was asked, so close that it appeared to be directed towards us.

" No, sir ; not a thing, sir !" came the answer.

Then, cool and distinct, we caught the following orders as we sat there holding our breaths, our hearts
beating so loudly that we nearly rocked the boat.

" Ready about ! Ready ! Ready ! Put your helm
down, quartermaster."

" Helm's alee, sir."

" Tacks and sheets ! Haul taut ! Main-sail haul !".

(An anxious waiting pause.) "Head braces! Haul well taut! . . . Let go, and haul!" (So firmly were these words impressed upon me that I never had to learn afterwards the orders for tacking ship.)

There followed a rumbling sound, shouts and orders, and then an explosion that ripped the fog and cut great gashes of scarlet through the gray opaque wall.

"Huh!" croaked the man next to me, with a shiver, "if that had caught us, eh!"

"Good-bye, Mary Ann!" the man in front commented hoarsely, looking back over his shoulder.

Mr. Spencer was leaning forward. "They think we're off there," he whispered, jerking his thumb over his shoulder. "Lads, you did well."

All was silence again, and the frigate gathered headway to the north.

But now, if I shall live to be a hundred, I can never get one sound from my ears. . . . To the eastward, and beyond the English vessel, sounded the high tooting of a fife! The first bars of "Yankee Doodle" was the tune it played. I almost leaped up to my feet, but the music was soon ended, for a rattling, swingeing crash followed a burst of blurred, red flame. I could smell the smoke from the frigate's broadside that reached us now. But it was not she that spoke the second time!—no, no!

" Kill-Devil's got the weather-gage of her, by Moses!" cried the sailor next to me, putting his arm about my neck and giving me a hug.

"Silence in the boat there," ordered Mr. Spencer, angrily.

A roaring, mingling of explosions followed. The men in the bow began to laugh hysterically, and even Mr. Spencer joined them.

"The *Young Eagle's* got under her quarter. She'll rip her hide," he giggled. "Hark! did you hear that? 'Tis the long twelve! Don't cheer, you fools!"

It was well he had given this order, for the men were about to burst into a shout. One of them dropped his oar, and was roundly cursed for it. But now a multitude of sounds came from the direction of the fighting vessels. Groans and orders, cries and firing, and above them all I could hear the comments from close about me, that in my ignorance I did not exactly understand.

"Old Johnny Bull's missed stays," yelled Mr. Spencer, laughing. "Ho! Ho! the sword-fish and the whale! Stab her again, Captain Temple, stab her again."

A distinct broadside! and then a wild cheer, followed by a confused roaring, with high treble shrieks, like a counter-tenor's note in a chorus!

"Bleed, damn ye, bleed," muttered the man next to me.

"Tiddley dido! That was our cheer," gurgled the cockswain, sawing to and fro in his narrow little box; but no sooner had he spoken than a blast louder and brighter colored than the rest ripped out.

"The frigate's broadside!" gasped the cockswain.

All was silence.

"God help us, they've sunk her!" the lieutenant groaned.

No sound for full five minutes!

Three or four shots now, and then silence again for a longer time. It appeared to me that the fog had lessened. A fine drizzle was falling, and we could see the outlines of a vessel not a quarter of a mile away from us.

"Pull, for your lives!" cried Mr. Spencer, waking up. "Pull, for your lives!"

We gave way together, and the heavy boat was soon hitting up a good pace and burying her nose as she rose and fell on the seas. The lieutenant took a glance at the small compass, and headed us towards the northwest.

"We're close to Nantucket," he said. "I can't make out the *Young Eagle* at all. *That ship's the Britisher!*"

We had rowed but a few minutes longer when, as if by a miracle, the mist cleared away and the sun shone forth. Clear and distinct a big vessel lay off to the eastward. The hated emblem of St. George flew at her peak.

"I thought as much," remarked Mr. Spencer to the cockswain. "She's grounded on the sand-bank. That's what Captain Temple counted on."

But hurrah! to the windward of the British vessel was a sight that gave us joy!

There was the *Young Eagle* at a safe distance, eating up into the wind, with her jib-boom hanging, and one of her yards aslant. Somehow Temple had found time to get up his top-gallant-masts again, for they were both in place. But now those on board the frigate had espied us; that was plain enough. She was not so large a vessel as she had first seemed, being of the smaller class, carrying probably not over thirty-two guns at the most. She was badly cut up from the effects of her encounter with the brig, however—her foretop-mast was gone, her main-yard was over the side, and all her running-gear in great confusion.

The fresh wind that had spoiled the fog was coming from the northward, and, as I have stated, the frigate had seen us; proof positive was not wanting, for a puff of smoke from one of the guns of her forward division leaped from her side, and the ball came spattering along towards us.

"Oh, shoot the shot!" laughed one of the bowmen. We were missed by fully a cable's length.

But the tide was against us, and with a good light to observe our progress, I noticed that we were making comparatively slow headway. The long-boat was intended to be rowed by six oars of a side. Now, owing to the extra men that we carried, there was only room for ten men to do the pulling ; and by some mistake the oars that we were wielding were not all of the same length, some of the cutter's having been put in through carelessness. The weight of the swivel caused us to be well down by the head, moreover, and the cockswain had to mind his eye to keep headed straight. All idea, or hope, of our getting back to the brig that day at least was done for, and to save ourselves we were making for the shore of Nantucket, distant about three miles. But we were not out of range of the guns on the frigate, and consequently were yet in danger.

"Come aft here, you men in the bow !" ordered Mr. Spencer. "She'll row better. Here, stir a foot !"

He looked back, and just as he did so there came another puff of smoke. I saw the ball smash into the top of a wave, strike the water again, and then, slightly deflected, it came right for us. I saw this first, and backed water, giving a shout of fear. The men in the bow gave a leap forward and tumbled in among us, sprawling over our heads and shoulders, and bruising shins and elbows, blaspheming and cursing.

If the shot had struck four inches lower we would have been sunk then and there. It caught the gunwale forward, just abreast of the grating on which the swivel was lashed. The poor fellow pulling bow on the other side gave a shriek and dropped his oar, clasping both hands about his head. I looked back and saw the blood trickling over his shoulders and through his fingers. A splinter had almost scalped him ! We yawed about and shipped the top of a sea, and it looked like the end of matters, for we were cut away to within eight inches of the water, and the bow badly stove and broken.

"Cast loose that gun and heave it overboard, two of you," roared Mr. Spencer. "The rest all aft. No ! Steady ! Debrin, you and Jones keep your place and pull—damn ye, pull."

I laid back with all my might, and so did the man
next to me. The brave lad in the bow had recovered
from the shock of his wound, and with another fellow
cast off the lashings of the swivel and dumped it over
the side. I can never forget the sight of that gory man
working there with his broad naked back red from his
head to his waist. As soon as it was finished he tumbled
weakly across the thwart. The men in the stern-sheets
were bailing with their hands, and one was using Mr.
Spencer's cocked hat with great effect, while Jones and
I were giving way at top strength and keeping with a
great effort the seas from broaching us. As the weight
was in the stern, we could ride, bar accidents, in half-
safety. All the oars were taken up again. The bowman bent over and tied up his wounded comrade's head
with his neckerchief, at the same time throwing his shirt
around him, and for this the other thanked him as he
might for some slight courtesy. But a new terror threatened!

Two successive shots that had been fired at us during
the confusion went wide, but to our dismay we saw that
they were lowering away a great barge over the Englishman's side, and that the men were sliding down into
her.

"Heigh! Look there! The *Young Eagle's* coming
down to pick us up, lads," cried Mr. Spencer, turning
about in response to a touch on his elbow from the
cockswain. "Pull now, and get down to it!"

He headed the long-boat more to the west, and we
could see that the *Young Eagle* had repaired some of
her damage, and had tacked in the direction we were
going. She would have passed almost within range of
the frigate, but all at once the latter vessel gained stern-
way (her top-sails had been aback for some few minutes),
and she worked off the bar! Our hopes of rescue fell.
Turning on her heel, she made out to meet our brig.

Now we perceived that the Englishman's sides were gashed, and two or three of the ports astern had been knocked into one big opening. But the barge was after us! Every man rowing in our boat could count her strokes. There was no use of making light of it—she was gaining at every jump, lifting high above the top of a sea, and then again almost disappearing.

There were twelve good men behind those long white sweeps, and they rowed a fine boat with speed in her, despite the load of uniformed marines. We were grunting with the weight we put into every backward swing, and Mr. Spencer was talking to us after the fashion of a cockswain to a racing-crew, calling out continually:

"Lift her, boys! That's the ticket! Pull altogether," and so forth.

My mouth grew so dry that I tried in vain to swallow. I could feel my head roll back and forward. Presently I began to row with my eyes shut, for it seemed an effort to keep my lids from falling. One of the men in the stern began to spatter us with water to refresh us; the sun was blistering hot by this time. The lieutenant stopped his cackling.

The stroke-oars were being helped at their work by two men pushing as the others pulled. I caught a dim sight of this, and wished that some one could lay hold of my sweep with me, for my forearms pained, and I felt gone in the pit of my stomach. How long we rowed that way I do not know, but suddenly I was awakened, as it were, by hearing Mr. Spencer say:

"Lads, you have held your own. Keep at it! Steady wins!" Then in a lower tone he added, "Get ready with those muskets."

This speech had called me to my senses, and it was almost with a shock of surprise that I found myself keeping up the stroke. My eyes had been closed so long that the light dazzled me, and at first I could see

nothing; but I felt better than I had before I closed them; and now to say something that is of interest: A refreshment often comes to a man whose muscles have apparently expended all their strength; and thus it was with me. I was working on my heart and nerves alone, on the very life of me, as it were, and to keep this up too long means ruin; that is its limitation. When my eyes could focus, what little breath I had almost checked.

There was the English barge *not three hundred yards astern!*

A despairing glance behind, and I saw that the shore was yet a half-mile off; the sea was breaking in little rolls of white on every hand, and we were in shoal water that had a peculiar yellowish look. I noticed Mr. Spencer kicking off his boots.

I closed my eyes again, for the sweat stung them, and I felt a blackness coming over me. But just then the crack of a musket sounded in front. It was followed by another—the English boat was answering!

I was wide awake once more, but in a dream apparently. The marines would stand up and fire, and then squat down and load again. I could hear the English bullets sing past.

"Ouch!" exclaimed the cockswain, all at once, as if he had dropped something on his toe. A ball had struck him on the fleshy part of the thigh, and he sat there rubbing it and cursing in such a comical way that the man on the thwart next to me laughed outright, in a hoarse, jarring fashion.

We were in the surf, and the British barge not half-pistol-shot away, when No. 5 on the starboard hand fell forward in a faint; the cockswain got another ball, this time in the wrist, that caused him to let go the tiller, and, a breaking wave catching us under the quarter, with a clatter we rolled over fairly end for end.

When I came up there was a tremendous seething

and bubbling in my ears, and, putting out my arm, I managed to catch hold of the tiller-hooks of the overturned boat, and hung on with all my might.

"Help me !" cried a voice.   I looked about, and saw the wounded seaman weakly swimming alongside.   I extended my hand to him, and observed that eight or ten others like myself were holding fast with straining fingers to the long-boat.

The English barge was backing in carefully and with skill.   We were not a cable's length from shore, and making for it, hand over hand, swimming with the ease of a porpoise, was Mr. Spencer.   I knew it was he by the gleam of gold lace on his high collar.   But the seaman had grasped me so tightly that I lost my hold, and there came to me the assurance that I was going down, and did not care at all.

CHAPTER XV

A PRISONER OF WAR

I SUPPOSE that a man who has been almost drowned—to the limit that all sense leaves him at least—has drunk as deep of death as a person can and talk of it afterwards. With a shifting light before my eyes, a throbbing pain in my temples, and a sickness all through me, I found myself knowing that I was breathing once more; but I was waterlogged, and when I attempted to move, I could feel that I was filled to the throat with some gallons of brine. All at once I doubled up with a spasm of choking, and in a minute I felt better.

I was lying in the bow of a boat—the motion I could feel distinctly—but owing to the thwart being immediately over my head, I could see nothing but a succession of sturdy legs and bare feet pushing against the stretchers as the men rowed.

Such an attack of hiccoughs racked me that it called attention to my having regained my senses.

"'Ullo, Bill, 'ere's another one come back from Davy Jones," chuckled a black-whiskered man, leaning over with his face close to mine. "He's swallowed a bloomin' volcano, from the looks of him."

"Where am I?" I faintly murmured.

"Wot a question!" was the answer. "This is the same old world, and full of trouble. Did ye take us for angels and me for St. Peter?"

"Help me up," I cried, in answer.

The man bent down and hauled me out by the shoulders
to a sitting position; then I saw how it was.

Prisonnier !

I was captured, and here was a fine ending to the glorious life that I had been anticipating !

I suppose now that if I had spoken all my thoughts
since I had left Belair, and even asked only a few of the
many questions that my common-sense prompted me to
keep to myself, I should have been considered stark,
staring mad, let alone being a simpleton. It was almost
ridiculous to look back at it and think that I did not
know certainly who was the President of the United
States, or anything about the history of the last two
years. If any one had told me that the British killed
their prisoners, I should not have doubted it, and what
was to become of me I had not the least idea, but I saw
that I was not alone in the strait. Out of the crew of
nineteen men that were in the long-boat, ten, including
the wounded seaman, were sitting dejectedly in the bow
and stern-sheets. Together with the Englishmen, we
crowded the barge uncomfortably, but not dangerously.

The British sailors appeared to be rather a beefy set,
and they were in high spirits over their success. A pallid young officer, with his hair standing up in tall curls
over his forehead, sat in the stern-sheets : he was nurs-
ing a wounded hip carefully, and half leaning against a
little midshipman, who had his arm thrown about his
shoulder.

Raising my eyes from the boat, I perceived that the
frigate was drifting with her topsail against the mast
only a few hundred yards from us. I began to feel a
bitter hatred of her, and it gave me pleasure to see the
long, white gashes in her sides, and to notice, plainly apparent, the effect of the *Young Eagle's* gunnery.

" Halloa, Johnny Bull !" cried some one behind me
with a laugh, " I guess you run against something, didn't

you, a short while ago? Ship looks kind of unhealthy, like a man's face with the small-pox."

I turned. It was Sutton, the foretopman, speaking. He did not appear to be very much depressed by his surroundings, nor did he fear the result of his impudence, to judge of his expression.

"Stow your jaw," answered one of the Englishmen. " There are worse things than small-pox."

I noticed that the man's face was pitted deeply.

"That's so," Sutton replied; "there's the cat, for instance. I beg your pardon for not thinking of it; I wouldn't slight an acquaintance of yours for anything."

There was some more coarse badinage, not worth recording, and we were under the shadow of the vessel. Many faces lined her bulwarks, and, a line being thrown to us, we grated softly, fending the boat off from the side. Then a rope-ladder rattled down, and not without some difficulty those in the bow began to clamber up; soon it was my turn.

When I reached the deck I looked about and gained an idea of the effect of shot and splinter; the dark stains, hastily mopped up, had a reddish tinge that was suggestive, and the loose running-gear that had fallen from aloft showed that Captain Temple must have used some of the missiles condemned by the English—and here, let me state, afterwards used by them ; to which I can make oath.

No one stopped work to interview us as we were being hastened below, but many were the looks of hatred thrown at us, and cutting taunts also in plenty. To all of these Sutton kept a running fire of replying, in which he was ably seconded by one or two others.

"Why, my old boiled lobster," he replied to a marine who thrust his great face over the hatch-combing as we descended, "if I hadn't ketched a crab, I believe we'd 'a' took your old hooker with the long-boat!"

A warrant-officer was directing our guards where to stow us, and under his orders we were huddled together down in the fore-hold, in the cable tier, where the only light and air that reached us came down through the chain-pipes.

I counted noses, and saw that there were in our party six sailormen and four landsmen who had been enrolled in our marine force. We presented a sorry appearance sitting there in the dim light on the flaked cable, the most uncomfortable thing to rest on that one can imagine.

What had become of the rest of us in the long-boat I did not know then, but as I found out afterwards, I might as well tell of it here.

There had been nineteen in all when we started; seven reached the shore safely, two were drowned— one of them, alas! the brave cockswain who had been wounded, as I have stated. Now as there is no report of this action to be found in the naval chronicles of Great Britain—at least, I do not know of any—it may be of interest to put down what we heard of it, although it cannot be vouched for. From the talk we heard I make out that there were nine killed on board the *Acastra* (this was the name of the frigate), and upwards of twenty wounded.

There were two killed on board the *Young Eagle*, and two wounded. In this, I think, I am correct.

If Captain Temple had been an officer in the regular navy, he might have deserved cashiering for such a fool-hardy bit of business as attacking so powerful a vessel when he might have escaped; he was the only one on board the privateer, however, who had reckoned her at less than forty-four guns. But besides this, after his glance at the lead, he knew where he was, and could have pricked his position to a certainty on the map. As Mr. Spencer had said, he had counted on the proximity of the sandbar. But to return to our unfortunate company down in the bowels of the English ship.

The groaning of the poor lad with the bloody head caused me to wonder whether this was going to be our prison cell, or whether we were placed there temporarily before moving to a better or a worse one. Sutton took off his jacket, and with an old hemp swab we found we made Mackie, the man I had saved from drowning, the wounded one, as comfortable as we possibly could ; but it was not long before he was wandering in his mind, and this depressed us all, for there is nothing so apt to cut one's spirits as the watching and suffering beyond the power of alievement.

We were sitting there in silence when a voice broke in upon us.

"I hear that one of you is an officer. Is there an officer down there ?"

"Yes," shouted Sutton, "there is."

Then he whispered to me, placing one hand on my shoulder, "Speak up, lad ; it will do no harm to play it so, and you may get a chance to speak to some one higher than these hulk-scuttlers. Make a plea for Ned Mackie, if you can, or the boy will die down here in this rat-hole."

So I stood up on my feet, and, gazing up at the circle of light through which came the cable, I cried, loudly, "What do you want of me ?"

For an instant I thought that I was going to be made the victim of a joke, as the man did not reply, but talked to some one evidently standing over him.

"Yes, sir," said he, " there's an officer, a midshipman, I dare say, in there with them."

In a few minutes we heard the drawing of the heavy bolts that held the small door that led through the bulkhead into the mid hold, and some one called, "Let that young man who spoke come here."

I stepped out; the door was closed behind me, and I saw it was guarded by two marines with muskets. Stumbling over barrels and boxes, I followed the three figures ahead of me up the ladder at an order from one of them, and soon I found myself on the berth-deck; then we went up another ladder to the gun-deck. We were evidently crowding on all sail, for the frigate heeled over to such an angle that the half-ports had been closed for comfort, but the water dashed in through several rents in her top sides.

A shiver passed over me, for the idea suddenly came that I was going to be hanged or thrown overboard, and this was emphasized by the sight I caught of four sailors carrying a limp dead Englishman up from the cockpit—that he had died under the surgeon's knife was evident.

From above came the sound of shouting and hurrying; the frigate came up into the wind, that must have freshened, and swung off on the other tack. As soon as this had occurred, I noticed that some one was coming down the ladder near where I stood. As he stooped under a beam and approached us, I perceived that the man was in a handsome uniform, with great epaulets and much gilt braid.

" One of the Yankee pirates, eh ?" he said ; but despite the import of the words his voice had a fine ring to it, and at one glance into his face I saw here was a man who would stoop to no mean revenge. His light-blue eyes were almost kindly were it not for the bent brows about them ; his face was extremely handsome and well moulded.

" Are you an officer of that brig ?" questioned the tall man, who I now made out must be the captain of the frigate.

" I am, sir," I replied, drawing myself up, and making a salute with my elbow at right angles and my fingers at my forehead.

With a quick glance at my position the captain made this statement:

"An officer, eh? But *you* are no sailor; you may be a soldier, though."

I almost faltered in my reply.

"I am instructor in cutlass drill, sir, and small arms."

The Englishman half smiled at this.

"A nautical maître d'armes?" he asked.

"Oui, monsieur."

"And speaks French in the bargain, by St. George! Well, well! What is the name of that vessel you belonged to?"

"The *Young Eagle*."

"Privateer, eh? I thought as much."

At this he called up the ladder to the spar-deck.

"Oh, Mr. Vyse!" he said. "I was correct. It was a Yankee privateer, and not the *Enterprise*, or any of their navy."

I was tempted to reply something, but held my tongue.

"What's your captain's name?" was the next question.

I gave it, and the names of the three other officers, but I was interrupted.

"Well, you can tell Captain Temple, with Captain Hilton's compliments, that he is the most impudent and most reckless scamp unhanged," remarked the gentleman, quietly.

"When shall I see him, sir?" I asked.

"Lord knows. Not for some time, I judge," was the answer. Then the captain turned. "Take him below again," he ordered to my guards.

They stepped forward, and each laid a hand on my shoulder. I pushed them off.

"One moment, sir," I began. "There is a member of our crew badly wounded down there with us. He will surely die unless something is done for him."

As I was speaking an officer had descended the ladder from above. I had seen the heels of his boots as he stood on the top step for some time. He was short and thick-set, with a mottled, reddish face. Captain Hilton turned to him.

" Mr. Vyse, you heard what this lad said. Pray see that this wounded man is attended to in accordance with his hurt, and his place of confinement changed if necessary."

" Very good, sir," the short man rejoined; but he had such a mean look on his face that I took a distrust against him.

When I reached the hold again and was thrust in once more among my companions, there was a deal of questioning.

" You should have said you were a lieutenant," grumbled Sutton.

" It would have made no difference with a privateer officer," put in another seaman, Edward Brown, a Long-Islander. " They'd hang us all if they dared ; and, mark me, they won't pamper us—'tis not their fashion."

I did not tell of my military salute, that was so involuntary, having betrayed me, but of course I can see it was the reason for the captain's quick statement about my being " no sailor."

It was pitch-dark down in our dank, bilge-smelling hole, and long after we stopped talking I could not fall asleep. The ridges of the cable worked into my flesh, and the muttered curses of the others as they tried to make themselves comfortable and found they could not mingled with the light-headed ramblings of poor Mackie, and a sound suspiciously like weeping from the corner in which lay one of the young landsmen, all combined to add to the misery.

Mr. Vyse had failed to carry out his superior's instructions, and there had been no one to look after the wounded man, nor had we been given so much as a pannikin of water; we were all suffering from thirst.

The welcome morning came slowly after an apparent year of night, and with it some relief, for we were given something to eat and drink. Weevilly bread, greenish salt-horse, and water that smelt unhealthy do not make a meal that is inviting, but it went. After it had been passed in to us through the entrance we heard a banging and clattering, and found they were nailing up this mode of ingress. Our next meal was lowered down to us through the circular opening overhead. It was but a foot or so in diameter, and thus we were bottled up, as it were, like flies in a jug. On this day Mackie was very low, and we all thought like to die. I doubt very much if any of us could have lived many days in that foul, close place, but we had to stand it some time longer, and the way out of it was like this:

The third day, at about noon, we heard the stirring and trampling of feet and a confused muttering of voices. I swarmed up the cable until my head was close to the opening, and there I listened. They were busy dealing forth powder and shot—I could make that clearly out. But now I heard the sounds of conversation close to me.

"'Tis the *Constitution*," said a voice — "at least, they say so up on deck."

"Then we're in for it," was the reply. "I've heard tell, messmate, that she's a sixty-gun ship in disguise."

"How far off is she?" was the question.

"About six miles off the larboard bow. You can see her from the ports."

"What's going on up there?" asked Sutton from below.

"They say we have sighted a ship, the *Constitution*; and they're clearing decks for action," I answered, much excited.

"The *Constitution!*" exclaimed Brown. "Then hallelujah! we're free men. Cheer up, my hearties!"

Sutton's reply to this startled me so that I almost slid down the cable. Three roaring huzzas broke from him, in which the others joined. Soon I felt the swaying of my support, and I saw that the foretopman was climbing up to me. It was a crawl of a few feet.

"It's a good thing, Debrin, that we are below water if we get to bandying shot, I tell you. See how she raked the *Guerrière*." Sutton chuckled.

But we could understand nothing from the confusion of sounds, until all at once I heard a voice I recognized speaking close to me. I knew the tones before I caught the words; it was Captain Hilton. In whatever he was saying I interrupted him.

"Oh, Captain Hilton," I cried, "for God's sake, help us! We've a dying man down here."

"Who's that addressing me?" questioned the captain.

"The prisoners in the cable tier, sir." I heard the answer given in a gruff tone, but most politely.

"That is no place for them," said Hilton, angrily, "and I thought I gave orders—"

The rest of his speech I did not catch, for a gun-carriage or something rumbled on deck in such a way as to drown it, but I thought I detected some expostulation from the other speaker.

We slid down, Sutton and I, to the others. Mackie was conscious, but so weak from his fever and suffering that he could not lift his head. When we told him the news he drew a long breath.

"It's too late, friends," he whispered. "I'm done for, I fear me."

We sat there now with courage growing, waiting to cheer at the first gun-shot; but all was silence from above. This continued for full ten minutes; then we heard the sound of laughter, and caught the words:

"'WE'VE A DYING MAN DOWN HERE'"

"The signal of the day, eh? I know her; 'tis the
Pique."

Sutton, who had understood, struck out with both feet
and arms, muttering an oath.

"'Tis one of their own vessels!" he cried. "Did you
ever see such luck?"

But my cry for succor, heard by the English captain,
had done us good, and that afternoon the barriers were
broken down from the entrance, and we were transferred
to a more comfortable place of confinement in a brig
near the steerage bulkhead, where at least we could sleep
on hard boards, and we were given a blanket apiece.

Poor Mackie was taken to the sick-bay. It was evident
that he was not long for this world—and alas! and alas!
in four days the news was brought to us that our messmate had died; his skull had been slightly fractured,
and the doctor wondered at his having held to life so
long. He was buried at sea, and I must say this, that
Captain Hilton proved himself to be a magnanimous,
big-hearted gentleman, for we were allowed on deck,
and a passage of Scripture was read before they dropped
the closed hammock overboard into the great graveyard
of the sailor.

As we went below Sutton observed to me:

"We're steering to the eastward. Yes, and we'll see
the inside of a prison where men rot, if tales are true.
We're bound for England, lad."

The time went by, and even the count of days was
lost. We sang songs, told stories, and played at draughts
with some rough checkers one of the sailors whittled
out. I wish I had here space to record all that passed,
for some of the yarns spun would be worth the reading.
I learned a great deal about the condition of affairs between America and England, and that, as my friend
Plummer remarked, "we had given the lion's tail a twist,
and a good one."

But there was plenty of time for thinking. Oh! how often I thought of Mary; of our meeting and our parting, and the way she had called " John, John !" to me from the pier-head. A great many of the yarns spun were of love — all about maids "with eyes black as coals "—but I declined to contribute mine. I related the incidents that had happened on board the *Minetta*, but the tale of the severed hand, as Plummer said, was "about the world ;" they had all heard it, so I listened more than I talked. I was always willing to sing, though, and picked up the airs in a jiffy.

Here is a fraction of a song that Brown used to chant —it had forty-nine stanzas :

> " ' The face that would smile when my pockets were lined
>   Showed a different aspect to me ;
> And when I could naught but indifference find
>   I hied me again to the sea."

With subsequent adventures too numerous to mention.

Another one of the choruses that was most popular was " Hull's Victory," and a rattling good sea song it was. I used to take the tenor, Sutton the base (in a way that would make the beams shake), and were it not that we were on short allowance in the eating line we would have been quite comfortable. Every day two of us at a time were allowed to take the air, in charge of a marine. Sometimes it was Sutton and I who walked together, and sometimes it was Brown or Craig, the landsman, who was my companion. Poor Craig ! His spirit appeared entirely broken. He had behaved bravely in the long-boat, but now his lack of heart was pitiful; he contributed little to our enjoyment, and the only person who ever gave him a kindly word, I really think, was myself. He spoke to me often of his home and of the sorrow it had given his mother to part with him.

I can vouch for this, that if he ever got back again,

there he would stay; for all desire towards adventure and roaming was killed within him.

I have not mentioned the other seamen by name purposely, for, with the exception of Brown and Sutton, they were an ordinary set of good and bad, who would have done well under competent leadership perhaps, but who displayed no individuality; they were all loyal to their flag, and did not appear much cowed by their confinement, though they quarrelled frequently among themselves. When I walked the deck with Sutton I enjoyed it most; he was an old man-of-war's man, and criticised the handling of the *Acasta* in a rather superior manner and a loud tone of voice.

Some of the foremast hands among the Englishmen were rather well disposed towards us, and many bits of tobacco they gave out of sheer kind-heartedness to our forlorn little band, some of whom had actually suffered from being deprived of the stimulant.

There was not a man-jack of us that was not approached at one time or another with the proposition to enlist in the king's service, the reward being full freedom from the moment of signing; but, thank God, there were no traitors forthcoming.

It happened that Brown and I were walking the deck one fine morning when the sound of "land, ho!" came down from the mast-head. During the last day or so we had sighted a number of sail, all English, but now this created some excitement. There must have been a mist on the water that had hidden the land as we approached it, but by the time our recreation was almost ended we could spy it from the deck as we passed the gangway—tall white cliffs showing above the horizon.

"That's Land's End," observed Brown, jumping up to look over the bulwarks, for of course we were not allowed to approach near a port. "Johnny Cutlass, my

son, this voyage is over.   In three hours we'll be in the
English Channel, and then for a little sojourn on board
the hulks, or maybe we'll be shipped direct to one of
their land prisons, where we'll find plenty of company, if
I don't miss my reckoning ; but keep up courage—things
might be worse."

We were the last to go on deck this day, but the news
we brought down with us started a cross-fire of talk and
questions.   All showed interest except Craig, who sat
there in his usual position, with his forehead on his
knees, never venturing a word.

CHAPTER XVI

IN DURANCE

WE were awakened early in the morning, and given an order to get our dunnage ready, as we were going to be transferred from the frigate to one of the prison-ships. The order to get "our dunnage" must have been a bit of sarcasm, as there was none of us who possessed a spare shirt to his back.

"Where are we, do you suppose?" I asked of Sutton, for the noise of our having come to anchor, and the attendant turmoil before and afterwards, had kept us awake most of the night.

"Plymouth, I take it," was the answer; "and we must have made a good run. I was here once, in 1799. It's a great town, if—"

"If what?" I interrupted, for he had paused.

"If you could only go where you chose," he responded, with a grin.

"We'll have a squint at it, anyhow," quoth Brown. "Come, my bullies, don't leave any broadcloth behind you. Look alive! you mustn't keep the gentlemen waiting."

A sorry procession, we went up to the deck in column of twos, under the guard of a half-dozen marines.

"They've hidden all of their scars," remarked Sutton, looking around him.

Sure enough, the ship's carpenter had been at work to such good purpose that there was little or no trace of the action with the *Young Eagle*. The bulwarks inside

and out had been freshly painted, and spare spars placed
in lieu of wrecked ones.

Our breakfast was doled out to us on the upper deck,
and then we were hastened to the gangway.

Such a multitude of bumboats and small craft I had
never seen as surrounded the vessel. Women and young
children crowded two-thirds of them, and hucksters and
venders of all sorts the rest; the sailors were gathered
in a shouting, hallooing cluster on the forecastle, calling
to those in the boats below them—wives and sweet-
hearts were there aplenty! But the crew had not been
allowed to receive anybody on board as yet, and our departure, being such a small number, created little comment. A launch was waiting for us, and one by one we
jumped into her stern-sheets.

I almost forgot I was a prisoner in looking about me.
I saw more ships gathered together than I had ever seen
in the whole course of my life. Some were almost twice
as large as the 74 *Plantagenet* that I had seen from the
deck of the *Minetta*.

We rowed under the stern of a great vessel pierced on
one side for sixty guns.

"There's the sort of a craft," remarked Sutton, pointing, "that Nelson and their admirals win battles with.
Curse me if she couldn't swing the *Young Eagle* at her
side ; eh, youngster ?"

And well she could, I think, for it struck me that she
was more of a floating fort than a sailing craft. Sheer-
hulks and vessels outfitting crowded in the inner harbor,
and the constant hammering, tapping, and picking of an
army of calkers filled the air.

When we reached the gangway on the port side of
the prison-ship we climbed up to the tall gallery, and I
had to smile. We might have been royal personages
making a visit, for such ceremony I have never seen
equalled. Passing between two files of marines, we

were inspected by three different groups of officers. They asked many questions, and for some time seemed to be very confident that Sutton was an Englishman. Seeing that he had some tattoo-marks on the back of his hand, they requested him to bare his arm, which he did, one of the officers saying:

"It's ten to one we'll find the crown or the lion."

"Neither them nor the unicorn," grinned Sutton, as he pulled back his ragged sleeve.

There, across the firm, white muscles of his forearm, just where the line of the sunburn on his wrist ended, was tattooed the picture of a naval engagement, one vessel sailing triumphantly away with the American flag as big as her spanker covering half her side. The other ship was sinking beneath the waves, and all that could be seen was her stern and a tremendous British Jack. Underneath the first was "*Bonhomme Richard*," and under the other "*Serapis*." The line of lettering that stretched across the top of this work of art read, "Three cheers for Yankee pluck!" It was the spirit of the occasion, without regard to historical fidelity, that the artist had caught.

"I have a more recent one if you would like to look at it," Sutton began, unbuttoning the collar of his shirt. But he had evidently shown enough, for the British officer passed him without any further objections.

At last our names were taken, and we went below into the foul-smelling air of the 'tween-decks. Five or six hundred men were confined on board this ship, and as the guards had a generous portion set apart for themselves, the prisoners were much crowded. But we were not going to be kept here long; and although the time seemed to go slowly and was certainly most tedious, only a week elapsed before we were informed that we were going to be taken to a large prison near the town of Bristol.

On the twelfth day we were landed on the dock in Plymouth, and the dry ground felt odd to our feet, I can tell you. As luck had it, Sutton, Craig, and myself were in the first draft.

There was a small squadron of cavalry and a body of infantry waiting to escort us past the town, which we walked through completely surrounded by soldiers, marching in column of fours. The comments from the townsfolk were various—some bitter and some kindly.

Poor Craig was so weak that Sutton and I took turns supporting him, but the seaman's feet, becoming very much blistered, I bribed, with my next to last bit of gold, permission from a van-driver for us to crawl up on one of the wagons.

It took us seven days to march from Plymouth to Bristol. We passed through towns and villages where we were fairly well-fed and treated, sleeping at night in outbuildings and stable yards; but so closely were we guarded that we found no chance to escape, although we were on the lookout for it.

I must say that I have always held an admiration for certain traits in English character, despite my prejudice already confessed to, and instances of kind and humane treatment were so frequent along the march that it could not be held to be a hardship altogether, although it was not an outing for pleasure exactly.

From Bristol, where we arrived in the afternoon, to the town of Stapleton, where the prison at which we were to be domiciled was, it is about seven miles, and the whole of the way thither we were escorted by a crowd of good-natured, kindly folk, who fed us, and were constant in the expression of sympathy.

At six o'clock we skirted the edge of a vast domain that I found, by asking, was the private estate of the Duke of Devonshire, and before we knew it we were halted in front of a long row of stone buildings, behind the barred gratings of which appeared hundreds of pallid faces. The buildings were surrounded by walls ten feet or more in height, on the tops of which sentries were patrolling their beats. We passed over a drawbridge spanning a ditch of some twenty feet in width and very deep, and going under an archway we were let in to an interior apartment in a body, and then out of a farther door, where we found ourselves in a wide open space surrounded by the brown, sombre prison-houses. The chatter of French sounded all about us, for the majority of the prisoners were Frenchmen taken in the war then being waged against Napoleon. They appeared to be a happy, garrulous set, and I believe could have been kept in order with a switch. The Americans, as a rule, had little to do with them.

I could write a book upon my life as an English prisoner of war, and it might not be dull reading either; but as these pages are to be a record of my adventures alone, I fear I would take up too much time if I should allow this fact to leave my mind.

But just a short sketch of what I saw there during the four months that I suffered with the rest may not be amiss. Why it was not longer that I stayed was due more to good fortune than to good management. But to come to that after a while.

The Frenchmen swung their hammocks in a building apart from the Americans, and were, as I said, more contented and less restless. The Yankees were constantly plotting to escape, and doing, I must confess, everything they could to make their captor's life a hard one. There was a great deal of grumbling and gambling, much rough horse-play, and yet a great deal to commend also in the loftiness of spirit and courage displayed by many. Sutton, Brown, Kemp, Craig, and myself messed together; the first two soon became prominent, and better men it would be hard to find. Kemp, the man who pulled on the same thwart with me in the long-boat, grew over-fond of the dice-box, more's the pity, and became quarrelsome, so we got rid of him. Craig was tolerated, and that was merely on my account.

All sorts of plans were proposed for breaking jail, and during the short period of my captivity I know of at least four attempts that were circumvented at the very last moment. Only one or two individual escapes occurred, and whether the men who thus took French leave were afterwards apprehended I cannot say.

A huge prison, in which are confined some five or six thousand men (our numbers were swelled every day by new drafts of American prisoners and Frenchmen) is much like a city. We had theatrical companies, markets, and exchanges, and men quarrelled and gambled, and plied their trades or callings to some advantage. Time passed quickly, although one day was much like another. We were well guarded and fairly well fed, although clothing and foot-gear were at a premium.

My size and strength had actually increased since I had left Belair. I stood six feet in height before I was nineteen years of age, and I afterwards added two inches more to this. In the sports, especially in the foot-races and wrestling, I found myself a leader. Of course no person could live in such a community as this, even for a short time, without picking up a great deal of useful knowledge, besides imbibing much also that would serve no one in good stead except perhaps as a warning.

I learned the history of our war up to date, however, and to show what good cause our country had in opposing Great Britain, I might record that here at Stapleton there were at least a thousand honest American seamen who had been impressed into the service of the King, but who, at the outbreak of the war, had delivered themselves up as prisoners rather than fight against their flag.

I understood that there were twice as many more at Dartmoor, but this was only hearsay.

My knowledge of the French tongue enabled me to converse with the Frenchmen, and I whiled away many an hour by talking with them and reading a romance so smirched by constant handling as to be almost undecipherable. A small volume of Shakespeare, belonging to an ex-schoolmaster, who kindly loaned it me, I pored over by the hour.

One day there came a little excitement in our life, and a great hallooing and huzzaing resounded through the yard. It was a reception tendered to some members of the crew of the luckless *Chesapeake* who were transferred from the hulks to join us. They were not of the riffraff who unfortunately composed part of her company, who had been paroled or held in Halifax — they were the volunteers from the Charlestown yard—*men who fought.* They had been accused of being deserters from the Royal Navy, but had proved themselves guiltless upon trial. (N.B. The English found but one man to hang among the *Shannon's* prisoners.) We got up an entertainment in their honor that lasted the better portion of the night. The dramatic words of brave Captain Lawrence, and the recital of the events of the action, aroused a fever of patriotism in the prison. The English made a big thing of their victory at the time, the newspapers being filled with it; and no matter how much of a veil their historians may throw over the other occurrences of the war, they will never fail to mention this one. But who can blame them? It was a fine fight, and there is no use in indulging in any 'ifs' at all.

Weeks went by and wintry weather came, bringing a great deal of suffering to the ill-clad and improvident; sickness and death were with us; cold and hunger make men selfish, and it was hard work to keep up one's courage—even the bravest hearted often gave way to fits of despondency. These were bitterly trying days—indeed they were.

Said Jack Sutton to me one cold night as we lay huddled up for warmth:

"Johnnie Cutlass, my son, I'm going to get out of this if I die for it. This is not living; and if I get a bullet in me, I'll thank the man who sent it there. Some day you'll find I'm gone—free or buried, one or t'other. I'm going to make a break for liberty, and never give up trying."

These words confirmed me in the idea of taking the first desperate chance myself. But I confided my intention to no one, and even Sutton did not know of the stoutness of my determination.

CHAPTER XVII

A FRENCH LEAVE-TAKING

THE evening of the 23d of November, 1813, I can set down in this chronicle in large, important letters; for on this date, by a combination of fortunate circumstances, I ceased to be a prisoner. It happened thus:

The officers attached to the military force stationed at the prison lived together in a small building at the southwest corner of the rectangle formed by the high walls. Through the building which they occupied a passage ran to a small postern-gate. On several occasions I had been over there bearing messages from the prison-keeper (I was one of the monitor officers in charge of the order of my section of the west wing). Of course I had never progressed farther than the small antechamber that opened into the guard-room and barracks, where I would wait to secure an audience with the commandant or one of his subordinates.

But on this day I was bound to see a strange condition of affairs—the orderly who generally stood at the door was missing from his post. It was past dusk, and as I pushed in I noticed that the entrance to the guard-room, usually filled with soldiers, was shut. I thought of giving a hail, but then, perceiving also that the entrance leading into the main building was gaping wide, impelled by a sudden impulse I stepped swiftly across the threshold into the hallway I could hear voices coming from somewhere, but a room to the right appeared to be empty; a candle was burning on top of a tall dressing-case, and there across the foot of a narrow cot lay spread the uniform of a lieutenant; and a great bearskin shako, with a tall plume, topped one of the bedposts.

Now methinks to do what I did then took more courage than anything I have ever attempted. I gave a leap sideways into the room, and closed the door behind me. Actually panting from excitement, I tore off the rags which served me for clothing, hid them beneath the cot, and, shaking from head to foot, I donned the uniform. Luckily the clothes were made for a large man, and they fitted to perfection. I glanced at myself in the glass as I put the towering head-gear on as a finishing-touch.

I was a strange-looking object. My hair, which was long, was done sailor fashion down my back in a pigtail, but the locks straggled over my cheeks; and, young as I was, my appearance would have been improved by the use of a razor. But I gathered my queue on the top of my head, where it was kept by the weight of the shako, and then I stepped to the door.

The voices had ceased, but I plainly perceived that some one was coming down the stone-flagged corridor— the jingling of spurs echoed along the walls! Hastily I closed the door, and extinguished the light with a pinch of my fingers. It was good for me that I had done this, for whoever it was gave the door a push and thrust in his head. How he ever missed seeing me (for I could have struck him with my knee) I cannot understand to this day. Perhaps the gentleman was far-sighted; but, moreover, he had been drinking, for *I caught a whiff of his breath!*

"Humph! Not here," he muttered, thickly. "A pretty piece of business."

Then away he clanked, with his big sword hitched under his arm, and I heard the slamming of a door to another apartment. It was one of the staff-officers. I knew that probably he came from the outside, and that

the way to freedom, or at least to the open air, must be
in the direction from which he was walking ; so I stepped
out into the passageway and tiptoed down it. Then thinking that cautious steps might attract notice, I changed
my gait to a military stride, and swaggered along with
chest out and shoulders back. My doing this was fortunate, for I went by the open entrance of a small apartment, where a young man in undress uniform sat reading
a book with the aid of a small lamp ; he glanced out at
me, but made no comment. I had affected to yawn, and
half covered my face with my hand.

Now I came to the end of the corridor, and here were
three doors : the one on the left shut, the centre one
partly ajar, and the one on the right closed with large
bolts. Looking through the door that was open, I could
perceive a man's leg stretched out on a chair as if he
were resting, so I turned to the one on the left. I was
about to draw the latch when from within I heard the
sound of voices in conversation.

"Good for you! Now another throw," some one
laughed. Then came the rattle of a dice-box.

There was nothing for it but to try the farther door,
the one that was bolted, and to do this I had to run the
risk of attracting the man's attention in the middle room.
Nevertheless I stepped by, and, giving a quick glance
over my shoulder, I saw that he was asleep, with his
mouth wide open and his hands thrust deep into his
pockets. With trembling fingers I drew the bolt of the
heavy, iron-studded door, and swung it open. It disclosed
another passageway much like the first, with rooms on
either side and a staircase in a recess at the farther end.

Good fortune still favored me. I tramped along and
found that to go out I had evidently to ascend the steps.
When I reached the foot and placed my hand on the iron
guard-rail, I almost gave a gasp of sheer fright. There
standing on a little platform at the top was a grenadier,

with his musket leaning against him. He had caught
sight of me, however, at this same instant—the hall was
dimly lighted with a flickering taper, and I was in full
view. I thought of immediate retreat.

But to my surprise the man instantly drew himself
erect and his musket snapped to a "present." Drawing
the heavy cloak that I had thrown about my shoulders
up to my nose, I hurried up the steps and returned the
soldier's salute in proper manner, but with shaking fingers, as I passed him.

Here I was in the open air, and from the entrance a
narrow causeway or bridge led to the top of the wall.
But all danger was not over, for at the farther end stood
two more of the red-coated gentry. One had called the
attention of the other to my approach, and there they
were, drawn up like two carved figure-heads. I should
have to go between them! But the light was very dim,
and only boldness could serve my purpose. So I gazed
directly at them, and with a great bound of my heart in
my throat I saw that the ruse was going to be successful. They presented arms as I brushed by.

A small flight of stairs led down the wall on the outside, and here the ditch was spanned by a foot-bridge
—on the bank stood another sentry! I had wondered
why I had not been asked for a password of some sort,
and now I feared that this last man would prove my
downfall, and that surely I would be stopped and asked
some question. I hesitated as I stood there half-way
down the steps, and in this moment I noticed the sentry
across the bridge bring his musket to a half-charge with
a ring of his accoutrements. In the dusk I could see
four or five figures approaching, and soon I heard the
sentry call them to halt.

I could not make out the words that followed, but it
was all merely perfunctory business I recognized, as the
approaching figures were officers. Now fear often gives

"THE MAN INSTANTLY DREW HIMSELF ERECT"

a man a judgment and cleverness that support him in
sore straits. There was but one chance, and I took it.
I turned about, retraced my steps, passed the two sentries, who saluted me once more, then again the third
man at the head of the stairway, and I was back in the
corridor.

When I had turned the angle of the passage I entered
one of the rooms, and crouched behind a curtain, holding my big hat in my lap. My teeth chattered so that I
feared the noise would be audible, and I had been just
in time, as, laughing and talking, the officers were approaching down the hall!

As I sat huddled in my corner I perceived that they
had some huge joke among them. They were walking
slowly, and I heard distinctly what passed.

"The idea of Tillinghast forgetting the countersign
strikes me as being grand," exclaimed some one, with a
guffaw at the end of the sentence.

"Ha! ha! ha!" laughed another. "I told you it
was the author of *Robinson Crusoe*, Tilly."

"Why, confound it all! I always thought that he himself wrote the book," roared a deep bass.

I recognized the speaker as one of the young lieutenants of the garrison—it was his clothes, by-the-way, that
I had on my back at the moment.

"I think the governor chose it for a play on words,"
quoth another. "A poor pun, even for him."

"Why we should require a password at all is more
than I can see," responded Tillinghast. "Come down
to my quarters, Carntyne. We have time for a hand of
whist."

They passed on. I waited a few minutes, putting two
and two together, and suddenly it came to me. *I had
the password at the tip of my tongue!* Hastily rising, I
stepped outside of the room. It was but a few yards to
the bottom of the stairs, and I heard the sentry hum-

ming a snatch of a tune, and keeping time to it cleverly
with the stamping of his feet in the measure of a jig. I
was afraid that if I approached him the way that I had
done before, he might look closer, so I made believe
that I was carrying on the fag end of a conversation
with some one, and answered an imaginary question
with a laugh (a trifle forced, I must admit).

"No, thanks," I cried; "you gentlemen are too much
for me. I must hasten. Eh?" (A pause.) "I shall be
back by nine o'clock, but I must hurry." Then I charged
along up as if the devil was after me! The inflexible
grenadier had hardly time to salute me; and I rushed
past the other two at the end of the causeway at the
same pace. They made some remark after I had gone
by, but I did not catch it. More leisurely I descended
the steps on the outside of the wall, and crossed the little
foot-bridge to where the last redcoat stood. His musket
barred my path, but it was a respectful attitude.

"The word, sir?" he said, slurring the usual challenge.

"Defoe," I answered. He hesitated. "Daniel Defoe," I repeated, restraining with difficulty a mad impulse
to close with him and pitch him headlong into the ditch.

The response to this was a backward step on the
sentry's part, and a stiff attitude of present arms. I replied with somewhat of a flourish, and hastened down
the path. It led across a sort of common, bordered by
twinkling lights shining from some vine-covered houses,
and in the stillness I heard the sound of a fiddle played
somewhere, and from another direction the voice of an
infant crying like a good one. What was I to do? I
knew little or nothing of the geography of England, and
to save my soul I could not imagine what would be the
best direction to take.

My first idea was to put as much space between me
and the prison-yard as I could, so I walked away from it

with that end in view alone. It grew very dark as the twilight faded, and I kept to the common until I plunged through a thorny hedge and made the road. It seemed to lead straight to the northward, which was as good for me as any other point of the compass, so I hastened along as fast as my legs could carry me.

The big military hat wobbled unsteadily on my head, and I thought how difficult it would be to make any sort of a fight with such an encumbrance to quick motions. But I reasoned I would attract a great deal of attention if I should discard it, so I slung it over my back by the plume, ready to clap it on if necessary, and went forward at a dog-trot.

The villages in this part of the country were so close together that I seemed hardly to leave one before I saw the lights of another. I was evidently on the highway, however, and, strange to say, I met but a few country people walking. They looked at me rather curiously, but did not speak. Thus I had traversed some twelve miles or more before midnight, and as there was a town of some size in the distance, judging by the lights and the sounds of two separate sets of chimes striking the hour, I determined to find some place where I could rest and think over the situation.

Close to hand was a cottage whose outlines I could just discern, and near it were some hayricks and some straggling outbuildings. I climbed the low wall, jumped, or, better, stumbled, across a ditch, and made my way through the farm-yard, intending to rest in the hay; but all at once the hoarse, rasping bark of a dog made me halt. That the beast was coming in my direction and was angry I could not doubt; right in front of me was a little wooden cabin, and thinking that the entrance to it might be open I ran straight up to it—I found a door with the first extending of my hand. It pushed open; I entered and swung it to behind me.

It was as dark as if I had suddenly become a blind man. The place smelt dry and musty; a strong, pungent odor filled my nostrils, not unpleasant exactly, but new to me. Reaching round with my foot, I touched something large and soft. For an instant I thought it was a living thing, but feeling with my hand I perceived it was a sack stuffed with some yielding material. I sat down upon it and began to think.

Now and then I heard a sniffing, whining sound that showed me that the dog—bad luck to him!—had found my whereabouts. Here was the position of matters:

If caught, at first glance I might pass for one of his Majesty's officers, but I could not stand an investigation without discovery. My hair would have betrayed me if nothing else, and apparently there was no hope but ultimate recapture, anyhow. Yet I did not despair, for I was young, and youth builds to suit its fancy.

As I stirred around a bit I discovered that the whole place was filled with sacks like the one I had been resting on. In this movement I must have made some noise, as the dog outside set up a furious yawping again, and I am afraid the language I used would not look well in writing—indeed, it behooved me to remain silent, so I stretched myself full length on the sacks, which I now made out to contain wool. They made a soft couch, and from thinking I must have fallen to dreaming on the instant, for I began to go over the events of the last few days, and from them I strayed back into the past, and, of course, I thought of Mary Tanner, and that drove out all else, as usual.

It seemed to me that again I was in the little garden under the shadow of the rose-bush. I could recall Mary's arch smile and the sideways glance of her eye. The imaginary conversation we held continued at great length, and then the scene changed to the sea, and I was captain of a ship, sailing, with a fair wind, to some country whose name I could not place, but I knew that there Mary was waiting for me.

All at once I awoke. I found myself with one hand in the breast of my brilliant red tunic, grasping close a little leather ditty-bag I had made from the leg of an old boot when on board the *Acastra*. It was strung about my neck by a thong, and contained all that I knew of that I could claim in the way of earthly possessions.

These consisted of one of the De Brienne buttons, a single gold piece with the head of King Louis on it, and a package of dried rose-leaves twisted into a small bit of paper.

It was gray dawn; cocks were crowing, and the bleating of sheep sounded from near by. With incredible swiftness the light spread, and soon I could dimly see my surroundings. I was in a small storehouse connected with a shepherd's cottage; utensils of various sorts lay tossed about, and there, under my foot, was almost the very thing I was longing for—a pair of sheep-shears, evidently new and in working order.

To perform the operation of cutting one's own hair with the aid of a glass and barber's clip-scissors would be no small undertaking, but to do it artistically with sheep-shears and in semi-darkness I defy a man to accomplish. But nevertheless I went at it, and disposed of some four inches of queue and the straggling elf-locks satisfactorily. (I wonder what the farmer said when he found this in the sack, and if he blamed it on the sheep.)

I tried to even matters up by the sense of feeling and touch, but it was but a makeshift job. Soon it was bright enough to caution me to be moving. The light that had come in entered through a small glazed window high up near the roof and beyond reach; so I opened the door, peered out, and thanked my stars that the dog was not in sight. The epaulets had not been hitched on the shoulders when I had helped myself to the uniform, and now with the aid of the shears some of the plume and the gold braid was disposed of, and thus, more magpie and less peacock, I might, I thought, pass muster for a common soldier, as it would attract less attention. But still I was a nondescript-looking figure, I must affirm.

The road was but a stone's-throw distant, and I quickly got over the wall and found myself standing there, not knowing what way to turn; in fact, I feared it would make small odds which choice was made—north, east, south, or west.

"No matter what happens, I shall have a yarn to spin," I said, grimly, to myself, as I stretched my stiffened legs and rubbed my cold hands together to start my chilled blood going.

CHAPTER XVIII

I KNEW that most likely I was in Gloucestershire;
and from a sign-post, pointing the way I came the
night gone, I learned that I had passed the towns of
Thornbury and Slimbridge. While cogitating how to
get a bite to eat something happened that put even
hunger out of my head—I heard the flourish of a horn !
Turning about, I saw the coach coming up a little hill,
swinging along at a good pace, with the leaders in a
gallop.

The boldest course was the best; so I leaned noncha-
lantly against a stone post that had cut in it " Eight
miles to Hardwick," and waited for the mail to come up.
The driver, a ruddy-faced individual in a multitude of
cloaks and a wide beaver, caught my attention even before I had time to signal him with my hand.

" Are ye off to Gloucester, laad?" he cried, drawing up.

"Aye," I answered. " Hold on, and I'll take a passage."

There were but three besides the guard on top, and I
clambered over the wheel up to the front seat before
the coach had lost its headway. I feared most dreadfully that the driver would begin to question me at once,
but, thank the powers, he did not. Keeping up a continuous clicking sound against his teeth, and gracefully
flourishing the long-lashed whip (catching the leaders
now and again with the end of it most cleverly), he
drove ahead without speaking.

All the time I was wondering how I was going to pay the fare with one French gold piece, when the red-faced man made this matter smooth sailing.

"'E better get off before we get into the town, laad," said he, "then we won't ask noo fare o' ye.".

"Thanks, very much," I returned.

"Not a bit, not a bit," he laughed. "A soldier on a spree wants all 'e can spend, eh?—pull up, hosses!"

I nodded, and we drove on in silence.

For a long time there had been visible a great square tower rising above the stretches of vineyards, corn-lands, and gardens. It was the first thing that caught the eye, and I began to speculate about it. But the near scenery was as delightful as the distant view. The day was more like spring than winter; every living thing seemed bound to make the most of nature's kindly mood. The country was interspersed with rich pastures in which fat, broad-backed sheep were grazing; the flocks saluted us with choruses of bleating and baaing; rooks and other birds chattered in the trees—all happy and all free! How I drank in these sights and sounds, craning my neck, and straining my eyes and ears! Beautiful residences of the aristocracy, with wide-spreading parks, were frequent on each side of the highway, and soon scattered houses overgrown with vines proclaimed that we were on the outskirts of the town. The tower that had been so conspicuous a landmark belonged to some great church; that was very plain, but I feared to ask for any information.

As we were about to turn a corner the driver pulled up his horses, and understanding him to mean that my ride was over, I quickly descended to the ground, at the same time giving an expression of my gratitude. The coach was barely out of sight when I saw ahead of me the swinging sign-board of an inn, and with that my desire to feed grew so strong that I fished out the gold

piece from my catch-all, determined to purchase a breakfast if it took the last penny.

Walking up to the entrance to the "Moon and Star-
fish" (this was the odd name on the sign), I went inside the tap-room, and found that the people of the inn
were preparing for their daily customers; the floor was
newly sanded and the pewters shone brightly on the cupboard. Calling for the landlord, I seated myself at a
table by the window, and a flood of self - conceit came
over me so that I almost gibbered with delight!

In a few minutes a bowl of coffee was at my elbow, a
thick fat chop decked in greens was putting strength into
my blood and spirits as it disappeared, my jaws worked
to a tune of my own composing, and I cared little for
the future—the present was good and given to enjoy!
But soon I was to be on a very different tack; for with
a clatter and clanking I recognized the approach of the
people I most dreaded to meet—the men who fight his
Majesty's wars and eat his victuals. Five soldiers entered from the outside!

They were petty officers, with stripes on their sleeves,
red coats with puffs at their shoulders, strings of bright
buttons, pipe-clayed cross-belts, and black gaiters.

They may have been handsome to look at, but to me
they were five living horrors! With a chill and a tingling back of my ears I pretended closer attention to my
meal. I knew they were looking at me, but they entered
the next compartment and called for ale and spirits.
When the landlord appeared I overheard the conversation.

"I don't know who the young man is," spoke the host
of the inn, as if in reply to a question. "He came off
the coach, I take it."

"He's an officer," observed one of the soldiers.

"You're wrong," corrected a second. "Where are
his shoulder-knots?"

"I observed him close," put in the one who had not yet spoken, "and now it strikes me he is part officer and part private. 'Tis the uniform of the Somersetshire Foot-guard. I know it."

I was almost choking in my efforts to bolt a great bit of meat, but from the tail of my eye I saw that two heads were thrust about the corner and that they were piping me off. So I turned my back and looked out of the window. The heads were at last withdrawn, but there came a laugh in a minute, and some whispering in which I caught the words, "curling-tongs and the barber," probably in allusion to my great need of both.

I am honestly very sorry that I never paid the landlord for that good meal of his, but I acted on an impulse that more than likely saved me total discomfiture. I was taken aback fore and aft, completely staggered with the idea that curiosity would pass bounds, and the gentlemen in the next compartment would begin to sift me. The window was wide open, and the sward on the outside came to within three feet of the sill; making no noise, I crawled out headforemost. Then walking quickly across the court-yard, I dodged behind a row of stables, and crept along beneath a line of hedge; and this time I did not take the big hat with me, but left it and the cloak mounting guard over the remains of my meal.

Now I really should have liked to have heard what the redcoats said, and I fear that the landlord could not have been complimentary.

The hedge that I was following ran up to a high wall, on the other side of which was presumably one of the parks of a nobleman or an aristocrat. By dint of scratching and hauling and sheer strength, I struggled over the top and came down on a level stretch of lawn, dotted about with handsome beech-trees, and farther on edged by a noble line of oaks. No one was in sight, and, driven by a nameless dread, I started running. A great bronze-colored bird with a long tail scurried across my path and tore up into the air with a whir, making me shy to one side, like a runaway horse; I kept up my speed but a few hundred yards, however, when the idea came to me that this would never do at all. So I threw myself down at the foot of a tree and tried to compose my ideas.

Off to the right, beyond a low hedge covered with a thorny vine, was a field that had once been grown with corn (wheat, we call it in our country), and lording it over this ruined domain, with its arms outstretched, was a ragged scarecrow. I think my next move was something that proves me far from imbecile. Leaping the hedge, I tore off my bright red coat and white breeches, and then, with mighty little on, I crawled, Indian fashion, towards the silent guardian of the fields.

Oh, they were very ragged indeed were his Majesty's habiliments, but there were enough of them to cover me, even if I did show bare at the knees and elbows, and hurriedly I hung them on, and, taking the flapping hat from off the straw-stuffed head, I was the scarecrow come to life! I had hidden the uniform under some handfuls of leaves and grass; and now to get out of the park and reach the road, where, by my appearance, I rightfully belonged!

The wall on the inside was so high and so well built that I could not reach the top, but as I went along I came to a little gate that unlocked by thrusting back a bolt. I opened it, and found myself in the kitchen-garden of a neat white cottage. The sound of a woman's voice singing in clear tones came to my ear.

CHAPTER XIX

FRIENDS IN NEED

FOR some minutes I stood there listening to the voice, and I made up my mind that the owner must be a young person full of hope and strength; I pictured to myself that she was a slender girl, and that probably it was her hand that tended the flowers of which there was a profusion in the windows.

Now it would be impossible for me to reach the road without going by the house, so I thought that the best way out of it would be to approach the back door, knock, and ask for a drink of water, even if I had to interrupt the fair singer in the midst of her warbling.

I was about to do this when the song came nearer, and before I had reached the end of the path a woman's figure appeared in the doorway. She almost filled it, so large was she across the shoulders; but immediately I perceived that she was the author of the clear notes nevertheless, for the trill died away from her lips as her eyes fell upon my sorry figure standing there before her.

"Well, well!" she exclaimed, brushing her hands against one another (they were covered with white flakes of flour), "and what are ye doing i' the garden? We want none o' ye about. Mizzle; d' ye mind me?"

Before replying I took a few steps nearer and glanced up at her. Her age was uncertain, and even now in my recollection I cannot imagine what it may have been. She was not gross or fat, but simply large—of great proportions every way. Her eyes were bright—nay, almost beautiful; her cheeks were red, and her mouth like a ripe rosebud; her throat was round and full, like a songbird's. If she had been a smaller woman one might have said that she possessed a plump prettiness, but her size honestly prevented this description.

"Madam," said I, making a low bow, and pulling the scarecrow hat from my ragged locks, "I might ask for a drink of water, and such was my intention, but I feared disturbing your sweet song that I was enjoying so." (You see how much I had learned — it was thus they spoke in the romance.) "I would go thirsty for long to hear it again," I continued.

At this she dropped me a bob of a courtesy and smiled.

"Was I tuning, then?" she asked. "I always do on fine days."

"May they come more often," I replied, again bowing. She blushed at this.

"And is it water that you're wanting?" she said. "You're a smooth-spoken laad. Come into the kitchen; I dare say a glass of milk would go better."

I entered the neat whitewashed room, and at a motion from the kind hostess seated myself at the table.

This day I had two breakfasts. I had done full justice to that set before me at the "Moon and Star-fish," but now I had to eat another, for there was placed before me a basin of porridge, a loaf of bread, a huge pat of cream-cheese, and a bowl of milk. As if to relieve any embarrassment that I might feel, the large woman, with an assumed air of unconsciousness, bent over her pan of dough, and took up her chant exactly where she had left off. Although the edge had been worn from my appetite, I finished the meal, urged by a sense of politeness even to scraping the platter. Then I arose.

"I thank you quite as much for the song as for the

repast, madam," I said, and I was about to add more
when she interrupted me.

"Perhaps you sing yourself?" she inquired.

In return I cleared my throat.

Well, indeed, it was a humorous situation. Here I
was, all dressed in rags, leaning against a high-back
wooden chair, and piping in a key that was a bit too
high for me a song I had learned from a fellow-prisoner
who had been a ballad-singer, or an actor, or something
like—lines all about a lady in a bower with a lover gone
off to the war. I shortened it by some half-dozen verses
and waited for her comments.

"A pretty thing," she smiled, humming the air over,
and beating an uncertain time with her hand, as if she
feared she had not caught the notes aright. Suddenly
I heard the slamming of a gate, and I perceived by the
change in the woman's face that I had best be going.
So, feeling that maybe I had done something to pay for
her hospitality by giving her a new tune if no more, I
backed out into the garden just as a thin, undersized
man came about the bushes; he had evidently made
entrance through the gate from the gentleman's park.
But I had turned about an angle of the house, and just
caught the woman's words of explanation.

"A poor laad to whom I gave a bit to eat, John," she
said; "that was all."

Then a sudden idea seizing me that perhaps the man
might recognize that the clothes I had on belonged to
the scarecrow I had robbed (he was evidently a gardener
or outside helper), I hastened through a hole in the front
hedge and hurried down the road. But the singing of
the ballad had suggested an idea to me. Perhaps by
this means I could keep body and soul together, so far
as eating and drinking went, and my adventure, I reasoned, might prove a most fortunate one.

I did not stop at the inn this time, but hobbled past

on the opposite side, and a five minutes' walk brought me nearer the heart of the town. Passing a number of people, who gave me a wide berth, and keeping straight ahead, I came to a square, or, better, the meeting-place of four thoroughfares crossing at right angles. Not far away rose the great square tower. It was so high and so massive that I walked towards it to obtain a nearer view, and stopped in astonishment before one of the greatest cathedrals in England.

Led by curiosity, I came still nearer. The great door was open, and I entered, with a feeling of awe, the dusky shadows. At the eastern end the light came through a great round window, shattering in a myriad of colors like a mass of jewels. No one apparently objected to my entering; in fact, I had seen no one outside but an aged gaffer sitting on the steps, with his chin resting on the handle of his stick. So I crept into one of the carved stalls and sank down in a corner.

I might have been in a dream, the whole thing seemed so unreal to me—so far from what the past had brought; and as if to make this feeling more assured a strange, grand music suddenly welled up from a recess to the left. I had never heard a church organ in my life, but I shall not get over my first impressions—never, 'pon my honor. I forgot my rags, my danger, my whole position, as I sat there fairly chained by the music that set me marvelling.

I knew nothing of religion except what I had gleaned from the family prayers at Mr. Edmundson's, and that was very little. Of course there had been some psalm-singers among the prisoners at Stapleton, and an itinerant preacher had once given us a sermon full of threats, of dire vengeance, and brimstone.

But now I realized that truly there must be a God, and that here must be His temple! So, overcome by some great sensation, I dropped upon my knees and gave thanks for my escape.

I was interrupted by a kindly voice, and, looking up, I saw that a tall man, with his white hair trimmed in a by-gone fashion and a black coat buttoned up to his white stock, was standing there in an expectant attitude looking at me. Whatever he took me for I do not know.

"Repent, son, and return," he said, in a soothing tone, bending forward.

I had feared that he was going to upbraid me for my presence, but his next movement deprived me of that idea entirely.

"Here, take this," he said; "and God bless you and direct you."

As he spoke he extended his hand, with a piece of silver in it, towards me. A sense of pride in that, so far in my life, I had asked alms of no one almost tempted me to refuse it, but fearing that he might put me to questions, I took it, mumbled some thanks, and hurried out into the sunshine.

I am sure that if he had been an American I should never have escaped without telling a story of some sort, but the English are of a less curious temper than we are, and if they interfere in other people's business on the outside world, they have a talent for minding their own at home, and to this I testify readily.

My clothes were so disreputable that I determined to spend part of the shilling in procuring a means of mending them. So I entered a little shop down the street, and purchased thread and needles. With these in my pocket, I set out immediately looking for a place to hide while at work.

Taking the wide road that led to the north, I followed it, and, passing by a common on which some lads were kicking a large leather ball about, I came to an inn, much more important than the one I had stopped at in the morning, surrounded by a court-yard with sheds and stables. A number of large carts and vans were resting here, and, crawling over the tail-board of one that had a wide canvas top, I took off my clothes and began repairing my numerous rents. It took some time, for the coat was threadbare and torn into jibs and streamers.

CHAPTER XX

A BEGGAR A-HORSEBACK

WHEN the tailoring job was finished I was in less danger of coming to pieces, and, despite what I had eaten, my stomach told me it was past the midday-meal hour.

Now where I was to go I did not have the least idea, and my heart went down like a lead. But *en avant!* There was no sense in tarrying ; ho ! for the highway !

As I went to go out of the court-yard to take up my aimless walking again, a tall chaise in which were two elegantly dressed gentlemen drove through the entrance gateway. I had to jump from under the horse's hoofs. Some of the inn servants, who had paid no attention to me, ran out from the stables at the sound of the wheels, and immediately in the doorway of the inn itself appeared a slender man, with powdered hair, who greeted the other two with a graceful salutation ; there was a trace of courtliness in it that was handsome. But my heart gave a bound as I turned curiously to watch the finely attired strangers.

They were speaking French ! Not the French that I had heard lately in the prison, but the French that my mother had taught me and that my uncle spoke.

" Welcome, Monsieur de Rèdun !" exclaimed the tall man in the doorway, "and welcome, Monsieur le Marquis."

" De Rèdun !—Monsieur le Marquis !" How familiar and natural this name and the title sounded to me ;

and then it all came back — "Gabriel Montclair de Rèdun, Marquis de Monseverat, friend of my grandfather, le Marquis de Brienne." I remembered that my uncle had made me learn this in the long list of stupid names. There were two sons, Georges Lucien and Guy Léon de Rèdun. The latter and his father had both lost their heads on the guillotine on the same day that my grandfather had lost his. Somehow the idea that there might be some help come to me from a man who bore the name of Rèdun crossed my brain. I paused a moment, then turned back into the court-yard.

The servants had led away the horse, and seated at a window that, owing to the warmth of the day, was partly raised were the three fine-looking gentlemen. I watched them for a few minutes, not knowing what to do. I could not hear the sound of their voices, so I came nearer. The shortest of the three, who had been addressed as "Monsieur le Marquis," was talking and gesticulating with his jewelled hand.

"Yes, yes. We will see the lilies again, my friends," he said in French. "Give this usurper time enough and the rope, and he will hang himself—a trite but true saying, my friends."

All at once one of them looked out of the window and saw me standing close to. I felt as if I had to do something to account for my presence, and the idea suggested to me by my singing in the morning was put into immediate practice ; why, except for the connection of thought, I should have chosen the song I did I know not, but it was a fortunate circumstance. I struck out into a little chansonnette, something in the nature of a serenade, that I heard my uncle trill in his high-pitched voice—a song that may have been a favorite with the gallants of King Louis's court.

I did not look in at the window as I sang, but cast my eyes upward in apparent oblivion to my surroundings.

As I began the third stanza (something about roses and hearts, I remember) I was interrupted by approaching footsteps. My voice had attracted the attention of the people in the court-yard, and a hostler was hurrying up plainly with the intention of sending me to the right-about. But if that was what he meant to do, he had to give it over, for a commanding voice in English, without the trace of an accent, exclaimed from the window :

"Bring that lad in here, some one."

Before I knew it I was following one of the servants through a passageway, and was ushered into the presence of the three men seated at the table.

"Where could he have learned that song?" one of them was saying. The short man was humming the air, but he stopped short upon my entrance.

"Who are you and what is your name?" questioned the large gentleman, addressing me in French as soon as I had crossed the threshold.

"Jean Amédée de Brienne," I replied, taking the name by which I had been known for the past few months, only giving it, of course, a pronunciation somewhat different.

"De Brienne!" exclaimed the youngest gentleman, starting. "Where do you come from?"

"From America, monsieur; but just now from the prison at Stapleton—whence I have escaped by a good chance."

I noticed that they were looking at one another in incredulity, so I spoke on, led by I know not what :

"Have I not the honor of addressing Monsieur Georges Lucien de Rèdun, son of the Marquis de Monseverat?"

"I am the Marquis de Monseverat!" exclaimed the youngest, starting to his feet. "My father is dead."

"And my grandfather perished on the scaffold with him and with your brother Guy," I returned, calmly.

The effect of this speech was wonderful. The two other men sprang up, and the taller shut the window suddenly.

Monsieur de Rèdun was for hurrying towards me with both hands outstretched, when he was restrained.

"Hold! Hold!" said the eldest. "Let us ask more questions. What was your grandfather's name, my young friend?"

I gave it, and the whole of my family tree, so far as I could remember it, on my mother's side. I answered all their searching inquiries. This took all of an hour, mayhap. Then in a few words I told of my sailing on a privateer, my capture and imprisonment. Before I had finished Monsieur de Rèdun had laid a hand on my shoulder.

"You are a grandson of le Marquis de Brienne?" he asked, excitedly.

"Oui, monsieur—of the councillor of the King."

"Embrassez-moi!" he cried, and, despite my rags, he threw his arms around my neck. "This is le Marquis de Soyecourt," he continued, after the salutation, indicating the short gentleman.

"À votre service, Monsieur le Marquis," returned the latter, bowing. "And, Monsieur le Comte du Saille, permit me."

The handsome elderly man with the powdered hair stepped forward. "Have you ever heard my name before, monsieur?" he asked.

"Indeed I have," I replied. "You once crossed swords—"

"With your father; he did me that honor," came the interruption. "We parted friends. Gentlemen, it is enough!"

They all gathered close, and the elder man kissed me on the forehead, after the manner of my uncle. Tears were in his eyes, and, relieved from the great strain under which I had been laboring, I broke down altogether; sinking into a chair, I wept, rocking myself to and fro. "Oh, God be thanked!" I murmured over and over.

As soon as I recovered myself I saw that they had placed before me wine and meat, and were refraining from asking further questions until I should have refreshed myself. The words which were whispered in my ear opened my heart and shut all fear behind. "Courage; you are with friends. We will not desert you," said M. de Rèdun, with his hand on mine.

I looked up from my plate (truly I had been well fed for a vagabond this day) and found my new friends in consultation. I could not eat, but I caught the word "clothes," and, looking down at myself, I reddened. I was mad to tear the horrid rags from me! Monsieur de Rèdun, as I shall call him, as it was he that afterwards became my patron, poured himself out a glass of wine, and, giving me a smile and a bow, came nearer. He was a very handsome man, of about seven-and-thirty, with a fine figure, and a well-turned leg that showed to the best advantage in his black small-clothes, for, like the rest, he followed a fashion a little different from the English of that time.

"Monsieur de Brienne," he said—"to your presence with us—I would like to ask you something of your father."

"He is dead," I answered.

And at this, God forgive me, I saw that I had deceived them all into thinking that I was my uncle's son, instead of his nephew! Now I reasoned if I should tell them my remarkable story, and proclaim that I did not know my father's name, and was all in a fog in regard to that of my mother, even although I knew so much about the past family history, I would put a sorry climax to a very good beginning. I regretted deeply that I should have' to let them keep on in the error ; but I spoke the truth, and I did not know it at the time.

"Monsieur de Brienne is dead?" repeated Monsieur de Rèdun.

I sighed, "Alas !"

"'Tis sad ! He had vowed never to set foot in England, or he would have been here with us," remarked M. du Saille.

"Instead of going to that wretched, far-off wilderness," quoth the marquis.

"'Tis a fine country and a fine people," I put in, quickly. "You gentlemen have little knowledge of it, maybe—"

"I condole with you on the loss of your parent," interrupted M. du Saille, turning the subject. "He was a strange man, and they say the best swordsman at court —*un vrai gallant.*"

"There could be no better," I answered. "He taught me all I know."

The gentlemen smiled at this, but the next question that was asked me by De Soyecourt caused me to start.

"Your mother was—"

"Named Hurdiss," I put in. "She was very beautiful and of high birth, but died in America, in the city of Baltimore, when I was but a child."

"Did your uncle leave no property? They say he took with him to America a large amount."

"I have this," I replied, producing the last of the buttons that had adorned the homespun coat that I had worn at Marshwood. "All of my property was consumed in a fire—everything," I concluded. "I am left without a sou, a relative, or a friend."

The gentlemen handed the button around.

"It is true. I remember that crest well," said the tall man. "And I remember well, also, your grandfather's beautiful daughters — and great favorites they were, as children, with the King."

"Yes," put in M. de Rèdun ; "and they married, after taking refuge here in England, one the Duke de B—rt and the other le Comte de B—illy." *

The short nobleman here spoke, musingly :

"After their husband's deaths they went to America, to seek their brother, probably, but they met with sad misfortune. Now I remember hearing something—"

My heart gave a great bound! Was I on the point of finding out my real name, and who I was by right and law ?

"Yes," I said, quickly ; "tell me, pray."

"One of them was drowned in a shipwreck," Monsieur le Comte continued. "Sad, sad, alas ! and the other married some nobody, and went to reside in the wilderness."

I rather resented this, for I yet cherished the memory of him who had carried me on his shoulder, but I said nothing.

" Hortense and Hélène, those were the names," said M. de Rèdun. "They looked much alike, although there was a year's difference in their ages."

" It was la belle Hélène who lost her life by drowning," observed Monsieur le Marquis.

"Pardon me," put in Monsieur du Saille ; "it was Hortense, I am quite certain."

Here again arose the uncertainty.

" Who was it, monsieur, that married the English sea-captain ?" I asked.

" Ah, was that it ?" returned the tall man. "I did not know, nor have I any recollection of having heard which one of the ladies made this mésalliance."

---

* I have purposely left out mentioning these names in this story for reasons. —J. H.

The other gentlemen had come to no conclusion, and thus I found out nothing, after all. This was about the sum total of the talking we did at our first meeting, although it gives no idea of the time we were at it, and I was soon led away by the tall man. I had caught the idea already that he was the landlord of the inn, and such was the fact. Indeed, a great many of the *émigrés* in England at this time were engaged in far less remunerative employments, and some had all they could do to put food into their mouths.

Well, when I had taken a bath I was much refreshed; indeed, I could scarcely imagine that I was the same youth who had been halting along the road-side, ignorant of his whereabouts and careless as to his destination a few hours before. I could hardly persuade myself that it was true.

As may be perceived (at least, I should think the fact was evident enough), I had ceased to think of myself as a boy. It was only at times that my age would assert itself in a manner that led me to indulge in prankishness and skylarking. Thus when the hair-dresser came to my room, shown up by one of the inn servants, I pretended not to understand English, and, in consequence, they spoke openly before me. So I found out not a little. In the first place, I learned that Monsieur de Rèdun and the Marquis de Soyecourt were supposed to be very wealthy, and that I had been taken by the inn people for the private servant of the former, who had lost his way when ill some time previously, and had but now found his master.

That night as I lay in a comfortable bed, after bidding my friends a good-night, I reasoned over the situation. I had been engaged as private secretary to the Marquis de Monseverat, and would start for London with him on the morrow. There was but one regret, and that was the small deception I had been compelled to make use of in regard to my name.

No one was ever in more confusion of mind than I was upon awakening at daybreak. But how easily we adapt ourselves to circumstances—at least, many of us. "What next?" said I to myself, when I had gathered my intellect.

Poor old Jack Sutton! what was he thinking? I breathed a prayer that I would see him alive and well again.

CHAPTER XXI

A GENTLEMAN VALET

I BREAKFASTED early with my titled friends, and during the discussion we held it was agreed that the best way to keep suspicion from me — they were quite as apprehensive of my being taken by the authorities for an escaped prisoner as I was myself—was for me to assume the position of private servant for the nonce to my patron and kind friend Monsieur de Rèdun.

We started about nine o'clock in the morning along the post-road to the eastward, with a trip of some hundred and ten miles before us, I was informed.

The two gentlemen drove ahead in a high-wheeled chaise, while I and the servant of Monsieur le Marquis de Soyecourt followed by the coach within a few minutes of their starting.   It was our intention to pass the night at Oxford, and we expected to reach London on the afternoon of the following day.

They had spoken very openly before me, and although they had not indulged in any explanations, I gathered from the earnestness of their talk, and from the substance of it, that they had not given up all ideas of dwelling once more in France, and returning to the grandeur they had been accustomed to.   Their bitterness against Napoleon was extreme, but with him out of it I do not see how they ever expected to live comfortably in a country whose inhabitants they hated as a nation ; for if the common and middle class of people do not compose a nation's blood and body, I miss my reckoning.

The view from the coach-top as we descended the
hill from the inn was extremely fine. The river below
took a bend almost in the shape of the crook of a man's
elbow, and enclosed an island covered with houses, connected with the shore by a large bridge. But soon we
had shut the view of the water behind us, and as we progressed inland the smell of the sea disappeared entirely.

The man Baptiste, alongside of whom I was sitting on
the second seat, had the impassive, expressionless face
of the trained servant.   As he was not disposed to be
communicative, and had evidently been told to treat me
with respect, I grew reserved, and out of caution I kept
silent ; but nevertheless my enjoyment was not prevented from being of the very keenest.

I could crowd these pages by detailing my varied sensations. I could have sung or shouted, so high were my
spirits. But I had to keep all this to myself; and being
but a lad, as I say, it was far from easy. Two or three
times I got down to stretch my legs, and thus I found
myself walking behind the coach as we entered the little
hamlet of Witney. In fact I did not know that we were
so close to a village until I saw the guard get out his
horn to toot it, as was his custom when approaching one.

Running after the coach, I swung myself on board
just as we rolled across a bridge over a small, clear
stream. We had taken on fresh horses at a place called
Burford, if I remember rightly, some short time back,
and we would not have stopped at the little place we
were entering (the driver was pleased with himself and
proud of the rate at which we had been travelling), but
as we went by the gate of a private park we were hailed,
and, looking over the side, I saw two officers in regimentals waiting to be taken up on the coach. One of
them had the uniform of the Somersetshire regiment
that had been stationed at the Stapleton prison, and I
recognized the man before he had seated himself as one

of my former guardians ! But he glanced carelessly at
us, and then stared rather insolently into the face of a
young country lass who was leaving home, or in some
trouble, as she had had her handkerchief to her eyes for
the past hour or more.

I need not have feared recognition if I had thought
for a minute, for I was something of a dandy in my way.
My legs were encased in gray breeches buttoned tightly
from the knee to the ankle. My coat, with its long tails,
was of blue cloth, with brass buttons, and the large velvet
collar roached up behind, almost swamping my ears.
My waistcoat had wide lapels (pulled outside the coat,
mind you), and was made of cream-colored satin. My
stock was of clean white linen, and my hat, that was a
trifle too small, would persist in getting rakishly over my
left eye, as if it understood that I was careless, happy,
and defiant of bad fortune !

Yes, I believe I could write pages of description of all
I saw and felt on this journey, but I am really very
anxious myself to reach the more interesting part of it,
and so resist temptation. We arrived at Oxford in the
late afternoon. I was delighted at the glimpses of the
old college buildings and the students playing at cricket
in the fields, while through the trees I could see that we
were near a river, as now and then the water would flash
into sight.

When we reached the inn at which we intended stopping, Monsieur de Rèdun, who had arrived already, sent
for me to come to his room. I was fully prepared to
carry up his box or to tend him in any way, as befitted
my supposed position ; but as soon as I entered the
apartment he greeted me with a smile.

"Monsieur le Marquis," he said, "be seated."

A strange tingling thrilled me as he called me by
that title, and yet I longed to tell him that I could not
claim it.

"I will explain to you," Monsieur de Rèdun went on, "that in London there are a large number of us who have been forced to take up residence outside of France. Your own story is so remarkable that, although, believe me, I myself do not doubt it, it would not be best to tell it to every one who might listen. Therefore, I pray you forget, as you have said, that you were an American, put outside from you the idea, above all things, that you have escaped from a prison of the English, and indeed, if possible, show little knowledge of the tongue—it is a frightful speech at the best, and racks the throat and ears. To people whom you meet you are Jean Amédée de Brienne, son of le Marquis Henri Amédée Lovalle de Brienne; your story is that you have come to England from America" (he lowered his voice and looked over his shoulder) "*to join us!* Ah, we need young blood and swords!"

"But, Monsieur le Marquis!" I interrupted, intending to blurt out the truth and abide by the consequences, "there is just one thing I—"

Monsieur de Rèdun playfully touched me on the cheek. "Never mind about that now," he said, smiling kindly. Then changing quickly to a tone of great seriousness, he continued : "You will understand everything in a short time. Perhaps some day your grandfather's great estates shall belong to you, as they must in the sight of God and the saints, and as the blessed Church allows it to be true. Then!" he exclaimed—"then we will whip this *canaille*, lash these dogs into shape, or drown them as they drowned us, eh? Ah, yes! The bubble will soon burst, and they will be glad to take our crumbs! . . . But no more for to-day; to-morrow you shall be informed. I know that you are to trusted, monsieur. . . . Say nothing. It is my pleasure to serve you. Be cautious with others."

Of course this touched me, and I doubt not I showed

it as I bowed myself out of Monsieur de Rèdun's apart-
ments, that were the best the place afforded. Our conversation had been held in French, and I have condensed
it somewhat; but the gist of what he said is here.

I had begun to grow very much attached to my kind
patron—for such I call him in this recounting—and I
also was much taken with the elder man, the Marquis
de Soyecourt; but he was not so frank or, if one may
say it, so simple as the other. I judged it best to let
matters take their own course for a few days, and to
stow my jaw upon certain subjects.

CHAPTER XXII

A VALET AND A GENTLEMAN

THE very best way to avoid falling into the error of becoming verbose is to be short spoken.

It is a great shift of scene. Place: London ; time: somewhere between the fifteenth and the twentieth day of December, 1813. Here I was, seated in a low-backed, soft-cushioned chair, with my feet on another, a linen napkin tucked in about my throat, and over me was bending a strange little old man who addressed me as " Monsieur le Marquis," as he curled my hair with a pair of hot irons. Now truly this was a change from being a prisoner at Stapleton, a scarecrow - clad figure doddering along the highway, or even from the position of a gentle-man's gentleman riding outside of a coach on the post-road. Yet all these three had I been almost within the fortnight, and what was I now? Why, " le Marquis de Brienne," who dined with noblemen, and had learned in these few short days to make pretty speeches to ladies of quality in silks and satins. What is more, I was fairly launched as a conspirator !

I hope that none who reads this will suppose that I was not sailing a proper course, or that I was living a life of deceit for the purpose of gain, just because I am gifted with an adaptable temperament. Oh no ! I hope I can say that what money I had I came by honestly, for it had been given to me with the intention that I should pay it back at some future time (I have paid it long since, to the last penny), and I was imposing on no one, unless it was my friend Monsieur de Rèdun, whose pleasure it was to do anything for me, and lastly there is nothing in all this that is intended as an apology of my position.

It cannot be said that I was luxuriously surrounded, despite that I was lolling in an easy-chair and having my hair curled by my own private servant. I was living in lodgings on the second floor of a house not far from Orchard Street, off Piccadilly, a house that had more the dignity of age in its appearance than an air of prosperity. I was the possessor of a suite of four rooms fronting the street.

The click of the irons ceased for a minute.

" Ah, Monsieur le Marquis, I remember well your grandfather when I was a young man, and he not much older! He wore his own hair, monsieur ; I never remember seeing him in anything else. It was much handsomer than a wig. . . . You resemble him much, monsieur."

This speech had called me back to myself, for at that moment I had been thinking of Mary Tanner and the old days on the hill-side at Belair. Yes, there was no doubt about it, she was much prettier than the Comtesse de Navarreins, with whom I had danced a quadrille the previous evening. What a strange career I had had ! Life was an odd book to read. Oh, that Mary could see me now ! How fine it was to be the nobleman !—How Mary's eyes would open !

But the old servant was waiting for me to speak.

" Ah, Gustave," I replied at last, making a wry face at myself in the glass, for the old man had given my hair a tremendous twist with the tongs, " I doubt that we shall see the old days again. From what I hear, France seems to be getting ahead fairly well without such men as my grandfather—the people seem to be able to look out for themselves and struggle on."

I glanced at the reflection of the old man's face. On it was a compound of expressions.

"Monsieur le Marquis," said he, quietly, "had they not killed the kindest master in the world I should be one of them to-day. It is that alone that made me leave my country. Could I but forget the guillotine and the days of horror, and that I really loved my King, I could rejoice in France's every victory! I had a nephew who served with the one who calls himself the emperor. Yes! ah! a great general, Monsieur le Marquis, this Napoleon! My nephew was at Jena and Eylau; he was wounded at Essling, and died bravely at Wagram. A man can have but one country, monsieur, think what he may—do what he can!—Pardon, Monsieur le Marquis, I weary you."

It rather surprised me to hear the old man speak thus, for his language was better than one might expect to hear from the lips of one who had been born and bred a lackey. But they set me to thinking, and his next question chimed in well with my thoughts.

"You have seen France, Monsieur le Marquis?" he asked.

"No, Gustave, I have never been there," I replied. "I have lived my life in far-off America."

Now with this word a surge of pride came over me. What was this France, that I had never seen, to me? What were the plottings of the little band of nobles who had been despoiled of what they call their rights? Why, *I* was an American! There was my heart! Could I ever truly enter in with all my will and spirit for the cause or the factions of another nation, an exiled government?—What reward was there for me? Aye, what reward? I remembered those brave men whom I had left in prison. (Ah, one can learn patriotism in a prison!) Edward Brown, and Jack Sutton, the boatswain's mate, with the stars and stripes as big as your two hands tatooed across his broad chest, came into my

mind's eye. Their country's flag was mine! The watch-word of Lawrence, that had been brought to us by the prisoners from the *Chesapeake*, rang in my ears as it had rung through the crowded prison—" Don't give up the ship !" Of a truth I was no Frenchman, though I could pass as such, and had done so.

Wondering what my messmates had been saying about my strange disappearance, I fell into a reverie of retrospection. Where were Captain Temple and the *Young Eagle?* Where was Si Plummer, who had loaned me his belongings, and who, I imagined, I could see with his bundle on his shoulder, chanting his song as he went over the hill? Where was the brave sailor who had thrown his severed hand at the feet of the English officer? And what was I, but a person who was allowing himself to become embroiled in a cause in which he had no heart—deeper and deeper committed every day to plots and conspiracies for whose method he had no stomach (yes, I may set it down—assassination, dagger, and pistol were spoken of !). Truly I had no place here! and a great wish came over me that I could exchange this borrowed finery, and this assumption of being what I was not, for a sailor's toggery, the wide sweep of the sea, and take up again my life on a vessel to whose peak I might look up and sight the flag for whose sake *my* countrymen were dying—for whose sake I should and would be fighting as soon as God would let me !

The door of the little room opened. Gustave had long since had my hair arranged to his satisfaction, and I had been sitting in silence I know not how long. But with the draught of air from the hallway I turned my head and saw a small dwarf of a man, who was a sort of a servant and boots in the house, standing there with the morning paper. I took it—the London *Times*—and read the head-line in the first column, " England's Disgrace !" in big black letters. And below it :—" Has

Another Vessel Been Lost in Single Action to the United States?" Hastily I read the rumored report (pity 'twas not true) of the capture of another forty-four gun frigate by the gallant *Constitution*. I laughed aloud at the *Times's* expressions of astonishment that such things should be, and then I threw the paper down and burst into a loud huzza.

Gustave had been watching me as if he thought I had suddenly turned madman.

" Is Napoleon defeated?" he inquired.

" No, no; not that," I answered, smiling to myself, and I think that I heard him give a sigh of relief. At this moment there was a tap on the door, and the old fellow laid down the fine plum-colored coat that he had been preparing for my wearing, and Monsieur de Rèdun was ushered in by him with a low bow. The nobleman closed the door behind him.

" Mon ami," he said, hurriedly, " I would speak to you alone." Gustave (he had been "loaned" to me by De Soyecourt) was too well-trained a servant to be told. He picked up a pair of boots and went out into the hall-way.

" It is arranged!" cried Monsieur de Rèdun, speaking quickly and excitedly. "Three of us must leave for Paris within a few days! A cipher letter has been received! The time is most opportune, my dear Blondin. Ah! and those turn-coats who have forgotten tradition, and licked the hand that humbled them, they will see how the faithful will stand before them — *Dabit Deus his quoque finem!* Yes, yes, mon cher Jean, we will see !"

He gave me an embrace, to which I confess I replied, because he was my friend, and then he continued: " You are the one to go with us—you, and De Soyecourt, and myself. We can face the danger bravely, mon ami! Consider the reward !"

Aye, there it was again—"the reward." What did I really care for it?

"I have an invitation for you to be one of a little partie carrée this evening," Monsieur de Rèdun went on. "I judge it is best that you attend— Eh, what's the matter?"

I was standing with my back to him, looking out of the window; he approached and placed his hand on my shoulder. I turned, and his eyes met mine. I was constrained to speak at once of what was uppermost in my thoughts. It required some courage.

"Monsieur de Rèdun," I asked, "what do you really think of me?"

"I think you are one who can be trusted," he replied. "In fact, on that I would stake my life; but—" He hesitated.

"But what?" I inquired.

"Well, then, I pray you not to take offence, there is none intended—but why should I not tell you? The manner of your joining us was certainly most strange, and in some minds it has excited a suspicion. That there have been spies among us, we know well; but you—"

I interrupted him. "Believe me, my dear friend, I would rather die than betray a single word of what I have heard, or know by being told. But listen"—I spoke earnestly and slowly—"one can be honest with a friend—I truly doubt the ultimate success of any scheming to restore the old régime. I have thought everything over carefully, and have come to a decision, my first statement put aside."

Monsieur de Rèdun said nothing, but stood there listening, with one elbow on the mantel-piece, while I continued speaking. It was some minutes before I had finished, but I told him frankly of my position and what I considered right for me to do. He was most attentive, and although once or twice I saw that he felt like making some interruption, he restrained himself.

"You have deceived us, then, in something; is it so?" he inquired at last, speaking cautiously.

"I fear me that I have; that is, I have allowed you to persist in a mistake." A long silence followed.

"You need not inform me in what mistake, monsieur," he said, quietly. (I noticed that he had dropped my title.) "I shall not even ask why you did not tell me this thing before; but, believe me, at this late hour I appreciate the confidence that you have placed in me. As to your misgivings in regard to our attempts to restore the better things, I shall say nothing, monsieur. If you have weighed carefully the matter, I shall not attempt to dissuade you. . . . But one thing, spoken as a friend, I must tell you: Do not, for your life, breathe a word of this to De Soyecourt, Du Saille, or to any of the others."

"Tell me, what am I to do?" I asked. "I am in your power—your hands."

"It would be wrong," the Marquis replied, musingly, but with a sad tone in his words, "not to help you, aside from the requirements of friendship. So do not fear."

"I do not fear; I do not fear," I reiterated. "But what shall I do?"

"You must come with us to France," was the answer, spoken in a low tone of voice. "Despite the embargo laid on trade and importations by the usurper, money works corruption, corruption means many things. It is a known fact that licenses to enter French ports have been sold to both American and English vessels. You are not safe in this country; come with us to where danger will be no less, but chances to follow your own ideas the better. I can explain that you have left for some French port when you desert us, and if you do not return I shall join in the general mourning, that is all. We will increase our party by one in order to keep up the original number, and I shall let you know as soon as possible how we intend to leave England. Good-bye, until this evening. . . . Au revoir, monsieur."

When he had gone I began to think and ponder over what had passed. Had I been foolish in being so frank and clear - spoken? A word from the Marquis, and I might be returned to the hulks or the prison-yard. Yet in getting out of England lay my only chance to escape or to carry out my plans. From what had gone before, I understood that it was intended to make a voyage across the Channel in one of the small smuggling-vessels that plied an adventurous and remunerative trade along the coast of England, despite the careful watching of the coast-guard vessels and the war-ships. But Monsieur de Rèdun's manner had chilled towards me—I felt that. My words had killed the enthusiasm with which he had always addressed me. I half feared that I had been rash.

CHAPTER XXIII

A DISCOVERY AT A DISCOUNT

NOTWITHSTANDING this set-back, we made rather a merry group at the partie carrée that evening. My restraint wore off; I almost felt relieved. *Il n'y a que le premier pas qui coûte.* To all intents, nothing had occurred.

The people one met at these gatherings were most interesting; the impoverished rubbed elbows with the affluent, but the manners of all were the same — the stilted courtesy, the bowing and scraping, and the gallant speeches. Young bucks and aged beaux, blooming young creatures and ci-devant beauties were gathered together, and, excepting the small-talk, gossip, and coquetting, the conversation was limited to the days that had been and the times that were to come—when the eagles of the usurper should give place to the lilies of the rightful heir of the throne of France—their France. Titles and great names were there—a surfeit of them— and exalted personages lent their presence on great occasions. I was presented to royalty in the persons of two future kings — one a very affable imbecile and the other a jaded rake—and I heard enough scandal to sink a ship.

Many English notables — lords and ladies, famous statesmen, and military leaders—would come to the crushes and routs. I liked them much better than I did the people I was supposed to belong to, all said and done. They are a fighting nation, and we Americans have more points in common with them than we generally admit (prejudice again, you see). But they did not love us, and often I had to control my tongue or I would have betrayed myself.

But here we are off our course with a vengence; no more side issues at present.

Monsieur de Rèdun (noble gentleman) treated me as if we had never held the conversation that had upset our first relations; he did not once refer to it. Our friendship triumphed over everything; he was kindness itself to me always.

One afternoon (the 18th of January), upon the breaking up of one of the little poverty-stricken courts, M. de Rèdun ran his arm through mine, at the same time saying, "I shall walk home with you, if you will permit me, Monsieur de Brienne."

We strolled along in silence, I waiting for my friend to speak. At last he did so, halting at my door.

"By twelve o'clock to-night you and I will start northward in a chaise, and to-morrow evening," he whispered, softly, "we will find ourselves in the neighborhood of N——, where we will meet the others, and embark, if the weather permits, in one of the little luggers that cut deeply into the King's revenue. If we land safely on the other side, you had best quit us at once. Leave it all to me. In five hours I call for you."

"Never mind the curling-tongs to-night, Gustave," said I, as the little old man came forward to meet me upon my entrance to my lodgings, "I am leaving London."

"To be gone some time, Monsieur le Marquis?"

"Yes, to be gone some time. But I shall not need you for two hours; you can go out and take the air for a while."

"Bien, Monsieur le Marquis."

The faithful old fellow left the room, and I thumped myself down in the easy-chair and gazed at the fire. I was thinking over two very curious things that had happened that afternoon that drove even my coming departure out of my mind.

It was at the reception of the Duchesse de Villequier. Late in the proceedings a tall, ascetic-looking youth was announced as "Le Duc de B—rt, Chevalier d'——," etc., etc.—no end of bobtails and pendants.

"Le Duc de B—rt!" exclaimed I to myself, looking at him closely. How odd! here was a remarkable adventure! In another minute I was presented to him.

"We must be relatives, Marquis," he said, languidly (by the way, he was a clerk in a draper's establishment); "that is, through marriage. My uncle espoused one of your aunts," he added, "'La belle Hélène,' she was called at court."

"I am charmed and honored at the privilege you extend, Monsieur le Duc," I replied, bowing. "'Tis most gracious of you." ('Twas this way we all spoke to one another.) My young coxcomb touched the region of his heart with his finger-tips, and offered me his snuff-box in the old-mannered way.

It was rather amusing. If he was my cousin by marriage, well and good; but if he was not, and was related by blood, why, it was a very different matter; it all depended upon who I was myself who he was. But he appeared ignorant entirely of the fate of the two fair sisters, and I soon tired of talking, so we parted. We ran across one another two or three times in the crowd, but I would luff up to avoid getting within speaking distance.

The other odd circumstance to which I referred was the presence at .the reception of the Duchesse of a gentleman named Hurdiss; he was from Cornwall, and had a son in the King's service—a lieutenant in the navy, I gathered from what I heard him say.

As I sat there thinking and watching the glowing coals I did not notice how the time had sped, and I was surprised to hear the clock strike such a late hour; before I had finished counting the strokes Gustave entered and lit a candle.

"'Tis growing cold, Monsieur le Marquis," said the old servant. "If you are going to face the weather to-night you had best dress warmly."

I was preparing to shift into some heavier clothing, and stood there, partly dressed, stretching myself before the fire.

"Pardon me, Monsieur le Marquis," said Gustave, rather timidly. "You are going to France?"

"Yes, and I shall not return to England," I answered.

"Monsieur le Marquis."

"Well?"

"How did you get that scar on your neck, monsieur? I have been minded to ask before—I have been afraid. Pardon my boldness now."

"I did not know that I had a scar there, Gustave." (A man, unless he has some especial reason for looking, seldom sees the back of his neck.)

"Take this small mirror, monsieur; hold it so. Now look in the large glass, monsieur."

I did as the old man directed, and there was a distinct red line, or, better, two red lines, that joined at the nape of the neck and ran nearly to my shoulder - blades in the form of an inverted V.

"I can't remember any injury, Gustave. I must have been born with it, I dare say."

"A birth-mark, monsieur—so? A strange coincidence, ma fois!"

"In what way, Gustave?"

"Why, in many ways, Monsieur; but 'tis of no moment."

13

With this he turned away, and began to thrust some of my belongings into a pair of heavy saddle-bags Monsieur de Rèdun had sent to my lodgings. But my curiosity was aroused.

"You have a story to tell," said I, half laughing, to the old fellow, who generally needed little encouragement to talk; "what is it about?"

Gustave looked up. "Le Duc de B—rt," he began.

I started. "What name was that?" I asked.

He repeated it once more, slowly.

"Oh yes; I had the honor of meeting him to-day. Well?"

"Not he, Monsieur le Marquis. I was speaking of his uncle, from whom he received his title."

"Ah, yes; go on—continue."

"He had a scar like that, monsieur—the trace of a would-be assassin's dagger. But that is not the strange part. He had a son who had, when born, the same marks, Monsieur le Marquis."

I was hard put to it now to conceal my interest and eagerness.

"How did you know of this?" I asked, making believe to yawn. "Gossip, eh?"

"Every one was talking of it, but I have better proof. My wife—a good woman, long since dead, Monsieur le Marquis—was the child's foster-mother."

"What became of the boy, Gustave?" I inquired, carelessly.

"He disappeared, monsieur. He would have been a relative, and about your age."

"Yes, a blood relation," I returned. Then I gave a sudden whistle. "Come, come, we must hurry."

Gustave went on with his packing in silence. I looked at my reflection in the glass.

"Bon soir, Monsieur le Duc," said I, bowing. "Mes compliments chez vous."

Then I made a grimace at myself and hurried into my clothes. When I was dressed I once more sat down before the fire and thought things over, and I came at last to the decision that it was best for me to adhere to my previous determination and not to allow anything to turn me.

CHAPTER XXIV

IN THE CHOPS OF THE CHANNEL

BEFORE daylight of the next morning my good patron
and myself were some thirty miles north of London,
driving through the county of Essex.   At about ten
o'clock we breakfasted at a way-side tavern, where we
exchanged our chaise and tired horse for two saddle
beasts, I having quite a tussle with mine as I mounted;
and then we pressed ahead all the afternoon, expecting
to be near the little village of N—— some time in the
evening.   It was damp and chilly, the prospect was not
fine in the way of scenery, and my companion was in no
talkative frame of mind.   It was strange; I was, so to
speak, a blind man in the power of his guide, for if I
should lose Monsieur de Rèdun I should be in a bad way.
At last I knew we were near the sea by the way the
horizon line cut straight across the sky.

I wondered greatly at my patron's knowledge of the
road and the by-ways by which we reached this particu-
lar bit of the coast.   For hours we had ridden across a
wind-swept plateau, seamed by many deep-worn paths
running in all directions.   In the earlier part of the
afternoon gibbet-like sign-posts had helped to point us
to the right direction, but as it grew towards dusk we saw
none of them, and yet never once had Monsieur de
Rèdun faltered—turning and twisting and yet keeping
the same general direction, until he had brought us to
the edge of the narrow height along which we were riding.   There was the dark water rolling and tumbling and

booming against the shore far beneath us. A slight mist was blowing inland that promised thicker weather. We turned northward, and finally we sighted a little cluster of houses, whose roofs we looked down upon from the top of the great cliff; and then Monsieur de Rèdun drew up and pointed.

"Your eyes are good," said he. "Can you see whether there is anything hanging from the window of the house nearest yonder small dock?"

I gazed intently. In the growing darkness I could make out a white rag or something fluttering from the window-sill, and so I reported.

"The signal," was the response to my information. "They are ahead of us, and all is well—let us make haste."

"Monsieur," said I, reining in my horse, "we will soon part, perhaps, and I am going to take this opportunity, while we are yet alone, to say a few short words. You are a nobleman by birth; it matters not who I am, but you have taught me that a man may be a nobleman by nature and by conduct also. I owe you more than I can repay—more than I can reckon. May you have no cause to regret your kindness to a forlorn and friendless stranger. God bless you! In words I cannot thank you!"

This sounded very trite and commonplace, I grant, but it was an attempt to express my honest feelings.

My dear friend looked me in the eyes. "You have grown close to my heart, mon frère, that is all," he responded. "Have you aught to tell me of yourself now that you would not have said before? Eh, bien, venez la dire."

"It would do no good. I have nothing more to tell," was my reply.

He clasped my hand.

"One question, and one only—are you a relation of le Marquis de Brienne?"

"He was my grandfather, monsieur. It is answered."

"Ah! so?—well, we may meet again in better times—I shall hear from you. Come, we must be moving. Nous serions prudents."

It was no easy job to urge our tired nags down the steep runway, and had my mount backed and filled the way he had when I first put leg over him, we might both of us have pitched headlong upon the roofs of some of the outlying huts, for they were scarcely more.

I supposed that this little village was considered of too small importance to be watched closely by the government, but it must have been apparent that it was not fishing or net-mending that kept so many stalwart sailor-men there. It would have been a fine place for the press-gang to have swooped down upon.

We drew up our horses before the house nearest to the stone pier or jetty that ran out some hundred feet or more from the shore. On one side of it was a small dock or basin large enough to give shelter to a half-score of fishing-boats about the size of those we call "dories" in New England.

As we dismounted, Monsieur de Rèdun gave a halloo, and a figure appeared in the doorway. I was surprised to see that it was Monsieur du Saille. He called back into the room as he approached us, and a man followed him out and took our horses.

"Ah, De Rèdun! you're on time, as usual, and I see that you have not forgotten your way," Monsieur Saille cried, as he grasped my patron's elbows in his two hands in a half embrace. Then he bowed to me without much effusion. "Good-day, Monsieur le Marquis!" was all he said.

I had not known that my host of the Gloucester Arms was going to be one of us, and so expressed my surprise at seeing him. He made no explanation, but I take it he must have been in London for some time, and that he had come direct from there, although I had not met him at any of the routs or parties.

"Why should I forget my way, monsieur?" my patron said, laughing, as he paused on the door-step. "Have I not travelled it every month for three years?"

As we entered the house the Marquis de Soyecourt was standing at the door, and greeted us in his usual reserved way. We were in a large room, and I noticed the smell of the same kind of tobacco that the sailors use on shipboard in the English service—a smell that seems to cling to them and to all of their belongings. But apparently none of the gentlemen had been smoking.

"Everything is most propitious," said De Soyecourt, as he brought forward two chairs from the table. "Dame Fortune smiles on us. But pardon me; you have not noticed Monsieur Rembolez."

It was then that I saw for the first time that there was a figure sitting back in the dark shadows in the corner of the room. I recognized the name, and as soon as the owner of it stepped forward into the light of the single candle I remembered his face, and that I had seen it in London. He was a sharp-featured, thick-set man—that is, big as to his chest and shoulders, but very light and muscular in his underpinning. His eyes were so black that they appeared all pupils, and his teeth were so large and even that I believe that he could have bitten a ten-penny nail in two with them, for his jaw also looked strong as a vise. I did not like the man, and, as I had good cause to remember afterwards, he on his part had conceived no great affection for me.

At the mention of my name he merely glanced up and showed his teeth, at which I was tempted to show mine in return, for the meaning of that display was rather ambiguous. He was to be the fifth one of the party, and I am quite sure he was not of Monsieur de Rèdun's choosing.

"A good night for the crossing," observed Monsieur de Soyecourt. "Did you see the lookout on the cliff as you came down, gentlemen?"

"I doubt not he saw us," returned my patron. "But he probably kept well hidden. Is everything ready? Is Captain St. Croix here?"

"Yes, and most of his crew within calling distance," returned the steel-jawed man, casting a look over his shoulder.

I saw no door, or anything that would suggest that there was an adjoining room, for the one we were in occupied the whole ground-floor of the house; but behind Monsieur Rembolez was a tall oak cupboard that reached almost to the ceiling. There had come a lull in our conversation; the Marquis and the host of the Gloucester Arms were talking in whispers, and Monsieur de Rèdun was engaged in pulling off his heavy riding-boots. All at once the low grumbling of men's voices in talk was heard, and then a round oath in good sea-faring English issued apparently from the tall cupboard. I fairly jumped as the door of it was opened outward, and a great, black-whiskered man stepped out of it. Then I saw where the smell of tobacco came from, for the smoke rolled out with him, and the ember in his long clay pipe was glowing.

Astonished, I looked past him, and saw that the cupboard concealed a good-sized trap-door; it was open, the top of a ladder extended through the floor, and the sound of the voices came from below. It was a most ingenious idea—the cellar to which this passageway led was not under the house, but under the garden at the back of it. The floor of the room in which we were was made of hard, dry earth, and digging there would have revealed nothing.

I found out, by questioning afterwards on the voyage over, that the two other houses which abutted on the in-

nocent-looking garden also had passageways that led to the smuggler's store-room.

The bewhiskered man was addressed by the company as Captain St. Croix, but I would bet a new hawser to a ship's biscuit that he was more English than French, although his accent was fairly good.

"It looks the night for our purpose, gentlemen," he said, politely, but in a gruff tone of voice. "We have brewed a punch below. What say you I send for some of it, and we will pledge a successful passage to the *Hirondelle*, eh?"

"And destruction to the Corsican upstart," put in he of the beady eyes.

The captain gave a hoot down the shaft and ordered some one to bring up the punch-bowl. At the same time he set about getting us something to eat from a rough sideboard near the fireplace.

Just as a man's head appeared coming up the ladder there were three sharp knocks on the door, and a tall fisher-lad in a dripping great-coat came in.

"It's thick and raining," he said, as he untied the straps of his tarpaulin hat. "I've seen the lights of the old boat. She'll be off the head in a few minutes."

"Then we must bear a hand," growled the captain. "So, gentlemen, let us eat and drink and dispense with ceremony."

I was very hungry, and fell to at once, as did the others, but I noticed that Monsieur Rembolez found time to propose his toast of destruction, which was accordingly tossed off. After that a constrained silence fell upon us, that no one seemed anxious to break in upon for some reason or other, but full justice was done to the captain's punch—by-the-way, a mighty strong brew it was. In half an hour, at a signal from the outside, we left the shelter of the house, and, hurrying down to the dock, we were all crowded into one of the row-boats.

Then pulling away, with three men at the oars, we headed against the driving rain through the half-darkness.

It was about eight o'clock in the evening, and the moon would not show until about two in the early morning—smugglers' weather, if there is such. Every now and then we could see a flash of light ahead, as if a lantern were being displayed to guide us, and in a few moments we were alongside of a small, low, freeboarded craft of about forty tons. We scrambled aboard without ceremony.

The *Hirondelle* must have had two or three other places at which she stopped to take on or to leave her cargo; I am quite sure she took on nothing from N—— that night, but her decks were covered with bales and boxes, tightly lashed in place. As it was so wet, I followed the four other gentlemen down into the little cabin, although my love of the sea was returning so strongly that I was tempted to stay on deck and court a soaking.

The little box of a place in which we were sitting was dimly lighted with a swinging lamp, and as we conversed of the plot and object of our trip (of which I shall say nothing) I could tell that we were travelling at a good rate of speed by the rushing and lapping of the water against the hull. The reason I do not give any full account of the venture in which I was supposed to be engaged is that I think, even now, I should keep it silent, as it concerns neither me nor my story, and it might be a breach of confidence to dwell on it.

My titled companions were not hardened salts, and coherent conversation soon became an absolute impossibility for obvious reasons. Small blame! The odor of that cabin was wonder inspiring—and, truly, smell is the snob of the senses! It is the last thing that surrenders to changed conditions; it revolts at unexpected moments, and overthrows all efforts of the will. The crew bunked aft, and mingled with the whiffs of damp clothing was the aroma of stale tobacco, cheese, rum, garlic, and pea soup—a bad combination for sensitive nostrils! It did not worry me very much after the first few minutes; Monsieur de Rèdun stuck it out through pride more than anything else, but the others lost a great deal of their dignity.

After a time we all fell asleep, however, most of us in a sitting posture, and I was the first to awaken. It was between three and four, and still raining, when I came out of the close, musty hole and breathed the fine air. I noticed we had shortened sail, and that a man in the bow was heaving the lead. He did not call out the soundings, but signalled them to the captain by motions of his hand. It was clear we must be in shoal water, but in how many fathoms I could not tell. All at once the man at the wheel threw the lugger up into the wind, and we pitched about, hove to, for probably half an hour.

Nothing could be discerned through the pearl-gray of the drizzle but the green, choppy surface of the sea stretching out all about us. Every one on deck was listening. I could see that from their attitudes, and I caught the infection of it, and strained my ears on the alert. All at once I detected a sound directly astern of us—the crew were evidently expecting something from the bow, and were all facing one way. I hearkened for a moment, to make sure, and then I knew that it was the sound of oars; so I spoke to the man nearest me. He clapped his hand to his head, and gave a long, low whistle, which was answered very near us by another.

In a few minutes the dark shape of a large row-boat could be seen approaching, and, going below into the cabin, I aroused the rest of the passengers, who gave welcome to the news—our friend Rembolez appeared rather nervous.

Where the lugger put off her cargo I do not know, for as soon as the five of us had clambered over her side into the barge, and Monsieur de Senez had given a handful of gold to the captain, the latter stood off, presumably to the southward, while we rowed directly to the east.

Not a word had been spoken by the rowers or the man in charge of them, and I was so interested in wondering what next was going to happen that I was perfectly satisfied to curb my curiosity and ask no questions. I was not anxious to anticipate, and felt really sad to think that I was soon to leave Monsieur de Rèdun—for what, I knew not. But "*vogue la gallère,*" said I to myself.

CHAPTER XXV

WE were off the coast between Dunquerque and Gravelines, and I should judge that the boat had rowed out some seven or eight miles to meet us. The men at the oars looked part Dutch and part French. They were a villanous-looking set, however, and the fellow at the tiller appeared little above them in order of intelligence; but while we were pulling straight ahead, the cockswain suddenly stood up and lifted his hand to call attention.

"Arrêtez!" he whispered, hoarsely.

The men backed water skilfully, but yet such headway did the boat have on that it required three or four efforts before we came to a stop. There, not ten lengths from us, lay a long white lapstreak, sharp at both ends. She had pulled almost athwart our bows! Had we been keeping any sort of a lookout we would have seen her before, as her crew must have had us in sight for some minutes. One glance at them told me that these people were not French! Rembolez had stood up almost as soon as the cockswain, and was looking forward eagerly, but I saw his face change to a puzzled expression.

"Les Anglais!" exclaimed the cockswain between his teeth.

A few strokes of the long oars that the men in the stranger craft wielded, and she was alongside of us.

"Un pilote?" said a voice with an execrable accent

and a drawling twang through the nose. "We want a pilot.—Avez-vous un pilote?"

"We have no pilot for you!" answered Monsieur du Saille in English. "Keep away from us."

At the same time he drew from the breast of his coat a small double-barrelled pistol.

"Who are you, and where do you come from?" put in Monsieur Rembolez.

There was evidently some consternation in the white boat at hearing the sound of English. The men were leaning forward preparing to take a stroke, and one of them hitched at the big knife in his belt.

But what was I doing at this very moment?

It was with difficulty that I was restraining an inclination to plunge overboard and strike out for the whaleboat.

It is almost past believing, but unless my eyes were playing me false there was something passing familiar in the figure of the big man who stood there upright in the stern-sheets, balancing a boat-hook in his hand. This aside, it would have required but a close glance at the wiry, strong-knit figures and the keen, sharp-featured faces, for one who knew, to declare that they were no English press-gang bullies, but Yankee sailor-men! What were they doing here?

I was trying to control my voice, which had left me in my astonishment, but the nobleman landlord did not notice my condition, and was still continuing his warning.

"Come no closer," he said—"at your peril. We have no pilot for you. Keep off!"

The big man in the stranger boat was evidently perplexed and at a loss what to do, when I found my tongue.

"Plummer! Si Plummer! Get me out of this!" I cried.

We were so near by this time that our oars were almost touching, but the astonishment occasioned on both sides by my sudden outbreak seemed to paralyze all hands.

"Who, in the name of Davy Jones, are you?" came the answer, spoken quickly.

"John Hurdiss, of the *Young Eagle*," cried I, throwing off my cloak. "Look alive! I'm coming to you!" Just as I was about to plunge overboard I felt myself grasped about the arm.

It was Rembolez who had laid hold of me! The words he hissed I did not catch, but in order to loose myself I drew back my free hand and caught him a blow fairly between the eyes. He did not relax his hold, however, but endeavored to throw me into the bottom of the boat. Although he was a powerful man, he probably did not know much about wrestling; I had the firmer footing, and, twisting him round, I turned the tables, and was forcing him away from me when he sank his great white teeth into the sleeve of my coat. Had he caught my flesh I might have lost the use of my arm, but, as it was, he laid hold of the cloth only, and the sleeve parted at the shoulder; but the little French cockswain now decided to take a hand, and sprang upon me from behind, but the result was to my helping. I just remembered hearing the sharp snapping of Monsieur du Saille's pistol, which missed fire, when I went backwards over the gunwale, and with me fell Beady Eyes and the little cockswain! I came up between the two boats. In the meantime both the crews were laying about with their oars over my head, and there was a lusty scrimmage going on. As soon as he felt the water closing over him, Rembolez released his hold, but the little 'long-shoreman in the striped shirt still held on, and before I knew it, some one grabbed me and him also, and, pulled us both over into the long white boat. Somehow the combatants had drifted apart, and with a quickness that was surprising the Yankees had got out their oars and were giving way.

I scrambled to my feet, and, looking over the stern, I saw that the other boat was after us, but they never could have caught us had they been pulling two men on a thwart. In three minutes they turned about and made off in the opposite direction.

"Douse my top-lights!" exclaimed Plummer, leaning forward and smearing the blood away from a slight wound on the side of his face. "Where, in the name of Tophet, did you come from, lad?"

"From an English prison, in the first place," I laughed, chattering from the cold; "but it's a long story. Oh, but I will be glad to see our colors again! I can hardly believe it is you, Silas! I'm mighty glad—but wait till I gain my wits."

The French cockswain here interrupted any more questions or explanations by an effort to jump overboard.

"Lay hold of him!" cried Plummer to the men in the bow. "Hold the frog-eater!" and in a minute they had pinioned the little Frenchman down. "Pull, larboard; hold, starboard!" Plummer ordered all at once, jamming the long sweep he was steering with hard down, and I, following the glance of his eye, saw outlines of a vessel not five hundred yards away.

"What ship is that?" I asked.

"The *Yankee*, privateer," my old friend replied, "Captain Jonathan Gorham; the luckiest vessel ever launched —that's honest truth! Oh, we've some yarns to spin, my son, and so must you, and, ecod! we'll have a time of it! I can scarce believe that it is you at all, lad—just as you said of me. How in—but it's the sort of a thing I might expect would happen on a cruise like the one we've had since leaving Buzzard's Bay!"

"Well, I have had some adventures myself, Plummer,"
I said. "That's gospel! And in the very first place,
I owe you a debt of gratitude for the loan of the clothes
and cap, my man."

Now, upon my soul, I did not mean to be condescend-
ing in my speech, but there must have been something
in my tone that caused the honest seaman to make a
change in his.

"I hope they brought you luck, sir," he said.

I noticed that he had said "sir" involuntarily.

"Indeed they did," I returned. "I'll have to tell you
all about it."

I glanced back through the mist. What were the
conspirators thinking or saying about me? I trusted
that Monsieur de Rèdun would find himself in no scrape
—because he had been my sponsor. And why the
deuce had Rembolez been so anxious to prevent my
leaving them? That was odd!

But now the bowmen were getting in their oars, and
we were close alongside of a large top-sail schooner, a
splendid bit of ship-building. She was hove to, and the
great main-sail was crackling, and the reef points keeping
up a continuous drumming against it; and the sound
was good to my ears.

"What have we here?" called a voice over the rail,
only a few feet above our heads.

"A pilot and a passenger, sir," answered Plummer,
pushing the whale-boat off from the side of the schooner
with his hands.

A short rope was thrown out to us, and, laying hold
of it, I clambered over the bulwarks and came down on
deck, where I found myself face to face with one of the
strangest-looking figures that I have met in the course
of my knocking about the world.

Before me stood a slight, stoop-shouldered man,
dressed in a blue broadcloth coat and an old-fashioned,

14

long, yellow satin waistcoat, over which protruded a stiff shirt-frill brown with snuff. He had on a pair of tight-fitting buckskin breeches thrust into heavy sea-boots. A hanger that must have weighed four pounds depended from a broad leather belt about his waist. The expression on his face was the remarkable thing about him. At first I thought that he was laughing at me, for his light blue eyes had such an eager twinkling light in them that they appeared to show amusement. His mouth was parted in a smile, and a continual lifting and lowering of his eyebrows lent the idea that he considered me or my appearance some huge joke.

"Is this the passenger or the pilot?" he asked, lifting a heavy cocked hat, and giving it a little flourish over his head.

"Neither passenger nor pilot," I replied, "but an escaped prisoner from England, who is anxious to get a chance to fight for America again. I was captured from the *Young Eagle*, privateer."

The man's voice had surprised me also. It was as fresh and young as a boy's. When I mentioned the *Young Eagle* he made a grimace as if he were about to whistle, but he changed it to an odd, rippling laugh.

"Oh, ho! Temple, of Stonington, eh! Such a reckless, careless devil! I know him. Good sailor, though. So you would ship with us?"

"Yes, sir," I answered. "And try to do my duty. Si Plummer will vouch for me."

"Oh, we can use you, never fear," the strange man chuckled. "And now where are we?"

"Eh?" I ejaculated.

"What's our latitude and longitude?" he inquired.

This was a puzzler for me, for I hardly knew one from the other, and could not have answered.

"Do you mean to say that you don't know that?" I asked, trying to fend off answering.

"Ha, ha! I haven't the slightest idea where I am," he answered. "I don't know whether I'm in the English Channel, the North Sea, or the Bay of Biscay."

This was told to me as if it were another huge joke, but I thought it was a strange condition for the captain of a vessel to be in.

"We're off the coast of France," I said, "not far from Dunquerque."

"Dunquerque?" repeated the funny man. "Ho, ho! that's fortunate. What may be your name, friend?"

"John Hurdiss," I answered, actually with a feeling of relief.

"Sounds honest enough. Pleased to make your acquaintance." From the gentleman's expression, however, one might have thought he doubted it, and was going to dig me playfully in the ribs.

At this moment Plummer, with two or three of the crew of the whale-boat, that was being hoisted in, came aft. They had the little Frenchman, who looked half frightened to death, with them.

"Here's the pilot, Captain Gorham," Plummer said, touching his cap.

The captain's reply to this, and the effect of it, almost took my breath away.

"Ah, Pierre," he said, "c'est donc vous? How is Madame Burron and the little ones?"

The little Frenchman drew back, and then fell at the captain's feet, grasping his hand.

"Ah, Capitaine Rieur, bonne fortune!" he cried, and he mumbled something I could not catch.

If it were not for the feel of my wet clothes and the sight of the crew standing there gaping at one another, I should have thought that I was dreaming.

CHAPTER XXVI

THE "YANKEE," PRIVATEER

WELL, I suppose if I were writing a tale of invention, I could imagine no stranger happenings than those I have recorded in the last few pages of this old ledger. But as almost everything has an explanation and can be sifted down to the why and wherefore, when we keep off the subject of religion and beliefs, I can make plain in a few words the situation. If "a ship without a captain is a man without a soul," truly a ship without a compass is a man without an eye. And that was what was the matter with the top-sail schooner *Yankee*, of New Bedford.

Four days before I had come on board she had had an encounter with an English ship that had offered resistance. During the course of the action the binnacle of the *Yankee* had been shot away, and the compass smashed to flinders. But the English ship had been taken, and was the *Yankee's* seventh prize in a cruise of less than four months. Captain Gorham had manned her and sent her home. Now the only compass left on board the *Yankee* was a small boat's needle in a wooden box. But, as Plummer told me, it was all out of kilter, and "as useless to steer by as a twirled sheath-knife." For three days after the last capture there had been such thick weather that they had not been able to get a sight of the sun, moon, or stars, and had sailed not by dead-reckoning, as the wind had blown from all quarters, but by sheer guesswork and the lead.

How it came about that Captain Gorham knew the

French cockswain was simple: Although the captain was an American born and raised, only a few years previous to the outbreak of the war he had done a little smuggling on his own account between Dunquerque and the coast of England. So what appeared at first to be most mysterious is really simple when we come to look at it.

But now to tell of what we did:

It had been Captain Gorham's intention, I take it, to run into Dunquerque Harbor, but owing to the representations of Pierre Burron, who stated that we might never leave it if he did so, this idea was given up; and, keeping the lead going, we took the wind on our quarter, and made off to the southward, the captain promising to put the little Frenchman on board the first vessel bound for his country, and pay him well for his services, if they were needed.

While we had been coming about, I, to show my willingness, had hauled lustily on the main-sheet and pitched in with the crew; and as soon as everything was going well, Plummer and I sat down against the bowsprit and began to spin our respective yarns.

Of course there was much to tell. Mine is known already, and Plummer's was but the recounting of the most unusual good fortune that had ever attended the career of a cruiser in any service, I suppose.

It seems that finding the *Young Eagle* had sailed before he had expected she would be ready, Plummer had delayed a long time before he had found a berth to suit his fancy, and then he had shipped in the *Yankee*, from New Bedford. From the day of their sailing they had had fair winds and great luck, capturing two vessels off the American coast, laden with supplies for the English army in Canada, two more on the high seas, and three, of all places in the world but almost under the nose of the British Admiralty, at the entrance of their own private Channel! In all these encounters they had lost but two men killed and four slightly wounded.

The manning of so many prizes had reduced the crew of one hundred and twenty men to twenty-two all told. Being a fore-and-aft vessel, this was more than sufficient to run her properly, and, although it was considered foolhardiness in the forecastle, old Smiley, or Smiler, as they called Gorham, had determined to make one more attempt to pick up a cargo before he started for the States; besides, the necessity of speaking some vessel and securing a compass had now become imperative.

"Tell me something of your skipper, Plummer," I said, after an hour or such a time of talk about ourselves. "He is of a certainty the strangest-looking man I ever met."

"Well, if you want to know the truth," Plummer answered, in a whisper, "he's as mad as the King of Bedlam—that is, to my thinking. In fact, on shore they say he is in league with the devil. But whether it is the devil or the powers above, he certainly carries a fair pinch of good luck 'twixt his thumb and his forefinger. You haven't heard him sing yet—wait till you hear him at that! It will make the flesh crawl on your back, my lad. But, hark ye, he's a good seaman, for all of his blithesome vagaries. And he can man-handle any two of us—mark you that, mate!"

The only other officer capable of navigation left on board the schooner was the third lieutenant, Mr. Carter, who had been one of the slightly wounded, and who yet carried his right arm in a sling. As Plummer and I were talking, the lieutenant came on deck, and ordered us to shake out the reef in the main-sail that we had taken in some time back, and set the top-sail and flying-jib.

The weather was clearing up and the wind going down at the same time. The sun now broke through the clouds, and by noon it was fine, clear weather. To the eastward we could see the low-lying shores of France, while to the westward the white cliffs of England shone plain to sight. A number of sail could be seen skirting the English coast, close in; nothing at all in the way of shipping could we make out on the other hand. But after we had altered our course slightly to the east, at three o'clock in the afternoon we made out a brown sail hugging the shore, and evidently endeavoring to make the entrance to a small port not far from the mouth of the little bay. We could see the houses and steeples plainly. I judge it was either Wissant or Ambleteuse; I think the former, but I may be mistaken.

It was evidently the skipper's intention to head off this little brown sail, and soon we saw that in this he would be successful, as the latter turned about, and started to run for it; but a point of land made her take quite an offing, and in two hours we were almost within hailing distance.

One of the 18-pound carronades was loaded, and a shot fired across the little vessel's bow. Down came the brown sail, and she lay there swinging and dipping like a wild fowl too frightened to escape. I have seen some clumsy craft in my time, but I think these vessels are the strangest-looking. She was a French lugger, only half decked over, with a great leeboard swung alongside, and had a conformation somewhat like the shape of the boats that boys whittle out with their jack-knives. There were five men in her, who appeared scared out of their wits, but their relief was great when Captain Gorham hailed them in French.

They had no compass, but agreed to set our pilot on shore, and he left us, grinning and delighted. Now we cleared away again, and left the Strait of Dover behind us, steering a course somewhat to the eastward of the middle of the English Channel.

I noticed that the armament of the *Yankee* was very similar to that of the *Young Eagle*, except she carried one less gun on a side ; but she was steady and quick in answering her helm — points that would have counted greatly in her favor in action.

In the evening, as I was talking to some of the crew below, a cabin-boy came into the forecastle in search of me, with an order for me to repair aft at once—the captain wished me. I had exchanged part of my citizen's clothes for some that Plummer had offered me, as my coat was minus a sleeve, and I hastened up. Captain Gorham was pacing up and down the little quarter-deck ; he halted as he saw me approaching.

"You will dine with me this evening, Mr. Hurdiss," he said. "And if my nose does not deceive me, dinner is on the table."

I bowed and thanked him, and we went down into the little cabin. Mr. Carter was on deck, and the captain and I sat down *vis-à-vis*. No sooner had he seated himself than he began to hum, or chant better, only without using words, beneath his breath. This he kept up even while he was feeding himself! As I was very hungry (it appears to me that I have dwelt upon my appetite rather often) I did not interrupt the music, and so for full five minutes not a word was said. At last Gorham pushed back a little ways from the table, and sang a few words to the same air he had been humming.

"And-now,-Mr.-Hurdiss, spin-us-your-yarn," he chanted.

So I began at once with the cruise of the *Young Eagle* and the fight with the frigate, for I did not consider it necessary to tell of my earlier life, or of my claims in the matter of high birth. It was the second time that I had told the story this day, and I probably hastened —one does in a second telling, generally. When I came to the more exciting parts, dealing with my prison life and escape, Captain Gorham hummed a little bit louder, and this continuous accompaniment urged me to speak faster, so I covered ground in great fashion. He played an obligato to my solo, as it were, piano, fortissimo, and all of it. When I had finished he arose and hushed his noise, as if he had been forced to bite the end off the tune against his will and inclination.

"Mr. Hurdis," said he, "we need some one here aft with us, and there's a berth for you—take it. I shall tell the men to obey your orders, as you will obey mine. You will act as third lieutenant, sir."

Then, as if this settled matters, he began to hum again, and went up the ladder to the deck, leaving me sitting there in amazement. Here was another false position! How fate had forced such situations upon me! It seemed a long time ago that I was supposed to be a French nobleman (oh yes, I was one), and I could scarce bring myself to believe that my rescue had happened only the very morning of this day. "Now," quoth I to myself, "if I refuse to accept this honor thrust upon me, I may do the very worst thing that may happen." It behooved me to balance matters carefully, to weigh and measure possible results.

I knew enough to give the orders under ordinary circumstances for the making and taking in of sail. I could, at a pinch, have stood my trick at the wheel. I could use enough sea terms to lead one to suppose that I knew more, but I knew none of the methods used in determining a ship's position at sea. I had no inkling of how to prick a course on the chart, and what a navigator did when he squinted at the sun through a quadrant I could not imagine; but yet, I reasoned, the captain and Mr. Carter would probably do all of that that was necessary. I could get on with the men, I felt sure, and why not undertake it? Thus I convinced myself that I could become a lieutenant—I had learned to box the compass while in prison; and thinking of this accomplishment made me smile, for surely we would have given something to have possessed one, even at the end of a fob.

The good ten-knot breeze held in the same direction all night long. I took the midnight watch, and felt quite proud of myself as the men moved to obey my orders to ease off the sheets when I thought occasion demanded it.

Plummer appeared quite pleased at my promotion (one might have thought he was responsible for it), and the other men had not appeared to take any dislike to their new officer; so I became quite tickled with the idea of my importance, and stopped my misgivings.

Mr. Carter was a very silent man, and I found it difficult to engage him in any conversation, yet I gleaned, from what he said in response to questions, that Captain Gorham was very wealthy, and many other things about him. (It is well known that he owned the *Yankee* himself, and a half-share in the *Teaser*, another New Bedford privateer, commanded by his brother.) So busy had I been all day that I had scarce bestowed a thought upon the friends I had deserted so unceremoniously in the morning; but after getting into my bunk I grew rather uneasy. Never would I forgive myself if I had brought any discomfiture to Monsieur de Rèdun; but he was equal to the emergency, indubitably—any one who knew him would have reasoned that much for certain. As to Rembolez, his conduct had been puzzling; for why should he have been so determined upon my not leaving his company? He must, as well as my patron, have been compelled to give some explanation to the others. Finding I could not answer my own interrogations, I quit, and soon fell a-snoring.

The next day was Sunday. I think I detected that Captain Gorham hummed psalm tunes during breakfast. Surely it was Old Hundred that he was repeating when I joined him on deck in the afternoon.

But it was no Sunday breeze, and we skipped along lively. In my opinion the *Yankee* would have been no match for the *Young Eagle* in sailing, but she would have shown a clean pair of heels to almost any English or French cruiser twice her tonnage.

During the day we had passed within some miles of a number of vessels, but they had paid no attention to us, and it was not until half-past five that we had anything that approached an interesting situation. We were somewhere off the island of Alderney, for the captain knew his position to a nicety, and was steering a little to the north—"to give the Casquet Rocks a wide berth," he told me—when one of the men aloft made out a vessel bearing down to meet us; she was carrying the wind so that if we kept on as we were we would pass near to her.

In an hour it could be seen that she was a frigate, but Captain Gorham held the same course undisturbed.

CHAPTER XXVII

I WITNESS SOME REMARKABLE PROCEEDINGS

IT reminded me a little of my voyage in the *Minetta* to note the anxiety of the crew as the *Yankee* bowled along. The big vessel that was to windward had evidently been reconnoitring the French coast; but she did not show any suspicion, and we approached one another as peaceably as were we two friendly merchantmen. All at once the frigate tossed out her flag, and up went ours in answer.

Needless to say it was the same as hers—the cross of St. George.

Mr. Carter had brought up from the cabin a canvas bag and a book, the edges of which were weighted with lead. "There she goes, sir," he said, turning to the captain; and as he spoke a little line of streamers crept up the Britisher's mast-head. The captain, humming carelessly, opened the book.

"Give them four, one, nine, three, seven, Mr. Carter," he said, in a singsong.

Five little flags that the lieutenant had picked out rose on our color halyards. To this day I do not know what they meant, but it was apparently satisfactory to the frigate, for she took in her signals, and we did likewise. Plummer gave me a wink as he gathered the bunting in as it fluttered to the deck.

"We caught these aboard the last prize," he said, "and just saved the book from going overboard. There's luck for you!"

I noticed that Captain Gorham's eyes were dancing as we passed by the frigate, about a quarter of a mile astern of her, but I was totally unprepared for what he did, and stood aghast at his orders.

"Stand by to cast loose and provide the long twelve!" he shrieked, in his high voice.

Mr. Carter made as if to offer some remonstrance; but the men, grinning, jumped to obey. We had the windward place now, and every advantage, besides it would soon be dusk.

"Ta-ta, ta-ra, ta, ri-ro," sang Captain Gorham, as he sighted the long gun himself.

As soon as he had trained it to his satisfaction there was a burst of white smoke, a roar, and we all bent forward to watch the shot. I gave a squeal of delight as I saw the frigate's mizzen-topsail yard break square in two and, with the sail, slam over against the stays. The captain of that vessel must have been a most surprised individual! He yawed about, succeeded in getting taken all aback, generally mixed up and scandalized.

"Show our colors!" cried Gorham, and I dare say the sight of them surprised the Englishman still more.

"Learned that little trick from John Paul Jones," continued the captain, with his voice at high pitch. "I sailed in the *Ranger* with him, and came back a quarter-master — started cabin-boy, gentlemen. But he once done that trick to the frigate *Boothby*, and, egad! with a craft not half the size of this one! Tidery dido dum— —ha-ha!"

"Were you on the *Bonhomme Richard*?" I asked.

"Was I? Eh? Diddledy dee, tumpity to. Yes, I was there. Didn't we give them bumpity-bang; bingity-bum slampity—slap! Guess I was," he added, suddenly whirling and jumping down the ladder into the cabin, as though he realized that he was doing something foolish. We heard him roaring away in a nameless chorus for some time as he paced up and down, and not one of us cracked a smile.

It was full five minutes, however, before the Britisher got upon our track or fired a gun. Then two of his shot went over us, and the rest went wide; but as we sailed three points closer on the wind almost, and legged two feet for his one, he fell behind; after two hours of it he tacked off eastward; and I wonder if he made a report of all this to their lordships!

I was below about nine o'clock in the evening when I heard the shouting of orders, and, gaining the deck, found Captain Gorham standing beside the helmsman, very silent, with his face black as thunder. Mr. Carter was leaning against the rail hard by, trying to appear unconcerned—the schooner had been put about.

"When I give an order, I want it obeyed without question, sir, d'ye mark that?" scowled Gorham. "That's what you're here for — to obey orders! I'm going back to France and pick up a compass — and a crew too, egad! This little cruise of ours is not over by a long shot."

Mr. Carter answered not a word; not a muscle of his face moved. I knew better than to say anything myself at that moment, but presently, as it grew darker, I crossed over to him.

"What's up?" I ventured.

"Heaven knows," the first luff responded, in an undertone. "You heard what he said. I simply asked 'Why?' that's all. 'Tis a piece of foolishness, to my mind—this putting into port—eh, eh, have a care; it won't do for him to see us talking." There was a silence of a minute, and then he went on, in a deep whisper: "Truth is, we've made a pot o' money, and I want to see home again, Mr. Hurdiss. I've been married but a year, and there's a wife and a fine bouncing youngster, I trust, waiting to greet me. Where do you hail from, if I may ask? You're too smooth spoke to have always been a seaman."

"I shipped from the town of New London," I replied, slowly. "But I don't think I have any home exactly—that is, in a manner of speaking—unless it is the ship I happen to be sailing in."

"I've heard men talk like that afore, my boy," observed the officer, rather kindly, "and when they do they have always the same reason."

"What's that, Mr. Carter?"

"Young woman in the case, Mr. Hurdiss."

I thought of Mary Tanner, and said nothing.

"If she ain't married to no one else, go back to her; and if she won't have you then, tell her you're coming back again after your next voyage—and keep a-coming, too. Women like men with gumption, no matter what they say. Your lady-love ain't married, is she? Ye look too young for that sort o' thing."

"No, she's not married!" I could feel myself blushing.

"Then pitch in, man-fashion, and win! Lordy, I know how 'twas with me — three years o' waitin', and 'twas worth thirty! I'll bet ye get her! Is she pretty? What's the use o' asking?—no one else like her in the world, o' course—that's what I thought at the time, and think so yet, b'gorry!"

Perhaps the kind fellow imagined I was going to spin him my yarn; but I did not, and most likely he would not have believed me if I had. Soon we were busy taking in the top-sails, and further conversation was ended.

Captain Gorham stayed on deck all night; only occasionally did he break forth into a tune. We kept heaving the lead every now and then, and kept a close lookout.

The next morning we were off the harbor of Barfleur.

"We won't stay here long," observed the skipper, who seemed none the worse off for his long night's work. "We're just where I said we'd be. By hemlock, I know the ropes of this place, and I could sail in here with my eyes shut! Load up those guns; I'm going to fire a salute before we come to anchor."

So I was to see France, after all.

CHAPTER XXVIII

AN OBSERVER OF HISTORY

WE stayed in that harbor almost six months to a day—
a bit longer than Captain Gorham expected !—but there
were sundry good and sufficient reasons for our sojourn,
and I did not make any complaint, although I wished
more than once we were out of it. I found a chance to
see a little more of the world, and took in vivid pictures
of some historical occurrences—or, better, the effect of
them—worth more space than I can afford to give in
this writing.

Why Monsieur Rembolez was so anxious to detain me,
upon my attempt to escape, I found out also, and what
became of my fellow-conspirators after they landed. It
would make a separate tale if I went into it; but,
as an old sea-captain once said to me, "Watch your
sails and mind your wind, or you'll carry your masts
ahead of your ship." Which is another way of saying,
"More haste less speed," perhaps. To take things in
order:

Barfleur is a fairly good harbor of a very bad kind;
the town itself is very small, and contained less than fifteen hundred inhabitants—scarce more than a village.
As a port of entry it was dead-and-alive when I first saw
it. The water is very shallow, the channel tortuous, and
the whole place filling up with sand. We came in on
a very high tide, but found bottom twice, nevertheless,
and a vessel of deep draught could not have entered.

15

But as Gorham had said, he " knew the ropes," and had been there often—* . . .

The people were tired of war—they had lost all inter-est in it. The news that the allies were pressing the Emperor hard, following so quickly upon the disastrous campaign in Russia, and Wellington's hot pursuit of Soult to the southward, prepared every one for the change that was soon to follow. Few able-bodied men were to be seen—nearly all of the straight-backed and vigorous were in Napoleon's fleets or his armies. Captain Gor-ham must have acknowledged to himself (he never did to any one else) the mistake he had made in supposing that he could pick up a crew so very easily. Only a half-dozen stranded American seamen did we find, and they were not of much account. There was one thing I was glad of, anyhow: on board ship the difference in our rank prevented me from seeing much of my friend in the forecastle. But on shore it was another thing ; although Plummer was always respectful, we were on a plane of equality there ; that I endeavored to show him in every way in my power.

.   .   .   .   .   .

—This was our fourth or fifth ramble out in the country. . . . When we returned to the little tavern we sought our usual seat in the corner, where we filled our pipes (by the same token, I used to smoke now and then—rather gingerly, as a school-boy does), and Silas delivered him-self of the following :

" A rum lot, these Frenchmen—a jumping-jack-in-the-

---

* Unfortunately, this chapter of Captain Hurdiss's narrative is presented in a very condensed form—not from any desire on the part of the editor to shorten it, but because these pages of the ledger in which the autobiography was written were loose, and the mice had destroyed whole paragraphs. In one case a page was missing com-pletely. The rest of the book was in a state of good preservation. —ED.

box nation. I don't know what to make of 'em. Here
comes along a new king who 'stalls himself in Paree, or
gets his friends to 'stall him—egad, the same thing!—and
what does *they* do? They jumps and hollers and cheers
'emselves black in the face, and tells him *he's* the captain
for them! And in about three weeks more trouble.
Give 'em four months, and they'll want the little soger
back once more." (They had him inside of a twelve-
month.) "Oh, I don't know what to make of 'em—dash
me if I do!" concluded Plummer, in disgust.

I laughed. "You are about right, but there's more to
follow; we haven't seen the end of it yet."

"I judge we've seen the end of this cruise, or, mayhap, the war, sir"—this was spoken in a deep-chested
growl. "We'll rot our timbers unless something's
done pretty soon. 'Nap' had more to do with our row
with John Bull than most people give him credit for,
master."

"Captain Gorham doesn't seem so anxious to get
away as he did—think you not so, Silas?" I asked.

"'Deed, I agrees; he's been on a musical spree for a
fortnight come Tuesday. Now, aboard ship, no one's
allowed to turn a tune but himself" (I had not known
this), "but ashore he'd follow in the wake of a beggar
with a fiddle for a mile. Any music but what he makes
turns him silly—like tickling some folks in the ribs."

This was almost a fact! If any one of the enemy had
attacked Captain Gorham with a broadside composed of
a bass-viol and a clarinet he would have struck his colors—to carry out Plummer's idea of it. . . .

"Think it over," said Mr. Carter. "I'd like to run
up to Paris and take a squint at the place—just to say
that I'd been there, Mr. Hurdiss."

. . . After a while I consented. We were to share ex-
penses, and I was to repay him from the prize-money I

might have coming to me from the *Young Eagle;* he told me it was probably no inconsiderable amount by this time.

Odd to tell, Captain Gorham gave us leave for two weeks; he was confined to his cabin, and maybe as an antidote to the effect of music upon his nerves he was indulging in some rather superior French brandy—but this may be maligning him. . . . It was on the 29th of March, if I remember rightly, that the allied forces entered Paris.   Louis XVIII. followed in a few days, and a fortnight or so later Napoleon formally abdicated. But when Mr. Carter and I arrived at the capital on the third day of June affairs were in a very unsettled condition.   People were afraid to speak the truth concerning their convictions or opinions.

Everywhere there was a "wait-and-we-will-see-what-will-happen" attitude.   The military — the defeated army of an adored leader—were disgruntled; suspicion was rife, and intrigue on all sides.   But Paris herself! such a city as she is! a world apart from any other! resembling nothing but herself—unique! magnificent! My knowledge of the French tongue helped me, and in honest Carter I found I had a splendid companion— simple as a child, tender as a woman, brave and generous to a fault.   Poor Carter! I often think of him (but I must mind my wind and sails); good times did we have together.

One day we set out from our lodgings—on the morrow we were to start on our return trip to Barfleur—intending to visit some place where it was rumored we might catch a glimpse of the King.   I had never told any one that once I had met him (this affable personage) in a gathering when I had more of a handle to my name than plain mister.   I knew he was not much to look at; but Carter was wild to see him, so we went.   But we never saw the new monarch, and we never got there.

As we turned about a corner of one of the streets approaching the Place de la Concorde, I came to a sudden halt. On the opposite side of the street was a well-known figure — my dear friend, the Marquis de Monseverat! There he was, looking, as the English say, "very slap" in his fashionable toggery; behind, following at a respectful distance, was none other than old Gustave!

Forgetting to make an apology to Mr. Carter in my haste, I ran across the street, and in another moment Monsieur de Rèdun, who with a glad cry advanced to meet me, had flung both his arms around my neck.

"Ah, mon chère Jean," exclaimed he — "you here! La fortune! Now who was right about the better days? They have come back!"

He said this with such a wild exhilaration that I knew he must be blind to the signs of the popular distrust.

"Are you alone?" he asked. "Come where we can talk. What are you doing here in Paris? Are you going to advance your—"

I interrupted him. "I am here with a friend—just to see the sights—merely on pleasure bent, Monsieur le Marquis."

Turning, I signalled Carter to come over to us. Monsieur de Rèdun frowned slightly.

"Does your friend speak French?" he asked.

"Not a word."

"I shall be glad to meet him."

Gustave had been standing near us, and I extended my hand to him, but he pretended not to see it.

"Your servant, monsieur," said he, bowing very low. The old man wore a sad, troubled look upon his face.

My patron received Mr. Carter in his most courteous manner, but the honest sailor was rather puzzled, and appeared to have lost his bearings, looking from one of us to the other awkwardly. In a word or two I ex-

plained that the Marquis was an old acquaintance whom
I had not seen for some time, but Monsieur de Rèdun,
seeing how matters stood, took both of us by the arms,
saying :

"Come, you have not breakfasted, I know. Allow me
the honor of having you sit down at the table with me,
messieurs."

So, arm in arm, we started down the street.

As we progressed Monsieur de Rèdun asked me so
many questions (speaking in English) about myself that
I had no chance to find out anything in my turn concerning his affairs. Carter was visibly thawing under
the influence of the nobleman's individuality, and even
laughed at one of his sallies. But the walk was not to
be without incident. The street curved in circular form,
and as we followed the dead wall, hugging it close, we
suddenly came upon three men walking linked together,
as we were. The one on the outside had an empty sleeve
and a cross with an eagle in the centre of it ; the one in
the middle had a fierce mustache, and a ribbon in his
buttonhole. I dropped back to allow the gentlemen
the right to pass, and as I did so I felt Monsieur de
Rèdun's muscles stiffen. But the on-comers did not
turn out an inch, instead altered their course, with the
result they ran afoul of us without an apology.

"Give place, give place," growled the man in the centre, looking as if he would like to devour us.

Carter, seeing at once that there was "a row on," as
he afterwards expressed it, was drawing back his heavy
first for the purpose of smashing the mustached one's
features. But Monsieur de Rèdun restrained him.

"Pray don't! pray don't!" he cried, "I beg of you—
'tis my affair. Pardon me."

With a great deal of manner he whipped a card from
his pocket and gave it to the gentleman in the middle
—the tallest one. The latter took out his pasteboard,

and, lifting his great hat, that came down to his thick eye-brows, he said, gruffly, but quietly: "Merci, monsieur!"

The one-armed man was standing opposite me; he bowed, and I could see the stump of his arm wiggle nervously.

"Et vous, Monsieur l'Anglais—donner moi le plaisir?" he said, speaking with a bad accent.

I knew what he meant, but I was not prepared for the emergency—that is, I had no card—and his taking me for an Englishman rather upset me; so I faltered an instant. Monsieur de Rèdun came to my rescue.

"These gentlemen are Americans; they have no part in our quarrel," he laughed, airily (no one had seen any quarrel, by-the-bye). "But I shall be glad to meet monsieur after I have met"—and he looked at the card in his hand—"after meeting Captain Molineux." Another exchange followed, and the Marquis turned to the third man, and asked, quickly: "And you, also—will you not favor me—Maréchal?" (I perceived that he spoke the title in cutting sarcasm.) "I should be delighted if you would consider it."

A grim smile and bow was the rejoinder. "Monsieur has too much honor on his hands at present. If one of his friends—"

I stepped forward.

"No," interposed Monsieur de Rèdun; "I beg of you, no, for the sake of our old friendship. This is my affair."

Everything appeared to be satisfactory to all hands. The three strangers raised their hats and went their way, and the Marquis again ran his arms through ours.

"The unregenerate Napoleonites," laughed he; "two more or less matters little! Come, allons; I have the appetite of a wolf."

I was a little angry at my having been cut out so unceremoniously. I would liked to have had a chance to show him how I could handle a small sword.

From the day of our arrival in Paris, Carter and I had heard nothing in the cafés but duels—duels and murders. For what else were some of them—these encounters with no mere chance of fatality—but certain death alone? Two men tied together at the waist hacking each other to death with short knives in the dark; the famous duel over the table between Colonel D—— and the Comte de F——, elbows on the cloth and a pistol in each hand; in both of these cases double funerals! Oh yes, of course, "le satisfaction"—that is to be considered, maybe. I should not like to *kill* a man, or to have him kill me, just because we differed in opinions. If I wished to end his existence it would be because of some deadly injury he would do to me or mine if he should live; then I should rid the earth of him, perhaps, if my blood was up and I knew 'twas my life he was after at the moment. In battle it is different; in the abstract it is the *cause* that justifies, and in the hand-to-hand struggle it is self-preservation. But I am moralizing, which is not my *forte*, anyhow; so enough of it.

When we had reached the café towards which Monsieur de Rèdun was piloting us, we entered and found seats in a small compartment behind a tall screen. The decorations of this place were all Royalist, and plainly new. A few men seated about rose, and bowed to the Marquis as we passed.

"And now," said I, leaning forward in my chair, "pray answer *me* some questions! You took things so coolly just now that I am constrained to think this must be an every-day occurrence with you, monsieur."

"I do not seek for them," was the return. "I try to avoid them if I can—'*odi profanum vulgus et arceo*'—but there are some that cannot be ignored. Those gentlemen were out for game; 'tis a favorite trick of ex-imperials."

"Have you nothing to fear? Are they so clumsy as that?"

"I have heard they are good artillerists." Monsieur de Rèdun shrugged his shoulders.

I turned to him again, smiling at this wealth of contemptuous expression.

"To change the subject, Monsieur le Marquis: What did you do after I plunged overboard from the boat, may I ask?"

"There was much talking, my dear Jean; but, not to disparage the importance of it, it was soon forgotten."

He chuckled at me in a curious way. We had been speaking in French for some time—Carter was too busy with a *ragoût* to pay attention. I looked at my plate in silence. What a remarkable nature—a man with two duels on hand, and tantalizing my curiosity just to amuse himself, as if the seriousness of his position had left his mind!

"We soon had other things to think about," Monsieur de Rèdun continued at last, his eyes twinkling. "There was a greater surprise in holding for us."

"What was it? Don't keep me in suspense, monsieur."

"Simple enough. We were all arrested as soon as we set foot ashore. Parbleu! they were waiting for us—had been waiting some months."

"Rembolez!" exclaimed I.

"Yes, Rembolez. You are quick, my dear Jean."

"I never liked him from the first. What happened you then?"

"We went to prison; I was there three weeks. I was to have been executed—ah, let me see—ten days ago; but other things occurred, as you perceive."

"Where are the rest, Monsieur le Marquis?"

"All here in Paris, and well. Du Saille is Colonel of the Garde du Corps."

"And Rembolez?"

Monsieur de Rèdun made a quick flourish and a thrust with his knife. "De Soyecourt," said he. I understood, with a shudder. There was much more of the same work going on every morning, and with much less reason for it.

"How long are you going to remain in Paris?" was the question addressed to me, after a moment's pause.

"We leave to-morrow afternoon."

"Why don't you stay here and try to prove—er—something much to your advantage. You know you can count on me; it might be possible. There's Gustave. Have you nothing now to tell me?—think."

"There is nothing to tell, monsieur, that it would repay me to dwell upon," I answered. "I could prove nothing, even if Gustave should try to help me. He may be an imaginative old man."

I saw that the old servant had been talking.

"The King has revived the Order of St. Louis; the estates are going to be handed back; King Henry's head is replaced on the cross of the Legion." The Marquis spoke earnestly. "I will secure you an audience."

I hesitated. I was not so much tempted as one might suppose. Failure meant ignominy. There was a great difference from being the unknown head of a great house beyond all doubt in your own mind and making other people believe it, with only a nursery tale and a gold button to prove the story. What was the use? as I once said before.

I shook my head. "No, monsieur — a thousand thanks; I go back to my ship to-morrow."

"What is your address here?"

"Hôtel Strasbourg, Rue Notre Dame des Victoires."

"You do not leave until the afternoon? I have a reason for asking."

"At one o'clock. We spend the night at Mantes, and start the next morning at daybreak on the road for Cherbourg." . . .

.   .   .   .   .   .

I had not ceased to quiver from excitement as I mounted into the diligence and seated myself beside Carter, who, of course, inquired where I had been. He told me he had cruised about the streets (when he had caught another glimpse of the Duchess in her carriage), succeeded in getting lost, and had just drifted into port by accident. For some moments I could hardly reply or even listen to what he was saying.

What a morning it had been! I could recall the very feel of the damp, dew-soaked grass underfoot, and the leafy arches overhead in which the birds were twittering—how unreal it had seemed!—and the whispering of the swords as the blades rubbed against one another. I was mighty glad that I had not called aloud to the Marquis that time when I thought he had dropped his point too far. Heavens, I had been near it! But, as I say, I honestly wished I could have exchanged places with him, for Captain Molineux was almost too much for him; his attack was terrific, but he reached too far, and I knew how to stop that! I really trusted that Monsieur de Rèdun's thrust had not reached his lungs. My patron had not wished to kill him, or *he would not have been so cautious.* Colonel Whiffen (a renegade Irishman) had turned rather pale when it came his turn, but he had not flinched; and how proud I had felt of my patron when I saw him shift his weapon, so as to meet the colonel at his own game—left-handed!

I should liked to have picked up the colonel's sword for him; but I suppose if it were given him back he would have wished to continue, and there would have been nothing for it but to run him through the arm, as Monsieur de Rèdun had done. I hope he recovered the use of it, for to go through the world with only one is bad enough.

When we were driving back through the Bois there had been an amusing thought come to me—under the circumstances amusing, I mean. I had wished that the Marquis de Monseverat and I could take up the foils for a friendly pass or two. His name as a swordsman was known about Paris already, and the saying was that General Fournier had avoided meeting him, and he was a man-killer *par excellence*.

When we had put some miles of open country behind us and the gleaming dome of the Hôtel des Invalides had faded from sight, I told Mr. Carter of the morning's doings, and, forsooth, he was like to quarrel with me for not having him along—as if I had had anything to do with it, except take up Monsieur de Rèdun's invitation to be present. I had noticed Monsieur de Soyecourt's manner had been coldly polite, and barely that. But this time I parted with my patron with every indication of affection on his part, and the promise on mine that if I ever came to Paris again or returned to France on a voyage I should let him know.

By the time Mantes was reached Carter and I were on good terms again, and had begun to exchange conjectures as to how long we would probably remain in that deserted harbor, and what Captain Gorham had been doing in our absence. Carter also told me more about his wife, and I in return, to confess it, told him a little more about Mary.

When he asked me where she was, I had to reply that I really was not sure, at which he intimated that he thought it was about time I should find out, and instead of growing angry at this—it was meant kindly—I agreed with him; and that made me sick for a sight of her, wild for the sound of her voice, and my dreams began again of the old times, and what she used to say, and how she looked as she stood there on the pier.

CHAPTER XXIX

DANGEROUS DELAYS

WE perceived upon our arrival that affairs were in about the same condition as when we left them at Barfleur. Captain Gorham and eight men, among whom was Plummer, were all we found on board ship. The rest were on a protracted vacation—it about amounted to that—in Cherbourg. This fine and interesting place is distant from Barfleur some sixteen miles. I had been over there thrice, and was destined to go there many times more before we got away.

Napoleon had spared no expense in making the harbor a wonder of marine engineering. True, Louis XVI. had expended vast sums in first, constructing the foundations of the great *digue,* or breakwater, situate about two and a half miles from the river mouth, but Bonaparte had stopped at nothing. What struck me with amazement was the fact that the French had not long ago swept the British fleets and all manner of sail out of the Channel with such a place to rendezvous. Four hundred vessels could swing in perfect safety in the protected roadstead, and the great basins, or artificial harbors—one for merchant craft and the other for men-of-war—were unassailable by man or by the elements. The Emperor had carved out of the almost solid rock a resting-place for his battle-ships three hundred and twenty-eight yards long by two hundred and fifty yards in width; at low ebb-tide there was twenty-five to twenty-eight feet of water in its shallowest part. I was told

that fifty ships of the line could find accommodation
in it !

There were a half-score of dismantled seventy-fours,
a number of frigates and smaller vessels of war, and fifty
or sixty merchantmen lying idle at the wharves, but
what was more interesting was the fact that there were
three American privateers all a-taunto, waiting a chance
to slip out of the harbor—yes, to slip out; for—will you
believe it?—Napoleon's proudest port, containing a marine force greater than the whole American navy of that
time, was blockaded by a small but watchful squadron of
the English—just sufficient in number to keep up a vigorous patrol; and there was not a French port on the
coast that was not in the same condition. With the ac-
cession of King Louis, and the "piping times of peace,"
it might be thought that their vigilance would be relaxed.
But no; to take a Yankee letter of marque or privateer
was as much of an honor as to bring in a French frigate !
This is not a joke, nor is it boasting; ask any honest
Englishman. At Brest, at l'Orient, at La Rochelle,
at Cherbourg, and many other places American private
armed ships, cooped up, were waiting for a chance to
elude the blockaders and escape to sea. Not a few
had followed this policy during the whole course of the
war, and had outfitted continually from French harbors
—notably, the *True-blooded Yankee*, the *Leo*, the *David
Porter*, and several more ; their adventures would read
like a romance.

Captain Gorham had a method in seeking out the
smaller and shallower places like Barfleur—the British
did not watch them so closely. But we were to be
blockaded, none the less, as effectively as if the whole
navy of Great Britain were to be anchored off the point
in plain sight of us, and to escape we had to run as great
a danger as if we had to pass their broadsides. This in
due time.

One day Mr. Carter and I had walked the five leagues to Cherbourg with a more definite end in view than mere pleasure. The English government was objecting strenuously to the court of the King against the privateers being allowed to depart and prey against their commerce. Owing to the friendship of the Prince Regent for King Louis it was rumored that the authorities would soon adopt measures to disarm every American vessel within the limits of the kingdom (needless to say, they did so before long), and this news created great consternation and stirred all to action. One of the three vessels in the harbor tried to run for it, with the result that she was so roughly handled by the enemy that she just managed to creep back and no more, mauled and maimed, to her anchorage under the neutral guns, where, the next day, she sank. Her crew made the shore in their boats, and it was to gain their services that Carter and I were on our way. Gorham had awakened from his lethargy; here was a chance for the *Yankee* to fill her complement. Why the English admiral had not heard of the presence of another one of the "sea pests" so near him I don't know for the life of me—he never sent a sail to watch us.

But to make a short story of a long one, we found the crew of the luckless *Orlando* lounging about the Chantereyne dockyard, disconsolate and forlorn. When they heard our proposition there was much excitement, and there on the spot we enlisted eighty men and filled our complement of officers. Arrangements were made that they should proceed to Barfleur in small detachments, starting after nightfall for five successive nights.

This changed the entire complexion of matters. In two weeks the schooner was outfitted and ready for sea, provisioned for a six months' cruise. A fine crew we had, if rather heterogeneous, but mostly able seamen and Americans, among whom were a half-dozen blacks.

I had been employing my leisure time in studying seamanship, and trying to pick up something about navigation, but—I confess it with shame—my pride prevented me telling of my real ignorance even to my friend Carter, and so it was, to my half-fearful delight, that I found I was to be retained aft as fourth officer. Plummer was promoted to be bo's'n, and a clever one he made.

One fine starlight night, with a favoring breeze, we raised anchor silently, got up our lower sails, and slowly made for the harbor mouth—the lead being heaved on both sides well forward. Shoaler and shoaler it grew beneath our keel — shoaler yet. The men all looked back at the skipper: his hands were on the spokes of the wheel, and he listened to the soundings with an anxious face. At last it seemed hardly possible that we were sailing—that we must be dragging, surely. Then there came a gentle jar and an ominous straining sound. We were hard and fast, and the tide at top flood !

Getting out sweeps and kedges, luckily we worked off backward, and succeeded in making deeper water, where we anchored : then the boats were sent out to find the channel. There was none ! The storm of three weeks before had built a sand-bar clear across the little bay. The *Yankee* could not have gone over it without lightening herself to the danger limit. We were prisoners !

Seven times in the next ten days did we make the same attempt with the same result, and the men went sick at heart. Mr. Carter grew morose, the new officers discontented : and it was hard to keep the people employed. This was the first week in August, the weather was hot, and for days the clouds had been absent. But on the 8th—a Sunday, if I am not mistaken—the barometer began to fall, and to the north the heavens looked dark and lowering. A large proportion of the crew had been given liberty, and the rest were yarn-ing or grumbling forward, cursing their luck as only sailors can.

When Gorham came on deck he looked at the sky; it was two o'clock in the afternoon. He turned to me and asked the hour, and just then four bells were struck, so I knew it.

"Mr. Hurdiss, we're going to have a blow, sir," he said; "make all snug."

Then he went below again and began to pipe a long chant in a minor key.

In two hours it was ripping and tearing out of the northeast, and the *Yankee* was jumping and heaving at her cable like one possessed. The bar was an expanse of smothering white.

It was flood-tide at shortly after four, and when I poked my head up the companion-way to see how things were holding, I noticed that the waves were running way up on the shingle, and that the small jetty was almost submerged. When I reported this Gorham leaped up from his berth, where I had heard him humming for some time; bare-headed he rushed up the ladder, and scarcely had he gained the air when he turned and shouted down to me:

"Turn out all hands! Ho, there — Mr. Carter and all of you—on deck and lively!" Then he rushed forward and trumpeted down into the forecastle: "On deck there, all you lazy dogs! Jump, dang ye!—come, bundle up! tumble out!"

"Cat and fish that anchor, Mr. Carter," he ordered, coming aft; "set your staysail, and raise the peak of the main-sail. I'm going to get out of here or sink her, begad! Now let's see how you can handle a wheel, Mr. Hurdiss."

CHAPTER XXX

A CUTTING OUT

WHEN I grasped the spokes of the wheel I felt a qualm of misgiving, but I soon found that the *Yankee* could be handled like a cat-boat; she felt her helm readily, and answered it with amazing quickness. But when we reached the rough water on the bar it required two to steer her, and I thought we were lost once for certain, for we grounded heavily; but in fifteen minutes we had an offing, well out from Barfleur Point. We bore up for a time, and then came about and headed southwest-by-west, tearing along at the rate of nine or ten knots an hour. I felt sorry for the poor fellows we had left behind us, but I was glad to see that Plummer and Mr. Carter were on board.

The twenty-four hours following began with an abatement of the wind and a rising of the barometer. Soon there was only a good top-sail breeze, with occasional gusts blowing, but the sea was so rough that we kept along under our lower sails only: all this morning we saw no sail, except an English frigate, hull down to leeward.

Captain Gorham sang to himself in a contented manner most of the time, and he had a right. We had seventy-five good sailor-men on board a lucky craft, and we were in the very place to pick up the richest prizes.

But to my surprise Carter said to me, as we leaned back on the cushioned seats in the cabin: " Hurdiss, I wish we had never put back into port, and that we had started for home—compass or no compass—six months ago ; and another thing I wish—"

"What's that, pray?" I asked.

"That old Sal, the cat, hadn't gone overboard yesterday ; some of the men say she jumped off the bowsprit and tried to swim ashore."

"Ten to one somebody heaved her over," I replied.

"But 'tis a bad omen, nevertheless," remarked Carter; "and last night I dreamed I was in a coffin, and it was too big for me—worse luck !—most uncomfortable."

"Well, that shows that you're going to reach land," said I, trying to encourage him.

Carter had lots of spirit, and brains to go with it; and it was a strange condition of mind for him to be in. I could not fathom it. But in half an hour he seemed to be his old self again, and at table was in fine fettle, so I almost felt like twitting him about his barometrical temper. I am very glad I did not.

We set the top-sails in the late afternoon, as the sea had gone down and the gusts ceased.

A pitch-dark night came on. I went on watch at ten o'clock, and did a great deal of thinking while I paced the deck. I was longing to see Mary Tanner, to tell her of my adventures. What would she say to them? I concluded it would be better to relate nothing of the discovery I had made in regard to my father's name—there was plenty to tell outside of that! When I landed in America I would start for New London instanter, and then (I had it all laid out) some day I would come for her in my own ship, as I had promised (I was always modest enough to imagine a very small ship)—nothing was going to interfere with *that* plan.

As I was engaged in counting up fabulous sums of prize-money, and wishing that old Jack Sutton and Edward Brown were with us (poor fellows, they were thinking I was buried by this time, I suppose), the lookout reported to me that he thought there was land dead ahead, as he could make out lights.

I ran forward, and, sure enough, I could see flashes here and there, and two or three steady points of light to leeward. I jumped below and called the captain.

"Have you held the same course?" he asked.

"Yes, sir; the wind has not changed."

"Oh, confound it, it can't be!" Gorham grumbled, as he ran up the ladder ahead of me.

He ascended a short ways into the weather-shrouds.

"That's no shore!" he cried to Mr. Carter, who had come on deck barefooted. "That's a big fleet bound out for the Indies—that's what it is, by Jupiter! Port your helm!" he roared to the man at the wheel, and the booms swung out as we got before the wind.

We bore straight down upon the lights, that had now increased in number and vividness, slackening our speed by taking in our top-sails one after another, and hauling all sheets well aft. By one o'clock we were almost within hailing distance of the two rearmost ships, whose lights we could make out very plainly; as we displayed none of our own, we were probably invisible, owing to the blackness of the night. The crew had all been called on deck, and the carronades and the midship guns were loaded. Thus, amid great excitement, but in absolute silence, we came closer and closer, until it was only a question of time when a lookout should discern our presence.

"Fleet sailing" was then the usual way that Great Britain carried on her commerce with the colonies. Under convoy of a 74, one or two frigates, and a half-dozen smaller men-of-war, the great fleets set out. Woe to the stragglers! The privateers were generally hovering on the track, and it did not do for any of the flock to stray from the protection of the watch-dogs.

The fleet we were heading for must have numbered close to one hundred sail. Every one swung a lantern on the foremast, and they seemed past counting. Calmly they sailed on without a thought of danger.

"Get out the whale-boat, Mr. Carter," intoned Gorham, quietly (he had been squinting through a night-glass). "The nearest vessel is a merchant brig! Now, Mr. Hurdiss," he added, turning to me and dropping his singsong for a moment, "take the carpenter and nine men, and board that brig. They're all asleep on her. Do it quietly, and fire no shot unless you have to. Here, take this cutlass—a slit throat stops a shout."

Almost before I knew it the whale-boat was ready, the men sitting on the thwarts with their cutlasses and pistols in their belts, and we had shoved off. I confess that I was trembling so from excitement that my breath came in short gasps, and I could not swallow to save my soul. The carpenter was sitting close to me on the gunwale.

"Old Smiler is going to see what that other chap is made of," he whispered, pointing to the faint glimmer a half a mile or so down the wind.

The last instructions I had received on leaving the *Yankee* were, if I took the vessel successfully, to douse all lights, make off to the eastward for an hour, and then crack on all sail, holding a course southwest-by-west. That would carry me, so I was told, clear of Lizard Head and out into the Atlantic, where Gorham would try to pick me up. The men, of their own accord, were taking quick, short strokes, with no noise in the rowlocks, that had been muffled with canvas strips. And in a few minutes we were under the stern of the vessel, that I made out to be a brig, as Gorham said. I could hear plainly the jarring of her spars as she rolled in the swell that we had felt for some time coming in from the wide sea.

The breeze was much lighter than it had been, and

we backed in under the stern, the better to row away if it were necessary. The man on the after-thwart caught the chains that run down to the rudder, and whispered back, "All's well!"

I stood up, and, straining my eyes, saw that within reach overhead was a row of four cabin windows; the second one on the left was open.

Thinking that it befitted my position best to be the first on board, I unshipped my belt, slipping one of the pistols inside my loose shirt, and then by standing on the shoulders of two men, I caught the combing of the window and wormed myself inside. I could see that I was in a fair-sized cabin, that a dim light came from a lantern hanging in a passageway forward; but my heart almost stood still after a tremendous thump against my ribs. There, not more than an arm's-length from me, I heard the sound of heavy breathing! Drawing the pistol from my bosom I stood still, peering to one side, with every muscle stiff as a harpstring.

CHAPTER XXXI

A CRUISE ON MY OWN ACCOUNT

As I hesitated, not knowing what to do, a line of sturdy fingers came over the edge of the cabin window; then a face appeared, and, seeing who it was, I leaned forward and laid hold of the carpenter by the back of his shirt to help him. He murmured something inarticulate, and I saw the reason why he could not get in through the window. He had his cutlass in his teeth, and I had to relieve him of it and do some powerful hauling before I had him inside lying on his back on the cabin deck. Then I closed my hand over his mouth, and, bending my head close to his, whispered: "Hush, for your life! There's a sleeping man within touch of us!"

But now the hilt of a second cutlass appeared at the window. I took it, and, enjoining silence on those below in the boat, the carpenter and I hauled in another man. We must have made some noise, but the deep breathing went on undisturbed until every man jack of us had come in through that window. But it was no place to hold a consultation. With my finger to my lips I stepped to the passageway, took down the lantern from its hook, and came back with it. The sleeper was snoring, and we saw that he was in a bunk behind a half-closed curtain. But now the reason for his sound rest was evident. As we pulled aside the cloth, ready to jump on him if he made a sound, we smelt the strong odor of rum, and perceived that the man had clasped in his arms a big black bottle, much in the way a child in a cradle might fall asleep with a doll.

"You can't wake *him*," said the carpenter, who was called "Chips" by the crew, and if I had not stopped him, I think he would have tweaked the sleeper's nose.

"One of you stay down here and guard him," I said. "Mr. Chips, you and those three men close the forward hatch. I and these five men will take care of the man at the wheel and the watch. Now, steady! Make no noise!"

They followed me out to the little passageway that led to the foot of the ladder, and I went up it softly. There were but two moving figures on deck—a man forward leaning with both elbows on the rail, and aft the binnacle light reflected on the face of an old sailor with a growth of long, white whiskers; his eyes were half closed, and his fingers were grasped tightly around the spokes. Followed by the men I had detailed, I jumped up on deck. The old seaman at the wheel made no outcry, for a visit from a boarding-party was probably the last thing he had in his mind. (He took us for some of the crew, he told us.) But when he looked at the handy little weapon that I poked under his nose, however, his jaw dropped, and without a word his legs gave way and he sat down backward on the deck.

In the meantime the carpenter had clapped a pistol to the head of the man leaning over the rail, two others found sleeping on the forward deck were held quiet in the same manner, and I heard the slam of the hatch with satisfaction.

I had command of the brig, without a word having been spoken above a breath!

I say I had command of the brig right enough, but there was to be a little trouble, after all, which came near to putting me out of the game altogether; but of that later.

In obedience to the plan, the light had been extinguished, the yards swung about, the helm put down, and we were steering northeast-by-east—going very slowly.

I was standing by the man at the wheel, trembling with the agitation of pent self-congratulation—I would have given a great deal to have relieved my feelings by a cheer—when I was startled by a sudden whisper.

"Who are you? Pirates?" asked a shaking voice at my side. I looked around. There stood the old sailor with his knees half bent, as if they refused to straighten.

"We're Yankee privateersmen," I returned, grinning at him.

"Much the same thing," he muttered — "pirates! What are you going to do with us?"

"Treat you kindly, if you make no noise," I answered, rather amused than otherwise.

This appeared to relieve the old man greatly. The carpenter now came aft.

"I've bucked and gagged the men I found on deck," he said. "You don't want to heave them overboard, do you?" he added, chuckling.

"For the Lord's sake, no!" I answered, quickly.

I had no time to find out whether the man was joking or not in asking this, for a flash of red fire tore out against the darkness less than a mile astern of us. Then a crash reached our ears. Some more flashes and reports in criss-cross, and then a burst of flame so bright that I could make out the outlines of a vessel from her lower yards to the water!

"For the love of Heaven, Mr. Hurdiss," cried the carpenter, "old Smiler has run afoul of a frigate, and no less! That's the end of him!"

As we learned afterwards, that broadside was the end of poor Captain Gorham, and the tight little *Yankee* also.

Poor Carter (at thought of him I groaned), he was never to see the baby face that was waiting for him, or to feel the loved arms about his neck again ; the little wife would watch in vain. And Silas ! A lump grew in my throat ; I was almost ready to pipe my eye, but one thing prevented—we soon had affairs of our own to look after.

The report of the first shot had caused something of a commotion below. I heard the sound of a cry and an oath, and, rushing to the head of the companion-ladder, I was almost knocked down by a great man who came up it on the jump. He was bleeding from a gash the full length of his face, but I recognized him as the one who had been asleep in the berth below.

"Demons ! Devils !" he shrieked, and, avoiding my grasp, he jumped for the side, and, before any one could prevent, went overboard head first, with a wild, unearthly scream !

I knew that a struggle must have taken place in the cabin, and, calling the carpenter to follow me, I jumped down the steps, and here is where the unexpected happened ! The lantern I had left there had been extinguished — all was pitch-dark, but I could hear a faint groaning to the right. I felt along the passageway with my hand, and as I extended it I touched something that moved ! At the same moment my wrist was caught in a tight grasp and a hand fumbled up my chest as if reaching for my throat !

"Who are you ? Answer, I say ! Who are you ?" muttered a voice, in unmistakable English accents.

For reply I laid hold of the reaching hand, and thus the strange man and I stood there close together—I could not reach my pistol, or I would have shot him.

"Who are you ?" he repeated, hoarsely.

I said nothing, but endeavored to wrench my hand free. The man, at this, began to shout.

"Ho, Captain Richmond, mutiny !" he cried, and threw his whole weight upon me, as if to bear me down.

"Ho, Richmond! You drunken fool, the men have risen!" he roared again.

I had wrestled with many of my fellow-prisoners at Stapleton, but I had never been against such a man as this heretofore. I almost felt my ribs go as he grasped me, but I got my hip against him, and we came down together, completely blocking up the passageway. I fumbled for my pistol, but could not reach it, and, taking me off my guard, the man shifted his grasp to my throat. I tried to evade it, but it was too late—I caught him by both wrists, and for a second managed to keep his thumbs from choking me.

"Get a light! A light!" I cried. "Help!—Hu—"

I had got my knee wedged in the pit of the man's stomach, and was pushing him with all my might, but even with this and the aid of my hands I could not break away. Gradually my breath stopped, lights flashed and danced before my eyes — I could feel my chest heaving as if my heart would come out of my body; then it seemed to me I heard an explosion far above me, and I knew no more.

When I drifted back to the sense of knowing that I was alive, it took me some minutes to haul in my ideas. At first I could not have told who I was, and for a long time my whereabouts was a puzzle to me. It might be the first question of any one to whom I should tell this, to ask why I did not speak, and thus find out the condition of affairs. But let me assure you I was doing my best to form words and sentences, and the only result was a whistling, wheezing sound in my throat. My voice was gone! At last I found strength to raise my hand, and I felt that I was in a box of some kind, and this puzzled me still more until I heard voices talking to one side of me, and I recognized Chips, the carpenter, saying:

"It was a quick funeral, Dugan! And how is the young gentleman?"

Then the whole situation came back to me clearly, and I knew where I was and all about it. I put out my other hand this time, pulled aside the curtains, and it was as I supposed; they had placed me in one of the cabin-bunks; it was the very one, by-the-way, in which the drunken captain had been sleeping.

"Well, sir," said the carpenter, "so you've come back to join us? It isn't every one who's been so near the last port, sir, and returned."

I tried to answer something, and it must have been an odd sight to have seen me sitting there dizzy and swaying, working my mouth without a sound forthcoming. Something was choking me — at last I made a motion; they understood that I wished a drink of water, and Dugan went to fetch it for me. It pained me much to swallow or to move my head; I can truly sympathize with any man who has been hanged!

They had put something in the drink, however, that made me feel a bit stronger, and I motioned for Chips to come close to me.

"Have we come about?" I whispered.

"Yes, captain," he replied, nodding his head and smiling encouragement, the way one addresses an invalid. "We came about some time ago, and are now holding a course southwest-by-west. Is that right, sir?"

I nodded. All I knew was that if we held this course long enough we would fetch up somewhere on the coast of the United States.

But the man's addressing me as "captain" pleased me. Yes, surely I was the prize-master of the brig, and the men looked to me to manage her. But I did not even know her name as yet, and there were many things that I wished to find out. So, taking Chips's arm, I made a sign telling him that I wished to go on deck.

"I thought you might like to know, sir," remarked the good fellow, "that this 'ere craft is worth savin';

she's got no end o' mill stuff and government stores aboard—much as we can make out."

The cabin had been lighted by the lantern hanging above our heads, and as we went down the passageway I saw that another light was coming from a small door that opened into a little closet-like space which contained two bunks. A horn lantern was suspended from the deck-beam, and a man with his head bound up in a bloody cloth was in the lower bunk.

"It's Fisher, the lad we left guarding the drunken skipper," said Chips, following my glance. "He was struck on the head with a bottle."

We were at the foot of the ladder, and I saw that it was from this place that the man with whom I had had the struggle had emerged. It was right here where I was standing that we had been fighting, and it was there we lay. I looked down and saw that the passageway had been lately slushed out, for a sopping-swab and a squilgee had been tossed in the corner.

"Where is he?" I asked.

The carpenter shrugged his shoulders. I understood with a shudder, and did not repeat the question—my ears still rang from the report of the pistol.

By the motion of the vessel I knew that the wind must be light, and glancing up as I came to the top of the ladder, I saw that the carpenter was well up in his business, and that in him I had an able lieutenant.

The brig had every stitch of canvas set, and despite the fact that she was very old-fashioned and bluff in the bows, we were making good headway, and rolling out two rippling waves that seethed and tumbled on either side of us.

It would soon be dawn. The sky was growing light in the east, and the glow was spreading every minute, so that I judged it must be in the neighborhood of four o'clock in the morning. I sat down on the edge of the cabin skylight and rested my elbows on my knees; and in that attitude I gave thanks that my life had been spared, and prayed that strength would be given to me to meet any danger that might come before me.

The dawning of a day is a very beautiful and holy thing to watch, especially at sea, with the red edge of the sun creeping slowly up against the horizon, and the expanding sense that one feels in his soul at the world's awakening. Had I a gifted pen, I should love to describe the sight I have seen so often—the growing of color in the water, from black to gray, from gray to green and blue; the red-tipped clouds, and all—but I shall not attempt it; I should fail. Even this day I noticed the beauty of it, but I began to worry about my throat (I was in great pain again), and wondered whether the pressure of the man's fingers had destroyed my larynx. But if I had lost power of speech, I knew that the carpenter would carry out my intentions, and that he probably could give the orders in much better fashion than I could. So it was not necessary for me to borrow trouble, although I hated to think of whispering for the rest of my existence.

Suddenly I thought of the prisoners penned in the forecastle, and I approached the carpenter, who was chatting with the man at the wheel, and asked him, with his ear at my lips, about them—whether he had held converse with them, and how many were they. He informed me that there were eight foremast hands and the second and third mates cooped up below, besides the old gran'ther we had found at the wheel. The only way they could get out was through the forward hatch, which he had nailed down. I walked to the bow with him, and saw that he had cut a square hole in the middle of the hatch-cover big enough to admit air and to permit of talking with those below. Half laughing, he leaned his face over the hole and shouted:

"HE LEANED HIS FACE OVER THE HOLE AND SHOUTED"

" Below there, ye Johnny Bulls!   How fares it?"

The reply was a chorus of cursing.   But at last one man succeeded in hushing the others, and I could hear his words distinctly.   He spoke with a strong Scotch burr.

"Who are ye?   Where are ye takin' us?" were the questions he asked.

"We're Yankees," answered Chips, "and you know that right well.   We're taking you for a trip to the land of liberty.   If you behave yourselves, and stop your low talk and your blaspheming, you'll have your grub in due time.   We're Christians."

There was no further conversation, and at this instant I was seized with a hemorrhage from my throat, and the carpenter insisted upon my turning in in the cabin, which I was not loath to do, as moving about seemed to start the blood.   I went below, and lay there all the morning, suffering not a little.   They brought me food, but I was unable to swallow it; and when I fell asleep at last, I was awakened in a few minutes, it seemed to me, by Chips touching me on the shoulder.

"It's near meridian, Captain Hurdiss," he said. "Hadn't you better take a squint at the sun?   The wind is getting up a bit, too, sir," he said, "and the glass has fallen."

I endeavored to get to my feet, but the motion started the trouble in my throat, and I fell back weakly.

"Never mind; you'd better keep to your bunk," said the carpenter.   "To-morrow you'll be up and about, I'll warrant.   I'll leave this bottle for you, sir."

I detected an anxious look in his face, however, as he handed me a glass of water and spirits.   Again I fell asleep, and awoke some time late in the afternoon, feeling much better.

The brig had a great motion on her, and every plank and timber was groaning and creaking.   I took a sip

out of the bottle, that was wedged in the corner of the
bunk, and although it scalded and burned me, it seemed
to give me strength, and I crawled out, and, stumbling
to the foot of the ladder, made my way up on deck.
The sky had grown black and angry. We were on the
starboard tack under reefed top-sails, and everything was
wet with flying spray. The *Duchess of Sutherland*, for
that was the brig's name, belonged to an era of ship-
building when they believed that every breeze must
blow over a vessel's stern, I should think. The way
she kept falling off was a caution. She appeared to go
as fast sideways as she did ahead, and such a pounding
and thumping as she made of it I have never seen
equalled. Most of the crew were on deck, and one of
them, a fine seaman named Caldwell, saw me standing
holding on to the hatch combing. He came up, touching his forehead in salute.

"She's a bug of a ship, Captain Hurdiss," he said.

I nodded, and glanced up at the aged, time-seamed
masts.

"It won't pay to carry much more sail, sir," the man
continued, as if in suggestion.

I beckoned him to put his head close to mine, and
gave an order to take in the foresail, for it was holding
us back more than helping us. Caldwell bawled out
the order, and jumped with the rest to obey it. I felt
so weak that once more I sought the cabin. I took a
glance at the barometer as I went by, and saw that it
was still falling—that we were in for a hard blow or a
storm I did not doubt.

But the rolling and tumbling increased, and the groaning and complaining of the timbers led me to believe
that the old craft was working like a basket, which was
exactly what she was doing. Suddenly she gave a lurch
so hard and sharp to port that I was almost spilled out
of the bunk, and, fear giving me strength, I crawled up

on deck on all fours.   The man at the wheel was doing his best to bring the brig's head up in the wind, the fore-staysail had blown out and was tearing into streamers, the men on the forecastle were gathering, ready to cut away the foremast, and I heard a wail from the prisoners below.

It looked as if we were bound to capsize, but at this moment something carried away aloft, and we righted. But the storm was upon us ; the tops of the seas scudded along the surface like drifting snow ; there was a fiendish howling in the rigging—I motioned with my hand for the helmsman to swing her off.   He understood, and soon we were before it, scudding under bare poles tow-ards the north.   Even then the *Duchess* made very bad weather of it, yawing and plunging badly.   Caldwell, whom I had appointed second mate, came up to me.

" It's safer to run, captain," he said, shouting in my ear.   "Go below, sir ; Chips and I will keep the deck."

As I could be of no use, I took his advice, and crawled into the bunk again, trying to assure myself that all was well.

It had grown very dark, although it was but seven o'clock, and I had lain there but a half-hour or so, hold-ing my breath every now and then as we gave a deeper plunge than usual, when the carpenter came rushing in.   Even in the dim light I could see the terror in his blanched face—his whole frame was trembling.

"God help us, captain !" he said, in a hoarse whisper. " I've just sounded the well, sir, and there's three feet of water in the hold—   Did you feel that ?   'Tis all she can do to work up out of a sea !"

CHAPTER XXXII

WRECKED AGAIN

I WAS almost stunned at the news the carpenter brought, and hastened out, making for the ladder—dizzy from sheer fright.

"Hush—wait!" cried Chips, as we entered the passageway—"there, you can hear it!"

I defy any one to tell of a more terrifying sound!

"Rig the pumps, and get to work at them," I squeaked, faintly.

"Aye, aye, sir," he answered, "but it will do no good. Lord Harry! she's opened up like a sieve, sir!"

The men were already, under Dugan's direction, shipping the brakes, and soon we had the water from below pouring on to the deck and running into the scuppers and mingling with that that came on board of us over the rail. But the wind increased in strength until it seemed that it would take the aged masts out of the brig, and it actually threatened to blow the clothes from off our backs.

Chips had gone to sound the well again, and I was holding on to a belaying-pin, and trying not to show how weak and fear-sick I was. Noticing that one of the men, a narrow-headed fellow with an ugly gash of a mouth, was not putting all of the beef he might into his stroke on the pump-handles, I slid over to him and laid hold myself; but the man endeavored to push me to one side.

"Hands off, Captain Jonah," he snarled; "it might

stop working! We had plenty of good luck until you came aboard of us. Hands off, I say!" he cried. "or we'll feed you to the whales."

I could have struck the man for his insolence; his words had been heard by two of the men opposite, and I saw that the result might be bad for me, so I replied nothing, but taking a firmer hold of the beam, I wedged him out of his position, ready at any moment to fell him if he attempted violence. I was the stronger, and at last I broke his hold. Where the force I now felt command of came from I cannot imagine. The man would have slid over against the bulwarks if I had not caught him by the shoulder.

"Go over on the other side and work, you shirker," I cried, and, to my surprise, my voice roared out the words in tones like those of a bull!

I gave him a push up the slope of the deck, and began heaving up and down with all my might and main.

But I had made a discovery. It was only my lower tones, my demi-voix, that were gone! For three days afterwards this phenomenon continued. If I wished to talk, I had to use the full lung-power that I possessed, and the result was a sound that would do credit to a boatswain's mate in a typhoon. It was as unlike my former voice as a broadside to the pop of a pistol—but I am wandering.

The effect of my treatment of the insolent sailor had been marvellous—not a disrespectful glance was cast at me thereafter. Soon the carpenter came up from below.

"We may have gained some three or four inches, captain, but no more," he panted, laying hold alongside of me. "I think the water is getting in forward too, sir," he added. "Can't you feel how she settles now and again?"

"Get out some of the prisoners and man the forecastle pump!" I roared at him.

He jumped at the odd sound of my voice, but made no remarks, and scrambled to the hatch in a jiffy.

"Four of you up out of that!" he cried through the hole, at the same time battering away at the fastenings with a belaying-pin. The hatch was flung open, and instead of four, all ten of the Britishers came rushing to the deck. They probably had been dying of terror down below, and one glance at us working away for dear life told them the condition of affairs.

Without a word they set to work, under the orders of their own officers, to get the spare gear out of the way and start the forecastle pump going.

The carpenter soon reported from the hold that we had gained some four inches, and were now holding our own. This was at the end of an hour's work by all hands.

I perceived, however, that it would be foolishness to work all the men to death at the outset, and that the sensible way would be to divide them into relays, even if the water gained a little on us.

So I told off my own men into two divisions, and sent half of them into the galley to get rest and a bite to eat. But the prisoners I drove at it, as we had fully two hours' start of them. They needed no encouragement yet, and one of them even replied, "Aye, aye, sir," to my orders to hit up the stroke.

All night we worked away, and the gray dawn found us still at it.

Fisher, the wounded man, I had mounted guard over the prisoners, arming him with a cutlass and a brass blunderbuss that I had found in the mate's room. I hated to goad men the way I had to, but I think my own people worked almost as hard, and needed less urging; the Englishmen, even though they had made some arrangement by which they spelled themselves in their work, had begun to fag, and lobbed their heads up and down at every stroke.

By noon the sea had gone down, and, probably owing to the swelling of the timbers, the leak had decreased. We had gained a foot and more on the water in the hold, and the carpenter found out that it was as he suspected—the water had been entering through a started seam ; and he said that if we could get to anchor, he thought he might be able to locate where it was. So I ordered all but four of the prisoners below. At first one of the mates demurred ; but I would admit of no talking, and at the sight of the pistols he obeyed me.

Now the great question was to find out where we were. By two o'clock I made sail, and seeing that the old barky did better with the wind astern, I ordered the helmsman to steer the same course we had been holding, and then I went below to rest.

I slept like a top—the sleep of sheer exhaustion—and it was six o'clock when Dugan ran in and awakened me, telling me that land was in sight off the starboard bow, distant about twelve miles.

But where were we?

I had some idea of our position when the storm had struck us, and I presumed that we must either, from the course we were steering, have entered the Irish Channel or gone up the west coast of Ireland itself ; but it mattered little ; we had to find some place to anchor, and, if possible, to repair our damage, and besides, I intended to land the prisoners at the first chance, as they were a constant source of menace to us, and so many more mouths to feed.

Coming on deck, I took the glass and climbed into the foremast-shrouds.

What an odd circumstance it was ! Here I was a full-fledged captain, and had never been aloft on a vessel above the futtock-shrouds but once before in my life, and that was when I had covered myself with tar and glory by climbing to the cross-trees of one of the ships at the wharves of Baltimore. But I went up as far as the topsail-yard, hanging on harder than was necessary, perhaps, and from there I took a sight at the distant land. I made it out to be a collection of islands, with what might be the mainland farther on to the north. After I descended to the deck I changed the course a few points to the east, and in a little over two hours we had brought a high, rocky shore close to on the port beam. It was an island, as I had surmised.

The sky had now cleared to a glorious red sunset, and I could discern the conformation of the shore. Two arms ran out to the eastward, and—a remarkable sight! —I saw that the island was split in two by a narrow crevice, and that on the southern point it dwindled down into a narrow spit, at the end of which rose a sheer rock like a tremendous castle.

The carpenter had started the lead, with the result of finding no bottom until we were well within the water embraced by the extending arms. At last he reported suddenly fifteen fathoms; at the next heave, thirteen; at the next, eight, then six; and seeing that it was shoaling so rapidly, I feared to go in nearer, so we hove to and let go our anchor.

The water was as smooth as a carpet, and with the stopping of the strain and working of the hull, the leak ceased pouring in, the carpenter reporting, after a trip to the hold with the lantern, that she was only weeping a little along her inner skin. I had kept four of the prisoners at the pumps, however, and now I called every one, and in an hour's time we had her nearly dry.

Ordering the Englishmen back to where they belonged, but thanking them for the good services they had done, Caldwell and I took the first anchor watch, and the rest turned in to sleep.

The huge shadow of the rocky cliff enshrouded us, and in the rear of the black silhouette of the island I could see the pale greenish blue of the sky in the west, with a few stars twinkling through it, and myriads of them gleaming in the deeper blue overhead. It was so peaceful and calm, and in such contrast to the scenes that we had been through, that were it not for the pain I still suffered I could have felt almost joyous, until I thought of that broadside in the dark of the night, and of Chips's exclamation—"The last of the *Yankee!*" War! what a horrid thing it was! The sudden hurling of men into the great unknown—men unprepared, and, perhaps, unfit to die!

This was a peculiar notion to enter the mind of a man who had chosen to act the way I had; I don't know why I harbored it, except that it has come, I suppose, to many men in moments of calm reflection — to be forgotten with the next excited heart-beat. Every now and then I would cast a look up at the sparkling firmament, and wonder if in those distant worlds they had such goings-on. I intended to keep awake, but Nature asserted herself, and, lying there sprawled on the deck, I fell asleep.

I awakened with a start, to find it was daylight. I noticed that Caldwell must have succumbed after I did, for he had rolled up his jacket and placed it as a pillow beneath my head. But the honest fellow had given in at last, and there he was, snoring away on the top of the forward hatch, with his arms and legs straggled out like a jumping-jack on the floor of a play-room.

Now if what had happened before this calmly dawning day appears strange or improbable to any one who may read, and if they are tired of the relation of these facts, which, I can say without boasting, are unusual to have happened to any one being, let them lay aside for good and all the reading of what is to follow. "Le vrai peut quelque fois n'être pas vraisemble." For what has previously happened is nothing to what I am going to tell, in my opinion, as I am a truthful man.

I shook Caldwell gently, and told him to go down and stir out the man who was doing the cooking for us, and have him brew some coffee and prepare breakfast. We had some fresh vegetables still left, for the *Duchess of Sutherland* had not been long from port when we had taken her.

Then, all alone, I gazed at the island in whose little bay we were resting.

A narrow stretch of beach ran from the foot of the cliff to the water's edge. The top was verdure-clad, and to the north some stunted underbrush grew along the crest. The strange crevice that I had noticed ran from the green slope, sheer and straight, to within twenty feet of the water's level. It looked as if it might have been made by the stroke of a giant's sword. The high rock at the end of the tongue of land to the southward resembled, in the slanting, moving light, more closely than ever a moss-grown ruin; but all at once I jumped for the glass. A thin, twirling column of smoke arose from a little hollow a quarter of a mile up the shore. By the aid of a telescope I could make out two or three huts, and some gray objects on the slope of the hill that resolved themselves into grazing sheep. I made up my mind, before I landed the prisoners and set to work stopping the seams, to row in and find out where we were. But the smell of cooking coming from the galley reminded me that with the exception of some sopped biscuit and a bit of fat meat that I had managed to worry down the night past, nothing solid had passed my lips since my struggle with the man in the passageway.

Running below, I asked the carpenter in to breakfast

with me in the cabin. He was my first lieutenant, as
I have said, and of course I knew, without his saying so,
that he had saved my life—with my own pistol, too, I
surmise ; but we never spoke of this.

"Well, Captain Hurdiss," Chips said, "a busy day's
before us. I think if we can careen the old hooker and
get that opened strake so we can handle it from the outside, we can take her across, bar another such storm as
we had last night."

"We'll make a try for it, Mr. Chips," said I, roaring
out the answer after two or three futile attempts to
speak quietly.

"You won't need a trumpet this voyage, sir," was the
rejoinder to this, at which I laughed, for the hot coffee
and food were restoring my spirits.

The men, too, were in an even frame of mind, and
when I ordered out the boat they went about it like
good ones. I saw that the prisoners were fed before I
left the deck, and then going over the side, I gave the
orders, man-of-war fashion, to "Shove off !" "Let fall !"
etc., and after a pull of a few minutes the carpenter and
I landed on the beach near the hollow in which the huts
were, and, finding a path, we ascended to them.

As we approached the door of the largest hovel, that
was built of sods and stones, a nondescript figure, with
just enough rags on to save it from appearing savage,
emerged. The man appeared a little frightened at first,
and was truly startled at the sound of my voice. His
reply I could not translate, although I had merely asked
him what island this was, and what was the name of the
coast that we could discern to the eastward.

At last, by dint of signs and repeating the question, I
made out something that sounded like "Ennishkea,"
and when I pointed to the island to the north the same
answer came. When the land to the eastward was des-
ignated he said "Muhllet à Blackshod" over and over.

I gave him a bit of silver, and the meaning of that he understood quite well, for he grinned and closed his fist tight upon it, at the same time giving a pull to his long front lock, and looking up at me knowingly out of his monkey eyes. I never heard such outlandish lingo in my life as the man spoke, but I remembered the sounds of some of the words, and when I got back to the ship I went into the cabin, and the carpenter and I got out the map that showed the coast of Ireland, for Chips insisted that the man was talking Gaelic, and that it was either Ireland or Scotland whose shore lay off to the eastward.

"Hurrah! hurrah!" I cried, suddenly, my attention arrested by a name. "Here we are, Mr. Chips! The island of Inniskea — and off here is the peninsula of Mullet that encloses the waters of Blacksod Bay."

So I knew where I was at last!

But there was lots to be done. Arming the crew, we took the fastenings off the hatch, and ordered the prisoners into the boat. We left them on shore with a barrel of ship's bread and a half-barrel of salt meat. And then we rowed back, and prepared to do some impromptu calking, and fit the old hulk in a better condition for putting to sea.

The *Duchess of Sutherland* was loaded with machinery for some sort of crushing business, and the rest of her cargo was cheap cloths and print-stuffs, probably for the East Indian market. According to her papers, she was bound for Calcutta.

The seam that had done most of the leaking was hardly a foot beneath the surface of the water as she lay on even keel, we discovered. It had opened up badly forward, and again amidships — so we set about lightening her first before we hove her down.

Rigging a block and tackle, we jettisoned some heavy bits of machinery, and found that the cargo had been very badly and loosely stowed.

" DOWN WENT THE *DUCHESS OF SUTHERLAND* LIKE A LITTLE
ROYAL GEORGE"

The brig—she had been outfitted in a hurry—carried four guns, short carronades of heavy weight. on her deck, and we shifted these to starboard side, and then we rigged out an anchor at the end of a spar; and I was surprised to see what a purchase we got on her, and how well all this answered for our ends. As soon as they could, the carpenter and the crew set about calking her with hemp from an old cable, whistling and humming away merrily.

They progressed finely with the job, and as there was nothing for me to do, I went aloft. I could smell the tar that they were boiling in the galley, and was hoping that we could finish our work in time to get under way that evening, when all at once I felt a jar, as if the vessel had struck something below, and it appeared to me that we heeled a little more to port.

In fact, our list was very heavy now, and the masts had quite an angle on them. I saw that the carpenter, who was standing in a boat alongside, had stopped work, and was looking curiously up at me. The seam at which he had been tapping was three feet and more above the surface of the water, and the ripped green copper of the brig's bottom was plain to view.

The carpenter laid his head against the side, and then shouted up, in a frightened voice :

"For Heaven's sake, Captain Hurdiss, there's water entering somehow !"

He and the men in the boat hastily scrambled up the side.

Just then there came another jarring sound. It was the cargo shifting.

I was hastening to descend, sick at the news, when I cast a glance towards the shore, and there I saw one of the prisoners, whom I had noticed standing on the top of the hill, suddenly wave his arms about his head, and come tearing down the slope towards where the others were grouped about a fire.

But this was not all. Through the cleft in the hill-side I could see the waters on the other side of the island. And in this narrow space, framed by the walls of the cliff, I saw a vessel just coming about in the wind! Another instant and she was gone, hidden by the dark mass of land. But so vividly impressed was this quick vision upon my mind that I can see it to this day, as firmly fixed as were it a painting that I had studied in its every detail.

As I reached the deck the brig gave another lurch, and our bulwarks were almost in the water.

" The cargo's all adrift, Captain Hurdiss!" shouted the carpenter, jumping up the ladder. "And we must have a bad leak in our top sides. The old tub is rotten to her heart," he added. "Don't stop for anything; she'll turn turtle in a minute!"

The two men in the dinghy had pulled off to some distance, and were calling on the others to hasten.

Now the rest, without orders, were tumbling into the boats, and even with my small experience I could see that nothing could save the *Duchess* from sinking where she lay. I looked towards the shore, and saw the prisoners in a body running up the beach towards the north. Just as I caught sight of them, they rounded a point of rock and disappeared.

But a strange shifting motion in the brig warned me not to tarry. What impelled me, I do not know, but seeing the glass wedged in the shrouds where I had planted it, I made for it, and, picking it up, jumped into the boat.

We had rowed but a few dozen strokes when, with a lurch, and a dull explosion as the forward deck blew out from the pressure of air, down went the *Duchess of Suth-erland*, like a little *Royal George*. But the only living things she took with her were a few half-drowned chickens in a coop near the galley!

Even the carpenter now showed signs of despondency, and what I told him about the vessel that looked like a great lugger with one mast, that I had seen on the other side of the land, did not cheer him.

"We're in for it now," he grumbled. "There's no prize-money in this affair. She's one of the King's cutters, and she'll scoop us surely."

"That's what the prisoners were scampering for," spoke up Dugan, who was pulling stroke-oar. "They've gone around to fetch her."

"Well, that's all they'll find," said Chips, pointing over the stern of the boat.

I looked back. Only a few feet of the *Duchess's* masts were visible, but there was a lot of débris floating on the water near them.

Dugan made the following observation: "That's the quickest move she's made for a long time, messmates. I'll wager money on't. 'Where are we going now?' as the pirate said when he walked the plank."

No one answered a word. The crew sat there in despair. My heart turned to lead in my bosom. What next to do?

CHAPTER XXXIII

A SURPRISE PARTY

"COME, lads," I cried, at last, "avast cursing ; don't give up! Give way together. We'll make for that old castle rock, and go ashore."

The dinghy was a few strokes ahead of us, and in a few minutes we had beached both boats in a little cove hardly twenty feet across. I had an idea in my mind of leading the crew to the top of the rock, for it appeared to me that five or six men from the summit could hold a score or more at bay with nothing but stones for weapons. A long resistance would have been out of the question.

But to my astonishment I saw that the spit of land which ran out to the tall rock was not more than thirty feet in width, and that it was rounded, as if at some time the sea had washed over it. Dugan and Chips had followed me up the slope. When we reached the top, which was not more than ten feet above the beach, we could see the cutter plainly. Through the glass I made out she had come to anchor, and that they were loading some casks into a boat alongside of her.

I handed the glass to the carpenter, who was next to me, and asked him to take a look through it.

"They're going ashore for water," he replied; "and mark my words, we'll soon be prisoners on board that toy thing. There's a fine wind-up to a lucky cruise, messmates."

We sat there and talked for a few minutes, but nothing was suggested that was any use considering.

Caldwell had picked up the glass, and had levelled it at the cutter again.

"Halloa!" he cried, suddenly, "there are the prisoners on the beach. Now let's see what they're going to do. I wonder if they'll think it is a Yankee trick," he added, with a half chuckle—"scuttling that rotten old junk?"

I took the glass from him without answering, for I saw no humor in the situation. A boat put off from the cutter and brought back two of the men from shore, and now, hidden behind a rock, we watched the proceedings in turn. The idea of getting water was apparently abandoned all at once.

The boat rowed to shore again, picked up the rest of the Englishmen, and then I saw that they were getting out the quarter-boat from the other side.

In a few minutes both were loaded down with men. I caught the glint of steel as they handed muskets and cutlasses into them, and then they pulled off to the northward to go around the farther end of the island, some of the ex-prisoners running apace with them along the shore.

But an idea had seized me that set my blood tingling!

"How many men does such a craft as that carry?" I croaked, hoarsely.

"Twenty-five to thirty," responded Chips, sullenly.

It had fallen dead calm; the smooth waves broke lazily against the rocks and the strip of beach, but not a breath of wind was stirring. I had counted twenty men besides the prisoners in the two boats that had put off from the cutter. It would take probably two hours to row around to the north shore of the island.

Surely it would do no harm to broach the subject in my mind to the others, and I did so in a few short words, speaking in hoarse whispers.

"Why not roll one of our boats across the neck of

land, and then row down and take the cutter by surprise?"

I did not know how this plan would be received, but when I finished they were looking at me eagerly.

"Captain, Lord love ye, I admire ye!" cried Dugan.

Chips grasped my hand.

"By Solomon! we can do it, sir!" he sniggered, and we hurried across to where the men were seated, a dejected-looking group, on the sand.

In twenty minutes the boats from the cutter were out of sight around the north shore cape, and we set to work getting the largest of our own over the barrier.

We pulled out the plug from the dinghy, filled her with stones, and let her sink.

Then we broke up the spare oars into rollers, and in five minutes, or a little over, we had made a launching of the small gig on the western shore.

I took a final squint through the glass, and could see no one on the deck of the cutter. Smoke was coming from a little funnel near the bow, and I judged that whoever were left on board had gone below for their mid-day meal.

The men muffled their oars with their shirts, and, with a sensation of hunters stalking some dangerous animal, we rowed slowly along against the tide. Truly it was like as if the quarry were asleep, and we feared awakening it before we got within striking distance. Every one breathed as silently as possible.

Now we were right under her stern, and I read the name, "*Bat*," in gold letters.

She was a tidy little craft, more like a gentleman's yacht than a vessel of war, and from three small ports on her sides poked the muzzles of brass six-pounders.

It was but the hoist of a foot to get on board; and, behold! there was no one there to receive us! But we had no arms; and, picking up a handspike and handing

"'SURRENDER!' I CRIED"

it to the carpenter, I led the way down the little hatch, followed by the other eight men, with only their closed fists for weapons.

Now if any two people were surprised it was the two Irish sailors who sat there eating with their knives from tin plates they held on their knees.

"Surrender!" I cried, pointing the telescope at them as if I had but to touch a trigger to blow out their brains, and before they knew what had happened, or could raise their voice, two of the privateersmen had them pinioned by their wrists.

"Cut that cable; make all sail and get out of this!" I roared, pushing up again.

The jib and foresail went chock-a-block with one heave. Never did men leap to their work so quickly.

Now as it was but a stone's-throw to the shore, I ordered the two sailors overboard into the water, and gave them one of the empty casks to help them make it safely. They were glad of the chance to go.

The main-sail was up by this time, the rope hawser had been severed by the blow of an axe, and we were making out to sea! The crew, all on deck, burst into three hearty cheers, and I led them, with tears almost rolling down my cheeks! "Is this actually happening? Can it all be true?" quoth I to myself, over and over. The men looked dazed, as if they doubted the evidence of their senses.

I wonder if the Britishers thought it a Yankee trick?

I did not leave the deck to make any investigations of the little sloop until we had covered some five miles, and the unreality of the situation had begun to wear away. I had found out that she sailed like a witch and that there was no sail after us, and so breathed more naturally and was minded to investigate. I do not know what burden the cutter was, but although she drew little water, she

18

was most seaworthy; and, a strange thing, her top-mast was set abaft the mast-head, something the carpenter had never seen before. I found out since that all the old "king's cutters" were rigged that way.

There was barely head room in her forecastle, and I was surprised to find that even I, tall as I was, could stand upright in the cabin, which was well aft.

This cabin was very handsomely furnished, with a long couch down one side, a handsome table under a fine swinging lamp in the centre, and a desk with many drawers off in a corner, lighted by a handsome sconce. A number of books were thrown about on the couch, and suspended from hooks against the white panels were a half-dozen beautifully executed miniatures; the door to a little cupboard was open, and I saw, hanging up inside, a number of uniforms.

I walked over to the desk and picked up a leather-covered volume that had "Log-book of the *Bat*" on the cover in red letters, very beautifully done. I turned to the first page. It started:

"A journal kept on board H. M. Revenue Cutter *Bat*, of four guns, commanded by Lieutenant *John Deerhurst*, R. N."

Near by was a letter just begun, and broken off short:

"DEAR COUSIN,—I wish some one else had this boat. I—"

Here it stopped.

The few words seemed so comical, under the extraordinary circumstances, that I burst into a roar of laughter. I had to take but one step up the little ladder to have my head above the level of the deck. Standing there I called Chips to me, and showed him the entry in the book and the unfinished epistle.

"It's witchcraft," he said, "and nothing less. You'll have to write an answer to that, sir, when we get to the other side."

The *Bat* was a little bit larger than our single-gun boats, and perfectly able to go across the Atlantic, or to sail anywhere, provided her provisions held out. We found by an inspection of the hold that there was more than enough to last ten men for a month and a few days over, although we would have to go light in the drinking line.

At once Chips and I set about preparing a routine. The crew were divided into watches, and I laid out a course that would fetch us in the vicinity of Boston.

On we sailed; everything was fine. For three days I had a most delightful experience, reading the well-chosen books in the cabin, and seeing that the men were kept employed polishing the brass-work and overhauling the forward hold, and so forth; for we scarcely had to trim a sail.

On the fourth day the fine breeze, that had held from the same direction almost continually, stopped as suddenly as if it had been shut off by the intervention of a great wall.

Before long a slight wind came out of the west, dead against us, the sea got up, and at five bells a large ship was seen coming down before the wind with all sail set. I swung upon the opposite tack to that I had been holding, and at this the large vessel changed her course, evidently intending to speak me. There was no way of my escaping, for if I had started to run she would have overhauled us in two hours. I could see her ports and make out she was a 44-gun frigate. At Chips's suggestion I got out the signal-book that I had found, and the little flags also, hoping that this would be all that it would amount to if she proved to be English.

"Jingo! she may be Yankee, and at any rate we're out-pointing her now," Caldwell remarked, eagerly breaking a long silence.

"Don't crow," answered Chips.

I looked around for an instant: my men looked very uncomfortable, and most of them un-English, in their wide striped jackets. Dugan—just the sort of Irishman to be found in every forecastle: a combination of wit, butt, and general fun-maker—had said something or other that had caused laughter, for our spirits rose at the prospect of escape. I had to call him sharply to order—the frigate was so near that I was afraid the gentleman with the glass would notice any unusual hilarity. He and I had been staring each other out of countenance over our respective rails for some minutes as his vessel drew swiftly upon us. The stranger was very curious to find out who we were, and intended to come close. And talk of nervous work! I grew so on edge that I almost wished he would fire a broadside—anything rather than this silent, suspicious approach. Alas! we could not weather him!

Soon the hail came: "What cutter is that?"

I answered, mumbling my words.

"What are you doing out here?" was the next question.

For an instant I was nonplussed. "Chasing a Yankee privateer," I replied, with an air of bravado.

"Where is she?"

"Got away to the south'ard."

"I'll send a boat on board of you."

This was exactly what I did not wish to happen. "Don't trouble, sir. I'll come on board of you myself," I replied, at the same time ordering out the only boat we had left, a little dinghy swung over the stern.

"Now, Chips," said I, as the good fellow came up pale but resolute, "this is a case of 'must obey.' We are edging up to windward, and it's going to thicken. If you can get away, do so; but be cautious. You know the cost of blundering—I leave it all to you. Get up to windward without exciting suspicion, and if you don't hear from me in two hours, clear away for home. No, better: get **the** windward-gage, and if you hear **a** pistol-shot, **or see** a handkerchief flutter overboard, clear out."

I saw that my reference to the pistol might have given a wrong notion, so I hastened to add: " I shall fire in the air, just for a signal; pray don't think I intend to take the ship all by myself, or do anybody harm."

This conversation was held under the lee of the frigate; in fact, we were so close to her that she shadowed us completely, and although we were both hove to, I knew that we could swing off before she could get the weather-gage. I feared doing this myself, but I hoped that my coming on board would disarm all suspicion, and that Chips might be able to carry out the plan.

From the southwest a fog-bank was approaching—I had made note of it—and the air was filled already with fine particles of moisture. It was no easy job to bring the little dinghy alongside. But we were able to do so handsomely, thanks to the good oarsmanship of Caldwell, and at last I grasped the rope-ladder that had been lowered from the gangway and came up on deck. The boatswain shrilled his whistle, and the side-boys touched their caps. A fine-looking officer stepped forward to meet me, saluting, and extending his hand.

"Your name, sir?" he inquired, looking at me keenly.

It would not do to hesitate. I was running risks, of course, but no half-way measures would suffice.

"John Hurdiss, lieutenant, commanding the cutter *Bat*," I replied. I had intended to make use of the name "Deerhurst," but my own had leaped to my lips involuntarily. A sick feeling came over me.

"Will you come with me to my cabin, Mr. Hurdiss? I'm Captain Mallet, of this vessel, the *Cæsar*."

I followed him at once. All the officers were regarding me with the greatest curiosity—I heard them whispering.

"Isn't it rather a strange thing for you to be in this latitude and longitude, when your station is on the coast?" the captain continued. "It may not be my province to demand an answer, but I think it would be best for you to let me have one."

"Why, most certainly, sir," I replied. "I don't think you will judge it so strange when you understand the circumstances." And forthwith I began a story of how I had chased a small Yankee privateer for the last three days, and that she had given me the slip but the night before. I went into so many details that I consumed some time in telling this marvellous story; but the captain was not satisfied.

"I shall make a report of this affair, and it shall be looked into," he said. "Go back on board your vessel, and return to your cruising-grounds."

I was sorely tempted to ask what business all this was of his, but I held my tongue, and we went on deck together. The fog-bank was all about us. The *Bat* was nowhere to be seen! I could not help showing my impatience. A gun was fired, and then another, and a third, but there was no response; of course not. I could imagine her with all sail set, pointing off to the west, safe and free!

I made up my mind to give her a good start before I declared myself. Soon I would be a prisoner, but perhaps there would be a little amusement. All eyes were upon me, and in the group of officers I noticed an old man in civilian's clothes. He was a distinguished-looking figure, and I overheard some one address him as Mr. Middleton.

"Middleton?" I repeated to myself. "Where have I heard that name before?" I could not place it, but somehow it had stayed in my recollection.

"What's the explanation of this, Mr. Hurdiss?" asked Captain Mallet, folding his arms and stepping in front of me. "Where's your vessel, sir?"

I shrugged my shoulders.

"That's more than I can tell you," I replied.

Just as I spoke there came the sound of a shot off to windward!

"There's my vessel," I continued. "Might I ask you to set me on board of her? I fear my little cockboat has gone astray."

"You shall consider yourself ordered on board your vessel, sir, with instructions to report to your superior at Dublin at once, to whom you will give this letter. I will take the responsibility of insisting on this."

"Are you bound there yourself, sir?" I questioned, respectfully, but still with an assumption of injured dignity.

"We are bound to Portsmouth," Captain Mallet answered, curtly, and he gave orders to one of the junior officers to call away the second cutter.

Scarcely had the boatswain finished shrilling the call on his whistle when the old gentleman in citizen's dress spoke up.

"As Dublin is my destination, Sir John, would it be possible for us to be transferred to this young gentleman's vessel? It would save us much time and trouble."

"I cannot order him to take you," replied the captain, "but if he chooses—"

The old man looked at me.

"There are two of us," he began. "We are anxious to reach Ireland. If you would do us the favor—"

I was anxious to get away without more parleying, as the boat was now rocking at the foot of the ladder. In fact, I feared that the *Bat* might have mistaken the intent of the gun and made off. But in this I maligned the gallant man who was acting as my lieutenant. The

firing had not frightened him—he had waited for that
pistol-shot! While there was a chance for my returning
he would not have deserted me.

"Our quarters are not so large as those of the frigate,"
I began.

"I hope that this is not asking too much," Mr. Middleton put in, earnestly, interrupting before I had finished.
"We are just from Halifax. If you only knew— Wait
till I consult for half a moment—just pardon me."

He hurried off.

"I'd rather not take any passengers; but I'll stand by,
Sir John," I said, turning to Captain Mallet, "and get
ready to receive them, if they wish to come. It is best
that they should be dissuaded, sir, if possible; we are
cramped for room." It was anything to get away—the
strain upon me had been something awful.

"It is as Mr. Middleton says. Would you refuse to
take him?"

"I think I could make him comfortable," I said, "if
you will allow me to row off and bring my vessel up
while he is getting his belongings, sir."

"Keep within hailing distance, Mr. Hurdiss."

"Very good, sir."

I descended the ladder, jumped into the boat, and
gave the orders to pull out into the fog. When we had
gone some four or five hundred yards, I made a trumpet
of my hands, and shouted:

"Oh, Mr. Chips! Where are you? *Bat* ahoy!"

"Here we are, sir!" came the reply close to us.

In another moment we were alongside, and the carpenter, in the uniform of a British quartermaster, helped
me on board.

"Mr. Chips," I whispered, hurriedly, "it is supposed
that we are bound for Dublin."

"It is a roundabout way we'll take to get there, sir,"
he said, grinning. "I bet Dugan you'd come back, sir."

"Never mind as to **that**." I answered. "Make all sail as soon as that boat leaves us, and let us **get out of** this."

"Aye, **aye, sir**. I don't like that big bully off there, and I'll be glad to lose her."

As he was speaking he was crowding the tiller over, and the *Bat* was getting her nose around to the west.

This manœuvre was interrupted by an unforeseen circumstance: the wind shifted a trifle—at the wrong moment, too.

"Hold hard, sir!" ejaculated Chips, suddenly, with a grumbled oath, "there's a boat close alongside of us." He crowded the tiller over just as we were about to get the wind on the larboard tack. **The result** was that we hung there in stays for an **instant**, and then slowly fell off again to our previous course.

I had been hugging myself with delight at the prospect of once more being free, and out of the depressing proximity **of** the frigate. With my hands jammed deep into the pockets of the Hon. Deerhurst's storm-coat, and the big cocked-hat pulled down to the top of **the** gold-laced collar, I had been prancing up and down on tiptoe like a youngster pleased with himself and his prospects, and now to be called upon to face disappointment made me more angry than anything else.

The gloom of the fog had been deepened by the dusk of evening, **and as** I turned I could just make out the great shape of the *Cæsar* to leeward.

"On board **the** cutter there!" hailed a voice astern of us, "here **are** the passengers for Dublin. In bow—way enough!" the speaker added, addressing his own crew; and with that the oars were tossed and boated with **a clatter**. Our bulwarks were grasped by three or four pairs of hands, and the frigate's quarter-boat was grinding alongside!

Giving the helm to Caldwell, Chips and I crossed the

deck; at the same time Dugan, followed by the rest of
the crew, started to come aft from the forecastle. I
waved them back. There, in the stern-sheets of the boat,
sat a woman's figure, huddled in a heavy cloak. The
old gentleman who was so anxious to reach Ireland
was sitting close beside her. A tall young midshipman
in charge stood up and gave me a curt salute; then,
speaking to the men forward, he ordered, peremptorily:

"Hand over that dunnage there, and be lively—all
asleep?"

"One moment, please," I said, speaking quickly to
attract attention. "I do not wish to appear discourteous,
but I think it would be best for Mr. Middleton to recon-
sider his decision to join us. My accommodations here
are small, and scarce fit for a lady. I should advise his
returning to the frigate—the young lady would not be
comfortable."

My voice, even to myself, sounded like that of a bear
with a sore head, for, as I have acknowledged, I was mad
clear through.

"You are bound for Dublin?" put in the young officer.

"That is where Captain Mallet has taken the liberty
to order me."

The old gentleman here arose. "Pardon me," he
said, steadying himself with difficulty, for the boat rocked fiercely every now and then—"pardon me, but we
will put up with anything; I have sailed in vessels no
larger than—than your fine little craft ere this. I am
most anxious to reach Dublin—pray take us, even if we
are unwelcome."

"I'd rather not," I growled.

"Of course if you refuse—" went on Mr. Middleton,
seating himself.

"Hand out that dunnage, you men in the bow!" put
in the overgrown middy, all at once deciding to assert
himself again.

I hesitated for a moment. Dugan and the rest were only waiting for a signal from me, I knew; but if it came to blows and harsh measures everything might go wrong. There was a lady in the boat, the frigate was within hail, and we were yet under her guns; I could see that her cabin lamps had been lighted.

In the meantime two large portmanteaus and a big box had been tumbled over on to our deck, and with a sudden gust of wind the drizzle changed to a downpour of rain.

"Look lively—bear a hand!" shouted the midshipman to us. "We don't wish to swamp here." But with a most surprising agility the old gentleman scrambled over our rail unaided.

"Good-bye, miss!" cried the middy; and before I knew it the draped and shrouded figure was assisted on board, and stood there almost beside me. The boat shoved off just as a heavy puff of wind brought our great boom sweeping across the deck.

"You had better go below to the cabin, sir," I said, speaking to my unwelcome guest in as polite a tone as I could manage.

"Oh, thank you, thank you," he answered. "Now I pray you not to consider us intruders. If you only knew—" There came another puff, the cutter heeled over till her rail was almost under, Chips began bawling to take in sail, so I lost the rest of the speech. When I looked around the old gentleman and his companion had disappeared down the after ladder.

"Boarded, and nigh to being took, by jingo!" chuckled Chips, as I joined him after we had clewed up our topsail and got in the jib. "So we're bound for Ireland, eh? Blow me if this ain't a rum go! Dublin bears about northeast-by-east. How long will we hold this course, Captain Hurdiss?"

"It's pretty dark, but the frigate may have an eye

on us. I'll tell you when to come about," I replied.
"Mr. Chips, I can't thank you for the manful way you
stood by me. But confound this last bit of business! I
hoped to get away before they came. I'm sorry. What
made you wait for me? I never expected it."

"Oh, I said you would be comin' back, sir. I knew
when I heard them guns you'd pull out of it. But, captain, what are you going to do with the passengers? Why
didn't you think to tell them we had smallpox aboard?"

"Why didn't you think of it yourself, you blockhead?"
I half laughed. "I suppose I will have to break the
news to them that they won't see Ireland for some time."

"'Tis that silly old gentleman's fault," quoth the carpenter. "Never poke your nose where it ain't wanted,
say I."

"He was rather insistent, come to think of it," was
my rejoinder.

"Rather hard on the young lady, sir."

"That's true, Mr. Chips; I've been thinking of that.
I intend to inform them before very long, however."

It was most unfortunate, but circumstances govern a
man's actions so strongly at times that he is compelled
to do things that are not agreeable to his feelings.

We dashed on, but without trimming for close sailing—
just killing time.

"I think we've gone about as near Dublin as is necessary," I remarked, after a long pause, squinting out
into the pitch-dark night. The rain had ceased, and although it was cloudy it looked like clearing.

"Very good, sir," responded the carpenter.

"Ready about!" he called to the men on watch.
"Hard-a-lee!" Then followed a heave, a flutter of canvas, and we were tearing back again over our track,
trimmed flat and doing finely.

"Bound for Boston town, now," laughed Chips; "she's
got her best side to windward!"

I had been thinking some serious thoughts for the last few minutes. What was going to be the outcome of all this? Here was Chips better qualified in every way to command a vessel than I was, and yet depending on me to bring the *Bat* into Boston. All I hoped for was to fetch up somewhere on the coast without going ashore. I hoped that I would not have to deceive him any further, and I almost came to the conclusion that it would be better to make a clean breast of everything, but common-sense as well as pride stood in my way. I could perceive that it would do no good. I wished that I had confessed my ignorance to Carter when we were at Barfleur. Poor Carter, he would only have been too glad to have helped me! Never again would I allow myself to occupy a false position if I could help it.

These cogitations were sent scattering by a question that tuned in with them.

"We'll have to take a sight to-morrow, sir, and there's one thing I meant to ask, if it is not too free. Have you wound the chronometer?—it might be wanting it. Did you note the log?" Chips asked this question in the most off-hand way.

I had seen with what care Gorham looked after the clock-in-the-box in the *Yankee's* cabin, and I knew how to do the trick.

"It should have been looked after," I replied to Chips's interrogation.

"What if it should stop to-night, sir? There isn't a turnip on board. I'd look into the matter, sir."

"I will," said I, starting for the companion-way. I went down a few steps before I remembered my guests; yes, though they had pre-empted the cabin without much ceremony, they were my guests, nevertheless. So I stopped, and knocked with my knuckles on the railing.

"Come in, sir," said a voice in a low whisper.

I bent down, and saw Mr. Middleton standing at the

foot of the ladder ; his finger was at his lips, the swinging lamp was lit, and he extended his left hand and drew me down towards him.

"I'm sorry to put you to any inconvenience," he went on, still whispering. "To-morrow you may find some other place to put us, perhaps. I had hoped you would have been down before ; I was near to coming after you. Hush ! pray don't speak aloud ; my granddaughter has fallen asleep ; you would not disturb her?"

I was about to tell him that he was welcome to the cabin (it could be divided in two by pulling the heavy curtain), and that I only wished to inspect the chronometer, when, without thinking, I looked past him, and saw a figure reclining on the cushions of the divan against the bulkhead. One glance—and if I were to lose my soul I could not but look again ! My mission and everything else went out of my head !

There lay Mary Tanner, fast asleep ! Mary Tanner and none other, as I was a living, breathing man !

How I concealed my perturbation I could never understand ; but I mumbled a good-night, and backed carefully up the steps.

Once outside, I closed the hatch and sank down beside it, my heart beating as it had never beat before, my breath coming in long gasps, and my temples throbbing as if my head would burst into pieces. "Mary !—Mary ! here?" I kept repeating to myself. What would she say when she found out the state of affairs ? I knew now why the name of Middleton had sounded so familiar.

CHAPTER XXXIV

THAT night I stood every watch. Occasionally I would fall asleep, to awaken with a start and a heart-lift to the realization that it was not a dream—that it was true! She was here!—here, of all places! Surely the providence that had watched over me had caused it to be brought about. I was a man now, thinking a man's thoughts, doing a man's work. Oh, to tell her how I had been waiting for this hour! I knew what to say—oh, I knew. How surprised she would be! Yet in a measure I felt afraid, and that I could not account for. What Mr. Middleton would say I did not care a rap—his case dwindled into nothing.

Eagerly I waited for daylight, and at last it came. Glorious and holy, fresh and new-born, the spreading light streaked the east, grew, widened, and caught our top-sails, until the canvas looked to be the pinkest silk. The cutter moved as if she enjoyed life, the very ripple of the water dashing off the bows sounded like happy laughter.

Caldwell was at the helm. He touched his cap to me, and in answering I discovered that I had still the heavy head-piece jammed down on my brows—the stiff stock and the massive gold-laced collar had almost worn my chin off; but all the rest of my belongings were down in the cabin, so of course I had to bide my time before I could shift into more comfortable duds.

"Have we an American flag in the locker, do you know?" I asked, turning to Caldwell suddenly.

"Yes, sir, I think I saw one." He called one of the men to take his place, and, going below, soon returned with a small ensign. "Shall I send it up, sir?" he inquired.

I nodded. Clear and bright in all its beautiful colors, up went to the peak the Stars and Stripes!

"It looks well," I observed to myself, but speaking the words out loud. My talking apparatus, I might mention, was almost normal by this time, although I could now sing bass instead of tenor.

"But why—why that flag?" spoke up a voice, as if in answer to my expressed thoughts.

"'Tis handsome; don't you think so?" I replied, turning to find Mr. Middleton (I knew why the name had puzzled me now) at my elbow.

"I have seen enough of it, young sir; 'tis getting to be most arrogant, with all the late successes it has had at sea. We Englishmen have not given the Yankee navy the credit it deserves" (and the Yankees won't get it in this generation either). "But pardon me," the old gentleman went on, nervously—"your name has slipped my mind—I should like to present you to my granddaughter when she appears."

"Oh, that will not be necessary," I replied, bowing.

He stepped back. "What do you say? What is all this nonsense about, sir? Answer me! My cousin is Lord of the Admiralty. I intended— But I shall report your conduct, sir! That flag; it is outrageous, sir!"

"Not at all, my dear Mr. Middleton. That flag is where it belongs. Allow me to explain—"

But I got no further in my utterances. Mr. Middleton lurched forward, and I had to catch him by the arms to keep him on his feet. Looking up in my face he tried to speak, but his jaw only worked convulsively without a sound.

"Grandfather ! Grandfather ! What has happened ?" (Heavens, how I thrilled !)

It was Mary Tanner standing there ! "What does this mean ?" she added, stepping towards the old gentleman with evident anxiety.

The old man could not reply.

"It means," said I, turning, "that Captain John Hurdiss has come in his own vessel to get you, Mistress Tanner." I half extended my hand—my voice broke.

I did not know exactly what would be the result of this speech, but if I had had any idea that it was to produce a sensation, the result certainly proved the correctness of my surmisings. Mary swayed for an instant, gave a gasp, and stamped her foot upon the deck. The flash of her eye had more kinds of feeling in it than one can describe.

"Traitor !" she hissed, extending her clinched hands at her side with the knuckles upward in a rigid gesture. Then she gave an inarticulate cry of rage, and, turning, hurried down the companion-way into the cabin.

Before me was standing Mr. Middleton ; his arms were folded, and his fingers clasping and unclasping nervously.

"What in the name of Saint Patrick have we here ?" he said, weakly. "What does this mean ? Who are you, and what are you ?"

"I am John Hurdiss, the commander of this vessel," I answered in return, folding my arms also, but keeping as quiet as I could (my heart had gone to ice). "I am a plain American seaman. You are my guest, sir, and believe me that no harm will come to you."

"You addressed my granddaughter just now as though you had some claim on her. We are in your power, but—"

"Stay !" I cried, lifting my hand. "My words may have been ill chosen, but mark this : I would put a pistol

19

to the man's head whose glance might look to harm her, as I would to my own if my thoughts could threaten treachery. Both you and she are safe, I pledge my honor!"

This speech, which really came from the depths of my being, had the effect of causing the old gentleman to relax his features somewhat.

"Thank you for this assurance," he said. "Will you tell me whither we are bound, and why you inveigled us, pray, to come on board this skip-jack? What plot is this?"

"Oh, pardon me," I returned; "it was your suggestion, and not mine. Every moment that I spent on board that frigate I was in great danger, and not only I, but these brave fellows who have stood by me so nobly. I almost warned you not to come. I did not know there was a lady with you. Since you have been on board I had hoped, or at least supposed, that affairs might have turned out differently."

"How so?" inquired Mr. Middleton, raising his eyebrows.

"The necessity for explaining my thoughts, sir, has passed," I answered, tersely. "I was mistaken."

How frequently it happens that serious conversation, aye, even tragic happenings, have been interrupted by something humorous or even ridiculous—a jackdaw at a funeral, or the bray of an ass interrupting a judge with a black cap on his head. Times when earnest attention has been turned to laughter are not infrequent, and the complexion of matters on the deck of the *Bat* was changed suddenly by just such an unexpected happening. We had been running free, with the sheet now and then giving a slap into the water, when the wind may have shifted a point or so, and as quickly as one might flip a shilling the great boom came swinging inboard with a rush. I saw it just in time to stoop, but it caught the old gentleman squarely across the shoulders and hurled him into my arms. Struggling to my feet on the other side of the great sail as it swung across the deck, I placed Mr. Middleton on his props again; but a transformation-scene had been enacted. The fine white curling head of hair was gone, and the very baldest-pated old buck I had ever seen stood there before me.

The incident took all the dignity and anger out of him as a pail of water takes the fight out of a mastiff.

"My wig!" he gasped.

Chips, who was at the tiller, had burst into a roar of laughter.

"Silence!" I shouted at him, too bitter to see anything amusing in the affair. I felt exactly as if I were acting in a trance, but noticing Mr. Middleton's head-covering was floating some rods astern, I ordered the cutter to be put about in order to pick it up; when I turned to speak to him he had disappeared into the cabin. I had the wig dried at the galley fire, and sent it in to him, with my compliments, a few minutes later. Then gloomily I paced up and down the deck. All the fire and life seemed quenched within me. I was stunned with the sadness of my disappointment. Oh, true enough, if I had known more about women I would not have felt so badly!

There was a little box of a berth, that had just room enough for a hammock and a narrow cupboard, at the foot of the forecastle-ladder, and I had taken possession of it, as, of course, it would not do for me to mess or bunk in with the crew. Now I betook myself to this seclusion, and, seating myself on top of a chest, I went into a condition of mind that only a few years before would have resulted in a flood of tears; but I was past that, and instead I fell to brooding in solitude over my hopeless situation.

There was a fine ten-knot breeze merrily blowing

when I emerged about noonday, and the little cutter was dipping into the waves gracefully, like a Mother Cary's chicken. Every one was in high spirits. All idea of my being a Jonah had faded from the minds of the crew. But I was filled with my huge disappointment. The bitter, miserable sensation had firm hold of me. Mary's conduct had been hard to understand; but what right had I to think it would be different! I had been flattering myself entirely too much, and then I saw what an injudicious and, mayhap, an unkind thing I had done, and regretted that I had not been more strenuous in my efforts to keep Mr. Middleton from carrying out his intention of leaving the *Cæsar;* but I believed that if I should have urged strongly against it, the cruise of the *Bat* would have ended there and then.

At one o'clock in the afternoon I saw the old gentleman come on deck; he was much agitated, and I noticed that he held his wig on with one hand as he approached. Lifting my hat, I bowed politely to him.

"A word with you," he began, nervously. "It is evident that you never had any intention of touching at Dublin."

"That, sir," I returned, "is the truth; I never had. Would you suppose it possible for an American crew to sail into a hostile harbor in a captured vessel and get out again?"

"You played the joke well on the Englishmen," he said, with a peculiar intonation.

"Yes; but they were Englishmen," I answered. "The Irish might be quicker-witted."

I knew that he was an Irishman, for he had a genteel touch of the brogue.

"Look here, my young sir," he rejoined, "I am a wealthy man, and my word is as good as a written and sworn-to bond. If you will land me on the coast of Ireland, anywhere, I will give you a thousand pounds."

"No money could tempt me," I replied, "to place the

freedom of my crew in jeopardy ; but this I have determined : if I meet a vessel bound for Europe, and can do so without great risk, I intend to place you and your granddaughter Mistress Tanner on board of her. More than this it is beyond my power to do."

At the thought of the shattering of my fond dream I sighed.

"You just spoke Miss Tanner's name," snarled the old man, looking at me fiercely ; "and your forwardness in speaking not long ago was most noticeable. I pray you, do you claim acquaintance?"

"Sir," I returned, "it is as the lady says."

"She says you are a stranger to her," answered Mr. Middleton, grimly.

"So be it," I replied, and turned upon my heel.

I did not see anything of Mary that day, but late in the evening she and her grandfather came on deck, and, arm in arm, walked up and down the weather side of the quarter-deck, I giving over to them, and pacing up and down the opposite side of the main-sail ; but my heart was big to bursting, and I was tempted again and again to step around the mast, and, standing there face to face with the girl that had given me the rose, demand an explanation. Oh woman ! who can account for your strange actions or analyze the motives of your inconsistencies?

As they went below, I happened to be standing so close that my presence could not be ignored, nor could I, without seeming rudeness, avoid speaking.

"I hope you and the young lady are quite comfortable, Mr. Middleton," I said, bowing. "If there is anything in my power I can do to add to your comfort, I pray you to command me."

Purposely I avoided looking at Mary as I spoke, and yet I was conscious that her eyes were full upon my face. She stood a little apart from her grandfather, and her little foot was tapping the deck impatiently. Mr. Middleton acknowledged my salutation, and replied with a certain peevishness that is shared by the very old or the very young when they consider themselves put upon in any way.

"The only thing that you can do is to redeem your promise, and set us on some vessel bound for Great Britain," he returned.

"I shall endeavor thus to redeem myself," I said. And then the two went below, leaving me leaning back against the boom, spiritless and dejected.

We were carrying a large square top-sail, and kicking up a great smother that showed that we were travelling well. The man at the tiller was humming softly to himself, the crew were lolling forward taking it easy, when I saw my first lieutenant approach. I noticed from his expression that he wished to speak to me.

"Well, Mr. Chips," said I, "and what is it?"

"I beg your pardon, sir," he returned, "but hadn't you better take a squint at the sun and see where we are? It may cloud up to-morrow."

I was in a quandary.

"Well, Mr. Chips," I growled, "do you suppose I don't know where I am?"

"The sextant is in the cabin, sir. But there is another thing," he added, touching his cap. "Would you mind calling me by my real name?"

"Why, isn't it Chips?" I exclaimed, in surprise, not knowing that this was the nickname applied to every carpenter afloat.

"My name is Philemon Cutterwaite, sir."

"Very good, Mr. Cutterwaite," I said; "I shall endeavor to remember it."

"Thank you, sir," was the reply. "Shall I get the instruments and take the time?"

As he spoke he stepped to the head of the companion-ladder and knocked. I could think of no excuse for the moment for detaining him, and, taking my silence for consent, he obeyed the answer from below to enter, and disappeared. But in an instant **he came** on deck.

"Captain Hurdiss," he said, "the **chronometer** has stopped. We must have forgotten to wind it, sir—bad luck to it!"

"Then **there is no** sight for to-day," I said, much relieved.

"I suppose not," was the grumbling answer. And then the good fellow went forward.

For two days we sailed on **as if we** had entered the trades. Seldom did we have to trim a sail. Every one was happy, excepting myself and my two guests. But not a word did we speak. When they took the air I kept below. I saw to it that they had the best of everything, and had detailed one of the men, who had been out in service, to look after the cabin and wait on the table. I was miserable, but determined not to intrude myself for any reason. **I was** acting not unwisely, but I did it without method.

CHAPTER XXXV

THE REDEMPTION OF MY PROMISE

I MESSED alone, either on deck or in my box of a cabin; and I had just finished my morning meal when one of the crew who had been aloft came down to the forecastle and reported that there was a sail in sight to the westward. This was the fourth day since my last exchange of-words with Mr. Middleton. When I came on deck I could just make out a faint spot against the western sky, but what course the vessel was holding I could not make out even with the aid of a glass. We held up in the stranger's direction, but shortly after eight o'clock it fell dead calm, our kindly wind stopped as if we had been blanketed, and the *Bat* rolled lazily about, fetching up occasionally with a jerk of her heavy boom that would send an echo-like sound rolling up the great main-sail. "Mr. Cutterwaite," as I shall call him hereafter, had given some orders during the watch while I was below, and I saw that the crew were making ready to get rolling tackle on her, as a preventive of the danger of carrying anything away by the continued slapping and romping. The sea that was running must have been the aftermath, so to speak, of a heavy blow, for it rolled from the southward, smooth and round, with not a ripple on the crest or a dimple to be seen on the sides of the waves. For ten hours we lay becalmed, and by evening the sail we had sighted had disappeared.

The sun was going down behind a streaky line of clouds that crossed the western sky in such a peculiar manner that, as they caught the red sunset color, the whole west resembled nothing so much as a great American flag. Even the stars were there, shining in the blue field. I was standing looking at it in admiration, when I turned suddenly and saw that Mary Tanner had come on deck, and was regarding the sight with wide-open eyes. Probably she had not seen me, but I determined to speak to her, and so came closer.

"See the flag yonder," I said, pointing.

She was startled at my presence, but quickly she gave a little frown, as if I had interrupted some pleasant thought.

"I see it," she answered, turning her head half away ; and with this she descended into the cabin again. I had whirled about and crossed the deck, determined not to affront her any more.

Bad weather came on during the next dog-watch—rain, and a cold, blustering wind pelted out of the northeast, cutting up a heavy sea, and making everything wet and disagreeable ; for four days and over this continued. I saw Mr. Middleton but once ; and as he almost accused me of dodging vessels that might take him back to Europe, our conversation was neither long nor gratifying. I caught but one glimpse of Mary, as she kept to the cabin.

The storm lasted nearly five days, to be more exact. We had run before it, and were well on our course; but I was glad to see the sun come out and the wind go down early one afternoon. I put on dry clothing, and felt more comfortable than I had for a long time.

Such a starlit night as this was I can never recollect seeing since ; and as it was warm I brought up a blanket to lie on, and determined to pass the night on deck. As I lay there watching the top-mast sway to and fro against the besprinkled heavens, I fell into wondering what was going to become of me—what should I do

when I returned to America? I could not imagine;
and it seemed to me that it was impossible that Mary
Tanner, whom I had grown to think of as the one
person in the world who might be interested in my life
(ah, the beloved picture of her waiting for me!), was
here within sound of my voice—here in my keeping, as
it were ; and yet affairs were sadly different from what
I had hoped or supposed they would be.

I was lying with my head almost on the edge of the
hatch combing, when I thought I heard the sound of
something like a sigh or a long-drawn breath ; I raised
myself on my elbow, and there she was standing not
three feet from me.   I could have placed my hand over
hers if I had so chosen !

"Mary," I said, softly.   She gave a little gasp and
turned.

"Pray do not go until you have heard a few words
that I wish to say," I went on, leaning forward. "If my
speaking to you is disagreeable, I shall not repeat the
offence a second time.   Listen ! I had not thought to
carry you away, but I had hoped some day to find you.
In prison I thought of this, and as a free man the
hope has been before my eyes.   Now there is nothing
left ! I have naught to offer you, but some day there
may come a time when I can do so (I was urged to
speak on thus by her silence).   You think me—"

"Oh, pray do not explain further, Monsieur le Marquis," she interrupted. "I suppose that you are going
on to speak of your titles and estates."

I started.

"What do you mean?" I said. "What do you
know ?"

"Only what Gaston informed every one in Stonington," she replied. "Poor loon ! they would have put him
in the mad-house— But you were going on to say, you
are—"

"A plain American seaman," I returned, "who would give his life to serve you."

I had risen to my feet and stood there looking at her. I had thought for a moment that her look had softened as I spoke—anyhow, she lowered her eyes—but just then Mr. Middleton's voice interrupted us from the cabin.

"Mary, child," he called, "where are you?"

"I am here," she answered, and she jumped below, almost into the frightened old man's arms. I clinched my teeth, and there was no sleep for me that night!

I made up my mind this time that I would not speak to her again unless she addressed me first. Two more weary days, and another stormy interview with Mr. Middleton! This one was held in the cabin at his request. I knew that Mary was listening to everything from the other side of the curtain, so I managed to keep my temper.

At last there came a rather important day to enter in the log. In the early morning hours it clouded a little, and an intermittent breeze blew up from the south. At daybreak we discovered a sail about six miles distant, bearing a few points off our weather bow. She was a small ship, and at the first glance at her Mr. Cutterwaite pronounced her English. We changed our course, and at the same moment the vessel did hers also, and when about a mile distant she broke out her flag.

"A Portuguese, by David!" exclaimed Dugan.

"We'd better try the British Jack, sir," suggested the carpenter.

I acquiesced, and soon the *Bat's* natural colors were flying over us. Instantly down went the Portuguese emblem, and up went that of England. The ship had come up into the wind, and was waiting for us with her main-top-sail aback, and her foresheets fluttering.

I called down into the cabin.

"Mr. Middleton," I said, "you can get your baggage,

sir. I judge we will soon part company. Here's your chance to take passage."

In ten minutes we were almost within hailing distance, and the old gentleman came on deck, followed immediately by Mary. Her eyes were red, and she looked, strange to tell, as if she had been weeping. It required all the strength of will I had to keep my lip from quivering as I raised my hat and wished her a polite good-morning. There was a strange, wistful glance, that I could not fathom, that she threw at me, and then she turned her head aside. I had donned the uniform of the Honorable John again, and, leaning against the lee shrouds, I raised my voice and hallooed,

"What ship is that?"

"The *Lord Lennox*, from Quebec to Liverpool. What cutter is that?"

"His Majesty's sloop *Bat*, from Dublin to Quebec," I answered.

"What do you want of us?" was the inquiry of a short, thick-set man in a beaver hat, who had mounted the rail.

"Can you take two passengers back with you to England?" I replied. "They are all ready."

Suddenly I noticed that the ship had dropped four ports, and I saw one of the guns run in and the toss of a sponge handle. Instantly the risk we were running crossed my mind.

"Stand by to cast loose and provide those guns," I said, holding the *Bat* up a few points so as to lessen our speed. "Arm all hands," I added.

"The guns are all loaded, sir," answered Dugan, who was placing a lot of cutlasses in a handy place near the bitts.

We were a fair bit less than one-third the size of the vessel we were nearing, and I saw that the men cast rather furtive glances at her as they set about obeying orders.

I was in a bunk in a large cabin. I did not know what it all meant, and I did not have time to speak. It was but a glimpse of consciousness I had, for off I went again; I remembered no more until I was awakened by the sound of whispering. Looking up, I saw that Cutterwaite and Mr. Middleton were standing alongside of me.

"Well," I said, faintly, "how fares it?"

"Another prize, Captain Hurdiss, and a good one," said Chips, bending over me. "We took the ship, sir. You're on board of her, and the cutter's in our wake. We're not three hundred miles off Cape Cod. The wind's fair, and all's a-taunt-o; but you've had a narrow escape. Now, stow all talk, sir."

"How long ago did it happen?"

"Nigh on to a week, sir."

"A week to-morrow," put in the old gentleman, speaking for the first time, and speaking friendly like. "Captain Hurdiss, I beg your pardon for my past conduct. My granddaughter and I—" He stopped all at once, and I saw it was hard for him to continue.

Oh, I could have cried for the joy of it, but at this instant I heard a soft voice ask:

"Is he speaking?"

"Mary!" I said, tremulously.

Mr. Middleton and the carpenter stepped the other side of the entrance, and the one whom I had always dreamed of as waiting for me came near. There was no pride in her face this time, and her voice shook as she whispered, softly:

"Sh-h-h—you must not speak!"

I put out my hand. She took it, and sank down at the side of the bunk.

"John, dear, forgive me," was all she said, and then— and then— Well, what is the use of telling more? Women are strange creatures. But suffice it. I had.

of a truth, taken the fairest prize in all the world. How she had won the old gentleman to her way of thinking I do not pretend to tell. I have never asked, nor did he inform me. But some women have a way with them against which there is no gainsaying. Mr. Middleton was a wise man, and this may account for it. As any one can see, my tale is told.

But I was not the only one under Mary's care. Dugan and three others were wounded, lying in the forecastle ; one of our fellows lost an arm, one of the enemy likewise, and one poor devil was killed ; six were wounded, including two officers. But we found under hatches ten Yankee prisoners, rescued (?) forsooth from a foundering American prize-ship. Without their help (two were officers) we would never have got the *Lord Lennox* into port.

I was on the deck when land was sighted. It was my own country that lay off to the westward ! I, the happiest man in all the world, was home again.

The happiest man ? Aye, that was truth ! for as I stood there looking at the land growing more and more distinct, I felt a touch on my shoulder and another on my hand.

"Mary," I said.

"Yes, John."

"Mary, I know not what awaits me in life, but I feel content—I can face disaster or fight trouble. I fear nothing when I think how much I have to live for. You are happy?"

"If you were a duke, John, I could not love you more and if you were a beggar I would not love you less." she said.

"Tell me something ; why did you call me 'Traitor' when I first spoke to you?"

"It was the uniform," she answered. "I did not understand."

"I was a loyal traitor then," I laughed. Mary looked up at me and smiled.

Five hours' more sailing and we were anchored in Boston Harbor. The *Bat* came up with the evening tide.

Thus ended my adventures. Before the war was over I learned enough navigation to go as first officer on another cruiser, and upon my return Mary and I were married. Since then I have made many voyages in my own vessels, always knowing that there was waiting for me when I returned the dearest little woman in the world, and were I a nobleman with vast estates I could be no whit happier, nor could I be so happy as I am at this very moment. Of that I am sure.

There is just a half-page left of this old ledger. As my story is done, I can but go over it again; and, in looking back, what a strange record I have made here, for I began as a child without a name and without a country, who chose both for himself. I had been a mysterious waif in a Connecticut village, an instructor in small-arms on board a privateer, an English prisoner of war, an alleged Frenchman among the refugees in England, a lieutenant of a fine schooner, and the commander of two vessels, all inside of two years. Yes, and had I not been a robber also? For I robbed an English officer and a scarecrow of their clothes, and an old man of his granddaughter. (Of the last I am prouder than I can tell in calm words.) And now I am a prosperous ship-owner, with nothing in this wide world to wish for, except that I were a better scribe. Oh, I might set down that I learned, of course, of the death of my uncle, and found out that Gaston had disappeared with the belongings of Belair, no one knew whither. I was sorry for this, for there was much that I would like to have possessed. As for any other title than that of an

American citizen, I care not so much as the snap of a finger; nor would my sons, I am sure, even if they had but to extend their hands to grasp it. They may read in this a great deal that their father has not told them, but it could make no difference, I am sure, in our relations towards one another. Edward Brown is in my employ, and so is Jack Sutton (on shore at this writing); Si Plummer is captain of a fine coaster, and I see him now and then. He has a great yarn to spin about the loss of the *Yankee*. Philemon Cutterwaite is a Boston boatbuilder. Temple, of the *Young Eagle*, was killed in a duel at some place in the Mediterranean. Mr. Middleton died in my house three years ago, a dear old man whose loss was mourned. One thing more: I might as well state I returned all the personal effects found in the *Bat's* cabin to the Hon. Deerhurst, who lives in Sussex, England, and, upon my last voyage to Europe, Mary and I spent three delightful days with my titled but simple friend and patron the Marquis de Monseverat.

THE END